MORE LIKE
WRESTLING

THREE RIVERS PRESS
NEW YORK

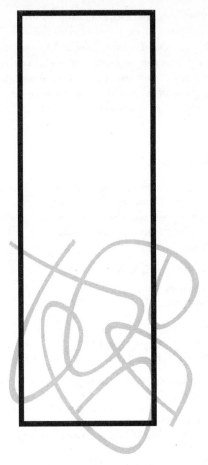

MORE LIKE WRESTLING

DANYEL SMITH

This is a work of fiction. All incidents, dialogues, and characters are products of the author's imagination and are not to be construed as real. In those few passages where actual place-names and well-known individuals are referred to, the situations, incidents, and dialogues described are entirely fictional and are not intended to depict actual events or to change the entirely fictional nature of the work. Any resemblance to persons living or dead is entirely coincidental.

Copyright © 2003 by Danyel Smith

Published by Three Rivers Press, New York, New York.
Member of the Crown Publishing Group,
a division of Random House, Inc.
www.crownpublishing.com

THREE RIVERS PRESS and the Tugboat design are
registered trademarks of Random House, Inc.

Originally published in hardcover by Crown Publishers,
a division of Random House, Inc., New York, in 2003.

Printed in the United States of America

DESIGN BY BARBARA STURMAN

Library of Congress Cataloging-in-Publication Data
Smith, Danyel.
  More like wrestling / a novel / by Danyel Smith.
  1. Problem families—Fiction.   2. Oakland (Calif.)—Fiction.
3. Sisters—Fiction.   4. Girls—Fiction.   I. Title.
  PS3619.M575 M67 2003
  813'.6—dc21   2002011349

ISBN 0-609-80993-8

First Paperback Edition

For my sister
Raquel,
and for my parents,
Janelle and Reginald

The art of living is more like
wrestling than dancing, insofar
as it stands ready against the
accidental and the unforeseen,
and is not apt to fall.

—MARCUS AURELIUS ANTONINUS
  (121–180)

MORE LIKE
WRESTLING

PROLOGUE

Paige and I are sisters.

Everyone always says how close we are. Teachers, friends, the random relative. Grinning or turning their lips down or searching Mom's gestures for meaning, that's what they say: *Paige and Pinch are so close.*

They don't know the half of it. They've no idea how hard we played—especially as little kids. Played like we knew just how ugly things could get.

Dashed and pedaled until we damn near popped.

Until we were sweaty and shades darker and almost in pain.

But we're from Oakland. And Oakland builds quality. Folks who creep but don't crawl. Melt down, but don't vaporize. I move around—Oakland, anyway. So I know the Bay Area creates righteous people who deal with splendor and sting, sham and certainty, gray velvet fog and lemon-glass sunshine—all while just getting from Point A to Point B.

I know this because I can *see*. I watch. And this place—with its indigo-green jewel of a lake and its underdog nature and dead downtown and Southern Negro mores and shiny liberal whiteness and slow-motion port and fifty-cent tacos and fern-cloaked hills and baby tunnels and beckoning bridges and Victorian crack-houses and modern manors from which you can see San Francisco twinkling and Marin sleeping and after that straight to God's cool pacific pond—it had to be

Oakland that pasted Paige and I together. It would be Oakland that pulled us apart.

Life, though, had a lot to do with it. And death, too.

THE year was 1989. April. I was twenty-two. Paige, twenty-four.

It had gotten to where my sister and I were living on opposite sides of the country. Maybe her husband had chosen New York City. Maybe New York was as far as either of them could envision.

So I was flying, on a Friday, to the end of my sister's imagination. Not to get her, or even to try and talk sense to her. I was going to see Paige. It's what she wanted, even if she didn't realize it. To be seen. Maybe I wanted her to see me, too.

Had been about six months since she and her husband left Oakland. By the time I landed at JFK airport, she and he'd been split up for about twelve weeks. Their two-year marriage had already defied lots of ugliness, and until they went away, I thought the relationship might last ten or twelve years.

The ride from the airport was more of a thrill than the flight. New freeway and new hotels—new to me, anyway. Close rows of houses and then a freeway that ran along the ocean, or a river, and then blocks and blocks of tall buildings with small stores on the first floors. A billion yellow taxis and stunted childless parks and then what had to be the Lower East Side. It's what my sister called her new neighborhood. Cab pulled up to the address, I got my bag from the trunk, and my head together to surprise Paige. It was cold. Cold as January back home. A fat man with a snug overcoat was coming out so I walked in without having to buzz. Walked up four flights of stairs and then knocked. Took a while before Paige opened the door.

'Oh my God!'

Put my hands on my hips, smiled like *ta-da*!

'Pinch you did not come all the way out here!' Her eyes

were dry, brown, and bright with fake life. She liked to say that eyes like hers were sold by the box and stuffed in otters' heads at natural history museums.

'I did I did!'

We spent ten minutes pulling in luggage, and she made me relate how, from the moment the thought came to my mind, I'd come to be where she was. Paige wanted details about who gave me money, the ride to San Francisco airport, and who knew I was traveling. I told her all while she sat across from me on a beanbag. Paige pressed her eyelids together and then started squeezing oil from the meaty part of her nose. Then she held a hand mirror to her face, checked her tongue for sores. There was nothing wrong with my sister. Not with her face, or her body, anyway.

Paige stayed in the weekend I was in New York, only left the grimy building Friday night to rummage the corner deli for tortellinis, bubbly water, honey, and the best of their second-rate lemons. She went to the sticky-floored store in nightclothes and a long coat, said to me on that Saturday morning that she'd moved to New York to get from California's hard-core, winterless beauty, and to bravely walk through blowing snow.

I looked at her, and then looked out the window. Said, 'What snow?'

Paige said she'd stopped looking for loveliness at Queens, on the way in from Kennedy. She hadn't looked at anything except what shone or made a lot of noise. Things were old enough to scare her in New York. The freeways were called highways, and were cracked and laneless. I nodded in agreement when she said that people's cars, no matter the color, were beaten, graying, and overworked. I picked up one of the books she had in a stack on the floor. A history of witches. Biography of Mary McLeod Bethune.

'There's no expectation of cleanliness here,' she said. 'The living is mean. And clannish.'

I could tell Paige didn't want to learn the place. We sat up and watched CNN or the network, not the local news, didn't glance at the local dailies still being delivered to her apartment in the last tenant's name. Paige hadn't memorized radio station call numbers, had yet to go out partying on the weekends at all.

WHEN the pilot said we were over Illinois, all I saw were brown, tan, and green squares of land. My first time outside of California. The furthest I've been from Oakland, ever.

I know Oakland is the best place in the world because I was raised there, went to school there, and because I've been, with my sister, on about a thousand field trips to Places of Interest around there. Paige was one to ask question after question of the tour guides, and she retains facts as long as they come in the form of a story in which the right people halfway triumph. I take in what the tour guides say, but I've always been more apt to remember what was going on during the field trip—as opposed to the history of Alactraz Island or Lake Merritt.

And just the fact that Oakland *has* Lake Merritt is almost enough. It's a big, park-lined lake, right in the middle of town. Plus there are universities all around the Bay Area, so even when they aren't, people seem smart and like they have some culture. In line at the post office, old Black Panthers tell stories about Huey and Eldridge and feeling like men. Not that Paige and I used to go, but people our age remember each other from Panther day care and free breakfasts. My mother does keep a photo of Bobby Seale holding me when I was fourteen months old—though lots of people in Oakland have photos like that. Mom says the Panthers gave the best parties.

People call our mother Gwen or Gigi, depending on whether they know her from work or from life. She was born in

Oakland, went to high school, a year of trade school, then she had Paige. Two years later, I appeared. Nine and a half months in her stomach, I must have wanted to stay. In the pictures of Mom, Paige, and I from that time, Mom looks about thirteen. Teeth need braces. Her brown eyes brilliant, happy, and terrified, like a girl on her first whirligig.

Before I was born, Mom left our father. Can't say that I'm bothered about it, but neither one of us would know homeboy if he was standing next to us on the BART platform. For a while we were coming up just fine. Mom got a lot of help from her grandparents. My great-grandmother had one daughter, an only child named Elizabeth. She's Paige and I's grandmother, and when Mom got herself a job at the phone company, and found a two-bedroom apartment across from San Antonio Park near East Oakland, Gram Liz made sure Mom had plates and cups and a crib and an iron at her new spot. Then Gram Liz moved to Los Angeles for a good job at Pacific Southwest Airlines. Gram Liz wasn't old school, or even very old.

Mom collected likenesses of pineapples—ceramic, wooden, metal, just little knickknacks. They sat around on everything. She told us they were a symbol of welcome and family affection.

'What's a symbol?' I asked Mom that.

'Something,' Mom said, 'that means something else.'

'Why have symbols?' is what Paige wanted to know. 'If you mean "welcome," why not just have a sign that says it?'

'Pineapples look better in the house.'

'But it's still a pineapple,' Paige said. 'It means food.'

Mom was at her jobs a lot when it was just the three of us. She did days at the phone company, half-nights bookkeeping for a place jammed with bolts of velvet. Paige and I would be up there sometimes. We pulled tassels from cartons, tied them to us and marched through groves of brocade. But for our great-grandparents, we never had baby-sitters. Mom could leave me with Paige from the time I was five. We had toys, watched television. One time I bruised my ribs jumping off the bed, but I'd have done that if Mom had been home. I had to go to emergency, and Mom told the doctor she'd been in the other room. We did fine.

During the week, after school, Mom took us to the library for books about glass elevators, and slaves who got away. Sometimes she told us stuff we didn't know—like that pickles were really cucumbers, and that Gram Liz had been defiant and bossy as a young woman, smoked Virginia Slims, worked on the naval base in Alameda, dated whomever she wanted, white or black, started social clubs with her girlfriends, and drank bourbon and pop from champagne flutes. Mom told us that Gram had never told her much about how life got lived or how boys were dealt with. Had let Mom grow up like a weed, but still close to the shade of the house Mom's dad had left Gram when he died at the veterans' hospital, from some type of hemorrhage, at twenty-four. Gram Liz never got married again. Didn't get along with Nannah or Grandpa. I couldn't imagine anyone rebelling against our great-grandparents. Or being anything but happy in their house.

In the tiny backyard of our own triplex, we read comics with a thick Chinese boy named Theo who lived with his parents, our landlords, in a front apartment downstairs. In our living room, there was a poster—it was of six identical human silhouettes, yellow, green, blue, purple, hot pink, maroon, each touching the other. All with afros, and looking serene. The caption was SOME OF MY BEST FRIENDS ARE COLORED. Mom tried to explain it, but I didn't get it.

In our room was a framed print that looked drawn by a child. Next to a shakily sketched yellow flower was WAR IS UNHEALTHY FOR CHILDREN AND OTHER LIVING THINGS. I didn't get that one, either—the words met each other, in a circle, in my brain. The poster wasn't a symbol, based on what Mom and Paige had said. The print stated the obvious. But if whoever made the poster meant it the way it was written, why would there be the need for one?

And why would it be printed in kiddy scrawl?

Like it was one thing and meant something else?

SATURDAY night, in New York, Paige complained of comets shooting around the curve of her head. She said she had a weight in her lower abdomen like it was two days before her period, a hotness in her ear. Her arms got an ache, it was there, it wasn't. Paige's eyes burned, she shut them, tried to will water to them, pressed them, with her fingers, toward the flat bridge of her nose. She swallowed bullet-sized multivitamins, palmfuls of Vitamin C, and dusty, green-smelling capsules of goldenseal root and echinacea. She said her pee was pumpkin—I could see it was infrequent. She said that it was probably because she was always drinking lattés with butterscotch or caramel syrups, always wondering what if any was the technical difference between the two. There were moments when her horizon tilted and only a deep breath of outside air would right it. Before she got in the bed with me, Paige stuck her head from her fourth-floor window. Let in a cold sour breeze. She shook her head purposefully, like there was water in her ear. We lay down head-to-toes—like we did when we shared a bed, which was rarely.

'I can't believe,' she said, 'you really came out here.'

PAIGE learned to braid her own hair one Saturday afternoon by the swings at San Antonio Park. Behind her, there was a sandbox, a seesaw, and sun. Gum wrappers and striped bus transfers under my Keds. I had on jeans with a cuff and a cotton turtleneck with short sleeves. Paige and I both had two braids that looked perfectly lopped off by our shoulder blades. Mom had done them.

In a looped-together rope of brown rubber bands I'd tied between baby trees, I wound and unwound my calf, bounced to the beat of *Winstons taste good / Like a cigarette should / Winstons taste good like / Uh ooo I / Wanna piece of bread / Bread too brown / Wanna go to town / Town too black / Want my money back* while Paige sat Indian-style on the edge of a hard mat that spread out under the swings.

'What are you doing?'

She shrugged. Then Paige took half her hair down, combed it through with her fingers.

I stopped bouncing. 'You're not supposed to take your hair out.'

'I know,' she said. In the summer, above her forehead and along her temples, Paige's dark hair turned the color of peanut skins. She separated her loose waves into three parts and folded them tightly over each other—knotting, then tugging to unknot.

She was seven and she was concentrating. I'd never even thought of braiding. It seemed a task that went on around me while I pouted. Complicated, tight, grown folks' business. It was what Mom did.

But Paige braided and unbraided until she didn't have to pause once on the way down, wound and unwound until she found a rhythm slicing through hair with thumbs, pulling locks around with pinkies, pressing and directing with the three center fingers, maneuvering daintily with the very tips as she made it to the oiled curl at bottom. She found her elastic band on the circle of mat between her legs, whipped it around the new tail.

I walked over to my sister, touched her new hair. It wasn't smooth and flat, and one of the three sections was much thinner than the other two. 'You braided it,' I said.

Then Paige unloosed the other side of hair and handled that one.

My sister was bigger than me, and always had been. She talked more than me. Ate more than me. With her new braids, she was even more clearly ahead of me. I wanted her to do my hair.

Paige felt her own plaits for tightness, then got up and sat in a swing. She had her hands on the chains but didn't push off, start pumping. Said to me, Do that other one, *I said it / I meant it / I'm here to represent it / I'm cool / I'm fine / I'm Soul Sister Number Nine / Sock it to me one more time.* We chanted while I bounced and wound through what we called Chinese jump rope even though Theo said he'd never heard of it.

At the apartment, Paige showed Mom her braids.

'Let me see! Look at you! That's *very* good.' Mom pressed and touched them, amazed herself.

After that, Paige was in charge of her hair and mine every schoolday. And she lorded it over me.

Most weekends, though, we were at Nannah and Grandpa's—Gram Liz's mother and father—just as Mom had been when she was small. Nannah moved to Oakland from Louisiana back in the 1910s. She followed our great-grandfather, who was a masonry worker, but then he got on with the railroad. Not that he was a redcap. Grandpa passed for white at work as long as he was able, ran a club car.

Known to grown folks as Mr. and Mrs. Louis Arceneaux—and it was pronounced Louie—Nannah and Grandpa lived in a one-story white-brick house in East Oakland, in the Flatlands. Out front, there was a small lawn, and on the side of the house was a long broad one with two flower beds. Nannah had bruised roses, bird's-foot violets, and a white-flowered forest of Great Solomon's Seal. She'd show us round black marks on the hose-like roots—scars from where the last year's stalks had emerged. The odd circles, she'd say, looked like the real, Solomon-from-the-Bible's seal. I always thought that's what a uterus must look like after babies—tattooed down deep and invisible. To make the whole pregnancy process seem worthwhile, people get to come up with names for babies, and fables to go along with them. I guess, in the end, you get a family.

Nannah let us pull weeds with her, and boogie through the sprinkler. Her hair was white embroidery thread, hands all wrinkle and fat vein, hard and cool as butter. She wore huge pretend jewels that should have swollen her knuckles from the tightness. My great-grandfather built her a cottage in the back-yard with fussy electricity and an oak door with a glass hexagon.

Nannah had always called it the Château. Pinch and I would sit in there and sip Coke with vanilla syrup at teatime from heavy highball glasses. Nannah splashed a tiny bit of Johnnie Walker in hers. The three of us played Go Fish in the château, and munched on maraschinos.

Nan can I? Nan can we? That's all that came from Paige's mouth.

No no no. Go next door, tell Mrs. McKnight I want you all to pick some of her blackberries. Don't go crazy. Paige, you know how many to get. And tell her I want some of her plums, too. And don't be playing over there all day around all those bees.

It's a fact that things were ordered and pretty back then. I know. I don't manipulate the sounds and pictures in my brain. Unlike Nannah and Paige, and Mom, my memory's detached from my will.

To remind herself that life was indeed all about a way-ward husband finally ill enough to stay home, about beautify-ing one's own land, about entertaining great-grandkids and having retired from cleaning other folks' houses, Nannah would casually say, highball sweating through the tablecloth, that her mother, as a child, had been a slave in a Catholic household outside New Orleans. All we could think to say was,

A real slave? It amazed us that Nannah was born in 1895. In New Orleans, from her father's shoulders, she said she'd seen Thomas Edison in a parade, when the streetlights changed from oil to electric. Nannah proved that the past, however disputed and hazy, had happened.

Sundays before dawn, we used to wake up, braids fuzzy, in her perfumed second bedroom, debating whether it was a Saturday or a church day. Nannah making applesauce from green fruit and cinnamon, with no sugar at all. Then with new perfect plaits she'd whipped together, we'd go to Mass and watch my great-grandfather pass a flat basket at offering. Nannah told us not to wave at Grandpa when he got to our pew, but we did, and then dropped in our two bits. Grandpa didn't wave or smile, but he nodded at us in a conspiratorial way. Like we were in the Catholic Club. His eyes were gray like mine.

On the way home, we divided M&Ms between us evenly in the backseat, candy by candy, color by color. We feared nothing except the serial killer on the news, and sometimes Grandpa. He had diabetes and so kept a frightening row of syringes in a blue plastic case. He was also going blind from glaucoma. On drives to the grocery store, when it was just we and he, Grandpa had Paige and I shout Red! Yellow! or Green! as we neared intersections.

It was 1973, so Paige and I had to be nine and seven. Seemed we mostly ate, read, and watched *The Lawrence Welk Show.* We ran down Nannah and Grandpa's endless driveway without so much as a glance over a shoulder. Not looking back—that's still my definition of joy.

Late Sunday afternoon Mom would come for dinner and take us home with her. We'd hop on the bus with wrapped roast beef and cans of creamed corn. Mom had groceries at our apartment, but Nannah sent food for the satisfaction she got from packing it.

On the route toward San Antonio Park, Mom pointed out fire stations and toy stores.

'What about tap? They have a dance school right on Park Boulevard,' Mom said.

'I saw it! I saw the costumes in the window,' Paige said. 'Yeah!'

'And maybe gymnastics for you?' Mom said, looking at me like she always did. With a little frown. 'The teacher said you were doing good in tumbling.' I figured she wanted me to talk more. But Paige knew the things to ask.

So I just looked at Mom. Knew she'd sign me up for whatever was right. There was no question in our minds back then about Mom. She faked an address so we could go to the better school in the better district. She made us eyelet dresses, got our photos taken at JC Penney, helped us bake hard little cakes in my Easy-Bake oven. And she wasn't much of a dater. Her high-school girlfriends had kids our age, so lots of evenings me, Mom, and Paige socialized with them, watching television, watching the adults, dizzy from Hula-Hooping, and from not having a worry in the world.

Paige, though, tends to forget the good stuff. She was in the District-Wide Christmas Pageant when she was ten, at the Calvin Simmons Auditorium back when it was still named after the City of Oakland. It's the only time she was costumed in the fluff and tulle of a princess. Instead of tap, Paige had ended up in ballet. Mom made her costume.

Paige sprinkled people with glitter dust, had white tights and rhinestone barrettes. Her own braids coiled by Mom into two neat buns. Paige touched kids with the silver star at the end of her wand and they disappeared.

She says she doesn't remember the performance, but I do. Paige got to do turns and leaps by herself in front of everyone.

SUNDAY morning, Paige at least showered, dressed in street clothes. She had a part-time job at a bookstore and had to be there by noon. She saw me to a yellow cab.

'Don't drink on the plane,' she said. 'You should have your wits about you when you fly.'

'You gonna stay out here?'

'Seems like it. Jessica's not gonna call. Ever. Everything's different except Mom. She's the same.'

Paige was right, especially about Jessica. They'd been tight friends at one time, but their days of hanging were over.

My sister isn't crazy, but she can be unpredictable. And it's not that her glass is half-empty. There's no glass, no water. And if there's a table, it's shaking. Maybe it's because we've always lived in Oakland, practically on top of the San Andreas Fault. It's an active rift just below the earth's rind that goes from Cape Mendocino, where I've never been, to the Colorado Desert, where I'll probably never go. I understand that the San Francisco Bay was created thousands of years ago by the fault's swings, and by the tipping and sinking of silt. But standing on the pier in Tiburon, or looking out from the Berkeley Marina at the World's Largest Natural Harbor, it just seems like the bay was created, complete and as is, by God. I'm clear on the fact that the bay's in a constant, invisible state of change. But I can't imagine it. The whole thing's so forever to me.

From the air over San Francisco, the bay was sky-dyed peacock blue. The Golden Gate Bridge a fancy hennaed crown. Olive hills, glass-gray skyscrapers, low red-roofed houses. Sparkling four-lane freeways stretched looped swooped carried people-filled cars in. Carried them out. I knew the pace I knew the colors knew them so well I heard *You're home* in the screech and careen of the wheels hitting the runway. In the silent ascension of heavy birds taking off, I thought I heard something else.

Paige always reminds me that God created the fault first, and that the bay, however sacred, is a by-product. She imag-

ines a thick russet shelf of earth grinding a softer one to powder. She imagines the fault spreading to a huge bronze wound.
Paige says that I can rest assured the mud plates will do as they
always have. They'll make us remember that nothing is promised. Not even the ground beneath our feet.

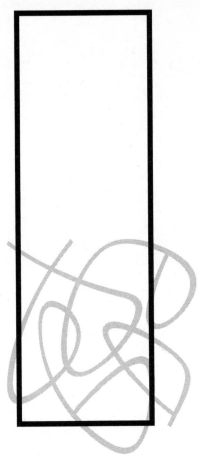

PART I
TEN YEARS:
1979–1989

Month: October (1978)
Day: Warm but cold Tuesday
Attitude: Happy, to an extent

Holy Jesus. Made Girls' League. It's just as important as student council, almost. Mom's happy about it. I should've known I'd get in. In Girls' League we get to have a 'little sister,' a seventh-grade girl who we, as ninth-grade girls, are supposed to be friends with, and show the ropes to. Saw a slim girl by the tetherball courts yesterday. I was over by the Ninth Grade Court, so the girl looked small and far away. She sat on the ground quietly, not playing, just watching two other girls fight for the ball. I thought the girl was white because of her long ponytail, and because she had on long sleeves. And I figured she was in the seventh because she looked friendless. I was going to go over, make her my little sister. The girl turned around right then, and I saw her brown hands and brown face. It was Pinch. She waved. The Girls' League teacher-moderator said it was okay for Pinch to be my little sister. The way I brought it to her, like it was a done deal, what else was the teacher going to say?

CHAPTER 1

MY MOTHER'S boyfriend, who'd been living with us for six years, stomped up to Bret Harte one day, twenty minutes after the dismissal bell rang. Warm, rain just gone, and windless, it must have been May. I had on a tan corduroy skirt and T-shirt. It was definitely 1979. In Oakland.

I was waiting in the crowded Ninth Grade Court on my sister, who I was supposed to be taking to the orthodontist. The court was four round tables with umbrellas, a school-sanctioned, fenced-in area along the perimeter of our junior-high-school playground—needless to say, NINTH GRADERS ONLY. Just as Pinch came up, moving like a turtle as always, except skinny as a piece of string, Seth walked up from the opposite direction. Drunk as a fucking skunk. Stupid as a motherfucker. In my head I was like, Damn, he didn't die today.

'Where are you supposed to be?' His face and neck were painted hard, rough brick red, and peeling gold horns had broken through the skin above his eyebrows. He hawked up something from his throat, then spit it out on the ground. He was talking to me.

I looked over at Pinch, who froze for the shortest second and then walked, at her same turtle pace, until she was near me, just inside the entrance to the court. Of course she wasn't allowed, because she was in the seventh grade, but no one said anything except Seth. Pinch's teeth were almost perfectly straight. There was no reason in the world for her to be going to get them worked on.

'Didn't I ask you a question? Paige!' His voice was sand and pink slobber. The knotty end of a tail had curled around one calf and rested on his foot.

My fellow ninth graders sat on benches, with instrument cases under their butts, and looked taller than they were. Some were purely alert, trying to figure out if he was going to kill people at random, or just me and Pinch. Some looked instantly wiser. They recognized the yellowy odors and bulbous eyes, if not the particular face. But they were surprised the schoolyard had been invaded. Oblivious clumps of kids ambled by the court, and from a nearby bungalow, short oboe and piccolo notes stamped the air. Band was the last period of the day.

Seth repeated himself, and I stared into his forehead, at the broad bottoms of the horns, where it must have stung when they pushed through. Staring just slightly above his eyes always put me in a daze when he was rambling. He'd say, *Look at me when I'm talking to you,* and I'd say, *I am.* Only the rare frown, pout, or tremble from me. That's how I played it.

Felt the still air on my eyes. Told myself to hold my chin up. 'I was about to take Pinch to the orthodontist,' is what I think I said. 'Was just on my way.' At my sides, fingers curled tight behind my thumbs. I glanced at Pinch, who was an arm's length away. For a twelve-year-old, she had soft, nine-year-old limbs. She was motionless but not stiff. Pinch's gray movie-camera eyes were thorough and hot with panic.

'I told you,' Seth said, 'not to be hanging up here in this court or whatever this little elitist bullshit is supposed to represent.' He had on creased navy suit pants and an undershirt and black loafers with no socks. There was a ring of had to be thirty keys in his hand. Seth looked at me with his iris and pupil indistinguishable from each other, and showed his carrot teeth. Black hair stood up on his scarlet-brown arms. The maniac was lost on a trip to pure hatred, but he'd managed to find me. And I never did *anything* to that fool. On the court I was scared and pissed at myself for being scared. Pissed at myself for even wondering what was his deal.

Seth said he was tired of my bullshit, took a step up and backhanded me across my face, his knuckles catching me right on the cheekbone. All those keys hit high near my temple, and like a fucking wimp I fell, the stupid slap pushing me down on the side of my kneecap, hip, and heel of my hand. He grabbed Pinch's wrist while I was still on the asphalt, on the white line that separated the court from the rest of the playground.

Dizzy. The reeling made me still and quiet. I had to get reoriented. Of course my eyes felt like they wanted to come out of my face, my mouth filled with water, I started sweating under my arms, on my nose, between my breasts. All that was normal. But I didn't like the fact that the spinning continued. Pain I knew how to accept—have patience, just let it get fainter and fainter. But even looking down and pressing my palms at the ground was no help with the slow twirl. The cracks in the cement and hard gray circles of gum spelled a message I couldn't decipher. My nostrils pulsed without permission. I could hear Pinch still breathing.

'Gimme your bus pass,' Seth said.

Shifted my weight so I sat flat on my butt. Got the brown leather cord from under my shirt and off my neck. Felt it rub against my face, felt it flip my hair up. I threw it in front of me, just beyond my feet. The pass and my house key were attached. Pinch got loose from Seth, darted out, picked them up, and then stood for a moment looking at me before Seth snatched the long cord back.

'Oh now Pinchy-Pinch wants to move,' he said.

He got in her tiny, lightbulb face. Might have been trying to gouge her eyes out with his horns. But every place on my body except for right under my eye felt shot by a huge needle of Novocain. Fingers fat and dead, legs splayed from my hips like a paraplegic's. Air licked at wetness on my face and I hoped there were no tears, I hoped there was a cut. Eyelids got heavy but I wouldn't blink. I watched his hands stuffing the cord in his pants pocket, was wary of his feet. I'd have to get up, though, if he fucked with Pinch. Even if I couldn't do anything, I'd have to get up just so she'd see that I had. But he was just teasing her, twisting up his face a half-inch from hers, calling her a baby, a waste. I pushed my tongue against my bottom front teeth, drank spit. *As if this is the worst,* I wanted to yell at his weak ass. I wanted to say, *Is this all you fucking got.*

'You can walk your ass home,' Seth turned and said to me. 'And if your little friends are really your friends, they *might* walk with you.' He looked at them when he said the last part, and a bushy-haired white girl who I barely knew had the sense—late!—to call for a yard teacher. Most of the kids began to inch off, then run, some lugging their trumpets or violas, some abandoning them for the sake of speed. 'Since you want to hang with these pussies so bad,' Seth called out—half to me and half to them—'since they're *so much more important* than getting your sister to where she needs to go . . . you see how much they like you now.'

He pushed Pinch off ahead of him. The turtle pace was gone. She had to jog a bit every few steps to keep him at a safe distance behind her. I knew Seth wasn't taking my sister to the orthodontist, knew she was scared but not crying, knew she was worried about me on the ground in front of all those kids. They weren't my friends. They were just other ninth graders, mostly fools from Band. Even Mom would know that. Seth had never been up to Bret Harte before, for anything. The only friends he knew of mine and Pinch's were kids on our block who knew enough to break wide when they saw him.

My sorry self still waited to rise. I had to. Even on the

ground I'd no sense of balance. A skeletal boy walked over with his big pores in his cheeks. Had hambone wrists, big flat ears, and a dollar-sized patch of silver hair. Sat not too far from me in Spanish II. Or Living Skills. He had my clarinet case and book bag.

'You can take the bus home,' he said, putting a transfer in my hand, 'if that's where you're going.' My face hurt and my knee was bleeding. He looked like the novitiates at my nannah's church. I'd never paid the boy any attention. Hadn't noticed the silver hair.

'I'm not going home.'

'Are you trying to wait for the yard teacher.'

In my head I said, *No. I'm trying to figure out if this is regular life.*

Then my true friend Obe—short for Obeden—came running up from over by the racquetball courts, wire-rimmed eyeglasses bouncing on his nose. He pushed in between Novice and me, and in his raspy voice Obe said I could come to his house for a while. Obe and I had become friends because he was one to save his lunch money to buy tropical fish, and my mother usually packed big lunches with liverwurst and canned puddings and Obe and I shared it all. I also loved, although not as much as he did, to watch Obe's fish in the big tanks his father built for him. Obe collected rainbow-finned fish that were finicky about temperature and light and food. He was always reading about them and scooping out the floating dead. When he spoke more than five sentences at a time, it was usually about the cichlids.

'He's not my father,' I said, like Obe didn't know that already. 'I hope those fools from Band know that.' I'd said it so Novice would know.

'They do,' Obe lied. 'If they don't, I'll tell them.'

'Don't tell them shit.'

I got it together to stand up—shook Novice and Obe off—

put the transfer in my bag. Plaid-shirted yard teacher sidled up and said, 'What's going on here.'

Novice and Obe barely looked over. 'Nothing,' they said together.

'What happened to your face,' the gaunt man said, with the whistle dangling from his wrist, and orange hair exploding from his ears. He waited on one, but didn't want an answer. I collected my stuff, started walking toward the bus stop on Foothill.

Mom always said that the thing about Foothill and MacArthur and all those endless Oakland boulevards was that no matter how far away from home you were, if you found one of those streets, you weren't lost at all. I got on the No. 40 bus with my book bag, my clarinet, my face fucked up. Rode west like a cowgirl. I was hazy and hated that I had to hold on to the seat. Said to myself, I don't want to get killed or raped or anything out here. But my ass is not going back to that house. I only wished I had Pinch.

That's all I was crying about. My sister was with that fool and who knew when Mom would get home. And what could she do, anyway? I couldn't go back, though. I wouldn't call. The bus was packed. I could see the gnarled, lucky people, their simulated concern. I *know* I was crying. Everyone knew, everything hurt. No one cared. I was on my own, and if Oakland was hell—and it was sometimes, in some parts, in bright light—at least it was mine and I knew my way around.

Passed a stop and screamed the loudest I'd ever screamed. Tall, bald, shrill shriek. I'd pulled the string that rang the bell, and the No. 40 kept moving. I screamed words, they had to have been words. I heard brakes screech but they weren't louder than me. Got off with my bag and case, and with vomit coming up my throat, burning along where the scream had torn.

I was fine, though, fine.

I wished and wished I had Pinch. That was the only thing.

CHAPTER 2

Right on the school playground, Seth jammed his thumb into the soft spot behind Paige's clavicle. Pinched her nose long and hard so she had to breathe with her mouth open and talk through gasps and heaves and humiliation. I thought he was going to kick her, but he didn't. This wasn't the first time. But I didn't think Paige would leave without me.

That afternoon, Paige didn't come home from school. Hours went by in our bedroom, and I got more confused, but took pride in her absence. Even during the most volatile moments at our apartment across from San Antonio Park, I'd rarely pictured me, Paige, or Mom away from it forever.

'You don't leave people,' Mom always said, 'at the first sign of trouble.' So until Paige broke out, I'd thought that was the rule.

That Ninth Grade Court night, Mom got home from work at about seven-thirty. She came to me and Paige's room, saw me faking homework, said, 'Where's your sister?' Mom still had on her coat, had her new canvas purse in her hand, and her keys.

I didn't say anything.

'She doesn't have anything this late,' Mom said.

Shook my head, No.

'I don't know where she is,' Seth shouted from him and Mom's room. 'So don't come in here asking me.'

Mom glanced at each corner of our room, like Paige might appear. 'You went to the orthodontist?'

'No.'

Mom sat down across from me, on Paige's made bed. My sister's pajamas peeked out from under her pillow. A paperback copy of *The Towering Inferno* was there, too. Mom put her purse next to her, held on to her keys tightly. 'Say what happened, Pinch.'

I wasn't going to say what happened, but I finally said, 'We left before she did.'

'Left where? Who's "we"?'

'Left the goddamn school,' Seth said. When he was drunk, he overemphasized the end of every word, like he didn't want to hear himself drawl. He leaned in the doorway, looked at Mom like she was young as me. Held a mug of something numbing. 'She'll be back here in a minute. Paige won't stay in the streets all night.'

All the way home from the Ninth Grade Court, Seth kept saying that Paige cared too much about silly things. 'All that school shit. Plays . . . and that trumpet. Involved in every goddamn club . . . waste of time . . . running around doing this, doing that . . . running the fuck around, *in* everything.'

I stayed paces ahead of him. Thinking, *It's a clarinet.*

'You ain't like your mama, Pinchy,' he said. 'Or your sister. You don't say a goddamn thing. So you'll be all right. Keep laying back. You can see when motherfuckers are coming for you.'

Then he said, 'Slow *down*,' and snatched me by the back of my shirt. Standing there three blocks from the apartment, Seth was in a sweat. I looked in his eyes, the whites were four shades of gray. Then he got my upper arm. Half-dragged me.

'Good thing you're cute,' he'd said as we turned at San Antonio Park. 'And gonna get cuter. Because you're dumb as a fucking doornail.'

In me and Paige's bedroom, Seth looked at my open

workbook, said, 'Finish that so we can eat.' He picked up
Mom's purse, made a motion for her to follow him, then
started down the short hallway.

Mom rose to follow but leaned over me first. 'Sit tight,'
she said in less than a whisper. 'Be quiet in here. Don't come
out until I get back.'

She left the room. I sat there. Seemed like an hour, could
have been ten minutes. She came back. Looked worried but
focussed.

'I'm gonna go search now for Paige. He's across the bed,
will be asleep in a minute.' Mom handed me the phone. 'If it
rings, pick up immediately. So he doesn't wake up. Whoever it
is, tell them I'm asleep, and so is Seth.'

So he's going to be here? With me?

'Pinch, I need you to do this. In case your sister calls. I
know you know what to say to get her home. You can do it?'

'Yes.'

'Okay. Your sister's going to be fine. You're going to be
fine. I'm going now. Be quiet as possible.'

The moment she left, I ventured out. Mom hadn't given
me enough phone cord to maneuver with. I wanted more, so I
could go deeper into me and Paige's room, not just sit up on
the bed like a target.

Noisy odors of hot sauce and liquor and cologne in the
apartment, but no noise. Gathered tangled cord, went and
stood by their bedroom door. Heard Seth breathing. Heard a
groan.

Throat tightened up. Sweat broke out on my nose. Walked
quickly, softly back to our room, dragging cord behind me.
Just as I got settled in our closet, moved shoes, and got a coat
over my knees, the phone rang and I about flew from my skin.
Heart beating like crazy. Answered it *so* fast, too.

'Hello?'

'Pinch?' *Yay!* It was Paige.

'Hi.' I spoke faintly.

'What are you doing?' She didn't sound like she was calling from a phone booth. And she sounded urgent but not hysterical.

'Waiting for Mom,' I said. 'She already came home. She
went to look for you.'

'Look for me where?'

'I don't know.'

'Who are you there with?'

'Seth.'

'Is he asleep?'

'Yeah.'

'For how long?'

'Not that long.' I was almost murmuring.

'Huh? You need to come where I am.'

Yes. Please. I don't want to be here. 'Where.' Spoke up the
tiniest bit.

'I'm, um . . . in Berkeley. You know how to get the bus to
the pizza place on Telegraph and Durant. Take the 40.'

'I know.'

'If I'm not there, wait for me. Or no, go to the big library,
Doe Library, to the reading room.' She began to speak
quickly. 'If I'm not there, go to the bowling alley under the student union. You know where that is. And if I'm not there, go to
Cody's Bookstore, by the maps and stuff.'

'Can you just stay in one place?'

'Okay I'll try. But you need to leave.' She paused, like she
was looking around where she was. 'I have to get off this phone.
Be careful. Leave that house right now. I'll find you. Or you'll
find me.'

'What about Mom?'

'Just get out, Pinch. That's all I know about right now.'

IT WAS going on fifty hours since the incident at the Ninth Grade Court. None of us had been asleep for longer than an hour at a time since.

Mom checked the three of us into a motel on University Avenue, by Cal. It was called the Eagle Point. In the Eagle Point room, Paige walked into the bath as soon as I came out. The bedspreads were thin. The bathroom was clean, the radio was old, and the television made a loud buzzing sound on every other channel. I flipped it off. Mom looked grateful for the lack of noise, and for me. Because I had found Paige, and then Mom found us.

Before the motel, there'd been burgers that neither Paige, Mom, or I ate, at a diner called Lois the Pie Queen.

Gram Liz had taken the hour flight up from Los Angeles, so before we went to the Pie Queen, we got her to the airport, so she could fly back.

Before the airport, we'd been at Highland Hospital. Emergency.

Between Highland and the airport, we went to Mom's daytime job at the phone company for a while. Old photos of us, with white borders, pinned on her cork board. In striped jumpers, on Nannah's side lawn.

By the time we got to the motel, I'd spent almost two days thinking my sister might have changed so much that she forgot who I was to her.

Paige opened the door of the bathroom, stood in the frame. She had scabs and dry elbows and hands. Ungreased hair and a frown. Draped in a giant black windbreaker, she also had on a red one-piece bathing suit and huge black sweatpants. In a haphazard way, she was dressed for work at Diamond Pool. She helped out up there, longed to be a lifeguard. In a pocket of the jacket, Paige stuffed a white pharmacy bag with tubes of ointments. Looked past the bruises on my neck and shoulders, to Mom.

I settled on the carpet between the beds. After what happened when I found my sister, I felt body-slammed, punched all over, or caught in a riptide. My body was overly examined. Jaws ached. Head missing clumps of hair. There'd been an accident. I had my own prescriptions, was glad to be breathing.

Mom slouched on the plastic chair near the pine desk. My sister hitched up the sweatpants, snapped closed the jacket.

Mom said, 'You should lay down, Paige.'

'I will later.'

'You're going out.'

'Yes, Mom,' Paige said. 'Going to work.'

'You're sure.' Mom sat up straighter, but her posture was missing something.

'Do I have on my uniform?'

Mom looked over at me. 'Take your sister with you, then.' Like my approval was necessary. I was exhausted and wanted to sleep.

'Yep,' Paige said. 'And what's your situation, Mom?'

'For just a while, I have to go over . . . deal with Seth.' Mom's posture and her voice were missing the poise of authority.

'Deal with what.'

We have lots of stuff over there, I wanted to say. *And Mom bought most of that furniture. There must be loose ends.*

'He and I have to . . . work out some things,' Mom said. 'I need to tell him you're fine.'

'That's what you need to do. Tell him I'm fine.'

'He's been worried.'

'He knows what he did.'

'He didn't know where you were.'

In my head I said, *He sent her where she was.*

'He didn't come looking for me.'

'Would you have wanted him to?'

'I don't want him to do anything but die.'

Mom, ask Paige how she is. Tell her to say what happened.

'Paige I know you understand . . . that Seth has a problem. Sometimes people need help.'

Paige's shoulders came forward like she wanted to hit Mom. Like she was getting her nerve up.

Mom said, 'I'll be back by here in a little while, after you get home from work. At like nine.'

'And what happens when you come back here.'

'We'll stay here for a short time,' she said, looking at me, and around the room. 'Then I'm going to try and work it out so maybe the two of you can stay with—'

I said, 'The two of us?'

But Paige was already clear on where Mom was.

'With who, Mom? Who can Pinch and I stay with?'

Silence in the vaguely lit room with the two double beds. Paige hadn't moved from the bathroom door. I fiddled with a skinny white vase that had been on the nightstand. Pulled at a folder that described laundry facilities.

Paige said, 'Say something, Mom. I'm about to be late for work.'

'Hold on. I'm talking. I want you to lie down, anyway. Now. Rest.'

Paige looked snubbed. Like she was an adult being called on childish behavior. She was a few weeks from being fifteen. I was glad Paige was back. I wanted to tell her to call in sick. She'd only had a birdbath, and I didn't know who the sweat-pants belonged to.

Paige said, '*Stay with who,* Mom?'

I wanted to hear a plan, too. An idea that didn't include Seth or the apartment across from San Antonio Park.

'Paige, give me a minute.'

'You've had a minute.'

'Listen. You don't talk to me like—'

'Tell me how to talk to you. Tell me so I know the rules.'

'Act like I'm your mother.' Mom wasn't indignant. She was too depleted for that. Her purse was on the empty desktop, one of the two straps torn and drooping.

'You are,' Paige said. 'And you should feel proud. I'm fine, Pinch is fine. No drug addicts here, no drinkers, nobody pregnant. I get good grades, Pinch hangs in there. So you're done, Mom. You got it. And you know what I think? I think you should rent me and Pinch a place. You can get Seth together, and me and Pinch can worry about me and Pinch.' One of Paige's eyes was smaller than the other. Cheekbone shiny with salve and still bloated from the Ninth Grade Court. Paige was talking madness.

'Rent you a place.'

'What other option is there? You already paid a week here,' Paige said. 'Can't keep doing that.'

'You don't know what I can or can't do.'

'You're right about that.'

Mom ran the print of one pinkie over the length of an eyebrow. The people at the telephone company had told her to take all the time she needed. Take the rest of the day if that's what was called for.

'Pinch, what about you?' Mom looked at me, through me.

'What about me.'

Hands in her lap. Short nails ragged, fingers nicked, the odd knuckle swollen. 'Are you all right?'

'Mmm-hmm.'

'You're going to put ice on your arm? You know how your skin is.'

'Yeah, Mom.' *I know I bruise easily. Know just how much I can take.*

'And you have those Ace bandages for yourself?'

'I have everything.'

Paige did call in sick, right after Mom left. Her Diamond

Pool coworkers were surprised she'd been thinking about coming in at all. The pool was the background of too many weird
times, a mirage of escape. Paige needed to quit that job, anyway.

In all her clothes, and still in her too-big flip-flops, my sister fell out on the bed furthest from the window. Dabbed oint-
ment on the side of one of her hands. Then she pulled the
bedspread over her legs and burrowed down so the windbreaker's collar was over her ears.

'Lay down by me, Pinch,' Paige said with her face to the
greenish ceiling. 'You need some sleep I think.'

I was scared, but after a while I climbed in. Felt like Jane
Eyre, climbing in bed with a loved dead girl. My sister was
cold. Her eyes were wide and vacant.

'Paige,' I whispered, 'do you hate me?'

Nothing behind my sister's eyes. Nothing in front.

I'D NEVER imagined just Paige and I living in a palace
with an ice-cream fountain in the kitchen, and a Ferris wheel
in the backyard. A fortress on a mountain where guinea pigs
and puppies lived all around, Easter-egg hunts happened
every day, and people figured out what I wanted just by glanc-
ing at my face. I didn't imagine those kinds of things. I never
even imagined an absence of tension. Or ease of movement.
Or long stretches of relaxed happiness in myself or Paige. But
that's how it was for a while, almost, at our new apartment.

We had the top floor of a house, a small two-bedroom
with hardwood floors, on the AC Transit No. 40 bus line. AC
stands for Alameda–Contra Costa. BART stands for Bay Area
Rapid Transit, and we weren't too far from the Merritt BART
station, either.

The landlady, Mrs. Vangelisti, was in Gram Liz's age
group. She worked millions of hours at her family's delicatessen
near Berkeley, lived alone in the two downstairs floors. Mrs.

Vangelisti's Mr. Vangelisti had died at Jonestown. She said he'd always called the house their pseudo-Victorian, so we began referring to our place as the Pseudo. We even had access to the washing machine on the enclosed back porch and the clothesline. Rent was cheap, too, because the Pseudo was in an iffy area of Oakland most black people and cops referred to as Funktown, and because Mrs. Vangelisti hadn't kept up with what she could have rented it for, not since her husband had been gone, which was actually fourteen years before he left for Guyana.

Mrs. Vangelisti thought Paige was at least in college or tech school because Paige carried herself like she was about business. She and I would get up, have cold or hot cereal and sometimes toast for breakfast. Mom gave us allowance and we had bus passes, so Paige took her bus to St. J's, I took mine to Bret Harte. The rule was to call Mom if you were going to be home more than an hour late from your last class or club of the day. And the office at school had Mom's home and work numbers on file in case there was an emergency. On weeknights, especially while I was still in junior high, Paige fixed something good like French toast or Hamburger Helper, or even a cut-up baked chicken with Stove Top and pickled beets from the can. Mom came by often. Made pots of spaghetti for us, or a bunch of enchiladas we could freeze. Mom paid our rent, utilities, and Paige's tuition at St. J's—mine, too, once I got there. She usually came by between punching out at the phone company and punching in at the textile place. Put new groceries in our refrigerator, checked in on us like a camp counselor.

DURING Easter break of my ninth-grade year at Bret Harte, Paige and I met Maynard.

I thought he was a dream. Maynard said, 'How you doin'' in place of hello. Said it fast, like it was all one word, and accepted 'hi' as a response. I found this suave. Plus Maynard

was muscley and walked lazily and was the oldest boy in
Upward Bound. UB was a weeklong day camp that Paige
signed us up for. It was supposed to help smart teens designated
at-risk-for-failure. Not like Paige and I were in some ghetto circumstance—like I said, the Pseudo was in Funktown, but it was
right off the lake. Right close to where small bungalows were
yellow-walled and tile-roofed, and closer still to stucco du-
plexes with terraces too short for a table, but big enough for
two chairs. Ceiling fans you could see twirling through bay windows. Paige signed us up because UB sponsored field trips. The
Psuedo was nice, but Paige loved a field trip.

After the second day of Spring Upward Bound, Paige and
I walked from the steel double doors of the East Oakland
Youth Center. UB was over for the day, and I was glad to be
out. Enough already with the representatives from Reading Is
Fundamental. The fake, indoor graffiti: LEARN TO TEACH
YOURSELF. And, CHARACTER AND CONDUCT SHAPE EACH
OTHER. I wanted to go to the Hallmark store in the mall, look
at the stuffed animals, and the statuettes they had of black peo-
ple in slavery times.

Stood there on the cement walkway next to Paige, button-
ing my sweater.

'You work up at Diamond Pool?' Maynard said to Paige
from the bus stop, which was right in front of the center. He
was grinning, for no visible reason. Back straight, shoulders
relaxed. We'd stayed behind a few minutes so Paige could help
the facilitator finalize the next day's outing. Thought we were
the last ones around.

'Yep,' Paige said. She was proud to be noticed, but suspi-
cious.

'Lifeguard?'

'Nah. Junior lifeguard.' We walked toward him. Maynard's skin like a Mission fig's—brown, then the darkest
brown. His shins and forearms glossy with the scars of an

asphalt upbringing. It was chilly for him to have on no jacket. His tennis shoes were wiped clean, and he had new laces. The elastic waistband in his sweatpants was stretched out. He had an oval spot of dust-gray hair just above his left temple.

'And what are you,' he said to me, 'a junior junior life-guard?'

'I'm her sister.'

'That's your job?' I liked him for asking that, even if he didn't know what he was asking.

'Slave labor.'

Maynard gave a little chuckle, then looked to Paige again. 'So it's the gold mines we're going to tomorrow?'

'Not mines,' Paige said. 'A river. With gold in it.'

'You picked this trip? Sounds tired.'

Paige was unfazed. 'You'll like it. You've seen wild mustard before?' The field trip was a train ride to Mariposa, where we were going to pan for gold. Hear about trail-finder Charles Frémont, see what was supposed to be the state's oldest courthouse. Right up Paige's alley.

'Mustard?'

'The plant. Not like ketchup. Yellow flowers everywhere on the ride up to Gold Country.'

'So you've been there.'

'I rode through it on the way to Sac a couple of times,' Paige said. 'When I was little.'

I remembered those trips. Wished that Paige had forgotten them.

'Where ya'll stay at?'

'Funktown,' I said.

'Wanna go over to Merritt Bakery, get something to eat?'

'Don't have money for all that,' Paige said. The bakery was also a café, and wasn't too far from where we lived.

'I got money.'

'Where,' Paige wanted to know, 'do you work?'

I wondered if he sold weed, or maybe crack. Wondered why he came to Upward Bound. There were other high-school girls there, but no other high-school boys.

'I got enough to go to Merritt Bakery and take you two.'

We went with him, and before the pie à la mode, their little push-and-pull was running smoothly. It was like they'd known each other for a while.

The next day, the three of us hung out in Gold Country, panning for granules, listening to the guides.

'Stop acting like you're not having a good time,' Paige said to him when the three of us got off by ourselves. 'You're trying to find gold as hard as I am.'

May was barefoot and ankle-deep in the shallow river. 'I'm having a *fine* time,' he said. 'I'd just rather look around, trip off what it would be like to live out here. This panning is bullshit.'

'You heard of El Dorado.'

'The lost city of gold. You're the only one who's watched a filmstrip? Did state history homework? Only one gone on these trips?'

Paige pressed her lips together, resisted gladness. The only thing better would have been if Maynard kept tropical fish in a tank. At Bret Harte, Paige had had a friend named Obe who kept fish. She adored him. He'd seen the whole Ninth Grade Court thing go down, though, so she cut him off. Paige missed Obe, a boy she could allow to know her privacies, a boy who admired her, didn't focus on her boobs, didn't laugh at brief histories of herself, or of San Francisco's cable cars. I'd liked Obe, too.

Paige kept her face to her pan, but I looked at Maynard. He wasn't flirting with her. He wasn't looking at me, either. Paige didn't even have to see his face. She'd detected the absence of judgment or ploy. Maynard stared at the riverbed, like maybe there was gold in the mud, after all.

From then on, Paige, May, and I partnered up for

Upward Bound confidence-boosting exercises. He said he had a girlfriend at his public high school. She was sexy, he said, and smart. Was going to graduate high in her class. He told us that his school was a rowdy one that always made a big deal about how their few "gifted" ones achieved collegiate distinction. I didn't know how May could be gifted one semester and then regular the next, but that's how he was classified.

'Lady up there called me "not achieving up to my potential,"' he told us on the last day of Upward Bound. 'Why you think they told me to come to this program? Supposed to inspire me, is the plan.' We were walking from Merritt Bakery toward the Pseudo. Every day after Upward Bound, we'd gone there for fried eggs and dessert, May proudly treating. Paige had never invited him in our place. We three stood out on the street, in front.

'Your mom home?'

'No,' Paige said. 'At work.'

'You can have company when she's not home?'

'No.'

Maynard should have said his good-byes. Paige could have shooed him along.

Out came Mrs. Vangelisti on the porch. 'Can I speak with you a moment?' Of course she walked toward Paige.

'I know. I'll have rent day after tomorrow.' Mom gave Paige cash, Paige passed it on. Mom could be late, but she didn't miss a month.

'Next week,' Vangelisti said, 'it's going to be due again.'

'I'm clear on that.'

'You shouldn't have loaned me this money, Paige.' Maynard went in his pocket, pulled out bills. 'I can get it somewhere else.' He handed Mrs. Vangelisti the money. Not like he was trying to show off, or get over on, or embarrass Paige. It was like Maynard had fathomed the fringes of an odd set-up, and found a path toward knowing more.

'This isn't all of it,' Vangelisti said.

'Day after tomorrow,' Paige said again. Now she was at a loss. 'I'll give it back to you,' she said to Maynard when our landlady walked away.

'You should. It's my mom's.'

Paige and I walked up the driveway to the front door. May stood on the sidewalk.

'Come on,' I said, and he finally bounded up behind us. It was a Friday, so we sat up there all afternoon and evening, watching television, eating pistachios. Paige washed clothes, I dusted my room. May sat around like he'd been over a hundred times, pulled soda from the refrigerator. Paige told him to rinse his glass, and he did. May knew without us saying that Paige and I lived there alone, that we could eat ice cream for breakfast if we wanted to, stay on the phone all night, or wear wrinkled clothes. Before too many more visits, he must have figured, too, that none of it was a thrill. He came over often, played music at a decent volume, danced his stiff dance, or read car magazines while Paige cooked or lay across her bed asleep or flipped through guidebooks or wrote in her diary. Maynard occasionally brought over his sister, Teeara, and her boyfriend, Todd. Tee was a bit wild, but Maynard kept her in check. Todd was wilder, and Maynard didn't let him come by as often.

When Todd was by, though, he sometimes referred to May's sexy girlfriend. Paige and I never did meet her.

MOSTLY, it was fun times. Tee, for one, had a get-a-party-started personality. She and Todd brought lots of food by the Pseudo. Usually barbecue, El Pollo Loco, or salmon croquettes from Lois the Pie Queen. They brought wild-berry wine coolers. Before long we met May's friend Donnell, and Donnell's girlfriend, Ch'Rell. Her skin was the sticky crown of gingerbread. 'Rell went to St. J's, too. I'd seen her and her man around.

All of us went over to the lake together on weekends, to the Grand Lake Theater for movies, and to free concerts at parks in San Francisco. Usually packed in Donnell's mom's Skylark. After school, we'd meet in Berkeley, by Cal, and stand around the arcade. Sometimes we congregated on the corner where there was a Mrs. Fields. We ate the cookies sometimes, when the chips were melty, but mostly we sat outside on milk crates or on the curb. Paige, Ch'Rell, and I in uniform. Todd's box radio screeching. May striding down the street from the record store. Donnell and 'Rell snapping about gas money. Me buying incense from one of the vendors that lined Telegraph Avenue. Sometimes Paige wasn't there. She still reported up at Diamond Pool.

Mom came through the Pseudo pretty often. When we weren't with our crew, Paige and I were over at Nannah and Grandpa's. Either just us, or us and Mom. Seth seemed a stumbling criminal, a faraway sandman. Though Mom and he still lived together, Paige and I never saw him. Small as Oakland is, I liked to think Seth saw me and my sister sometimes, and was too wobbly, or too ashamed to step our way.

Grandpa was getting sick. Back when he first went blind, he'd at least turn his face in the direction of voices. Grandpa still had comments, but now he spoke toward whatever way he was already facing. He barely left his house, not even for sun in the château. It was shivery with dust and spiders, anyway. The icebox had been warm since I graduated elementary school.

Even when it was nice out, as it was one fall morning when we were by there with Mom, Nannah wasn't much in her garden. We'd gone by at the crack of dawn to check on them before getting on the road to Los Angeles, to see Gram Liz.

Sitting in her oven-hot kitchen, Nannah gave us a check for school. 'Give it to Sister Leone,' she said.

'Okay,' I said, even though the science lab was named after Sister Leone, who'd been dead since before we got there.

The El Salvadoran lady from the church who came to Nannah's to change the sheets and cook food for the week was saying *Vete, vete* to the three of us. So we left, and before we even got on the road good, Mom took us clothes shopping at the nice mall in San Leandro. Once we were on Highway 5, we played loud music in Mom's tan Toyota, grooved to songs from her day. Laughed about Mom's bizarre work friends, brought her up to date about class work and school dramas. In the two years we'd been living at the Pseudo, Mom rarely discussed Seth beyond saying, offhandedly, that he was crazy. Paige had just started the twelfth grade, and Mom had still never said anything about the way shit had gone down. Never said a word about how she could still live over in the apartment across from San Antonio. Not like the Pseudo was so far from there.

So it was jolting when Mom turned down the radio and said, 'Seth was let go from his job at the hospital.'

'For real,' Paige said, pretending boredom. 'When.'

'About a little over a year ago.'

I said, 'A year?'

Paige said, 'So you've been paying all the rent?'

'You could say that.'

'Hmph. And ours.'

'Seth got sick.'

'Sick how?'

'Not well.' Mom was cautious. 'Seth wasn't always the person he's turned into. There were times he helped me when no one else . . . Maybe you all don't remember so well, but Seth used to be . . . more . . . normal.'

'As compared,' Paige said, 'to who.'

I said, 'Is he still over there? By the park?'

'I actually put him on a plane a few days ago.' Saying this, Mom was more assertive. 'To Springfield. Illinois. His sister—'

'His sister wants him?'

'I said he was sick, Paige.'

'Fuck that. He's *been* sick.'

'You're cursing in my car now.'

Subject changed. Stillness for a while.

Then Mom said she was looking at some houses to buy. She was grazing the foreclosure ads, especially for places out in Contra Costa County, maybe Martinez or Walnut Creek. She could get a place that needed work, she said, for almost nothing.

I looked to the backseat. Paige was stiff.

Faced forward again. *Walnut Creek? Who wants to live in Walnut Creek? What about hanging with Maynard and Teeara and Todd? What about the Pseudo? I'd gotten used to it. We had a way we were there.*

Fingers light on the steering wheel, Mom controlled what she could—the car, and the conversation. She instructed us about moments in which we could afford to be gracious. She'd always liked the topic.

'It's when someone who should be happy for you isn't,' Mom said. 'That's a time. And when you know, inside yourself, that you are clearly better than the person or episode you're dealing with, that's another time. And anytime your life is going well, you should be extra-compassionate.'

Neither of us said anything.

'You can't expect everyone to act as you would act.' Mom talked directly to the windshield. 'They aren't you. You can't go around, frustrated, saying, "If it were me, I'd do this or that." It's *not* you, and you don't know the other person's constitution or footing. All you can do is be you, and do the best you can for you. And your sister.'

I guessed she was speaking to both of us.

Then Mom reminded us that job applications always had to be filled out *completely,* and that being mature meant putting on a smiling face, even when you wanted to howl. Mom eyed my black eyeliner, reminded me to use makeup sparingly, because once I started wearing it, I wouldn't want to ever be without it. She let us know what our best physical qualities were. For me it was my eyes, my small frame. For Paige it was her hair and her legs. Mom said for us to accentuate the positive.

She was hungry for agreement though, so she backtracked. 'Really, Paige. If I was sick, wouldn't you want someone to take care of me? If you were sick?' Mom lived to say that the Golden Rule was golden for a reason. 'Imagine if you had a problem, a sickness that you couldn't . . .' Mom left it alone.

Paige scowled out the window at cows and carrot fields, at ancient Jack in the Boxes, and at the world-famous Anderson's, where we'd never stopped for the pea soup. My head bobbed with every bump in the road.

'Mom,' Paige said, 'just say why you stayed so long with Seth.'

Mom's turn to be quiet. Miles of California slapped by like a belt.

Rolling into Bakersfield, Paige said, 'Tell us the real deal about whoever is supposed to be our actual dad.'

'You met him once,' Mom said, 'you just don't remember.'

We knew this story.

I said, 'Why haven't we met him again.'

'He wasn't a very good man.'

'How do you know,' Paige said, 'that he's not good now?'

'He would've reached out. We aren't that hard to find.'

'We've moved,' Paige said.

We've moved apart, is what I wanted to say.

'Nannah and Grandpa have lived in that same house,' Mom said, 'for a hundred years.'

'I'm going to look him up.'

'You'll get your feelings hurt.'

No, Mom. You'll get your feelings hurt. Except I had no way of knowing her feelings. But for the salt in her voice.

Paige twisted her mouth.

Remaining silent was easy for me.

Mom then told us tales about the Dad, about him being all Haight-Ashbury and loving nature, about him having sold cars when he'd lived in Berkeley. On this trip, she slipped and mentioned his mustache. That was news.

There were miles of poppies along the hilly highway just before the northernmost borders of the county of Los Angeles, and when I saw the orange-red dots, I knew we were still an hour from Gram Liz's. But Mom charmed time when she told those bright blurry Dad stories. We ended up at her mother's in what seemed ten minutes.

Me in front, keeping Mom company. Paige in the corner behind me, jaw on her collarbone, satisfied to sleepiness by familiar crumbs.

CHAPTER 3

The Acorns got thick at night. Desperadoes idled.

Boys with cold curved shoulders patrolled. Boasted. Laughed like they owned laughter, and could do with it what they pleased. We knew some of them, from the No. 40, or M-B Mall. But Paige and I didn't go too often to the Acorns at night. What for, when May was always at the Pseudo.

'They always wanted Acorn to be like it is,' May's towering mom said, waving her ball mitt of a hand. 'Raggedy.'

May lived in West Oakland, in the Acorn housing projects. A cluster of short apartment buildings just repainted brown. To hear Paige tell it, in some fake long-ago time, when the Acorns existed for war workers and their families, the area was meant to be the 'fruit of the land of oaks.' The Acorns weren't *the* projects. They were *a* project, in the true sense of the word.

POST NO BILLS. Me, Paige, and May's mom were walking back from the liquor store. At a clip. It was late May. Light blue sky and perfect puff clouds. We passed a construction site where they'd been building at something for the longest. Signs said there'd be a Safeway, a check-cashing place, a Winchell's Donuts, a McDonald's. POST NO BILLS. I thought they meant for companies not to post their receipts, not to make public that people owed them money. Maynard had corrected me months ago.

'Read the Acorns' history,' Paige said to May's mom. 'Talk to people who were young in another time.'

'I wasn't young in another time?'

'Another other time. There was forced segregation back then. Fights. And people segregating themselves because . . . just because. Riots and stuff, way before the sixties. Police arresting black people for wearing mink coats in the summertime.'

Paige was so heartfelt, she couldn't see May's mom poking the fire. 'Why for wearing coats? It was against the law to be hot? To look dumb?'

'War wages! War wages gave black people money. They felt they could walk where they wanted. Act how they wanted. They had good jobs! Right down here at the shipyards.' Paige's elbow flipped vaguely west. I saw the dikes of the port. I wasn't exactly sure what a 'shipyard' was. Big ships, I guessed, being built. Lots of men in hard hats with hammers. Paige made it seem like the shipyard days were glorious. The Acorns a plush, busy enclave. Everyone walking around, shoulders back. Sun beaming on mink.

The Acorn buildings huddled around parking lots in boxy cul-de-sacs. We walked into the one that spread before May's family apartment. Overalls and boxer shorts set out to dry on porch banisters. Like big pigeons, Ch'Rell, Donnell, and Todd perched on a car that had been sitting on slit tires in the same space since we'd been visiting May. Todd's box radio blared. *No color lines,* the deejay pronounced after playing a song with a mesmerizing chorus. *Increase the peace.* So many times, we'd all sat there, crunching on Cheetos and drinking Tahitian Treat like it was one. May making rough plans for whatever afternoon lay paved and indifferent before us.

'It's a *quail,*' Paige was saying to May's mom as we neared the front door of the apartment. 'That's California's state bird. Not an eagle.'

'How,' May's mom said, 'do you know all this.'

Seth used to lecture Paige about history until she was

brain-dead. From our bedroom, I'd hear Seth say, 'But today niggas ain't shit.' That's when I knew he was done for a while.

And Seth had meant his today, the today of the moment he said it. Now it was ours.

May's mom told us to hurry up. Her son had already left for the gym. My face got warm. It had to be pride. All of us were going to see May play basketball.

M A Y was a forward, but not the captain. Even he admitted his game was selfish. Before the first jump ball, though, girls were sweaty from yelling *Go!* and *May!* Now six feet, big-boned, and smooth but for the few fluffs on his chest and pits in his forehead, Maynard was cute, but his feet fell fast, heavy, and flat. Too flat to get a scholarship.

He held his chin up, though, and the tops of his ears seemed taped to his head. He wore contacts when folks our age who were nearsighted had glasses. I screamed his name, too. Was glad to know him in the way so many other girls thought they wanted to. He and Paige still didn't seem to like each other in a boyfriend-girlfriend way. But she fed him lots of times after practice. He slept on our couch on weekends.

Paige was almost eighteen, thought she was grown with her ceramic nails and ladylike posture. I thought so, too. Teeara was two years older than May, lived in the same apartment with him and his parents and her two sons by two different fathers. Teeara's hair was layered with precision, and curled meticulously. I could never remember the name of Teeara's eldest son's father. He walked the straight-and-narrow, ran on the hoop squad at San Francisco State. We never saw him.

Teeara's younger son's dad—that was Todd—sold a little dope on the weekends and evenings in a certain Acorn parking lot. He was a cashier at the Super G in North Berkeley six-to-noon. Everybody in Oakland seemed to at least know of everyone else, and because Todd was selling, people knew him even better. May was often around Todd, so folks were starting to know who May was, too.

His mom sat tall in the stands, three vodkas deep. Next to me, breath all hot. Beige eyes bloody, beige face flushed and cakey. To the group of parents on the other side of her, May's mom said, 'All y'all need a son like mine.'

May's dad kept one eye on the ball, the other on the door where Todd was holding court with three poorly disguised crackheads. May never seemed embarrassed about his mother or father. He'd sometimes pause on his way home to get a vial of crack for his pops, and counted his mom's money for her. She sold weed by the nickel bag.

'Keep sixty for yourself,' May's mother had told him that afternoon, before the basketball game. Looked at us when she said, 'Take your friends to the show.'

May's mom liked her son, and us, in the way that even the most distracted people make time to pee. She had to like Donnell—he and May had been boys since bantam football, had been hanging out, off and on, since they were nine years old. Donnell's head was big and round, his neck skinny and his skin cold oatmeal. He'd been going out with Ch'Rell since eighth grade. Her mom had been a housewife, and Ch'Rell's dad was a ponytailed white man, did something for the City of Richmond.

After the basketball game, we were on our way to San Francisco, May driving Todd's fresh Jetta. Ch'Rell and Donnell had gone about their own business in Donnell's car.

Todd was in the backseat, between Paige and I. Had one leg stretched straight between the two front seats. He sucked on a joint, then a Camel, then back to the joint. Paige on the Camel with Todd. Me trying to be on the joint, but Paige watching me like a sergeant.

Teeara was up front with May, in a pouty silence about

something. The rest of us haughty and hollering to each other about the crackheads on San Pablo Boulevard. They were drooly with brittle hair and just blank not there. Lacking and wanting. Feeble from feeling everything. Running like hell to, running like hell from. Lips scabby, feet ashy, walking a slow curve around life. Rolling down San Pablo, I barely thought about May's father. Because he wasn't news. And because May was driving flawlessly.

'Paige,' May said, looking directly ahead. 'You and Pinch get enough to eat?'

'Mmm-hmm.'

'Need to stop at the store for anything before you go home?' Easy and happy, like it was his car.

'Nope.'

Not everybody on the street was a crackhead. At stop-lights, May looked at girls with juicy shapes. Looked long at a coppery girl with a small waist and round, high butt, she was holding hands with a date. May stared at her, spiteful. Mad that he needed another guy's seal of approval before commit-ting even his gaze for too long. May was different than Paige. She only liked guys whom she confounded. I hadn't seen May with a girl he really liked. But when he was flirtatious, it was with dizzy chicks who were shameless when they met him, about having screamed his name from the sidelines.

Tight as it was in the backseat, Paige didn't let the side of her thigh brush Todd's. With her finger, she touched the back of Teeara's neck. To get her to loosen up. Tee flinched but didn't turn around. If my boyfriend were Todd, I'd be pissed, too.

'So you're gonna be at Hayward,' Todd said to May.

'What it looks like.'

'You gonna be up there for real? Or you just gonna be up there fucking around with it. Like Paige's gonna do, up at Cal.'

'You talking to me, or Paige.'

'He's not talking to me,' my sister said. 'And he needs to stop talking about me.'

Todd laughed, coughed tightly on weed smoke. He had on sunglasses. So stupid.

'I'll talk to Pinch, then,' Todd said. He pushed the glasses up on his forehead, shifted his butt on the hump. Turned his rubbery face to me. 'You starting to look like a real girl, Pinchy. Got a little body now.'

That's why I didn't ever try really hard to smoke weed. Hated smug, blank marijuana eyes with their built-in excuses.

'Mmmmyes you are.' And he pinched my cheek.

I looked at him, didn't cringe. *Jackass*. His thumb and finger still squeezing my face. He still had the joint in the hand closest to me. Had reached over with the other. He was pressed into me.

'Tee,' Paige said, 'talk to your man.' I sensed my sister's antennae quivering. She ran her thumb up the pale side of her fingers, one by one.

Teeara kept quiet, didn't look back.

Todd ran his palm over my breasts. Gave one a tough squeeze. Tapped it. Said, 'We all been waiting on these.'

I squirmed, flattened. 'Don't touch me. Punk.' I wasn't loud. I was never sure of what level of anger went with what offense. And Todd's eyes muddled my head even more.

Todd giggled. Faced the center again. Hacked up a loud laugh. 'Punk,' he squeaked, like it was amusing I'd called him that. I pushed at him with both hands, didn't want any part of him touching me. He laughed more and was about to put the joint to his mouth again when Paige grabbed his dick. She'd turned in the cramped space and caught him by the nuts, too, with force. Held on. Todd shrieked, started trying to kick and swing at her, but he couldn't close his legs because of the way one was hemmed up between the seats. He couldn't hit Paige hard because it was too small back there. My sister let go, but the commotion of Todd's wild wriggling made May veer over to the curb and stop. Teeara held on to her door. Todd was doubled over, but his elbow still jabbed me over and over. His narrow hips tried to scoot, but there was nowhere to go. Then the joint was on the seat next to his thigh, still burning, and he flailed and struggled to put that out with his hand. 'Fuck!'

Paige got out of the car, and Todd pushed her as she stepped out. She didn't fall.

We were all out of the car. Todd was bent over, seething at Paige. 'Bitch. Stupid bitch-ass bitch. Should slap the shit out of you.' He moaned, a loud hum, and held on to his lower stomach. Tee didn't go to his side. Paige stood near May and me. She didn't look glad or sad, but she didn't look scared either, so I wasn't.

'Fucking bitch.'

'Shut that shit up,' May said.

'Fuck you too.'

I looked around. Paige watched May and Todd. I was reluctant to look at Teeara.

Todd looked at her, though, hard, and she got back in the car. He straightened up some, took small steps toward the driver's seat. Got in carefully, then drove off with gusto.

Paige, May, and I walked two blocks to an AC Transit stop. Stood behind the bench.

'That's what you felt you needed to do?' May said. 'Fight him? Whyn't you say something?'

'You were in the front,' Paige said.

'He touched you on your chest, Pinch? You like him?'

'No I don't like him,' I said. 'I liked him as a friend. Like we're all friends.'

May searched my face. 'Why'd he reach for you like that?'

'How does she know?' Paige said. 'She was just sitting

there, and Todd's conceited, high self felt free. What did you want me to do, Maynard, sit there?'

'No,' he said, and looked at his hands, then at his surroundings. He was surprised by where he was standing, by the sudden turn of events. 'I was right there, everything cool, we're going to the city.'

'Todd's retarded,' Paige said, 'and getting more retarded ever since his name is getting known.'

'Have that sixty. Was going to Pier 39.' May was perplexed. 'He knows y'all are my people.'

And Tee's your sister. But I didn't say that.

After about five minutes, Todd and Teeara rolled up. Stopped with a bounce and screech. Todd smiled, taut and closed. 'Get in,' he said.

I looked at Paige.

'We're cool,' she said.

May said, 'Nigga, press on.'

'Whipped,' Todd said, 'and ain't even got no pussy.' Then he made his wheels singe and scream as he bolted off, the square butt of his Jetta doing a wide swerve.

The three of us got on a bus, and after a few stops, I put my head in Paige's lap. She didn't put her hand on my hair or anything, but she let me rest there.

Only about eight people were on the bus, but May stood the entire way to the Pseudo, one hand on the bar above him. He watched people, watched them watch the rushing boulevard. 'So I'm supposed to beat his ass?'

Yes. Come to my rescue. Usually, May's presence was a shield. But he'd never had to forcefully protect Paige or I from anything. Tee either, for what I knew. Maynard loved his sister, but liked us more than he liked her. He'd little patience for Teeara's ways, but Maynard endured all of Paige's moods—like when she got crabby about Mom, or when some negro she'd met hadn't called her back. And when May wasn't staring into the food Paige made for us, skunked by his own problems, May told my sister she looked good, that she was doing good with me, and that she'd get into a good college. He mainly told Tee to shut up. May iced Paige down with his calm, and when the three of us were together, him taking us out to eat, and just so very steady, I could see him churning beneath, but he soothed me, too.

Maynard was glad he could always come over to the Pseudo, and that there were no grown people around. But sometimes he said, 'This isn't so fair.' He didn't like that we were alone. Of course, he wasn't alone at the apartment in the Acorns, and he didn't like that, either. *No, I've changed my mind. No need for rescue. Don't fight Todd, Maynard.* I'd never seen May violent, or even truly angry, but all I could think was, *You'll probably hurt him.*

Donnell came by to pick May up from our place. Minus the detail of the 'pussy-whipped' comment, Paige told the lame story. Made it funny.

Donnell didn't find it amusing. Ch'Rell laughed and laughed. So did Maynard and I, in the end.

A B O U T a week later, Paige graduated from high school. It was June 1982. May and Donnell graduated from their school, too.

Paige's class sang songs from *Fame* and *Hair* at baccalaureate Mass. Mom and I went in new dresses, brought Paige a huge bunch of white daisies. Paige's mouth stretched wide and her face went starry when she sang about the body electric in chorus with two hundred other seniors. She was glad to hold her flowers, and to be lost in the group.

After Paige's graduation, Gram took us to a seafood dinner at this place called Spenger's near the Berkeley Marina, and then we rode out to Mom's place in Walnut Creek. Mom got on the freeway without saying anything, and Paige didn't argue.

We'd been out there before, at Christmas, around the time she moved in. It was almost the country in dusty WC, about thirty minutes by car from the Pseudo. And Mom's house had needed fixing from the basement to the roof.

'I got a really good price,' Mom said.

'I hope you got it for free.'

That's how it had been between Paige and Mom at Christmas. And pretty much every time we'd gone out there since.

In June, it wasn't so different. Except Mom had begun pulling up old carpet, and it looked like she'd spent every free moment with an SOS pad in her hand. Her place made me think about the Pseudo. How neat we kept it, and how Mrs. Vangelisti had just had the walls painted cream instead of white, and how Paige and I decided one day to pour Drano down all the drains, every two hours over an eight-hour period. We had ivy in plastic pots, spices in the kitchen cabinets. A glass sugar dish and colored paper napkins. Gram Liz had given us a cabinet for our stereo and TV. We had the MY BEST FRIENDS ARE COLORED print on our living-room wall—and I knew what it meant. Nannah gave us pink sheets and pillowslips. And our drains moved fast like they never had.

Mom said, 'There's a bedroom for each of you here.' She didn't seem nervous at all, but I was. 'Small, but nice. Just like at the Pseudo.' Mom called it that, too.

'Mom, I told you I got into Cal.'

'I know, and it's great.'

'So I can't live way out here.'

Not true. She could be to Cal by BART from Walnut Creek in fifteen minutes.

Paige had told Mom back before Christmas that she was applying to San Francisco State and to Cal, because both were

cheap and the nuns at St. J's had told her she would get into
SFSU with no problem, and that she should try for Cal even
though she didn't have straight A's. Paige had a million
extracurricular activities, good SAT scores, plus she was black,
and they needed black people at Cal. Mom had sounded fine
with the plan. Paige filled out all her own applications and
stuff. Hadn't spoken with Mom again about college until she
had acceptance letters from both schools. It was like Mom
knew Paige would get in, would handle what needed to be
handled.

Was it a compliment she was paying to Paige—that we'd
be all right? Did Mom think her daughters were so bright, and
so together, that we'd figure out what needed to be figured out?
It had been three years at the Pseudo, and we were fine.

But Mom stood before us, pretty much saying for us to
leave it, and to come out to Walnut Creek. We were in the
kitchen. New linoleum, scrubbed tile, cardboard boxes of tea
on the open shelves. Of course I didn't ask a thing.

'They gave you some aid, didn't they,' Gram Liz said.

'Yep,' Paige said. 'I got some.'

'Well that's what the good news is. Because your mom
can't go on paying all that rent over there where you are.'

'Mom, be quiet.'

Gram ignored our mom. 'Paige, you need to pack up and
get out here. It's nice.'

Our mother tried to maintain her Mom demeanor. At first
I didn't recognize Gram's expression, but it could only have
been the pickled face of one near a bed of her own making.

Mom opened the cupboard, pulled out three saucepans
before she found a small kettle. 'This is a really big day!' she
said. 'I'm going to put some water on for tea.'

Gram looked at her as if she were a lost cause. I didn't
like it.

Paige's eyelashes were touching the bottom of her brows.

I decided to flow with Mom's upbeat behavior. 'I guess,' I said to my sister, 'I'll have to start showing you some respect.'

Mom said, 'You will, Pinch. You will. Cal's a good school.'

It was all very singsong and Paige listened like she knew the tune.

'You both have been doing a fantastic job over there at that house,' Gram Liz said, 'but you need to come home with your mother.'

'I think Pinch and I are going to stay over at the Pseudo.'

'Pinch is fifteen,' Gram said. 'Pinch is going to do what your momma says.' Chic in her cream suit, Gram squeezed my shoulders like she'd met me at a party long ago, was pleased to see me, and was just as pleased she had someplace else to be.

'Paige I can't tell you what to do,' Mom said. 'You're grown.'

Like that's news.

We cut a lemon pound cake Mom had baked. Paige drank the tea, and drank in Mom and Gram like tonics too weak for what she had.

I said, 'Mom, Paige is tired.'

Then I examined Gram Liz's model teeth and white swoops of hair. A jade brooch lay like a flat green eye against my grandmother's lapel. I thought it might be pinned through to the flesh. Nannah had given it to her. Gram always talked about how the brooch would go to Mom, and then from Mom to Paige. I didn't want it.

Gram Liz said, 'Tired. Yes. Good. I am, too.'

Month: April 1983
Day: Shining Wednesday and a warm night
Attitude: Nostalgic, but for what?

Woke up at about eleven, dozed until noon. No work today, no school. Failing History 42D for sure. Korean War, Populists, Women's Movement. Who can sit in a big room and then recall minor facts? When I was asleep the radio was on. The songs were in my dreams. Donna Summer doing 'State of Independence.' Myself and some girls from St. J's dancing to it. Then Kool & the Gang jammed 'Tonight.' I saw Clark Gable (as Rhett Butler) singing, 'Not yet a man / But ready to try.' Then someone said, 'Kool's making a video over at Macy's!' So I ran to see. And there the band was, singing. A mob of girls from St. J's were there, some in uniform, some not. I guess I miss high school. When I got up I made Pinch and me some macaroni and cheese and scrambled eggs. Food always tastes good when you're hungry. Yesterday was Mom's birthday. She's thirty-nine, a very young thirty-nine. That lady will always be a child. She pouts and giggles and acts silly as hell. I love her more than anything. I'd emigrate to Greenland before I hurt or humiliate my mother.

CHAPTER 4

I FINALLY stopped working at Diamond Pool, got a part-time job at a real-estate agency. It paid more, and I had to start paying some rent at the Pseudo. In August, I began classes at the University of California, Berkeley. After a semester and a half, I quit. Cal's a city unto itself, and I didn't know the bee-lines. The campus dialect—talk of 'histograms,' 'E-con,' and 'sections'—slowed me like slanted rain.

St. J's prepped me for the actual material. But in high school, it had all been spelled out and straightforward. Blue-plaid pleated skirts and penny loafers for us. Gray-white pink nuns still in long habits. Lay teachers cared if I showed up or not. Liked me when I got A's, told me how much more they expected of me when I got B's. I read geometry and history texts like they were regular books—straight through, some-times twice, and way before I was required to have. In religion class I was into saints like Bernadette who nobody believed in until they discovered the disease she had, the pain she'd been living with and never mentioned, maybe even never felt. And field trips—to the symphony at Calvin Simmons Auditorium, the aquarium at Golden Gate Park, the aviary at Lake Merritt—I even helped plan those. At St. J's, I got to go where I wanted to go.

There was something being offered at Cal aside from steep walks to marble halls, but I'd no idea how to grab it. Folks seemed to be working toward a planned freedom. Like if they did appropriate things, then good, adult, moneymaking things would eventually, but surely, follow. That philosophy made no sense to me. There's no order to good things, and because you act right does not mean you get stuff. Or get happy.

I guess I was unable to dredge up my Mary McLeod Bethune attitude. Mom had given Pinch and me her biography long ago. *She Wanted to Read* was the title. Mary had courage. If I'd been born in slavery times, my ass would have been depressed as hell, hacking away at sugarcane. Too scared to live, more scared to die. Other kids plugged into study groups and tutors and went to class most every day. I failed midterms, skipped finals and ten-minute appointments with assistant deans. My friends were pretty much living like me. She wanted to read. I didn't think I was supposed to be at Cal, anyway.

Maynard and Donnell were at Hayward State, taking about one class each. May wasn't friendly with Todd anymore, and neither were Paige and I. But since Todd was even more busy selling dope, and he still came over to see Tee, the idea that May and Todd were associates became pervasive. May's rep—as someone who'd be dead soon, or in jail—was whispered at every party. He liked the status. So silly the way he puffed out when folks in the Acorns glanced at him with curiosity.

Meanwhile, Ch'Rell and Pinch were still up at St. J's. And I had this boyfriend, Teddy, who went to UC Santa Cruz. I liked Teddy. We drove around, went over to the lake, and we had sex every time he came up to Oakland, which was every weekend. We had the first sex I liked. He made comments about my chubbiness, but that didn't stop him from squeezing and licking every single part of me. In the relationship for about four months, he'd begun eyeing cuter, happier girls. Maynard, Mr. Magnanimous with his paper crown and stream of wanna-be beauty queens, said Teddy was 'good for me.'

Pinch thought Teddy was an asshole. Pinch who thinks of each boy in Oakland, except for May, as a baby tornado.

Teddy picked me up from Cal one afternoon, before I dropped out. Honked for me up by the law school. His car was brown and the hatchback slanted like the back of his head. I had books in a backpack, played it like I'd been in class all day when really I'd been at Yogurt Park, reading about California missions and eating vanilla, then sat for an hour by the inverted fountain on Sproul Plaza, watching the cloudy water like a fucking crackhead.

He hopped on the freeway, which was the quickest way possible to the Pseudo. Teddy said, 'It might be good if we see other people . . . but still see each other.'

I nodded. 'Is that right.'

He pulled a ragged toothpick from his mouth, tossed it out the sunroof. Fished through the plastic well behind the stick shift until he found another. They were the red-washed, cinnamon-flavored picks, came in tiny, waxed sleeves. Teddy said, 'But I hope you don't hook up with any of Maynard's friends.' The picks stained his mouth and tongue.

I hated him for one second, but then still wanted to be his girlfriend.

To him I said, 'We'll still hang out sometimes, right?'

To myself, I said, *I am Maynard's friends.*

SO THAT weekend I approached this guy named Major at a hotel suite party in San Jose, given by Maynard and some people I knew and some people I barely knew. San Jose's about forty minutes south of Oakland, and I sometimes partied with kids from the state university there. On scorching days, when people got blacker than they were ever supposed to, you could smell the garlic rigs as they rolled through San Jose from nearby Gilroy. The eighteen-wheelers rumbled north toward Oakland and San Francisco, or to the Camp-bell's factory in Sacramento, or south to Los Angeles and San Diego. The boxed bulbs, so lavender they should have reeked of it, were supposed to stay cool under tarps, but damn near roasted in the sun.

The Hotel Triumph was tall and rectangular, new and worthless. There was a broken fountain out front and an asphalt driveway. Localites used the place as a restaurant, a club, or a hall—rarely did tourists or salespeople pull up with loads of luggage and tales of bumpy flights. The hotel got a new name—The Paramount, The Cardinal, The Summit—with every new group of investors. This time it was a group of second-string pro athletes from other parts of California, and their weak glamour lured people by.

There was good liquor at the small party where I first saw Major, and dull dips and celery and olives. I skipped the food and sipped my rum and lime. There was no reason, in my mind, for vegetables to look dead when you could drive ten miles in any direction and pluck milky red berries from low bushes or tug turnips from the soil. You could pull cotton from the plant not fifteen miles outside of San Jose, taste a bland Chardonnay grape, pick almonds and cherries. I knew. I'd done it on field trips.

Major was playing cards by a window with May and Don-nell and another guy named Oscar. One named Cedric was kicked back, along with two other boys in low chairs. I didn't know their names, but I'd seen them working over at Round Table Pizza by Lake Merritt. They drove big, brand new Beemers, so I assumed they were in the streets. What else would it be?

Some random chicks lay on their bellies across the bed. A detective movie was on mute. I'd never seen the girls before, and barely spoke. Ch'Rell was in the tiny foyer, sitting on the floor with a beer and a fashion magazine. Maynard had brought a boom box. Had the volume up, but not too loud.

He'd called me that Saturday morning. Blowing my phone up like he was retarded.

'Wake up,' he said. 'Wash some clothes, do your hair, whatever you need to do. You and Pinch are coming to San Jose tonight.'

'For what?'

'Just get on BART, call me from the Fremont station at like . . . seven-thirty. I'll pick you up.'

In what? I wanted to say. 'Why are we coming to San Jose?'

'Some fools chilling.'

'And you need girls.'

'Yeah.'

My eyes were still closed. I could hear Pinch in the front room, flipping between *Soul Train* and *Superfriends.* 'I'm not bringing Pinch down there to hang out with a bunch of drunk-ass—'

'Nah, nah. It's some guys from Berkeley High. Home from some school out in the country somewhere. Out there running track. Bring Pinch. Ch'Rell said she's coming down.'

'That's 'Rell.'

'What's Pinch going to do down here but sit up and take mental pictures? These guys are straight-up. It's Nebraska where they go.'

I saw snow in my head when he said that. A state shaped like a fat gun. Cornhuskers at the Rose Bowl.

'*Lincoln,* Nebraska,' May said. Like he knew about it.

'I'll be down later.'

'Just you?' He sounded upbeat, and a little desperate. How boys can sound when they need to impress other boys.

At the card table, Major was smiling, and held a speckled

mint between his front teeth like a trophy. Seemed like he won a hand. It was almost Christmas of my freshman year. I'd passed one class. 'American History 42D: Civil War to the Present.'

Their game was moving slow, brothers drinking, forgetting whose turn it was. So I walked into the sharp, shallow conversation. Easy.

'Your friend looks like this boy I liked when I was in, like, the seventh grade,' I said to the room. To see who'd speak up.

Major looked over. 'Me?'

When I nodded, Major said, 'Did this boy like you back?'

I said no and Major said if I played my cards right— laughs from May and Donnell with their vodkas neat in water glasses—my luck might be different this time.

The tall boy named Oscar said to Major, 'Oh, negro, you think you got game.'

I winked at Oscar, sweet. My wink said, *Oh, negro, I'm who's got game.* He sat with his butt on the edge of his chair, long legs stretched out straight. Wide, wiry shoulders. Eyes like flat root beer. Oscar tipped his glass toward me. Slightly.

'I don't have cards,' I said to Major.

Major told me to come by him and I could play with his.

Hoot. *Ow!* Hollers. Laughs. From the guys and from me.

Ch'Rell peeped her hefty head through the doorway, saying, *What? What?*

Major was big-time drunk that night. I saw the Big Man show he was putting on and liked it—I was starring in it, after all, in full female regalia, for the few minutes it was clicking. Then Major got up from the table and walked me out to the hall.

'You like this privacy?' He looked up and down the bare beige passage.

'Mmm-hmm.'

We stood there. Me leaned with my back on the wall. Him facing me from about two feet away. We both had our drinks.

'May's your cousin?'

'Like that, yeah. You in school?'

'Chilling with my mom right now.'

'Oh.'

'You in school?'

'Yeah. At Cal.'

'Oh,' he said, with an extra-long O sound. Acknowledging that it was a big deal.

Stillness. Sipped drinks. I squinted at him, trying to figure out if he was in any way crazy. He took it to mean something else.

'So I really remind you of someone?' The way he asked me, all serious and sincere, made me sink down onto my butt, back still against the wall, and answer him in a way that would make him feel good.

'I said that in there hoping you'd be the one to speak up. I thought you were cute.'

He sat down opposite me. 'You still think it?'

May and them were whooping inside. I heard the one named Cedric talking about how Major had walked right into some pussy and how it must be nice to be a pro-football-playin' nigga who jus' gets sistas walkin' up on him and damn near asking for the D-I-C-K. I vaguely remembered Cedric from Bella Vista Elementary. He was cute, but he was too cute. I could never love someone who'd had it easy. Major and I walked back in the room to a quick hush. Like people thought we'd been having sex in the stairwell. All we'd done was exchange numbers on a lipsticky cocktail napkin I tore in half. I looked at May with my chin down and eyes up, like, *You got something to say?*

On the way back to Oakland, in a clean car I'd never seen before, I asked May, 'So who's Major?' We'd left Donnell and Ch'Rell in San Jose for the night. Real couples usually got the room after a suite party.

May shrugged. 'Maybe he went to Castlemont. With Ted.'

'Teddy went to St. Mary's. But I hear your smart mouth.'

'So you and Ted chill with other people, no problem?'

'Am I asking you whose car this is?'

'What?'

'Okay then.'

It was late but not that late. May found a radio station he knew I liked, and kept the car at seventy all the way back to Oakland. I knew he liked the station, too. We went by this place called Mexicali Rose, split a carne asada burrito. Got a cheese enchilada for Pinch. May said he had to get the car back.

'To who?'

'I thought you weren't asking me.'

'Why you got secrets.'

'I don't have secrets from you.'

'Bullshit.'

'You love me. I'm your pal.'

'Who you taking the car back to?'

'And here we are,' May said, pulling up to the curb, 'at the fabulous Pseudo.'

Pinch was flipping channels in her pajamas when I walked in the door. Put my coat and all on a kitchen chair. Nothing had changed, not a fork moved, all day. Went back to the living room.

'You eat?'

'Yep,' she said. Looked at me, pissed she hadn't been along.

'It was tired down there. I'm tired.'

She said nothing.

'Got you Mexicali Rose,' I said.

'Was Ch'Rell there?'

'Yeah.'

'Mom called.'

'Saying what.'

'Where were you.'

'Hope you said about my business.'

'Said you were at a party. She asked why I didn't go. Told her you thought it might be rowdy. That I had homework.'

'Did you? Have homework?'

'Did it. Pretty much. Was Donnell there, too?'

'Yes, Pinch.'

'So you all had fun.'

'I told you it was tired. What did you eat?'

'Cereal.'

'Go get that enchilada.'

We went in the kitchen, she ate at it.

Pinch had a choice, whether to go to Walnut Creek and stay with Mom, or stay with me at the Pseudo. I couldn't have afforded the Pseudo without Mom paying some rent for Pinch. With her new house, Mom didn't need to be paying my rent. I think it was my graduation day when Mom let me know that. 'You're eighteen,' she said. 'Grown. And you need to handle your own shit.'

I'd wanted to say, 'I know how old I am,' but didn't.

Pinch hadn't chosen to stay with me because she felt she had to. At least that's what I hoped. Pinch is my blood friend. She knows all. Knows why. It's easy, natural for me to love Pinch, because she doesn't expect anything at all. Pinch stayed with me because she was used to it, not because she felt sorry for me. Aside from Seth, I don't know how different from Mom I actually was.

Pinch rinsed her dishes. I watched her slink into her bedroom. Aside from that, I wondered if her ass had moved all day.

MAJOR called the next morning, before noon. By seven he was sitting in a spongy flowered chair Gram Liz had bought us from the Goodwill.

'So how old are you?'

'Twenty-three,' he said.

'And you're staying with your mom?'

'Over on Eighty-seventh.'

'My nannah and grandpa stay over there.'

'I been playing ball,' he said. 'In the Canadian league.'

Major was wide. He was an average height, but his chest, hands, forehead, and thighs were vast. A body more interested in across than up or down. I watched Major trying not to watch a lone roach crawling along a crack in the cream wall. When Major's eyes drifted from mine, it was only over to where the insect was progressing, centimeter by centimeter, toward whatever little roach place it was going. Not like we really had roaches. Just every once in a while.

'There's another one,' Major said buoyantly, pointing out a roach hours later when we were sitting on the couch drinking apple juice and eating Pinch's graham crackers. His fingernails were ridged and had brown moons ascending. The skin at his knuckles was thick and ashy. Major ended up falling asleep on the couch, his head on a pillow covered with a Humpty Dumpty case I'd been sleeping on since the second grade.

I stayed awake for a while, then dreamt of being on an amusement park water ride. I was happily fastened in a fake log, the ride was taking me through a fake mountain. The first time around, I screamed ecstatically. The second time, right before a coiling cascade, the track disappeared and the log sunk slowly down beneath the clear water, me strapped in. Chest full of air, eyes open and stinging, I fought with the buckles, freed myself, and was getting toward the surface when I woke up, throat beating, relieved to be dry. Major stayed quiet, and I watched him awhile. He was submerged, like sleep was water. He'd found a bluish abyss that cushioned him from noise, movement, weightless touch. I was frozen with joy at waking, frozen with shame for letting him drift underneath.

After that night, two or three times a week, Major would drop his mom off at her job in the morning and then come pick me up, right after nine A.M., in her beige car. We'd go get Denver omelets from a spot in North Oakland called Lois's, and then drive over to the house Major lived in with his mom.

We were sitting on the cement porch there, cursing the gray lawn. There was a collarless cat in the driveway. 'Shoo,' Major said. 'Get on!' The orange thing spoke, and then walked away, tail high and swaying. Major nodded hello to the mail lady. We went inside.

There was a sofa set in the living room of Major's mom's house—it was supposed to form an L, but the room was too short, so it formed a C. Matted blue shag stretched from wall to rosy wall. Major opened the front and back doors for a draft, but the house, even just scoured and perfumed, smelled like cabbage cooked too long and fish fried on Fridays.

'You could probably get a job up at Cal,' I said. 'At the gym or something.'

He paused, considered the idea. 'I hadn't thought about going up there.'

'You being a sports person, I mean.'

'I got hurt,' he volunteered about why he'd returned to California. 'Snatched on in a wrong way.'

I didn't know what to say to that.

It wasn't even noon yet when Major said, 'You hungry? I am. Let's eat, huh?' There were hard yellow plastic vats in Major's mother's refrigerator, shrouded in aluminum foil.

So we got bowls out, heavy bowls that Major's mom probably beat cornbread in or tossed a salad for two. Major and I filled them with mounds of cooked white rice and baby lima beans, halves of chickens roasted in mustard, and stacks of broccoli. He poured vinegar and water over his. I spooned on jellied drippings from the chicken. We both topped ours with slices of American cheese, then ate our stews, blistering from the microwave, from the edge of the bowl toward the center. Put gnawed bones on a paper napkin. I bit steaming flowers from the broccoli and passed the stalks to Major. To wash it down there was Pepsi with brandy. Then Major laid his head in my lap, asleep. The TV was ancient, built into a cabinet with speakers. *Come on down!* we heard the announcer say with feeling, and then paid attention for a second to see who got chosen.

On another day Major said, 'Let's drive downtown,' and we did, and then went over by the campus, where people I knew saw me holding hands with a large, inky man. People looked at Major because he was so black, and because he was shaped, if looked at head-on, like a square with a smaller, rounded square for a head. His grin looked warm from across the quad, but up close it was chalky, dry as dust.

'He's a pro football player,' I said. 'He's home on waivers.' Not even knowing what waivers were.

Curious jealous girls raised their eyebrows, looked at me real hard. 'We're just friends,' I said, knowing they'd believe otherwise.

Major was uncomfortable with the inspection, said, 'Paige, you wanna get some ice cream?'

I said to the girls that I had to go.

Most days Major and I would eat, then sleep in his mom's house until three or four in the afternoon, and then he'd drop me back at the apartment in time for Teddy to call, in time for Major to drive up to the curb in front of the insurance company where his mom worked. His mom was in data entry.

Some afternoons, though, I went with Major to get her. *Look at her son,* the other women would say, in their brilliant suits with shoulder pads and elaborate buttons. *Look how he picks his mother up.* Major greeted them with softly spoken compliments, and they patted him on his hard arm as it rested on the door. Some of the women, bitter at the bus stop, wondered loudly why he had the time to be there. According to Major's mom, the people in her sector were tired of talking about a football team from another country. I pictured them believing her, nodding as they soaked teabags or sprinkled creamer in their coffee. They probably just wanted Major to be on a team they had heard of.

I wore a green rayon sundress with a scoop neck the day Major and I had sex. We'd dropped off to sleep after chicken thighs and zucchini and yams. We'd shared brandy from an old purple mug that said, in white letters, ST. MARK'S PEEWEE FOOTBALL—THE BIGGEST LITTLE MEN IN NORTHERN CALI-FORNIA. I woke up to Major wiping at the sleep in the corners of his mouth. His breath smelled stale, then rich, like frothy milk, or sugar browning, and I breathed it in. Major put his nose to my scalp, then scraped his teeth across the back and sides of my neck. He pulled my chest from the top of my dress. The wires in my bra pinched the skin over my ribs.

Yellow stretch marks welled out from under his arms and over his solid breasts like age circles in a tree trunk. I ran my finger across them.

'They don't hurt,' Major said. 'They never hurt. I never noticed them until one day they were just there.'

Major and I kissed for a long time and then I climbed off him, damp between the legs and not even out of breath.

I was seated next to him. My brain in a shrug.

'Feel like I love you,' he said. 'The things we do, the way we hang out. How you try to help me.'

I didn't look at him but I held his hand. 'I don't think you love me. Plus you know I sort of have a man.' Walked toward the bathroom. For all his might, I slipped my hand away without half-trying.

'I know,' he said. 'You know I know that.'

I guessed Major got a little high at night. I didn't think he was on the pipe, though. Maybe rolling some crack up in a joint. Rubbing some on his gums. Like that. Besides, Major ran around sometimes with those Round Table boys. And he always had money to buy me food. He was around dope, maybe sitting with it, or counting bills or something. I don't know. I only thought he got high because his eyes looked weak enough to want it.

I spent daytimes with Major. Two nights a week, when Teddy was up from Santa Cruz, I was off fighting with him. He was always telling me I needed to pull it together.

'Don't you want a house someday?' That was the kind of inane, suffocating shit he asked me.

'Not really.'

'If you don't want stuff, you'll never be successful.'

'Oh, well. You have your version of success, I have mine.'

'What is yours?'

'Being here. Not having people bring me down.'

'Bring *you* down? When are you up? Like, have you been going to aerobics?'

'Every day,' I said. 'Not.'

'They're free up at the school!'

'Yep they are.'

'I don't even think you're *in* school. You never act like you have to study. Even naturally smart people at Cal have to really work just to keep up their GPAs.'

Teddy, all crooked teeth and two majors. Talking to me about GPAs.

'Sometimes I think you're not the same girl I met,' he said.

'Who'd you meet?" I wished I could hurl a curve into his fast straight life. 'Who do you think you met?'

'A cute girl with goals. Your apartment is so together, I just thought—I mean, I know you're only eighteen, but with your situation with your sister, it just seems like you're older. Maybe that's why I expected a lot—'

'A lot of what? Of me wanting a house? That's what would

make me okay to you?' I didn't like the way he said *situation*—like I was in a sorry one. I sat up in the seat, faced him as he faced the road. 'You don't need to ask yourself who you met. Just look at me good. I'm the same girl. You're the same motherfucker I met, too.'

But then Teddy would lie close to me, warm arm thrown across my stomach, thumb hooked around the ribbonlike waistband of my underwear. Like I was his. Like he was a regular boy with a regular life, and I was his. He'd kiss me in his sleep, and let me alone for a while about how my life was going.

I was nineteen when I stopped seeing Major. The last time I saw him, he stood in the driveway of Pinch's and my apartment for forty minutes, asking for me to come down, saying he'd sold his mom's car for two hundred dollars, that his mom had kicked him out, and that he was hungry. It was fall, still warm, and Major had on a hooded sweatshirt. His hair, usually trimmed almost to the scalp, was about three-quarters of an inch long, and pressed in on one side. I had never seen him with hair. Hated the way it looked.

I'd never seen him act like this. Major was pleading. He had forty-five dollars! Didn't I wanna go over to Lois's Place? Get some grits or some pie or something from over there? Couldn't I please come down, Paige, please, damn. Could he come up? Plee-ee-eeeze? He yelled the word long and hard like a cheerleader.

I thought we was tight, he said, and he was screaming. *I thought you was my people why you actin' like you don't know a brother Paige? I'm getting better about it why can't you help me instead of just leaving me out here like this? It's so fucked up the way you're doing me right now not even caring or trying to help. Maybe you don't get high Paige maybe you don't maybe you don't even have to. You think you so fuckin' fly you ain't like me you ain't never had to deal with my shit you ain't never even asked me what happened in Toronto. You never said why'd you come*

*back Major you never said why'd you go. All you ever said was
Major come pick me up Major can you drop me by here Major
can I lay up at your crib Major I need to be back home by such
an' such a time. Major don't your mama need the car back. You
never said Major why'd you come back or Major why'd you go.
It was ugly Paige I know people told you they always happy to
tell on somebody I was trying so hard Paige and nobody even
noticed nobody even said I see you Major I see you trying. They
just want to talk about me when I'm down fuck me in the ass
stomp on a brother's back like he's not shit Paige and I thought
you was different you was rollin' with me and I thought you
would be there. But I see you just like the rest Paige. Down for
a nigga as long as he's pulling his own weight but when a nigga
gets weak he's on his own. That's cool Paige that's cool I know
those kind of motherfuckers Paige and I thought you wasn't one
of 'em.*

Major was hoarse and still trying to holler and I leaned
way out the window, soot from the frame making a hazy black
stripe across the bottom of my blouse. I told Major to go on,
that he was tripping.

I was leaning out of the window. 'I'm sorry. I'm sorry I'm
sorry I'm sorry.'

Maybe it looked like I was about to go down, because
Pinch pulled me back. She told him I would *not* be coming
out, and that my boyfriend was on his way. 'Go!' Pinch
shouted down. 'Do something about yourself.'

I sat on the floor, eyes hot, balling my fists so that my nails
lifted bits of skin from the palms. Major was down there, walking away, yelling that people ain't supposed to do people like
this. *Paige, you ain't right,* was the last thing I heard him say.
All his words had come out like wild vomit. The last four were
clear as spit. I had to go into the bathroom, wash my face, and
change my shirt. Teddy would be by.

'Major's trifling,' Pinch said. 'I don't know why you got involved with that pipe-smoker.'

I was wiping my face with a cloth, eyes closed against the soap, trying to erase melted mascara. I opened my eyes, saw the shower curtain behind me and the green-tiled wall. Saw the shelf behind me with the apricot scrub and the mint masque and the loofah sponge and the peach salts. Got up on the mirror, touched it with my nose, leaned back and tapped it with my finger. I could only see what was behind me.

Pinch was all, 'Are you getting it together?' I looked at each corner of the bathroom in the glass, checked on the toilet, sink, and tub from different angles. The mirror didn't show me. I stared at it, at the dried flecks of toothpasty saliva, at the streaks from the spray cleaner, at the shiny metal frame that bordered it. I hoped my face was clean.

'Paige!'

'Here I come. Damn. Trying to unpuff these eyes.'

'I don't know why you're doing all this crying, anyway. I mean, do you care about him like that? He's not a dregs-of-the-earth kind of crackhead, but Major gets high a lot, Paige. Why are you acting like he doesn't? You're stupid sometimes.'

'I forgot you know everything.' I was still staring at the mirror, waiting to appear. 'Major does not smoke the pipe.' I came out of the bathroom. I didn't know what all Major did or didn't do. In bra and jeans, I searched for a shirt. I saw twenty-four-hour deodorant, spread it under my arms. Saw extra-strength lotion and rubbed it into my elbows. 'Maybe he does some other shit, but—'

'Paige, he sold his mother's car for like twenty-five cents. That's a basehead, okay? That's a fucking crack addict.'

'You've seen him smoke crack?' I stopped and looked at Pinch, who looked back at me. 'Then shut up.' She was angry but she didn't—and she never did—look at me like I'd sprung psycho from Mom's stomach. I said, 'Help me find a shirt? You know I have to be ready. Why didn't you let me go down.'

'I wasn't holding you back. If you wanted to go down, you should have took your ass down.'

'You told me not to.' I was yelling at Pinch, and she was being mature, not yelling back. I still hadn't found a shirt. I knew I looked crazy, was acting kind of crazy. I avoided the mirror in the front room. I knew Pinch could see me.

'If you wanted to go, don't act like you couldn't have.'

'So I should have gone? Why are you going back and forth? I wanted to help! I was trying to get downstairs. You saw me!'

'I saw you yelling downstairs, Paige. I didn't see you going.'

Teddy rolled up the driveway of the Pseudo and honked. I asked Pinch if I looked all right, asked her if I should go downstairs, and to the video store and then back over to Teddy's friend's place to watch it, and then eat less than I wanted and talk about classes like I'd been to them, and about the phone bill for which I needed to borrow money. That's what I think I said. That was the language I felt.

Pinch said, 'Yes, go.'

So I went in a pink blouse and matching lipstick. I imagined Major with soiled clothes and filmy teeth. With wet eyes and horrid breath. I thought of him thin and pointing at people he didn't know, telling them all his personal business, and talking faster than he ever did.

Flew down a rib of highway with Teddy. It arced through a grimy, colorless part of California that didn't go anywhere except to someplace not that far and right back again. I pulled down the sun visor, glanced in the checkbook-sized mirror, saw only the green and white signs for Cupertino behind me, and swarms of low cubic concrete buildings that made up what people were calling Silicon Valley. We flew past the building that housed the Toyota–General Motors alliance. I saw it in the tiny mirror, squat and impenetrable, and counted in my mind six people I knew who went there daily and told me about the hourly wage and the benefits and of the overtime dough there that was phenomenal. I heard in their stupid, condescending tones that they hated the place, my pseudo-pals with sociology and African-American Studies and mass-communications degrees, driving around in new Volkswagens and secondhand BMWs, telling me I didn't need my degree to get on at that place, and that every job wasn't on the floor, or on the line, or however they phrased it. I heard it in their piercing voices that they mistook my inertia for cunning, and that sometimes made me smile.

I tried to concentrate on what video to rent, what section to go to first, and decided on Action, knew Teddy would fall quickly asleep serenaded by bullets ricocheting and cars detonating and the sight of a woman bound and sloppily gagged by a man with a scar he should have died getting. My hand went again for the sun visor. I stared into the mirror and everything that was spinning behind me. Teddy gave me a big scold—ripped into my twirling reverie. I folded the visor back. Hadn't seen my own eyes or nose or forehead or hairline.

With the air-conditioning and the radio on, I stayed in the car when we got to the video store, thinking about a time when I was riding with Major and Major's mother in her beige car, watching myself in the window of a San Jose Rapid Transit District bus. It was of a bowed, shatterproof material you could see out of but not into, and my face looked gaunt in it. I stared for as long as the bus traveled alongside us, and Major's mother had watched me as I raised and lowered my eyebrows, puffed out my cheeks. Major's mom had said, 'What are you *doing*?'

When the bus turned onto Junipero Serra Boulevard, the broad street with the car dealerships and so many streamers and American flags it looked like champions were getting welcomed home every day of the year, Major said, 'Let it go, Paige,' and smiled his arid smile. I knew if I'd been in that car with Major alone, I could have hung my head out the window, contorting my face like a daddy over his newborn. If Major and I had been alone, Major would have followed that bus down Serra all the way to Milpitas or even Bakersfield, or wherever it was I was trying to go.

Teddy got a murder movie and we watched it, and a few months later he told me he wanted to really totally break up.

'I need,' he said, 'a woman with motivation.'

'I'm motivated.'

'To do what?'

'Get through life.'

'What's that mean? To you? Big, small, short, tall, we all get through life.'

'I'm motivated to finish school, and for my sister to—'

'I'm not trying to sound fucked up, but I look at you and it just seems like you're . . . lazy, or constantly . . . discouraged or something.'

'So encourage me, then.'

'See that's what I mean. You're not happy.'

'Yes I am. Not every second. But I'm supposed to be just naturally happy? All the time, every minute? I thought that's what a relationship, a boyfriend was for. You make me happy, I make you happy.'

'You have to have a . . . base. Paige, I have to go.'

'Go where?'

'Go from the relationship. I'm not trying . . . I *promise* I'm not trying to be fucked up—'

'You *are* being fucked up. You're being so fucked up. Who are you? Perfection? I hate you, I hope you *die*. I hope your whole life is a fucking failure. I hope you never meet a girl who wants to have you. You don't know who I am, how I live. That's why I don't tell people *shit*. They wanna talk to me about happiness. Having a base. What is that? Who has that? If you're happy, *fuck you*, and I don't believe you anyway. I've used up my quote unquote motivation. There's a limit on that shit. You talk like you know something when you're just an ordinary nigga from an ordinary house. Pull over. Let me out. No I said *let me the fuck out.* I hope the ground opens up and swallows you alive. You're evil. Conceited. You're a weak, fucking soft-ass punk.'

That's the kind of thing Teddy told people I said. I know I was loud. I hope I did say all of it.

A few days after that discussion, Teddy called Ch'Rell in a panic, said he thought I might kill myself because I'd called him at about four in the morning and cleared my throat twice before I'd said, 'You need to come back to me. Come over. You love me. The way you touched me, made me feel stuff, made me cry. You don't want me to be the same girl you met, you want me to change. You should want me to change, but it's not that easy. I don't always think life is fine. The sky is falling. It is. I can't hold it up. I have motivation, though. I just need you to try and give me some more. Or wait with me until more comes.'

I know that's exactly what I said.

So to Ch'Rell, I was like, 'He thought I would kill myself?'

Because of what? I wasn't raised like that. Mom always said that even if she had an agonizing, incurable disease, she'd never commit suicide because just her luck, they'd find the cure five minutes after she died. Kill myself? Not. My voice might have been trembly when I was on the phone with Teddy, but I'd practiced my words. I'd told him that I wanted him to please come over and see that my face was back in the mirror. Then I said, No, no. Could I come over and show you in your mirror that my face is back in all mirrors again? He said nothing, so I told him that I'd be okay and such a better girlfriend. I'd go to aerobics up at the school. Still no real response, so I hung up the phone by pressing the button. Then left it off the hook.

He ended up telling Ch'Rell that he wasn't ever going to call me back. He said he was tired of my bullshit. Told her I'd been screaming and seeing the world through eyes he didn't know about.

So when Ch'Rell called me at home to see if I was all right, my stupid ass told her that, yeah, I'd called Teddy, but that I'd needed Major. Ch'Rell said she'd run into Major's mom at church and Major was gone away. His mom, Ch'Rell said, had asked during that part of the service, that Major's friends pray for his recovery. And also—and this was the part that Ch'Rell seemed a little too glad to tell—Major's mom had asked her in the parking lot afterward if I was seeking help myself.

Major's mom had the nerve to ask Ch'Rell if it was drugs with me. Or if it wasn't, she'd wanted to know, *What was it?*

CHAPTER 5

We all met Jessica at the same party when I was eighteen.

Jess who'd been raised with her mom and white dad, in a house with a lap pool, way up in the hills, Above Upper High.

That's what we called it. Above Upper High. Most referred to the area as the Oakland Hills. Or just the hills.

If you took High Street all the way up, suddenly you were in chic Montclair and the rest of the hills, up near where the Mormon temple sat like heaven's west veranda. You could see the temple from miles away, from the highway, and especially well from the Flatlands. At night, the bone blocks of stone glowed in a dome of gauze light. The temple was just east of the Claremont Hotel, and if Lake Merritt grounded Oakland, the Claremont and the temple were the steeples that stretched our town heavenward. Paige used to point out the temple, tell Mom that she was going to live there when she grew up. *That's my house,* she'd say when she was seven. *You can visit me there.* I was with Paige once on a field trip to the Mormon temple. It was manicured and solemn, and the view of Oakland was expansive. But she and I both thought it looked better in darkness, and from far away.

Jessica and her people lived up near the temple, on Elysian Fields Road off Skyline Boulevard. Fluorescent tennis balls and horse manure in the gutters. You could see four bridges from their living room.

The pristine crimson Golden Gate.

The Bay Bridge, gray snaky-spidery.

The San Mateo, plain as the city it was named for.

The succinct San Rafael that ended on the northwest side at San Quentin.

The suspension bridges, especially, could make you want to climb up as much as cross over.

Jess's place could make you thrilled just for the view. The living room and deck built out from it were held up on stilts, along a gorge. A good ten-second earthquake would send the place crumpled to the bottom. Potted rubber trees, gas grill, blocky redwood furniture and all. But earthquakes had come, and the house still stood. Earthquakes would roll through again. They always did.

I'd sit on that deck alone while waiting for Jess to get dressed, or with Paige, who always thought the sturdy expanse teetery. The stateliness of Jess's parents' house made me want to scramble from it sometimes. On my knees.

I enjoyed the deck, though. Way Above Upper High, starlight and the infinity of the Pacific hypnotized me to imagining I was someplace else.

THE night we met Jessica, Maynard was serving at this bar way down the hills from her place. A place called Peony's on Lakeshore Avenue. It was across the street from Merritt Bakery and near the Park Theater, which showed mostly kung-fu movies and occasionally hosted film festivals featuring short movies by Asians, and also black and white and Latin people from other countries.

Paige was sitting in Peony's with Ch'Rell and me. Paige was barely twenty, so you know 'Rell and I weren't supposed to be in there. The place was small and lined with leather stools and mismatched chairs. Enough room for a pool table and two tables that had the video game Centipede built in. The lights on the walls were hollow plastic candles with clear flame-shaped bulbs. Briefly unburdened people in waffle-stompers dusted salty fingers on their clothes. Ch'Rell had a nickel in her loafer where the penny was supposed to go. She and Paige were on their second tequila sunrise, both had rosy ceramic nails two and a half inches long. Back then, I was not to the level to be getting my nails done once every ten days, so my hands were homemade, but they looked neat. Negroes we knew well had not yet started selling crack.

The deejay was like fifty, was sipping brandy with a warm waterback, playing the Whispers' 'If You Just Say Yes' from a 45. Then Teena Marie sang about a Portuguese love. Teena Marie was a short white girl who sang with soul. She had another song about being 'out on a limb.' It was my favorite, because it seemed like regardless of the risk, she was going for love. In my mind I replaced Teena's man with my life. I'd been on plenty of limbs with other people. I wanted to walk out on one of my own.

As the youngest people in the bar, we were like San Francisco white people in Oakland for a night—slightly awkward, but like we had the most right to the most fun. We swirled glasses so the ice talked. Asked for more grenadine or for another lime wedge—like we had certain ways we liked our cocktails and wouldn't tolerate imperfection.

This guy Oscar walked in the bar, shook off his coat. It was a heavy one, the kind you'd need in real everyday snow. Made him seem sophisticated, versed in some other way of life. He was tall and with a receding hairline disguised by the shortest haircut possible. I'd seen Oscar run fast when he was a senior. Was high in the bleachers when he flew over a hundred meters' worth of hurdles like they weren't even there. Fatless legs like bulging drumsticks. One would jerk up, toes stretched skyward, thigh and calf extended to a driving horizontal line. Oscar's friend Cedric, with his slim yellow self, ran the 440 and went the distance with the white boys. Both always sharp in their varsity tracksuits and fresh New Balances. Cedric, especially, walked an inch off the ground. Had heard they'd gotten scholarships to someplace back East. I'd never spoken to either of them.

'Where's Ced?' Maynard said to Oscar. May was behind the end of the bar, not washing glasses or straightening bottles. Deep in his second brew. 'He didn't come with you?'

'Parking,' Oscar said. He nodded at us, then looked back at Paige and said, 'I haven't seen you in a long time.'

Ch'Rell said, 'You guys know each other?' Then her lips set, one molasses slug atop another.

'How's Major?' Oscar said to Paige, ignoring Ch'Rell.

'You know better than me.'

'Why's that?'

'He's your boy,' Paige said. 'I haven't seen him.'

'I thought he was your boy. That's what it looked like—'

'Two years ago?'

'I'm just trying to pick up the thread of the story.'

'Because it's so interesting.'

Paige looked at me and mouthed, *Retarded.* She was nervous, keeping her back to him, turning her head slightly toward him when she spoke, but never turning around in her seat.

Oscar had his foot on the bottom rung of Paige's bar stool. 'So what else's been up, then?' he said. 'I been out in the cornfields. Bring me up to speed.' He didn't lean in too close, but he did touch the hair on her shoulder. Boys who favored girls with long hair liked Paige. She kept it up, too—warm pressing combs, amber African hair-grow potions made in Texas, her head wrapped in satin scarves when she slept alone. Thought her hair made up for her square butt and inability to be glad for more than twelve seconds at a time.

Paige leaned further into the bar. He smiled at me, like he

saw she was nervous, and knew I saw it, too. I liked him for her then and there.

'This your sister?' I liked him for that, too, because Paige and I didn't look much alike.

'Yep.'

'Does she talk to you with her back?"

Paige swiveled around, looked in his face, said, 'Nothing's been up. Been at State.' She meant San Francisco State, but she was lying, anyway. Paige was working at the real-estate place about thirty hours a week. Made half-assed moves toward re-applying to Cal.

Maynard handed Oscar a wet bottle of beer. Then Cedric came in, hollered at the guys, then looked at Paige and Ch'Rell and I, said hello. Maynard ducked from under the bar, went over with his two beers, sat across from Cedric in a booth.

'What about pool?' Oscar asked Paige.

'Don't play.'

Ch'Rell said, 'She sure doesn't.'

Oscar glanced at Ch'Rell, then said to Paige, 'That's not what May said. May said you're excellent.'

Paige shot a look at Maynard, who was all teeth. He was happy. All of his people were at a place where he was in charge. And now there was a little minidrama between Oscar and Paige. His smile said, *Paige, Oscar's playing you.*

Why was *I* getting excited?

'May didn't say that about me playing pool.'

'He told me you *always* win. Said he makes money betting on you. Said you even beat him sometime.'

'Now I didn't say *that*,' May yelled from the booth, still smiling. Cedric drank his beer.

Paige got up to play. Ch'Rell watched the game, while Donnell lurked behind the bar, pretending to be bartender. Maynard and Cedric kept talking and toasting what, I didn't know, until May said, 'We should go over to Jack London, to the Rusty Scupper, get our groove on.'

A place called Jack London Square sounds all *Call of the Wild*, but really it was a roofless shopping mall, built along the waterfront at the end of downtown Oakland. Thursday at the Scupper was basically Negro Dance Night. The line to get in was long and almost segregated by sex. Females at the front with hems high. Stretchy fabric stretched over supple plumpness and dainty trophy waists and you could tell who had a baby at home by how delirious they were to be unencumbered and other girls were thrilled in a less glaring way to be free of the good-girl maneuvers they'd been given ovations for since kindergarten. There were sisters who'd gone straight from Catholic school to San Jose State to taking LSATs. Sisters next to them who'd had babies in high school but pulled it together to graduate and then go to UCSF.

There were sisters in hundred-dollar heels who'd already made it to the other side of the scruffy velvet rope. A father or an aunt's friend had got them jobs the summer after their senior years at the Wonder Bread or the Mother's Cookie factory, or at the Coke plant—three vestiges of job security laid parallel with the train tracks in East Oakland. Places with flues and fiery cursive logos, brick castles that sweated fat and yeast and beads of imagination. These girls were supposed to stay on just for the summer and then go to Laney Junior College. They were supposed to transfer after two years into the Cal State University system. They were supposed to get jobs that required casual coordinates and a daily BART ride to the city.

Instead the girls got used to the habits of labor and the sinewy men in hair nets and short sleeves who worked the kneading machines. Learned to stop feeling superior to the ladies who looked just like themselves but with moles and longer automobiles, with outwardly unflappable husbands and photos of small groomed dogs. The girls missed Laney registration and missed it again. These were the ones who'd come to the Scupper early. They were ready for Long Island Iced Teas and gin grapefruits and Cape Cods. Ready to pet and dance and even balance on the pier railing and stare at the water and not regret anything because the check was steady and it wasn't time for grief yet, anyway. I ran into all these girls at the jammed beauty supply store between the MacArthur BART station and Payless Shoes. We'd be buying hair texturizer in bulk and pinkie-sized curling irons or blow dryers with the comb attachment and finger-wave gel called FREEZE!

Toward the back of the line were the boys in tweedy pleated slacks and tasseled loafers with no socks. Dark shirts and fake designer watches. The corny adopted boys, and churchy boys, and ghetto boys with thorough parents—they came up from Stanford, a half dozen each from Cal and San Francisco State, all newly aware of their increased social currency. We knew them from around.

But the boys more familiar to us—the ones more familiar with us—Paige and I didn't even look their way. Boys who rang up sales at the Cost Plus or pruned shrubs for the Department of Parks and Recreation, boys who were at Laney who also managed their parents' Flatland apartment buildings and went home to sleep in their parents' homes Above Upper High. A few boys with just-sanitized hairlines who quietly sold crack to pay what their grants didn't and their moms couldn't at private schools like the College of Arts and Crafts or USF. A huddle of cats who sold crack and had never graduated high school, who got new Corvettes tinted glittery green, grew their hair out long and got it pressed straight and then curled into ringlets, wore velour jogging suits with dress shoes, had two babies both two months old by two different women, claimed East Oakland or West Oakland like it was Palestine, got their 'Vettes or Grenadas detailed twice a week, sucked Tootsie Pops and fondled tiny guns in their pockets, cruised Lake

Merritt on glorious Saturdays, turned out dances at Cal's
Pauley Ballroom by picking fights with brothers defensive
about their good manners, good grades, and plain rides. They
were my Oakland, these boys, and when they weren't being
rude—when they were sweet, and they could be sweet—they
made me feel as I felt about my neighborhoods and usual
routes. Comfortable and clued-in. The boys could be crazy,
but mostly we knew what they would and wouldn't do.

WE HAD to be the most chill little clique in line. The
bouncer saw Maynard and said, 'How many you got?' then let
us all in ahead of everyone, and for free. *Cloud nine.*

Paige maneuvered her way through the swarm of damp,
buzzing people at the bar, got herself another sunrise, walked
out on the pier. I stood at the sliding glass door that led out.
Paige liked the drama of standing outside in the mist, smoothing her ponytail, looking all stoic. Not me. I was excited to be
in a real club. Decided to tell people I was almost twenty-one.

Cedric followed Paige out, pointed to a small inflatable
raft attached to a cruiser, said, 'That yours?' and Paige had to
laugh. Paige must have remembered Cedric from Bella Vista
Elementary, if not from track meets. He used to get teased
about his big bronze afro.

Paige said, 'That thing would sink in five seconds.'

'Not if I was paddling,' he said.

'When are you guys going back to Nebraska? How is it
out there, anyway?'

'Lotta white people,' Cedric said.

'There's a lot of white people everywhere.'

'It's not even that. There's just . . . nobody out there. We
don't—'

'You're not going to leave are you?'

'Nebraska? Or from right here talking to you?'

'From Nebraska, silly.' Paige was big with calling people silly or crazy when she thought they thought she was cute.

'Nah, nah,' he said. 'Don't think I'm leaving Nebraska. But I never say never.'

Ch'Rell spotted me in the doorway watching Paige and Cedric, rolled her eyes, then passed me and walked out on the pier. 'Paige, you got some money? I don't and Donnell's tapped.'

Paige reached in her purse, walked back in the club with 'Rell without so much as a bye to Cedric. He stood there. I followed my girls. It was steamy inside, throbbing. The bass was climbing up under my jeans, shivering the hairs on my legs, vibrating the cotton threads of my tank, steady thumping, pressing in on my breasts, pushing at my butt and back. Paige's shoulders started rolling before she could buy Ch'Rell and Donnell's drinks, then Oscar pulled at her hand with two of his fingers, said, 'Let's dance.' Paige told me later it felt like he said *Let's drive to Baja, eat tacos al pastor on the beach, drink tequila so crisp it hurts our teeth.* Like he said *Have you been in the ocean naked before? Let me unbutton your shirt, I like your body.* Like he said, *Thank you, baby girl, the things you do make me feel better than usual. I can see farther than you and what I see is not ugly or shameful or solitary. The ground will stay beneath you the sun will rise sizzling orange every day the darkness will be cool and full of peace.* She said it just felt like he said that and she'd no time to ask herself why. The music was past blaring, and Oscar's longest fingers had been touching the very center of her palm.

The two of them danced on the tiny rectangular dance floor, it was crammed with couples, a swaying substitute cosmos that Ch'Rell visited to pull money from Paige's purse while Paige barely got off beat. Oscar was moving with a cocktail in his hand he held up high. He kept giving Paige sips of it until there was no more and he was saying words in her ear his lips all up on it because how else could she hear in that world and then that song came on with the lunatic bass and the monotone voice that said over and over again, 'I need a freak / I really do.' Brothers were stomping on the beat, all together, almost marching. I thought they'd end up in the water beneath us. A gangly boy dragged me on the floor. He had on a black and yellow golf shirt with Greek letters stenciled on the back. I led him over by Oscar and my sister.

He said, 'I'm Evan.'

In my head I was like, Cool, dance.

I heard Oscar say to Paige, 'You dance like this with everybody or you just dancing like that for me?' and it's not like Paige wasn't grinding her body against his and like she wasn't turning her swirling ass around to his groin and not like when she turned back to face him he didn't pull her hips close to his. They weren't looking in each other's eyes except for every once in a while, they were mouthing the words of songs and raising their arms every time a new jam was mixed in. Sweat was flowing, the deejay was not fifty, he was not playing the Whispers. New songs were sending bolts from the five-foot speakers. Every pump of bass, every otherworldly shake of metal bells was a body blow—every rap original and bizarre but still like it was assembled from the cells of my brain. The new music was familiar as my own pulse, genuine and particular as the warm place at the top of my legs.

My face was wet like I'd been crying. In unison, Paige and I did old steps we knew, and new dance steps like we'd invented them or had at least known them from last lives. There was a bliss being wound up, I could see Paige and Oscar coiling and uncoiling, limbering for the tangle and burst. Then I went weak, felt desperate, and like a trespasser. Always paying more attention than I could afford.

My steps slowed. Took in the black and gold boy I was dancing with. He had his own steps, they were sharp and fluid and his eyes were half-closed. I felt like if he was making love to me, he could go on like that for a long time. Thick, soft fuzz above his upper lip. He was browner than me, so like an avocado seed. Lips the exact same color as his skin. Not more pink nor more brown nor more red. His whole face—even his eyelids, and under his eyes—was matte, all of a piece but for the eyebrows and baby mustache. Lips full and dry, like he told the truth. He repeatedly raised one of my open hands with his index finger and mimicked my slack moves. It made me feel nimble, was a reminder that he'd picked me specifically.

I waited for this Evan to lick his lips, offhandedly, just to moisten.

He didn't even smile.

He put that same index finger softly on my lips, though. And finally showed some teeth.

So did I.

Then, smooth as one person, Ch'Rell and Donnell were next to Oscar and Paige. I spotted Maynard a few couples away from the rest of us, dancing with a girl whose hair went to the middle of her back. It was only for a few flashes of the mirrored ball that I'd let my eyes stray from my sister and friends. The longhaired girl danced like Maynard wasn't even there, had her arms crossed high over her chest, hands on her own shoulders. When a song she apparently loved whirled in, the girl looked up at the flashing light, then out the window into the dark, whipped her wrists and did sliding steps that barely jibed with Maynard's moves at all. He was in his own rhythm, plowed through the same unadorned stomp-slide again and again, each time with more power, and with less attention to his partner or us, until he seemed remote and enchanted.

After an hour, it had to be, we were all standing on the pier and Cedric was still there cool and moist, but due to the drizzle, not the sweet sopped journey from which the rest of us had just returned. He was talking to a girl we didn't know, her hair and clothes and face were not soaked to dripping, she was not mopping herself with paper napkins, not panting or on the verge of saying, *I cannot believe how we were dancing*, or *The only thing we can do now is tongue-kiss and hope it leads to the lushest sex and the truest love.* She dangled a drink by her thigh. Cedric did know enough to turn from the girl and say to us, 'I should have come in there with you guys.'

'Paige.' Oscar was wringing out the hem of his T-shirt. 'So what are you about to do?'

Evan came out on the pier, too. Tugged the back of my hair. On the dance floor, I'd already told him my name.

'Your haircut's cute.'

I had a puffball for a style after all that sweat, but willed myself not to touch it. Paige had cut it into a bob. Right to the nape of my neck. My earrings showed really well when I pulled the front back behind my ears with sparkly blue barrettes. Barrettes matched my bracelet. Bracelet matched my choker. Blue blouse buttoned to the neck, but tapered tight over my ribs, flared over my waist.

'I'm from Seattle,' Evan said.

'That's different.' I'd never met a black person from Seattle. Never met anyone from Seattle.

'You're from here, I guess.'

'Yeah.' *What to say?*

'I go to UC Davis.'

'I'm transferring to San Francisco State.' Such a lie. Took it straight from Paige's mouth. I was barely at Laney.

'Sophomore,' he said.

I nodded. Didn't know if he was talking about him or me.

'Davis has horses. Everyone thinks it's boring up there, but it's not. I like it better than Seattle.'

What was he talking about? Maybe he was as tongue-tied as me. Maybe my hair wasn't that much of a puffball. Paige was right there looking at Oscar, then over the railing at the water. It smelled like fish and deepness and faintly of salt.

Oscar's face was serious but wide open. 'You want a ride home?'

'Yeah,' my sister said. 'Come on, Pinch.'

I said bye to Evan. His eyebrows bent to a frown. His eyes were dark, taking in my whole face. Without charm or nervousness, he said, 'You should ask me out.'

I was about to pee on myself. Not really. But he was talking to me like I was on my own.

'I'm serious,' Evan said. 'Or give me your number.'

Paige was calling, so I yelled it to him as I went in her direction.

He jogged after me, said, 'You always run behind your friends?'

I said, 'That's my sister,' and he looked corrected but not cowed.

Paige called after me again.

I told Evan our phone number in a normal voice, and like a real lame-o I said, 'Good luck in school.'

Hopped in the backseat of what turned out to be Oscar's mom's old car and listened to my sister and him say things about mutual acquaintances. She asked him when we pulled into our driveway if he wanted something to eat. She fixed him a can of Campbell's and poured him a big glass of Pepsi with ice, but he'd lain across her bed with his shoes still on and was asleep. Paige came to my room in her panties and a clean tank top, said, 'I'm going to have sex with him. You think?'

She left me, and after a few hours they woke up to the jazzy station Paige had her clock radio alarm tuned to. She said they made love twice, and took a shower together, then made love two more times, and then slept until eleven and Oscar dropped Paige off at the real-estate place.

He left for Nebraska five days later, and there were long-distance bills in the hundreds of dollars. Carefully chosen greeting cards were exchanged, two or three a week. The pastel envelopes came to our place bulky with sticks of red-hot gum. Oscar dropped out of Nebraska three months later and came back to Oakland. Paige took care of the long-distance bills, spread them out, over months. It was one of the last bills either one of them had anything to do with that she paid. For a long time.

Evan ended up calling me two days after the night at the Rusty Scupper. We talked from midnight until sunrise. During the first two hours, Paige told me about every half hour to get off the phone. For a change, I argued her down.

Because Maynard went home with the girl he was dancing with, the evening at the Scupper had endless repercussions. The longhaired, wrist-whipping girl was Jessica and she got pregnant that very night, like it was her job.

CHAPTER 6

Before we ever knew her, Paige and I used to spot Jessica at this other club called the Dock of the Bay. She had her pick of the boys with the neatest hands and the most subtle, assured ways. We never hated her for it because Jess looked bewildered even as guys lined up white zinfandels for her at the bar. I did crave her San Francisco–bought clothing and jewelry, though. Paige always said that Jess had 'her own style,' which was the highest compliment my sister bestowed on other girls. We tried to find our own style at MacArthur-Broadway Mall. At the Ten Dollar Store, or at Petrie's from round racks of miniskirts in twenty shades of bright. Korean girls in surgical masks sculpted Paige's nails at M-B Mall, too. 'Don't go changin' / To try and please me' on the radio as she paid a dollar extra for the quick-dry coat. Got our shoes two-for-the-price-of-one at the Wild Pair. Bought tiny shrimp in massive coats of fried orange batter and ate them from a stick while searching Woolworth's for café au lait panty hose and lotions that promised to heal cracks and rejuvenate.

I liked the way Jessica came out to clubs and parties alone. Made her seem unimpressed. And like she knew enough to act as though partying were trivial. But based on how Paige and Jess clicked, by the way Jess fell into our circle, and by the way she inhaled Maynard in like five seconds, I was of the mind that Jess didn't have many acquaintances from whom to detach herself, let alone friends to truly chill with.

She had her parents, but Paige and I had each other, and our crew.

When Jess made her announcement one night at the Pseudo, Paige looked for a few seconds doubtful, then wowed. I thought Jess and May were ensconced in a real adult state of affairs. May was sitting on the couch, stacking and unstacking tin coasters.

'I'm thirsty,' Jess said, and walked into the kitchen. 'Lady with a baby!'

'You're sure,' Paige said, looking at May.

He stopped, looked up. 'Yeah she's sure.' He said it with the kind of soft resolve grown sons give mothers in movies. *I love you*, the shameface says, *but I'm changing. Our relationship will be different, but that's the course of things.*

'And you guys are happy about it.' Paige's question had less to do with Jess than with May, and how he was starting to live.

Maynard hadn't said he was selling crack, and maybe he wasn't. He could have been helping his mom more with the weed-selling. But he acted as if he were slinging—the straight-spine walk, his beeper, his distracted, busy attitude, his new, easier way with strangers. Quickly, he'd gotten used to people's too-quick or too-long glances. There was disgust sometimes in the nods toward May, even from folks in the Acorns. Nosiness in the glances, and fear, too. May took the consideration however it came.

He gave a short bland shrug. 'I mean, yeah. We're happy.'

Paige didn't seem jealous. More worried that May was zooming into love, money, fatherhood, into a different self. Maynard's hands were stronger, and face harder. His voice deep and warm with us, then deep and gruff when he was on the phone with Tee, or his mom, or in a coded conversation with someone we couldn't pinpoint. The gray spot in his hair was less out of place.

'Baby'll get here,' May said, 'baby'll get taken care of.' He hadn't had a real girlfriend since the faceless one from high school. May seemed proud of Jess's body and face, and the fact that she reserved them for him. Now she was going to have their baby. He'd probably already done the cartwheels.

Jess walked back into the living room with iced tea. That's how I knew Paige liked Jessica. My sister hated liberties, but she hadn't minded when May took them, and she didn't mind them from Jess.

'I'm going to tell my mom and dad—give it one more week to be absolute,' Jess said. 'And I'll tell them at the same time that we're getting married. My dad'll want to hear that.' It was relief on her face, and in the way she sighed after her tea was gone. Like she'd been going fast and found a lull.

'Ah,' Maynard said, 'maybe he won't want to hear that last part.'

Jess looked at Paige, said, 'Dad doesn't know May like I do.'

In my head I said, *You think you know him after four weeks?*

'Your dad don't wanna know me.'

'You guys are actually getting married?'

'Yeah, Pinch,' May said. 'It's the thing to do. Hell yeah.'

His hair had just been trimmed. He was in a new gray jogging suit and pristine running shoes. Maynard was at Hayward State part-time, and was lounging through fewer and fewer hours at Peony's. In the month Maynard had been with Jessica, he'd little time for conversations with me, or with Paige except to ask her when was the last time she'd talked to Oscar. Her answer was almost always 'I just got off the phone with him.' May would ask me when I was getting a boyfriend. I told him, even when I didn't, that I had things going on. Evan still called me, but homeboy was in Davis.

Aside from me, it was Jess who my sister wore out with worries about Oscar. Sitting in Peony's on a quiet night, I noticed how quickly Jess had evolved into mistress of the establishment by befriending the dusty deejay and playing video games for cashews with the older regulars. Jess always wore like thirty different thin gold chains on her left wrist, and they hung elegantly when she raised her arm for anything. She wore coats and coats of mascara, made her eyes look romantic. I caught Maynard looking at Jess as she talked to us, trying to quantify his luck. She'd started to blow off her classes at the University of San Francisco.

'Oscar already loves you,' Jessica said from behind the bar at Peony's, with her gold teardrop earrings and hair in a bun at her nape. 'Stop tripping.'

It's not like you had to be a genius to figure that out. The six-hour phone calls the notes the bubble gum and grape lollipops Oscar sent Paige. He even had my sister take the bus to this rehabilitation center in West Oakland where his dad lived. I went with her, sat outside with obliterated old men who smoked cigarettes and said I was pretty. Paige was to 'check' on Oscar's dad, and to give him twenty dollars that Oscar sent back to Paige in a greeting card. We brought Oscar's father fish 'n' chips and Winstons. He was drained and anxious and told Paige and I that we were angels.

Jess said, 'Oscar's got you dealing with his family, too?' She thought that this was very deep, and telling.

It must have been, because within three months, Oscar moved back to Oakland in a fit to be married. Paige was twenty-one, Oscar was twenty-two. My sister didn't talk to me about marriage or a wedding, so I didn't think she'd do it. Still, with Maynard preparing to marry Jess, and Jess having a baby, things started to fast-forward.

Paige and I didn't discuss it, but Oscar pretty much moved in with us. She paid attention to him, washed his clothes, usually fixed breakfast and dinner for us both. She listened when he talked about his plans to transfer to a computer school. About how he hated Nebraska, had been on academic probation, had only about two years' worth of units. He spoke about getting a job, part-time, at Federal Express. Oscar seemed to have money, though. Not a lot, but he bought bathroom soap, and a rug for the short hallway. Wine and pork chops and a VCR. Kept gas in his mother's ride. We never met Oscar's mother, but she'd lost her license, so he had access to her car almost all the time.

Maybe Oscar and May were selling crack. Donnell and Ced, too. I wasn't pissed at them if they were. It was like smoking cigarettes. You wish the person wouldn't do it, because it's unhealthy, and leads to early death. But some cigarette smokers don't die of it. Some smoke for a while and then stop. Lucky smokers die in their sleep at eighty-five. They risk death, freedom, health, virtue for the lifting feel of smoke in their limbs and brain. And to achieve rebel status behind a cloud of smoke. Secondhand smoke affects friends and family, but they stay around for the love of the smoker. The rebel smoke gets in their lungs, stays in their clothes.

If you're a dope dealer, you sell for the freedom of the money, the standing, and for what you believe is the standing up. I see them, know them. Boys with just-waxed BMW M3s with BBS rims and Yokohama tires. They smile easy, but not completely. They honk and say, *Sister, you don't need to be on that bus stop. The No. 40's gonna be awhile. I can't give you a ride to where you're going? Okay. I'll see you again. I seen you before.* And before they pull off I see under the raw smile that they sling for the warped, strengthening sense of purpose. See it on their faces even when they're leant up against the back of a dusty OPD car, legs spread, arms spread. They're pissed, and beyond frustrated. Scared. But along with all that is a look that says, *I was doing what I needed to do. Doing what makes me feel, for what I know of it, like a man.* I wasn't going to look down on our crew if they did start moving crack. So I was secondhand selling. Paige, Jess, and Ch'Rell, too.

I CAME home from Laney on a stale afternoon, heard the television tuned quietly to a *Wild Kingdom*–like show. With barely a sound, I shut the screen door behind me.

'That's you, Pinch?'

'Yeah.' Put my backpack down. Knew by the fact that it was just before five, my sister was still at work. 'Paige here?'

'You know she's at her job.' He was stretched out behind a bottle of Corona.

Started into my room. I hadn't been around Oscar, just him and me, for an extended conversation. I began moving stiffly. Stomach tightened, had that readied feeling. I was primed, but who could lurch from the blocks faster than Oscar?

'Pinch.'

I froze. 'Huh?' He could see me from where he was sitting.

'You want a beer?'

'No, thanks.'

'Come talk to me for a second.'

I didn't turn around. 'Come talk to you?'

'For a second.'

'For a second?' *What did he want?* It's not like he'd ever acted any way but nice, but people stun you.

'Don't talk to me, then.'

Went in my room, made the bed. Picked up clothes from the floor, wiped my nightstand. Pulled hair from my brush, put it in the wastebasket. Then I dusted my little collection. I saved African Americana. Tiny Sambos and slaves. If Mom's pineapples meant 'Welcome,' my plaster slaves meant 'Bad times are over.' I'd seen a woman on the news talking about her real, antique collection. She liked the stuff, she'd said, because it symbolized that the past was fucked up, but it's past and she's not embarrassed about it. The woman hadn't said 'fucked up,' but by her taut expression, it's what she'd had in mind.

I crouched down to put my shoes, pair by pair, in neat rows on my closet floor.

'Straightening up?'

I lurched up into my hanging clothes, disturbed hangers. Felt stupid.

'You all right?' Oscar said. 'Didn't mean to scare you.'

Sat down on my bed.

'I just kind of crashed in here, didn't I?' He seemed even taller when he was by himself.

'It's not that.' I was looking at my Sambos.

'I'm not talking about just this minute. I mean overall.'

'I know what you mean. And I don't mind you being here.'

'But you don't like it.' He stayed just outside my room. I appreciated that. It was gracious. I wondered if he was feeling that he could afford to be that way.

'That's not true.' I looked at him. I was telling the truth.

'I'm here all the time, and I don't want you to feel . . . put out. I got you something. Not that—'

'What something?' I got a little happy.

Oscar stepped in, handed me a shiny white plastic bag. Inside was a bunch of ponytail holders in every color. My hair was too short for a ponytail, but that wasn't the point. There was a bracelet in there, too. Of green oblong glass beads. And a matching anklet. I'd wanted an anklet. Jessica had anklets.

'Paige told you I liked this kind of stuff.'

'Yeah she did. I told her I felt bad about just coming in here and sort of . . . changing everything.'

'Nothing's really changed.'

'But it will.' He went back to where he'd been sitting.

I knew he was right.

A few minutes later, Oscar said, 'You want to go with me to pick up your sister?'

I put on my bracelet and hopped in the car with him. We rode around Lake Merritt with the tape deck blasting music Oscar'd said for me to pick. I rolled my window down. The afternoon, all blocked up with boring Laney classes and BART rides and being broke, didn't seem so stale to me anymore.

Paige worked in a dark brown office building across from the Oakland Museum, near the county courthouse. She waited out front in her skirt and blouse, with her purse and her low heels. Hair neat in a ponytail. Before she saw us, her manner was distracted, like a person who'd run out of cigarettes, a person who had things to do that wouldn't get done unless she saw to them. If I didn't know her, I'd have thought my sister was a regular woman from Oakland with a job and responsibilities. Sitting there with my favorite songs playing, I figured Paige's responsibility, her distraction, was me. Standing there with that giant brown building behind her, she looked like no one so much as Mom. Facing forward, but really looking back. Punching out of one place, about to punch in with me.

I moved to get in the backseat when we pulled up to her.

'Cut it out,' Paige said, and hopped in the back. She kissed her man on his shoulder. He turned around and squeezed her knee.

'So I'm your chauffeur now,' he said, pulling out into traffic.

'Yes. My chauffeur forever.'

'I'm teaching you to drive.'

'One day, maybe,' Paige said. 'But even then you'll drive me around.'

'You won't want me to then.'

'Yes I will.'

I looked back between the seats, saw my sister's face go placid.

I mentally crossed my fingers that on no day ever would Paige say to me, *Oscar used to not be how he is now. He used to be a nice person who helped me. He used to be normal. That's why I stay.* Because this time I'd remember the niceness. I'd have known it, seen how Oscar made her happy, and maybe my judgment wouldn't be so clear-cut. About her or about Oscar. Or about Mom.

M O M didn't come to Paige and Oscar's wedding. The way Paige told her, on the phone, 'I think Oscar and I might get married next month,' I don't think Mom really believed her. I know I didn't until Paige started looking in her closet for what she had white.

On the wedding day, Paige and Oscar didn't seem to notice that no parents were there. It was just Paige and Oscar, and me, and Paige's old boss Kirby, from Diamond Pool. May and Jess and Cedric were there, and Ch'Rell and Donnell.

Oscar wore a starched canary shirt buttoned to his throat with no tie. When I lined up his hair for him along the nape with his electric razor, he smelled like Paige's vanilla lotion. She wore a white wool skirt Mom had given her a while before, and a creamy round-collared blouse with mother-of-pearl buttons. Paige held silver-white flowers as she made her promises. She and I had walked to a florist the morning of her nuptials, pointed through a foggy glass refrigerator door. 'I'd like those, please,' Paige said to an older white woman with brown-gold caulk holding her teeth together. 'The puffy ones.' I got my nails done—lengthened, airbrushed coral-to-cream, diamond rhinestone on the left thumb—for the occasion. Really I got them done because I had the money. I'd gotten a job at the Planned Parenthood right near San Antonio Park.

A few weeks after Paige and Oscar's wedding, there was

an Oakland reception for Maynard and Jess's Las Vegas
elopement at the Lake Merritt Hotel. May's parents had gone
to Vegas with them. They didn't come to the Merritt Hotel.

Jess and her mother, Sandra, planned the event with a
Chinatown theme. Shrimp tarts hovered above blue flames.
Cold crab rolls shed confetti-like sesame seeds. Todd was out of
town, and Teeara was there in spaghetti straps and with her
baby boys. Donnell stood near a tray of gold buns wet inside
with mushrooms. The room was crowded with streaming lanterns, weak conversations, and silver balloons on curly strings.
Oscar's father, who'd known Jessica's mom since high school,
pushed his way through the dangling tails to get to clearer air
near windows. He'd come with us on a pass from the rehab
place, and seemed to like it when he wasn't in a crowd.

Sandra's voice was tinny, her thin chocolate wrists rammed
through clunky bangles. We'd met her before, but this time, Jess
said Paige and I's last name. Her mother was surprised.

'You two are Gigi's girls? I didn't realize that.'

I don't know why that was such a shock to us, when so
many people in Oakland knew so many other people.

Jess's mom and her husband, Roland, said cordial quick
'thank yous' to dozens of 'congratulations.' Then Sandra dove
into weighty chats with the food personnel. She had to keep
the rainbow of food curving toward mouths. It would keep
folks from pressing about what Maynard did for a living, or,
for that matter, what was Jessica's career plan. Paige and I
sipped wines Jess's mom said were from France or Spain or
anyplace but nearby.

There were white women at the reception with long earrings, and hair too long for their stage in life. They loved Sandra's earthenware. She was a pottery person, an artist, and
people knew of her because of it. Dr. Roland's black and white
dental friends paced with their white and black wives. Jess's
hair was swirled into a smooth knot. Her mother had done it

for her, and twisted in tea roses. Paige, Jess, and I were near a counter stacked with gifts. Rising above all the white boxes was a lamp. It had to be five feet tall, and should have been on the floor because every time somebody walked by the counter, or set a gift on it, the heavy lamp trembled, like it wasn't level on the bottom. Enameled gray, and pressed in with mirror, mother-of-pearl, and jet, Sandra had molded it. Even the shade was of clay, but pounded thin, and with slit after slit, so light could shine through.

'Maynard and I really appreciate everyone coming out today.' Jess was holding his hand, spoke into a standing microphone. 'We thank you, Mom and Dad, for everything.'

Jess was teary. You could hear mews of support from people.

'A lot of you have known me since I was a baby'—she touched her own rounding stomach—'and now I'm here having one of my—of our—own.'

There was applause.

'You all don't know Maynard,' Jess said, 'yet. But the thing I want you to take away from today is that . . . with him I feel completely . . . safe.'

There was attentive silence. A momentary desire to believe she believed.

'I'm in a whirlwind,' she said with an edgy laugh, 'but in a cocoon at the same time.'

Oscar, Paige, and I were standing near Sandra and Dr. Roland. Blue-gray eyes damp, his full lips stretched over capped teeth. Slowly he curled and then spread his fingers wide and taut as a starfish. Repeated the slow stretches until Jess's short speech was over.

'May,' Jess said, 'is there anything you want to say?'

May looked out at the throng, then over to where we were standing. 'Just,' he said, not even into the mike, 'that you said it all.'

Then Cedric raised his glass from the crowd. He didn't need a microphone. 'May and Jessica rushed off too fast for anyone to have actually *been* the best man,' he said. 'But seeing as I'm the best man here—next to the groom and'—he smiled toward Dr. Roland—'the Root Canal Man, I have a little something to say.' I rolled my eyes. Cedric had come back from Nebraska not two months behind Oscar and, with a whole lot of fake complaining, moved back in with his father. I'd never seen either of Cedric's parents. The dad was supposed to be a bus driver, drove the No. 40. Cedric said his dad's personality was kind of plain. Said his father wasn't one to call out the stops, or speak to people when they paid their fare.

Ced didn't have that plainness. His tie was loose. Belt buckle, tie bar, new shoes shimmery and bright as shame. He had a swingy grace he hadn't when he'd found Paige earlier, as she was signing the guest book. Cedric had said, 'Don't you look nice? Green is your color. I didn't get a chance to tell you how happy I was for you—for you and Oscar, I mean. He's a lucky guy. I hope he knows how lucky.'

Paige had said, 'Thank you,' about three times.

Now with his glass up, waving balloon strings from his face, Cedric said, 'I've known May for a *good* while. We've run the streets together. Had big fun. Too much fun.'

He got some laughs.

'All of a sudden I'm surrounded by real love between people my own age,' Cedric said. 'We're making big moves. Taking care of *ourselves*. No disrespect to the older folks—but I hope we figure this *love* thing *out*.'

Cedric got more chuckles. Good-natured, and knowing better.

'I just want to wish May and his bride all the best life has to offer.' Maynard walked over there, and as May hugged him, Cedric said something that got muffled in the embrace.

Sounded like, *It's time* or *It's our time* or *Keep trying.* Then Cedric went over and embraced Jess, too.

There was spotty applause. Tears had run down Jess's face. I felt like I was at a play. Not like my friends' actions were insincere, but like they were being carried out before an audience too early.

Donnell sat in a chair against a wall. Held an empty champagne flute on his knee. Ch'Rell was standing, then bent to rub her Achilles. Donnell handed her his glass, she walked to refill it. Paige was in a conversation with Oscar's dad. Oscar stood with his hand moving in a small circle at the bottom of Paige's back. I was by the champagne fountain. Jess and Dr. Roland were standing there alone.

Jess said, 'Be happy for me, Dad.' He was filling his glass, hadn't made a toast. 'May swept me off my feet. I really do love him.'

Her father said, 'You must.' His fleshy face was pushed forward and down. Cheek flesh close around his nose, forehead flesh crowded his eyes. Dr. Roland's chin, rosy and full, spread out over his neck like a robe. I wanted him to throw his head back, say what he felt.

Maynard came over, stood next to his new wife in her flowing ivory trousers and announced lame sacrifices as evidence of his love. 'You know I had a lot of business to take care of, wanted to cancel the party,' he said to me.

What business? If it's more than Peony's, then say that. You don't have to say it to Dr. Roland, but you can say it, straight out, to us.

'I wanted no part of this madness,' May said to Dr. Roland. 'This reception stuff. But I didn't nix it because Jess would have been upset.'

'Yes, she would have,' Dr. Roland said.

May didn't seem nervous, but cross. He wasn't getting the

response he wanted. 'I was gonna be a bachelor forever, but I guess I'm on lockdown now.' He put his hand on the back of Jess's neck. 'Cream of the crop,' Maynard said of Jessica. 'Can't nobody say different.'

Bachelor? Who says that?

Maynard said, 'Thanks for helping us with this celebration, but it's not a hardship for me. That's how it's going to be for my wife. Whatever she wants.'

But you're living in the apartment in San Francisco where Roland's paying the rent. So what, exactly, is the deal?

'That's all I can ask,' Dr. Roland said. He saw his wife nearby. He kissed his daughter's hand and stiffly shook Maynard's.

Then he went over to Sandra. Together in a doorway, they were like the last two bowling pins. Shaky from the charge of yet another ball, Jess's parents braced and hoped against a spare.

CHAPTER 7

Not long after the wedding, Teeara's man, Todd, came back from Las Vegas. He'd stopped going to his day job at Super G, went out to Nevada to make some real money selling crack with some other slinging-type fools from the Acorns. Todd didn't pack any clothes, just got in the car with some scandalous negroes and got on the highway. He sent Teeara money home in FedEx boxes, tens and twenties mostly, rolled up and bound with blue and green rubber bands. The flat boxes came about twice a week. Teeara was flush that spring. Nails done, hair done, babies all Gapped out.

Deep-summer Saturday. Paige, May, Oscar and Cedric, Ch'Rell and Donnell and I sweating on the long low step in front of May's parents' apartment. The door was open. I could hear the television, and the occasional curt mandate from May's mother to Teeara.

We'd put money together for burritos. Extra sour cream, extra chicken, extra cheese, extra everything.

'Get out of your hands, Pinch,' Ch'Rell said, with food in her mouth. 'Like you're the first person in the world to get your goddamn nails done.'

It had become habit. Running my thumbnails under my fingernails, checking them for perfection, admiring the fact that all ten were even, pleasingly curved, and bright. I got all the fills I could afford, didn't like the nails to lose their luster, or look in any way ragged. Even at my job, when I was helping people's kids build Lego towers, or wiping down sinks, or fil-ing filing filing, the nails were classy. Mature. I sure didn't want sour cream under them.

Paige said, 'May, where's Jess?'

'She'll be by.'

Right then Todd flew up in a dirty Beemer. I put my food down, stood up. Paige rose in front of me. Oscar kept eating, Cedric and Donnell, too. All three, so cool, staying seated. May at least looked up from his food when Todd came to a stop, all across the faded yellow lines. He'd been going fast.

First thing I thought was, *Nice car. Homeboy came up.* Slung low, the car was sandy-covered, hummed angrily, and then sighed when Todd slammed the door. 'Where's Tee?'

'What's up man?' Maynard said, putting burrito remnants in a bag and slowly standing. 'What's the problem.'

Oscar stood almost as May did. Cedric and Donnell stood, too.

'I need to talk to her is she in the house?'

Okay, but why was there so much perspiration below his nose? So many creases so deep in his forehead? Why the drying split lip? The smear of dust and grass on his cap?

'She's in there with the kids,' May said squarely. He set his legs apart. Purposefully, he didn't look at Ced, Oscar, or Donnell. Like he was confident, or wanted to seem confident of their presence. 'Why you breathing all hard?' May didn't glance at Paige, Ch'Rell, or myself, either.

Todd's eyes shot back and forth along our crooked line, from May on one end to Ch'Rell on the other. He saw the space between Ced and Paige, rushed between them and was in the apartment. May scrambled in after him and it was a big scramble after that, all of us falling through the front door.

May's parents were sunk in the couch. A coffee table was crowded with ashtrays, jars of banana baby food, forks, and *TV Guide.* There were quarters and nickels on the table, and a lighter stamped with I LEFT MY HEART IN SAN FRANCISCO. Atop a color TV showing the ballgame were broken pencils and plain matchbooks. May's mom tuned in to the commotion, but stayed still. May's dad dazedly watched the Athletics.

Standing there in flustered huddle, all we needed was Scooby Doo.

Oscar said, 'Todd ain't crazy.'

Ch'Rell said, 'He looks crazy.'

From inside the front bedroom, Todd's voice was hoarse. All I could make out was something like, *Tell me.*

May was already leaned against the bedroom door, waiting, and Oscar and Cedric and Donnell hurried after him. Teeara yelled back something like, *I don't know* and *It was mine,* then she said, *I'm not sorry* and *You shouldn't have fucked with me, you should have known* and *If you gonna play me out, show me the fucking respect of*—and then came a series of thuds and shocked screaming and Maynard was pushing at the bedroom door and tugging the handle and each baby inside was making a distinct soft noise, not crying but crying out.

Me, Ch'Rell, and Paige inched further toward the bedroom door, but May's mother swooped between the guys and us. She called out, 'Tee, baby! Open the damn door!'

I edged my way up, though, right beside her. Paige had my wrist, but I twisted it free. May got the door open, and when the guys fell in, I was right behind them.

Teeara was laid out, her head halfway under the bed with its chenille coverlet, but anyone could see she was unconscious and her right eye lay on the floor like a white yolk someone had handled carefully. Saw veins, and straight into Teeara's head. There was no blood, but the arm you could see was bowed, elbow pointed in the wrong direction. Maynard's mother started with these hyperventilating, whooping shrieks. In their flimsy crib, the babies had turned into sirens, bright blinking and loud.

Paige was behind me, outside the bedroom. 'I'm calling 911,' she said. No one paid her any attention.

Oscar and Ced kept Maynard from Todd, who was yelling at Teeara like she could hear him. 'What's the deal?' Fear pulled Todd's voice flat and brittle. His ripped lip was more inflated than when he first rolled up. 'I'm here now,' he said. 'Tell me what's the deal.'

Oscar had May from behind, arms around May's stomach. Ced pushed May's upper body from the front. I felt fire grazing my face and arms, air like from an oven boxing my head. Heard an old phone clang to the floor, then something else falling.

It was May's mom, getting to her knees, pawing at her daughter.

'Where is it?' Todd said.

Teeara was still.

'If you smoked it I will kill your ass.'

Kill. This was Todd. Pastrami-buying, breast-grabbing Todd.

Oscar said, 'Pinch go help your sister!'

I was entranced, though, by the luring, acidic way May was talking to Todd, saying, like it was a dare, 'Say that to me. Turn around and say that shit to me.'

Todd turned to May, neck muscles taut and a shiny film on his rough face. *Was it tears? Sweat? Didn't seem aware of what he'd done to Tee. Was she dead? How could she die?*

'Nigga fuck you,' Todd said. 'I'll say what I want.' Then he called Maynard 'boy,' like they hadn't both come into the world the same year, one Aries, one Leo. 'You shoulda been watching her ass while I was gone, anyway.'

May pushed against Ced and Oscar, but his voice wasn't huffy. With the same burnt sweet tone, he said, 'What's in your hand, Todd?'

'What's mine.'

I backed out of the bedroom, ran to the small junky kitchen. Paige was speaking to a 911 operator, and Ch'Rell's body was so slanted toward her, I thought she might tip over. The operator was asking Paige the number of the building and Paige had just never known it, so Ch'Rell ran out of the apartment to see if there was a number on the building and finally Maynard's father, who was sitting there on the sofa, aware but not moving, said, 'Ten-eleven.' Then Todd zipped by us, looked like he had a small steel jack in his hand, didn't look at anyone. Ch'Rell ran after him.

I heard Oscar say, 'Take care of Teeara, May . . . cool out, man . . . it's about her right now. Get your nephews.'

At the same time, Todd's BMW burned off, and Ch'Rell ran back in. 'Todd's gone,' she said, and then a dented ambulance rolled in where Todd had been parked. Oscar ran past us and out the front door.

Ch'Rell and I followed as Paige loped outside, stood on the sidewalk away from the cement step and looked around for what? *Maybe Todd killed Teeara. Maybe she's in a coma. Where did Oscar go, is he leaving us? May must be pissed. Or sad.* My sister grabbed my arm when she saw Oscar pull up. We clambered in the car as Oscar maneuvered from the lot.

Paige said, 'My backpack!' but Oscar kept twisting the wheel. I saw May's mom put her thimble-sized suede pouch of reefer in her purse and check on it once more before she got in her car to follow the ambulance. A pulsing group of Acorn people had congregated to see who'd been broken or punctured or dented or dead. I didn't see May's father, hadn't seen him get up from the couch at all. I didn't see May or Ced or Donnell, either.

When Paige went by a few days later to get her bag, she told me Teeara had a patch and it seemed okay.

By the time Paige and Ch'Rell and Donnell and I went

over to the Acorns on Thanksgiving weekend, we all knew
Teeara had the glass eye. May had told us, of course. And
everybody in Oakland was talking about the incident, and the
one eye. People had overblown details about babies being
thrown from the crib, and May's mom hitting Todd. When
people at my job or fools up at Laney brought that chitchat to
me, I let them glory in their little tales. Denied I'd been there.
What could I add that was juicy? No one would want to hear
about the rawness inside her head. Who could bear hearing
about the orphaned organ on the floorboards, so indecent, so
distinctly in the wrong place? No one would care about the
transformation of Todd by worry and ego and fury and greed.
That makeover was common in Oakland. And the misery and
meanness that surfaced in May as he defended his sister was
too difficult to explain on Laney's quad full of second-besters.
Too much to go into between abortion intake-interviews. It
had seemed, in the thump and scream of that July Saturday,
that May was defending Teeara. But later it was clear that
Maynard was defending Maynard. Jessica'd missed the graph-
ics, but maybe when she'd said her dad didn't know May like
she did, she meant that she already knew May better than any
of us, as well.

Thanksgiving Saturday, when Paige and I approached
the Acorns, we saw Ch'Rell and Donnell outside on the
cement step. Paige and I walked in, saw Teeara at the kitchen
table. Sons in a nearby playpen with stuffed Muppets and a
big round See 'n' Say. I picked it up. Cow went Moo.

Paige moved her hands from her sides to her hips to
across her chest to hitching up her purse. I picked up the thick-
set, littlest boy, took the pacifier from his mouth, kissed his
hair, tickled his toes. The older boy, the two-year-old, looked
happy in his nest of toys. He'd already learned to fake a face. I
got hot suddenly in that claustrophobic kitchen, held the small
baby tighter than I was supposed to. Those kids had seen the

MORE LIKE WRESTLING 113

whole everything that deep-summer Saturday. They'd seen the deep days before, and would see the ones ahead.

Teeara's pretend eye bulged like it might pop out. *At any moment I might see inside her head to bone and curds of brain and capillaries snarled around compasses and a violet in a glass jar barely touched with water. Why am I imagining things? That's Paige's job. Why can't I just look at her and say, I'm so sorry this happened to you? Why, when things are insane, do I shut my mouth and gaze? Who named me fucking silent witness? Why don't I hug Tee and say, Girl, you look good, you still look fine. You can still get a party started. Let's go to M-B Mall get our nails done. Let's go out tonight and dance.* I watched Paige take a long blink. Then she finally looked Teeara directly in her eye. See and say. Smiling was important, and so was pacification. But I hoped Tee's boys would say what they needed to, when they could.

The baby I held giggled. He didn't mind my grip. Tee turned my way and curved her lips in a small grin. Maybe Todd had seen the violet, and May the compasses, because Teeara looked relieved. She looked half dead, but thankful at the same time.

Paige and I had taken the bus over, but Donnell and Ch'Rell took us back to the Pseudo. We'd been to Mom's for dinner on Thursday, so had the best leftovers—ham slices, potato salad, cornbread stuffing, Gram Liz's gravy. But I wasn't hungry.

In our driveway, Ch'Rell said, 'That shit is sick.' And she looked sick when she said it.

'What we should be is happy that maybe Tee can only see half of us,' Paige said.

Ch'Rell said, 'Way Todd was, she needs to be happy she can see at all.'

'She can see all of us,' Donnell said. 'The one eye is completely fine.'

Ch'Rell and Donnell didn't get it. I squeezed Paige's wrist, but she didn't look over. I wanted her to save spacey conversation for when we were alone.

'Maybe Teeara can only see the good part of us now.'

'There's no other part,' Ch'Rell said, 'of me to see.'

HAD on a sweater, a coat, and a green knit cap the windy wet day Paige and I went over to Maynard's parents' with Oscar to meet May. Got out of the car, and flat streaks of cloud seemed two feet above my head.

Teeara looked pretty high when we walked in. Her mom was diapering the boys and May was looking at Tee like she was Mongoloid and had made a mistake she couldn't help. We were waiting on Jessica to go up near Cal, to the record store, and to get some pizza. Maybe buy Christmas trees.

Teeara lay on the couch in that crammed living room and put her good arm up, said, 'May, stop,' when he hadn't said anything. She said, 'I'm sorry. I'm sorry. Damn.'

Maynard, dressed to be out the door, was leaned against the window ledge. Faint sun eked in around him, put him in gray silhouette. 'I don't know why,' he said, 'you had to act so stupid, fucking with this nigga's money and then Todd—'

Oscar shook his head.

'Fuck,' May said. 'I don't see how this motherfucker felt like he could come up in here and completely change a situation, somebody's face, somebody's life, from one thing to another. Come up in here and just *change shit*.' Both his eyes were the shiniest tense wet brown.

Teeara started saying how she knew Todd had been sleeping with this white chick from UNLV, and also how she felt like the money Todd had marked off for her hadn't been enough to keep her sons up the way she felt they needed to be.

May said, 'I know the story,' then listened to more of it with his eyes closed.

Jessica was past late.

Tee asked May for a hundred dollars. Said she'd pay him back when she got her shit together.

Things were shifting. But like the dirt beneath us, things had been shifting all along.

CHAPTER 8

Oscar was on his way to pick Paige and I up from their new apartment. The three of us were going to the aquarium. Chilly midday Sunday, half-light and wanting to pour. Purple-tinged air and mist wispy enough to inhale—that was normal for Oakland in December. It wasn't an average day, though. We were about to feel *samiel,* as Paige's friend Obe used to say. A blistering arid wind was about to blow through, and it was almost New Year's.

Oscar and my sister had moved to a small, newly renovated two-bedroom apartment building on the side of Lake Merritt opposite the Pseudo. It was a nicer part of Oakland, over by Fairyland. We used to go to Fairyland with Mom, or with Nannah, get all excited about walking through the door of a huge boot that belonged to the Old Lady Who Lived in a Shoe. Paige cherished the elaborate puppet shows, and we both liked the big Magic Keys. Turn a key in a Talking Storybook, and a dramatic voice would bellow out a scene from *Alice in Wonderland,* or something like it. And maybe a princess or Little Red Riding Hood would walk out of her cottage and say hello. Paige says that Fairyland supposedly inspired Disneyland, but Disneyland is Fairyland to the ten billionth degree. Still, it was fun to ride from story to story on the Jolly Trolly, eager to turn another key.

Paige's new building was mixed with black people, white people, some Mexicans and Asians. People with jobs. Couples and singles, a bunch of kids, too. Oscar'd told Paige he'd been 'making a few easy runs,' for 'some guys May knows.' There weren't any straight-up crackheads in their building, but anyone who liked to mix crack with reefer and smoke it up in a Zigzag had already begun to count on Oscar, rain or shine. For crack or weed.

'I don't want to go to the aquarium,' I said. 'You guys go. Somebody's gotta let Oscar's dad in.' He was coming by. I liked Oscar's dad. Addict or not, he was cleaned up, and I could kick it with him. Plus Paige gazed at the fish like she wanted to leap through the glass and float in water temperature-controlled for her species. I didn't feel like being around her when she was like that. And I'd been to that aquarium with her enough times to last me my whole life.

'Oscar's father has keys.'

'Dang. He might as well move in.'

'He just might. You didn't want that second room.'

I ignored that comment. Paige had assumed, from the moment she found out they got the new place, that I was going to move in with she and her husband.

'Why would you stay here by yourself?' she said to me that day at the Pseudo. Oscar'd dropped us there, after having given us a grand tour of their new apartment.

'Just because,' I said. 'I want to. You're married, and you should be . . . like, a total wife. To him.'

'You like Oscar. You two get along.'

'We do we do. It's not even that.'

'You didn't like the second bedroom?'

'What are you talking about? Like I can afford to be choosy?'

'You're choosing to stay here. How broke will you be, anyway? I mean, I can give you some money, but it would be better if you came over to the new place.'

I shook my head.

'You need to stop being stubborn or whatever you're being. What are you gonna do here all by yourself? You gonna cook? Who're you gonna talk to?'

I thought I might call Evan collect.

A few days later, I helped her unpack her things at their new apartment. Paige was arranging her body condiments in their bathroom, when Oscar came to me and told me to move in with them.

'You need to be with your sister.'

'You all need to be by yourselves.'

'I knew this was a package deal, from the get-go. She's not gonna be right without you staying here.'

That's not the way I had it figured. Paige had a man. He sold crack, but he was nice. And they didn't have any kids. They could just be them. Paige could, maybe, just be her. Without me.

'She's already not right,' Oscar said, 'just at the prospect of you staying at the Pseudo.'

'Doesn't it get on your nerves? Her sister always being right there?'

He shook his head. 'You want to stay over with Vangelisti, stay.' He reached in his pocket, gave me some money. 'That's what Paige was paying?'

'Yeah.' I didn't know how much he'd handed me.

'One more time. Paige would be happy if you went in there and told her—'

'Paige knows you're giving me this money?'

'She told me you might need some money. You know she doesn't straight-out ask for anything.'

THE prospect of the aquarium hung over me. At Paige and Oscar's apartment, she rushed around, applied cream to her hands and face, found lipstick. I had my coat, my bag, was ready as I was going to be.

'So you're fine with Oscar's dad living here?'

'There's nothing to be fine with yet,' she said. 'Get your stuff. Oscar sounded weird. He's just gonna honk.'

'See. He's sick of me always being around.'

'Did I say "sick of you" or did I say "weird"?'

'Where's he coming from?'

Paige shrugged. 'You know how he's acting. I asked him where he was and he acted like I called him stupid. Like it's a big question, some big secret, where he is when he calls.'

'He was with Ced and May and them?'

'You think I asked him that?'

'Aquarium's boring,' I said. 'Been there too many times.'

'You like the penguins. You're going.'

I like them because they have personality. You like that controlled environment, the rigid feeding times. But I got my pocketbook and crawled in the backseat of Oscar's used Mustang. It was shiny red, though, and new to him. Air dam in the front, body lowered. Vogue brand tires with a white-and-gold stripe, and a curb-finder that scratched the cement before his wheels could. Oscar should've had the dealership embroider my name on the rear upholstery. His stereo system was supercrisp, even turned all the way up. His hair was buzzed to the tightest fade, his ear pierced a second time. With composure, Oscar periodically assessed his surroundings. Absentmindedly, he touched at his beeper.

Money was really starting to be made.

This was 1986. People had just started calling Oakland Cokeland.

Who knew the genesis of them all selling?

Exactly what May, Oscar, Ced, and Donnell were doing—what their fingers clutched, how their voices changed, who they negotiated with, how and where they stood, drove, congregated, if they fought or were scared—all that was unclear.

They never said, 'We sell crack.' They never said anything

about it, really. Not in front of me. And not in front of Paige, as far as I knew. And since no one had yet rolled up on us talking about *I didn't know your man was hawking rock over on Fifty-first off Telegraph. Damn! I thought that nigga was an athlete and all,* Paige liked to think Oscar was selling at some imaginative level. Involved, but in a way that was reflective of his intelligence. Besides, negroes on corners got shot, or arrested, sometimes twice a month. So what else could she think, and still act normal?

It had been quick.

First the boys had regular money. Then they regularly had more money than they should.

Then it was obvious—the consistency of the money, even over a month's time, was proof. Proof, when a brother had no twice-a-month check from a job.

Plus, there were the *accoutrements.* The watch that showed up on Donnell's wrist. May and Oscar frequenting the barbershop on Shattuck Avenue that catered to brothers who could drop forty dollars from the chair. And Cedric had become truly dapper. Nixed the jogging suits for bright billowy slacks and longish, silky T-shirts. Dress shirts with mandarin collars worn with sharply pressed jeans. And there were the new apartments. Nothing grand. But the apartments were nice. Nicer than our place across from San Antonio Park. And before Seth went crazy, I'd loved that apartment.

Paige and I figured Oscar to be making about eight or nine hundred a week. May and Ced seemed to be making more. Donnell, somewhere in between. Whatever Donnell was making, Ch'Rell was about him doing more.

She and I were making our own little moves. 'Rell was working part-time at a bank in Berkeley but was ready to quit, and to get pregnant and married. I was taking yet another computer class at Laney and had been promoted to peer counselor at Planned Parenthood. My boss, a plump, businesslike Mexican woman with three daughters at St. J's, said I had an aptitude for listening, and should reconsider the classes I was choosing at Laney. I told her I would, but hadn't. Was happy for the minuscule raise, and a shared desk. As for the aptitude required, if you've ever missed your period or had chlamydia, you qualified for my job.

OUR crew had started eating sometimes at the Foothill Smorgasbord. Across town, way east of the lake, it was open until one hundred o'clock, seven days a week. Occasionally Ced was there by himself when we arrived. He'd see ex-girlfriends with toddlers he'd make a big deal about looking at real hard—'You never know!' he liked to say, licking his soft serve.

We'd sit up there and talk about who was dating whom, who was vain and who was lying. It was only the middle-aged women who talked about the murder rate in Oakland. The newspapers were counting them—headlines said it looked like it would get up to maybe ninety deaths that year, over sixty of them black males. The ladies discussed how many Oakland street-level negroes were getting shot not once, but up to seven times. Talked about how the guys were living a dozen hours after surgery. *Just long enough to say to their stupid little friends, in one of those overrun hospital rooms, exactly who pulled the trigger.* That's the kind of thing the ladies said when they were murmuring about The Climate.

They meant the crack wars. The nephews they'd lost the grandsons they sent money to in San Quentin the neighbors' boys they half-wished would get arrested. We heard them, all whispery. *Way the climate is now, the youngest ones, the babies, they're the only hope.* The ladies didn't care if we heard. They glanced at our table, all superior, like we needed to know better. *These boys. Think they men.*

I hated when they said that. Like they were so right. Like they knew so much. Like the young men of now weren't the babies, the so-called hope, of yesterday. Like the current babies—Teeara's babies—were going to grow up and be so upbeat, so perfect. Those ladies, sitting there with their felt hats and their wigs shiny underneath and their meaty arms quivering and their brown eyes going from warm to molten to gazing with muddled awe at the young negroes there all manicured and with mustaches trimmed slender. These were the quote unquote d-boys. They crowded the Smorgasbord, too.

Leaned back in chairs, the boys had on Pierre Cardin watches and Ralph Lauren golf shirts. Herringbone necklaces, gold ear hoops. Beepers clipped on backward. They packed their plates, sat with their kids' mothers or their own mothers. *Eat up, get everything you want,* the boy might say. *No, no, let's go. Come on. We're not eating dessert up in here. Let's go on over to the Häagen-Dazs, get some of that swizz-almondchocolate.*

The ladies watched as the boys paid with big bills. They saw his kids in Nikes and backpacks, and emblazoned sweatshirts from Macy's. Over dessert, with their heads high, the ladies would begin talking about the robust cheerfulness of the children. *That's nice, though,* they'd say. *How he gets all that for his kids.*

ON THE Bay Bridge. Oscar pushed the speed limit over to Steinhart Aquarium in Golden Gate Park. We ran up wide granite steps, paid admission, practically jogged to the penguin exhibit. We'd just missed feeding time, though, when like sixty gray Argentinean birds came sliding down pretend dunes, gleeful fiends for silver fish. The maniacal gratitude of the birds was the reason I remained fascinated. When the fish were devoured, and the birds basically just remained still, I wondered if the penguins minded captivity any less because they couldn't fly.

'Come on, Pinch,' Paige said. 'Next time.'

We walked over to the Fish Roundabout, stood in the center and looked up, waited for the hammerhead shark to circle above our heads. Parents on benches reprimanded remote nine-year-olds. A Brownie troop turned purple in the blue-green light. With waxy arms raised, they pointed fingers at this sea snake, that porpoise, giant salmon, or dolphin. Paige waited. No matter how many times she saw the hammerhead—all the field trips, the dates, it had to be at least twenty times—she had to keep proving to herself that such an inconceivable creature existed.

'If the hammerhead's not here,' Oscar said, 'we can go check out the coral reef thing.'

'It'll come around.' Paige turned his way. 'You look funny. Why'd you want to come over here all of a sudden?'

'It makes you happy.' Oscar's mouth was dry. He had to lick his teeth so his lips wouldn't stick.

'I'm always happy,' Paige said.

Oscar laughed loud enough that a few people turned toward us.

Paige kept her face up toward the Roundabout, said, 'I am so.' The massive hammerhead finally swam by. From the neck down it looked like a regular shark with the big fin, but its flattened, horizontal head was shaped like the profile of a mallet, with an eye at each end. Paige nodded, and seemed assured that all things were possible when the gray-brown, twelve-foot thing brushed against its side of the glass wall. Its white belly bumped against the glass, and Paige jumped a little along with it.

She and Oscar moved to a bench by a shallow pool with the magenta sea cucumber. Paige reached in, said it felt like a tube of Jell-O rolled in Saran Wrap. From where I was leaning, against a column across from them, it looked like a red octopus had lost a tentacle. Paige wasn't supposed to be touching it. *You, out of everybody, you read the display cards, know the difference between a darter and a fluke—you know you're contaminating the cucumber, just by the touch of your hand.* But I'd been through it with her before, about handling exhibits at the aquarium.

'I have something to tell you,' Oscar said. He was looking at Paige, but then he looked at me, too. 'Me, Cedric, and Donnell and Maynard were on our way over to North Oakland, driving the streets, and—'

Paige said, 'Where were you all coming from?'

'We'd been over at the Smorgasbord,' Oscar said, and then hesitated.

Paige stopped focusing her eyes on his. Anticipating. I knew she wanted to go soft. Float along like a jellyfish. Bend with the blows.

'Todd was standing with a partner of his,' Oscar said. 'This big nigga named Bam from Berkeley who gets people's credit crystal-clean for five hundred dollars. You know Bam.' He looked at me. I didn't know Bam. Oscar picked a sea star from the pool, turned it over in his palm.

'May told Donnell to go over there,' he said. 'And then we pulled up. Then May got out of the car real fast, he pulled out a gun I didn't even know he had and he shot Todd in the foot and when Todd dropped to the ground holding it, he was howling, shoe leaking crazy blood. I was like, What the fuck? May shot the nigga, no problem. Like, there was the gun, he shot it and I was just happy Todd was holding his foot and not his chest, you know what I'm saying? Then May told Todd, "Shut the fuck up." We're all just standing there and Cedric looks scared but not that scared and Donnell has May's back or he thinks he does. He's all trying to look tough I don't know how I looked and then May says to Todd, "Shut your mouth. Up in my momma's house on some bullshit. Pussy. Disrespectful motherfucker." Paige! I'm standing there, I'm hearing all this, and I'm like, This is my boy, May, and he's really standing over a bleeding nigga with the gun that shot him. And I'm not saying May's all calm, but he's calmer than us and he's talking like he's fucking Boss Man King of the World or something, he's all saying to Todd, with the gun kinda pointed at him, it doesn't have to point, you know? The fact that's it's even a part of the conversation is enough, and May's saying, "I think you won't fuck with my sister or her kids or my mother again. I think you'll show anybody in my mother's house more respect than you show your own mother. I think you need to learn how to handle your business like a grown man." '

I finally said, 'What? Uh-uh. May was not saying all that like that.' He could do what he did, he could sell crack if he wanted to, but there was no way he was talking like that. Thinking that. Doing that. Maynard could turn into a lot of things, he could grow up, get stronger, get married, have babies. He could even stop being our friend. He could expand, but he couldn't transform into something unrecognizable. He couldn't submit to the worst parts of Oakland. Not completely. 'You're exaggerating. May doesn't get mad like that. He doesn't talk like that.'

'He was.' Oscar was talking fast, and low. I leaned in. Paige sat as she had been. 'I fell into being a lookout,' Oscar said. 'It was like out of a movie. I was standing there, I swear I was trying to be cool, but I was tripping, I was freaking out from the loudness of the shot, I knew the cops would come, and Donnell even started bugging so hard his mouth fell and stayed halfway open. Okay so then Bam reached in his pants just that quick, Paige, he reached in his pants like he was about to do something, but he hadn't seen Cedric, Cedric cracked Bam in his gut fast as hell, had him gasping, and May shot at Todd again or, I don't know, it could have been Bam, but it looked like May missed on purpose. We got in our car, parked under the freeway, watched Bam go get his gray El Camino and help Todd get in.'

Paige stared ahead at a platinum swarm of yawning anchovies. She'd brought her husband into focus for a moment and then pushed him back to blurry. 'Must've taken him,' Paige said, 'to Highland.'

I'd been to Highland Hospital a couple of times. Visiting folks. And on Ninth Grade Court Day. It was the county hospital, but no one called it that, they called it Highland. They had good doctors, a lot of them black, but it had gotten so the workers haze you, and half the patients look like they're about to kill you or themselves out of dejection or rage or longing or some familiar combination. Always new moms in there on Tylenol walking around stunned by pulpy frowning infants in plastic carts. Wheezing old people with old-people ailments segregated from the violent-crime victims by a piece of white fabric stretched between four metal poles.

The doctors, man, they ain't even going to try and get the last three bullets. That's the kind of thing I overheard when this boy Jerome we knew from Oakland High had been shot seven times and Paige and I went to see him. He lived, but he walked slowly after that, and his right arm looked like a long shriveled yam.

Jerome was bound in gauze and cuffed with ID bracelets. Tubes up his nose and another one speared into the artery in his left hand. The day before he was almost dying, he'd been wearing a forest green Adidas running suit and had seven thousand in hundreds rolled in his fist and was in North Oakland by the old empty Merritt College peeling his girl off a few to go to the Hilltop Mall with and he was leaning against the stop sign pole with a toothpick in his mouth head shaven but for some fuzz, body like the most bitter smooth brick of chocolate your mother told you a thousand times was not for eating was not sweet was meant for melting and needed sugar. That was him. That fool took me to the movies once.

And maybe he could have been Cedric or Oscar or Donnell or Maynard, but they weren't on the corner like that, doomed.

Not one of our boys was the type to be laying up in Highland, giving the others the name of a newly marked One, *the light-skinned one who went to Skyline High back in the day, the one who drove the white 2002, the one who hangs out in the lot at San Antonio Park.* Our boys weren't going to be moaning for morphine in one breath and saying in the next, *Yeah, yeah, that's where that nigga be at. Get him.* Our boys weren't typical vengeful ghetto negroes, swooping from Pine Sol–smelling hospital rooms, complete but for velvet capes and swords in sheaths. This is what I thought when I thought about it, which had only been a few times, and recently.

But now this, with May. And what I thought was I didn't want to be a visiting girl at Highland. And for some reason it became crystal clear to me that I would not be one of the girl patients at Highland, either, a girl with big bruises, or a baby with what Nannah used to call a cad of a father. A girl trudging by in confusion masked as relief, rage dressed as resignation. Trudging by saying, *Be strong, Andre* or Little Jimmy or Jerome or whatever the boy's name was. Saying, *Be strong,* to herself. Old ill men nearby totally weak but rigid with disgust and disappointment and jealousy and fear.

Our boys were not resigned, blatantly or intimately, to dying young or doing two-to-five or five-to-ten or moving into a huge home with no previous inhabitants out in hot dry Danville, away from the OPD and other dealers who wanted to kill them or jock them. Oscar, Maynard, Cedric, and Donnell had regular dreams for regular stuff. And they'd only just started slinging. It hadn't been long at all.

AT THE aquarium, I stared at the electric eel and the electric ray. Couldn't see the display card, to read how they could even *be* electric underwater, or why an aquatic animal would need, in its world, to be electric, anyway. To defend itself, that's what made sense. But there were other eels and other rays in the sea that weren't electric, and it's not like they'd died off.

Oscar said my name.

'What?'

'Your sister said she'd be right back.'

'And?'

'You think she's mad?'

'Did you ask her?'

'I mean I told her the whole story.'

'It's good you did that,' I said. 'Why'd you guys start selling?'

'Come on, Pinch.'

I waited.

'Craziness. I'm going to look for your sister.'

I sat there with the water slowly swirling above my head, and heard behind me a pack of kids. One had on a birthday hat, and a tour guide was telling them about the sharks and the hammerhead and the electric eel, and I thought about when Paige and I were little and Mom gave us parties, there were always burgers and a piñata and Twister and coconut cake.

And how on regular days we'd come home from school, to the apartment across from San Antonio, play on the clay tiles in the kitchen until Mom got home. This was when we were real little, before Seth was vile. Back then he brought pale frogs' legs to fry and warm crabs cracked and wrapped in newspaper. Turkey legs to smoke and oxtails soft and stringy—we sucked bones and laughed. Hadn't had these thoughts in a long time.

Puppy brown with a blowy black afro that swayed slightly when he moved, Seth took steamy showers, had razors and kept a well of change in a blue jar on his nightstand. He was portly, and a sharp dresser. Seth had gone through half of medical school. Worked in hospital administration—ran a tight wing at Kaiser Permanente. A benefit of his job was that people who sold X-ray machines took him to meaty dinners in lobby restaurants of nice hotels.

Sometimes Seth would bundle us off to his favorite trout pond. It was near the top of Upper High. The stocked pond was surrounded by dense low trees, and after tossing pellets in the water, the fish gathered and you flung your line in and everyone caught dinner. Seth paid by the pound. The flip of fish through our hands made us giggle, but we took his scaling and gutting lessons seriously. Seth would go fishing for real off the coast near Eureka sometimes, about four hours north of Oakland. Bring home salmon or perch or real trout with the rainbow. Fry us pinto abalone, sometimes take Paige and I crayfishing in Sacramento County's cold creeks. The steep banks were rough with roots and greased with glowing dead leaves. We inched down sideways, arms tense and just out from our sides. Clinging to ivy, white spiders like pinheads swarmed over our wrists. Paige and I grabbed at switches, screamed we'd fall.

Seth said, 'And what'll happen if you fall.'

'It'll hurt.'

'Well then,' he said, already laying traps at the bottom, 'don't fall.'

We didn't. We might have held on tighter, taken steps more carefully because we were nervous. Maybe we were lucky. Maybe the riverbanks weren't so steep or slippery as we thought then, or as I remember them now. But I remember things pretty well—like the Fourth of July when we were in Seth's Buick on the way to Sac for his friend Victor's barbecue. The car was tan and built to seem always surging forward. We eased past Sac's downtown, then by loops of homes with yellow-white lawns. Sac heat was comatose lightning. Lulled by it, and the engine's buzz, Paige and I stared at air.

A short way from Victor's, on an asphalt road covered with soil, a gray snake lay centered. The thing wasn't big, but was big enough to see. Seth slowed to roll by it. I scooted toward Paige so I could see from the window. The tongue flicked.

Seth said, 'Look at him! Don't be afraid to look a snake in its eye.'

Paige hung out the window almost to her waist. 'Will he do it again,' she said, 'stick his tongue out like that?' I peeked from behind her.

Seth backed over the snake, ran over it, backed over it fast, ran over it again. He narrated his own show, spit sludge and mud. Mom shrieked. I held tightly to Paige's legs and the armrest. Still out the window, the top of her body swerving with the Buick, Paige was screaming. She pulled herself in when Seth stopped, her palms gray from holding on to the outside of the car. She wiped them once on her pants and then clenched the fabric in her fingers. She took in noisy breaths through her mouth even as we started moving again.

'Sissy punk twanny-baby crybaby sissy—shut up,' is how it went from Seth to Paige.

Mom said Seth's name.

'You can shut the fuck up, too,' he said. There was glee oozing from *you* and *fuck*. His lips came back over his canines and he pressed on and off the brake slowly so the car lurched and we slid and grabbed at door handles and couldn't calm down.

The liquor had got good to him. He must have loved it. The courage it gave him to be the foul motherfucker he was.

Mom held on to the wrapped cake she had on her lap.

I finally yelled 'Mom!' and she turned to look at me, forehead lined, eyes wide, question mark on her whole face. Then she instantly turned her attention forward again. We were three or four blocks from the snake when Seth ran a stop sign and crashed into the rear side of a brown car. I don't remember impact, just afterward all of us quiet, and the car ticking like a flawed bomb. Mom was twitchy around the eyes, lips extra red, tops of her ears hot, cake at her feet, fingers spread and braced on the dash. Sun striped the backseat. I was on the floor, Paige's nose was bleeding. Drops fell from one nostril over her lips, down her chin, soaked a chocolate spot on her red shirt. She put a hand, then a sleeve, to her nose. Seth leapt from the Buick, whirled and cursed the brown car as it sped off. I wished Mom had the nerve to slide behind the wheel, point the car back toward Oakland, and just roll.

'Paige,' Mom turned and said, shaky. 'Hold your head back. I'll get you cleaned up when we get there. Hold your nose.'

When we get there? We're still going?

That was life, though. Absurd shit went down, and things just went on. The Buick wasn't bad off. Seth got back in the car and we drove on to the party. There was venison on the grill, pork ribs, and some salmon Victor had caught that morning. Mom set her lemon pound cake out between a store-bought pie and the firewater. Dense and golden, somehow it looked as good as it had when we left the apartment.

Victor was talking loud to Seth. 'That woman of yours is a diamond!' He was kicked back on his parked motorcycle like it was a recliner.

Paige and I listened, licked spicy yolks from deviled eggs. Flakes of my sister's blood were on the paper tablecloth, on me, on Mom, on everyone but Seth.

He kicked back with a Coke and something that killed bubbles. 'Course she's a diamond,' he said. 'She's with me.'

We came home that night, and by the next afternoon, Seth was either still drunk or drunk again. I'd seen him drink before, but this was different. And I wanted to know why it began in the first place. Maybe someone had knocked out his sister's eye. Maybe everything for him had been nice growing up, so he hadn't learned to play a bad hand when it was dealt. Maybe his whole life was a bad hand. Maybe Seth was disappointed in how things had gone down in his life, and how they hadn't. Maybe he hated himself for not having been a Panther. Or for letting Oakland affect him in such a way that he spat on even his own occasional happinesses. They proved his guard had dropped, if only for a millisecond.

Shit, maybe his parents had been addicts. I'd never know. Mom would never tell. So I had no context for Seth's behavior. If I'd been privy that July weekend to the source of his evil, I could've understood why Seth stormed outside with his livid jar of change—all silver, no pennies—and poured it over our building's hard lawn. Then stood there in bare feet, pants unbuttoned but not unzipped, sweater stretched and hanging over his hippopotamus belly, kicking at coins like a clown might, with yard-long shoes. With shoulders back and arms loosely raised, he said, 'You little assholes better come get this. This is for *y'all*. Find every cent.'

Theo and the neighborhood kids were in front of the next building. Scared to dive for the money, scared not to. Paige and I'd been standing, as he'd told us to, behind him on the front porch. Seth pointed at us to scramble. Me and my sister got down gingerly on the grass, started picking up coins. We kept him in our sights.

I started crying. *People just change. For no reason.*

Paige passed me nickels. 'Keep looking,' she said. 'Act like you're looking.'

Within minutes, though, Mom came and got us. Her all red again, and wet and inspecting, bracing, hurrying to get us in her car. The three of us rode and rode, and Mom calmed down and so did we, but we had uneasiness because we didn't know how long it would be before our driveway loomed before us again. Too soon, we were in it again, and Mom walked in the apartment seemingly normal, like she knew how things went and things, at that moment, would be what they would be, but whatever they were, she and we could handle it.

We didn't see him when we walked in. The three of us, doing surveillance. Their bedroom door was closed.

In our room, Paige read at a book. I refolded play clothes in my bureau. Mom might have been in the kitchen when Seth opened our door. Eyes blue-black and red veins swelling. Lashes heavy, lips lazy, set in a face warped and droopy with heat and going maroon. He spoke quietly. Looked at me, which was rare. 'Watch your sister, Pinchy baby. You don't want to be like her. Fucked up already.'

Paige wouldn't look at me when he left. Her face stayed in that book.

Mom came in. Paige ignored her. My sister must have been eleven. For her, I knew the creamy ceiling of our room had lifted up and off and the blue walls were dimpled and cinchy to climb and she and I were already up and over one and at Theo's for noodles in broth and a show called *Run, Joe, Run.* I knew Paige would tell me her brave thoughts later. Talk me to sleep with stories about field trips to pebbly beaches, and train rides through red mountains.

'Seth loves you,' Mom said to Paige. 'He loves me, loves your sister. He's just not happy . . . it's hard for him to accept other people's happiness. You two are naturally happy. And you're doing good, too, just living your life.' Mom's wrists were thin. What could she pick up with those wrists? Her long fingers were shaking. Hair all over her head.

Then she looked at me.

What was I going to say?

'Happiness is just difficult,' she said. 'I *know* you all don't believe the things he says. The unpleasant things. I know you don't believe them. Because here I am telling you the truth about how good you are. He doesn't mean those things. Life brings you things you don't want to deal with, but you deal with them because it's what's right. He's having a problem dealing.'

Mom's mouth was trembling. She gave the worst wobbly smile. Looked beyond tired. And tense, always red, and damp.

Paige wouldn't look at her.

'I want you and Pinch to be happy,' Mom said. 'That makes me feel good. That's what'll make me feel better. Make all of us feel better. But I'm fine. This is going to be fine. Just watch. I'll call you to eat. What's that face, Pinch? Don't look sad. Be happy, now. You'll see.'

PAIGE sat next to me on the bench by the crimson cucumber tentacle.

'Where'd you go?' I said.

'Pee.'

'Oscar's looking for you.'

'What do you think? May's not right.'

'At least,' I said, 'he's not afraid to look a snake in his eye.'

Oscar walked up.

'I forgot to ask you,' Paige said to him. 'Did the police ever come?'

'No. I mean, not that I saw.'

'Is Todd flipping? What's he going to say? Where's May, anyway?'

'Home with Jess.'

Jess and May had moved to a rented bungalow in Alamo, about twenty miles north of Oakland. It was in a dusty development where the houses looked similar to each other and you picked them by floor plan. Jess and May had a skylight in the foyer, the only one on their block.

'Doing what? Chilling after he shot somebody?'

'I don't know.'

'How are you feeling?' Paige said, 'You're a part of it, Oscar. In a legal way. What if Todd tells?'

'He won't. I was part of what happened to Teeara, too.'

'This isn't ridiculous to you? I mean, I saw what Todd did to Teeara, but—'

'You didn't see. You didn't go in the room. May shot Todd

in the *foot*. He'll be all right. I'm about to go over to May's.'
Oscar looked the same as he always did, except for abrasions
on the back of both hands. He kept rotating his right wrist. He
looked the same, except different, in the way familiar people
are recognizable, but softly distorted, even in good dreams.
'You're tripping,' he said. 'I'm trying to tell you. I got this.'

In the car Oscar held Paige's hand whenever he wasn't
shifting gears. Played the radio loud enough that the windows
vibrated, and that people next to us at intersections looked to see
who we were. Three cool-ass niggas in the old-but-not-classic
Mustang. People rolled their eyes, shook their heads, looked
straight ahead—or smiled if they had their radio tuned to the
station we were jamming. Oscar had special, boy-type woofers
under the rear window of his car. The bass punched through
me, then roughly rocked me, in short bursts it almost stung me.

Paige said, 'Do you have some of that Vitamin E lotion?'

Before I could answer, Oscar turned down the volume
abruptly, said, 'Promise you won't say anything to May, Paige.'

'Like what?'

'Like anything.'

*May's our friend, been our friend. But we aren't rolling with
him like Oscar is now.*

When we got in front of their place, Oscar kissed Paige
with his mouth open, said he'd call her later.

In her new kitchen, Paige boiled ramen noodles, sprinkled in salty bouillon powder, stirred in discs of carrot.

I said, 'Oscar'll be fine, right?'

'Did I ever tell you that the second time Oscar came over
to the Pseudo, when he left, he said, "Love you"?'

'The second visit?' Of course she'd told me.

'That second visit was deep. In the bed, he was holding
me unbelievably close. Then he held me a little away from
himself, looked at me from head to toe, and he said, "Can all
this be mine?"'

It still sounded thrilling, though, even hearing the story for about the fifth time. 'And what did you say?'

'I said, "Isn't it, already?"' She laughed a little. 'Because over and over again, kind of to the beat of himself going back and forth in me, he'd been all, "Tell me how you feel about me, tell me how you feel about me, tell me that you love me."'

'Did you tell him?'

'I told him I loved him.'

'And did you?' I hadn't asked her that before.

'I thought that I should love him. And I believed that if a million things about me and the world changed, that at some point I would.'

She said she'd woken up with his wet breath between her shoulder blades. He recounted scenes from his youth that my sister didn't know enough to believe were tragic. That aquarium day, over ramen, while Oscar was off doing God knows what, Paige told me that her husband did things that got on her nerves—eating with his mouth open, for one, and caressing the chub of her belly like it was flat as a model's. She thought that by touching her mushy stomach and not complaining, Oscar was somehow mocking her. And the way he mentioned love, she said it made him seem ignorant. Or boastful—as if he could know what love was.

'After that second time, though,' Paige said from behind her soup, 'I was always putting on my gardenia perfume for him. Doing every little thing I could to have him come over and say, "Love you," again.'

Absurd shit goes down, and things just go on.

We ate the ramen, had wine coolers. Even though he had keys, Oscar's dad rang from downstairs. I let him in. He had some food, smoked his cigarette, fell asleep on the couch.

From a pallet in the second bedroom, I heard Oscar come in at about four.

JUST when we'd been ready to leave the aquarium, ribbons of water unrolled from the sky. Oscar had run to get the car while Paige and I waited in the chilly marble foyer. Behind inch-thick glass, tiny moon jellies opened and closed themselves—slow, ghostly, thimble-sized umbrellas. Egg-yolk jellyfish, like egg whites, really, set loose in warm water, hung in blueness brilliant with electric light. But it was the perfectly evolved mackerels that hypnotized Paige. I could see why. They moved in schools. Each one the same. Shaped like thin footballs, and with skin cut from God's silvery fingernails, the fish were simple and streamlined for getting where they had to go.

CHAPTER 9

It was the next spring. Late spring. Cool and lasting forever.

Damp from the bath, laying up at the Pseudo by myself, deciding whether to get dressed or put my silky outfit in a bag, go over to Oscar and Paige's to get ready. The clock radio Paige left behind tuned to the Quiet Storm station. Sax-filled, stretched-out instrumentals of soul songs vaguely remembered.

Looked at the numbers. Six P.M. Needed to rise up.

I'd already pulled my hair back in a tight, slick twist. Plus a pom-pom of crisp curls poofed from beneath it. Cinnamon cellophane dye made my brown hair pop with maroon in good light. Had mixed Vaseline with pink gel in my palm, took a toothbrush to it, then combed down my baby hair so I had a feminine border laying along my hairline. Gave my sideburns a tendril, flattened it against my jaw with the mixture. The whole crew was going for drinks. Cool place called Carlos O'Rourke's.

We went out a lot. Brought the party wherever we went.

Phone rang. It was Mom.

'What are you doing?'

'Laying here,' I said. On my stomach, in my sweats, across my bed.

'You talked to your sister?'

'Talk to her every day. Four thousand times a day.'

'I talked to her today.' Like it was a news flash.

'And?'

'She seems fine.'

'Why wouldn't she?'

'You know how she is,' Mom said, 'better than me.' Could hear her washing dishes. Pictured her at the sink, looking out the window at her Walnut Creek yard. Phone between her ear and shoulder. Seeing where the sprouts were.

'Why's that sound like an accusation?'

'I'm just saying you know how she talks to me. Like she's so bitter. That boy seems to be having a good effect on her. That's all I'm saying.'

Said what I'd said before. 'She's not bitter, Mom. She's bitter with you.'

'Bitter with me.' *Rush rush* went the faucet water. *Clink clank* the plates and pans.

'She talks to you crazy because you don't talk about what she wants to talk about.'

'What's she wanna talk about?' *This is how Mom acts. This is the kind of thing she says. And she's for real with it.*

'Mom. Please.'

'No, seriously. What exactly does she want to talk to me about.'

Flipped over on my back, sat up. Took a breath. 'I've told you and told you. Talk to her about Seth. Why you stayed and what went down.' *Why he was the way he was.*

'What's there to say?' With an abrupt squeak, water off. Nothing in her background but the sputtery whir of a far-off Weedwacker. 'It's over. Been over. It was bad. None of us should have had to deal with it. I've put it behind me. All that's not something I like to think about, let alone talk about.' *So frustrated that you haven't passed the nonchalant gene on to Paige. So certain you passed it on to me. Well, you haven't. And there's no place where I can sit and erase all the effect anyone has ever had on me. It's what I want, though. Peel myself mentally nude.*

'So it's only what you wanna talk about. Can it be about what Paige needs to hear?'

'Nothing I say'll change anything.'

'So then you are saying that things could have or should have been changed, been different.'

'Of course I'm saying that. Of course I wish none of that craziness had happened.' *Thank you. A person needs to hear that, at least. You and Paige never even get to this point.*

'Can you say that to her?'

'What's it going to change?'

'Your relationship with her!'

'Don't yell into the receiver.'

'Mom, you know what? I'm getting off the phone with you.' *So you won't start saying that people from your generation 'keep counsel with themselves.' And please, I can't hear you say that you've never been depressed one day in your life. You say it when you're lighthearted and beaming, in the moments when even Paige greets you with buoyancy. No one has ever not been depressed ever. But when you say it, Mom, it seems possible because you chirp it between comical stories and you're wearing a cute outfit and zipping around to fun places in your car. Your masquerade makes me weak. Worse than a lie, though, would be if you were telling the truth. Because then what are you made of? And if we're made of the same, if we're going to let mean things happen to us, and not feel them, not let them scar us, or become so adept at covering up, then I'm scared for what we'll allow. Of what we'll do to, and accept from, other people. For all the train- ing, I haven't grasped the lesson. Haven't honed the practice of being in a stupor and wearing happy at the same time. Happi- ness is hard, Mom. That must be why you fake it.*

I'd never say any of that to my mother.

'Where,' Mom said, 'are you going?'

'Over to Paige's, we're going out.'

'Drinking?'

'Yeah. Drinking, Mom. Drinking ourselves into oblivion.'

'Don't say stuff like that.' Water whooshed back on. 'All right. Call me tomorrow.'

As soon as I hung up the phone, it rang.

'What, Mom?'

'Hello? Pinch? It's Evan.'

'Oh hi. Yeah, it's me. Sorry.'

'You all right?'

'Yeah. How're you?'

'Cool.' His voice had green-brown tones, woodwind notes. 'Long time, right? You upset with your mom?'

'A little,' I said.

'This a bad time?'

Yes! 'No. Not in any way. Evan. Can I ask you something?'

'No I'm not married, and I don't have a girlfriend.'

'For real.'

'For real I'm still single.' He laughed at himself.

How? When you dance the way you dance? Sound the way you sound. Kiss the way I know you must. So soft, so nice. So sweet. 'Why'd you leave Seattle and go to Davis? Go to another state, I mean, instead of going to, like, Washington State or something?'

'I guess I wanted to see something else.'

'Like what.'

'Don't know. Maybe I was tired of Seattle.'

'What's there to be tired of?'

'Stupid people. Everything. The past, I guess.' He paused. 'Not that it was so bad. But it is the past.'

'Do you have a fucked-up one?' *Say it. There has to be something.*

'Do you?'

Said nothing.

'Pinch,' he said. 'Question for *you.*'

I braced.

'What's your real name?'

Oh, that question. 'It's Pinch.' *No one's asked me that in a long time.*

'It is not. Why do they call you that?'

'I call myself that. Because I like it.'

'So it's gonna be you playing the hardhead.' He wasn't frustrated, but he wasn't amused.

I didn't say anything.

He said, 'You seem like you're ready to get off the phone.'

That's what you seem like. 'I should probably go on ahead. Going over my sister's.'

'That sounds right.'

'What's that mean?'

'Nothing. Just that whenever I've called you, ever since I met you, you've almost always had to get off the phone because of your sister, one way or another.'

Is that true? No. I didn't say anything. *It's completely true.*

'So,' he said. 'I guess I'll talk to you later.'

Call me back when I don't have to go meet my people.

'Hello? Are you there?'

'I'm here,' I said. *Still right here.*

'Look. I'm going to Seattle for my mom's birthday. Weekend after next. You should come with me. The bus ticket isn't even that much. See Washington for yourself. Since you're not from there, you might like it. See something other than Oakland for a change.' His voice had started to sound piped in.

'There's nothing wrong with Oakland.'

'There is if that's all you know.'

I'm in a good place. Why do you make me feel like I'm not in a good place?

'Say your real name, Pinch, before we hang up.'

'Why?'

'So I can feel like, after this weird conversation, at least I got to know you better.'

'We used to talk all the time,' I said. 'For a minute, we did.'

'What happened?' *Trueness. That's his tone. And interest.*

'There's just a lot going on.'

'School? You have a boyfriend. Or it's your sister?'

'And my friends.'

He paused. 'You're not coming to Seattle.'

I like you, but I don't know you like that. Can't get my head around Seattle. Clock's changing, numbers flipping. I have to meet my folks. My sister. And Oscar. See Jessica. Hear about her and May's son. About Ch'Rell and Donnell's newer son. Ask about Teeara, how she's living. Spy on Cedric's antics. Sit up with my people at a cool place and sip cocktails. Make judgments about who's smart or stylish or dense. Hang out. Laugh at things that aren't funny.

'Seattle does sound nice,' I said. 'But I don't think so.'

Said stiff good-byes and then gathered up my outfit. Red skirt and a redder top to set off my freshly dipped nails. Red and white hoop earrings, matching bracelet. Pushed red suede pumps in the plastic grocery bag with everything, then plopped out on the bed.

Got up quickly, grabbed my stuff, and walked out the door.

I stood across from the Pseudo, waited on the No. 40. Brutal night for May. Had to be forty degrees. Oscar would've come get me, but I felt like the bus. Scrunched my eyebrows for a flash, at myself—at the realization that I was taking the bus because I wanted to be alone. I hadn't moved in with Paige and Oscar. I'd said it was because I wanted them to have their space. But I'd wanted mine.

The 40 didn't even go near Paige and Oscar's. I just liked the route. Knew every dip in the road.

Months ago, I'd moved my clothes and my African-Americana collection into what had been my sister's room. She'd left behind her fluffy beige throw rug, the clock radio, and not much else. The room was larger, and with tan curtains instead of the blinds I'd peeked through in mine. There were built-in drawers in the closet, but Paige had accidentally painted them shut not too long before she moved out. So I put my panties and T-shirts in the bureau, set my collection on top. It was a room I'd be proud to have any boy in. But I never invited Evan down from Davis. Even though it was only ninety minutes from Oakland by car or bus. I hated that Evan presented me with options. *I can go to Seattle, Washington. To Davis, California. I can have other friends.* I knew I could, but no one ever said I should. Not even me, to myself. It was why Evan went back and forth between making me mad and making me want the crowded solitude of the No. 40.

Stepped off the bus a few miles from Paige and Oscar's. Stood by a Lucky's Food and across from a crowded Pep Boys' parking lot. A Mexican catering truck laced the air with boiling corn flour, cilantro, and seared beef. Got two bulging tacos and began walking the eight blocks over to MacArthur so I could transfer to the No. 57, get to my sister's.

Moving to my new bedroom had been simple as pie. I didn't feel older or smarter or a sense of accomplishment. I wasn't scared to be in the Pseudo by myself, but I was over at Paige and Oscar's all the time, anyway. It was like being promoted at Planned Parenthood. Rungs stretched horizontally ahead of me, land brushed my toes. Big deal moving to the big room. No stretch in the journey, no respite at the destination.

'Then at least,' Evan had said, 'tell me your real name before we say bye.'

'You're tripping.'

'"Tell the truth,"' Evan said, '"and you don't have to remember anything." It's a quote. Mark Twain.' Evan said he had more than twenty quotes taped up in his dorm. That they helped him look at the world from an objective place, whenever things got convoluted.

That struck me. The quote, and that he had a plan for avoiding chaos.

'My real name,' I told him, 'starts with a P.' It was true.

OSCAR'S dad had been living with Oscar and Paige for about six months. He didn't seem to mind my constant presence, and I liked his. Lean, and balder every day, he'd been living hard for a long while, and mostly seemed the contented kind of tired you get right before you're about to get into your made bed and sleep without setting the alarm.

Paige was dressing, so even the living room smelled like hairspray and banana lotion. She was relentless with the scents, and with rubbing things into herself. Always trying to soothe something. I was restless, had been ready to go.

'The red suits you,' Oscar's father said.

'Thank you.'

'Reminds me of the girls in Spain.'

'I didn't know you went to Spain.'

'Used to love the bullfights.'

'Sounds gross.'

He laughed. 'The knickers the bullfighters wore, I wanted to get me some of them. All the girls, the girls in their bright dresses, they loved those bullfighters . . . the swords, all the blood, and the bull was always just big and dumb and mad.'

'What else would the bull be? With somebody teasing it, getting ready to kill it?'

He laughed again, and I did, too. On the arm of the couch was Oscar's father's black vinyl address book. When I went to sit, the book fell on the floor.

'Oops,' I said, and reached for it. It was so old and ragged, loose pages that had been tucked against the thin spiral splayed on the floor. The tabs with the letters of the alphabet, except for P and for XYZ, had long fallen away. The pages were frayed, and the names and numbers, written in pencil, had softened to the palest gray.

I saw a map on the inside back cover of the book. Drawn in ink were five-pointed stars. Indented with a ballpoint, pressed in hard.

'The places you've seen?'

'Some of them, yeah.'

Wiesbaden and Madrid and Rome had red stars. Milan, Mexico City, and about ten others. Even Seattle. Oakland didn't have one. Not even San Francisco. I placed the leaves back as well as I could. He trusted me with the job, lit another cigarette.

'How old is this thing? Why do you keep it?'

'I keep everything,' Oscar's father said. 'And everybody.'

I ran two fingers over his map. Paused, let my ridges fill the hollows.

CARLOS O'ROURKE'S was right on the water. Felines tore around the slimy rocks the place sat upon. It was a big square restaurant at the north end of the Berkeley Marina between a chain hotel and a grocery called Goosey's, where lobsters with black-banded claws waited in tanks. Glass barrels of lemonade glowed pink with grenadine.

We went to O'Rourke's a lot until the management put up a sign that said, NO MOBILE PHONES NO HATS NO BEEPERS NO JEANS NO ATHLETIC SHOES. The staff had been perplexed and stiffened by the sudden slick blackness of the place. Plate-glass mirrors reflected tens of negroes into the hundreds.

I saw Maynard as soon as we walked in. He was posted up at a table in a good corner, with an excellent view of the bay. Over the last year, May's big priority had become having on whatever was most gorgeous. He'd long since smoothed his hair with no-lye, had it pushed back into a short wavy shock.

'Nice suit, dude,' I said to him.

'Calvin Klein,' he said, then tugged my skirt hem. 'Nice red.'

Ch'Rell was there in a black leather skirt so tight it rode up her hips. Donnell reclined in his chair like a dental patient. I kissed Jess on her warm cheek. Paige did, too.

Cedric walked over from the bar when he saw Paige, Oscar, and I. Sharp and high as a whistle. Ced had been having the barber cut multiple parts in his hair, and wearing diamond studs in both ears. Around us he was the same old Ced, but when he was at parties, I saw him speaking with fake deference, giving consistent eye contact. Gold chain showing, him smelling good, but not too much too good. Cordial, intimate, ivory smile barely broken into teeth and a relaxed stance that said, *Whatever interrupts me, I'm ready to handle with ease, and then we'll pick up where we left off, which was me making you want my attention, want what I have.* That's how Cedric played it. He gathered light. I loved to watch him. He liked to watch my sister.

'Hey, pretty ladies,' he said, smiling like it was his birthday. Under the aftershave, he smelled like a weed plant. Shook Oscar's hand and embraced him. Pulled out chairs, with a flourish, for Paige and I. May looked at Ced like he was doing too much.

The two of them were always getting pulled over, questioned. It happened to Donnell and Oscar only occasionally. Was hard at first, to hear about it, but the guys didn't speak of it angrily, so the episodes became ordinary quickly. And since the cops hadn't beaten them—at least that I knew about—and because they had never been actually arrested, the police thing seemed, at worst, a toll. Oscar occasionally mentioned by name the cops he dealt with. In a joking way. So it didn't seem like our guys were doing anything truly wrong. More like they were doing an arbitrary wrong. Like truancy. Or like driving well, but without a license.

'Life was real then,' May said, nodding toward Alcatraz Island. You could see its few lights from the window, hard proof there'd been whole other ways of dealing with people. 'If you fucked up, you went to the Rock. Stayed until you died, period.'

'None of this bullshit in-and-out,' Cedric said.

Donnell picked up fried mozzarella. 'You better knock on some wood around here.'

One good look around and I saw Todd in the entryway. Looked the same as ever except for the limp, which I thought he exaggerated for pity and Paige thought out of pride. Todd had on a black linen shirt not tucked into black linen pants, crocodile sandals, and a gold bracelet that could have been a shackle.

'Here this fool comes,' Jess said way under her breath.

'Haven't seen him,' Paige said, 'in six months or something. Was at the record store on University. Neither one of us spoke.'

Only fifteen months had passed and people could barely remember there'd been a time when Maynard hadn't shot Todd. A time when Teeara didn't have an eye that only looked like it. Paige still found it hard to believe she was married to Oscar. Jess and Maynard had a six-month-old son. Ch'Rell and Donnell had a baby boy, too, named Yannick, after the French tennis player, born three months after Jess and May's Zachary, whom we all called Ree. *If I ever have to have someone help me lift a stroller down the BART steps*, Ch'Rell was apt to say with a bottle to Yannick's lips, *please kill me.*

May must have ordered us drinks as we'd walked in because a slim, friendly Japanese waitress delivered to each of us our usual drinks. She'd waited on us before, and was less witchy about it than some of the others. I sipped my peach schnapps on the rocks. Paige shook her brandy and cola. No one was talking much because Todd was sitting not far from us, at the bar, chomping on spicy fries. Because of his gimpiness, everyone knew that Todd and Maynard weren't kids any-

more. Minutes went by and still our table didn't fall into con-
versation. Todd finally looked over, then pulled out his phone.
It was fresh. May had one, too, but it was chunkier than
Todd's.

I couldn't hear what Todd was saying into his phone. But
he kept looking over in our direction, saying something and
then chuckling. Kept putting fries in his mouth and gulping
something O'Rourke's had on tap.

'Can we go over to the city?' Jessica said. 'To the Wharf?'

Maynard didn't look her way, or answer.

'I don't know why I even get Mom to baby-sit,' Jessica
said to Paige so May could hear. 'If this is the shit we're coming out to do.'

Waitress dropped off another drink for May.

The manager of Carlos O'Rourke's was a white man with
solid shoulders and arms and a heavy stomach. He didn't
touch Todd, but asked him in a formal, chilly way to leave. He
didn't ask Todd to please put the phone away, he asked him to
leave. The manager glanced at himself in one of the huge mirrors, looked mad at himself for being nervous, and madder at
Todd for making him know how nervous he could get.

The situation was tense, but it was entertainment.

Todd said he'd finish his call in the men's room. The bar's
buzz dropped to a hum as Todd hobbled through the mass of
varnished tables and soft chairs, talking more loudly than was
necessary, and making sarcastic apologies. Then he saw a
white woman at the part of the bar closest to the front door,
talking on her mobile. He looked at the room, even toward us,
put his hands up in a shrug like, *You see this shit?* Then sat in
one of the chairs near some people we all knew and spoke
even more loudly than before into his phone. We were way
across the large room and could hear him clearly.

'Much money as I spend up in this muthafucka,' he said
to whomever was on the other end. 'Like a nigga can't have

nothin', do nothin'.' He stood, limped over to near where she was at the bar. 'This female can talk on her shit all night, but they want a nigga like me to leave.'

He stood right next to the pale woman whose breasts and belly were stressing the few buttons of her black blouse. She put her phone on the bar. When Todd still stood there next to her, she put it on her lap, sat there tall and wooden. Todd inched closer to her, set his boxy phone on the bar where hers had been. They were half a foot apart. She didn't look at him. Her pointy profile faced me. Even that was a mix of dread and slow burning.

'And you wanna know why I still can't stand that fool,' Maynard said. 'Always starting unnecessary shit.' May's voice was low. He looked past Jess's ear at Todd, past Todd to the front door. May wore no jewelry, was dipped in spicy cologne. He sipped his third snifter of Grand Marnier. Smelled like orange rinds in the compost bin.

Jessica's gums showed when she smiled her big real smile.

'Don't *you* start unnecessary shit,' she said with only her teeth showing. Jess had on white stretch pants, new Nikes, and Nike footies. She and her loose, washable silk blouse smelled like roses. I never understood wearing a silk blouse with stretch pants. Unless it was a two-piece outfit made to go together. But Jess pulled it off, just like how she wore tennis shoes on a Friday night to Carlos O'Rourke's—when it was crowded with everybody from professors to people with good jobs to retirees to us and people we saw at other places we tended to go.

Paige had on heels, hose, and a tight acid-washed jean skirt. Hair sprayed into a flip. Jess's outfit made it seem like we'd all made too much of the evening.

The chubby manager stood near the podium where the hostess usually said that the wait would be at least two hours for dinner. He glanced back and forth between Todd and the front double doors of the restaurant. Donnell shifted in his seat, then tilted his head toward the manager. 'He probably called downtown.' Donnell had the new habits of talking softly and letting his hair grow out some. He, too, drank Grand Marnier, barely looked at Ch'Rell.

Room droned steady and almost soundless, like a refrigerator. Manager had an elbow on the podium, nodded appreciatively and apologetically while his fat head got more pumped by whispery support from older people white and black. They'd gathered doggie bags and jackets, started a thin exodus. The chic people, white, black, and otherwise, glared at their food or tried to talk and eat as they had been. Even when Todd started yelling into his phone. A negro acting up was no reason to ditch brook trout with brown butter and a view of the bay.

'This spot ain't shit, anyway. Little-ass servings not enough to feed a fucking flea . . . drinks is fucked up, too. Need to bring my mama in here teach these fools how to make some potato salad, fix some red beans and ham up in this motherfucker.'

I giggled, and Paige did, too. May and Donnell watched Todd with deadpan expressions. Jess sipped at her club soda. Ch'Rell tugged at her skirt, which called attention to the run in her tights. Ced lounged with his whiskey. Ran the knuckle of his index finger across his mustache. It was the only thing that made him seem bothered.

The manager must have called the police because suddenly four were there, asking all the young black people for their IDs, and asking for IDs from some of the younger white people, too. The patrolmen seemed familiar with Cedric and Maynard and Oscar and Donnell. Familiar with Todd, too. I was with Oscar once when an OPD car rolled up next to the Mustang. The cop said, 'Oscaaaaaar,' all condescending. 'Light day for you, huh?' Oscar drove on when it was his turn.

At Carlos O'Rourke's, Maynard put down two one-hundred-dollar bills for a ninety-six-dollar check. Pleasant waitress slid by with the quickness to collect it. We all stood up as May did, just when three of the police officers walked over to where Todd was sitting. May tried to sit back down, but there'd been the commotion of us trying to rise and a rangy white cop walked over. Oscar put on the serene look he gets when he's wrong. Donnell swallowed the last of Ch'Rell's white rum.

Oscar leaned into Paige and I. 'If you have to go home without me,' he said, 'tell Dad I'm with Ced on a run.'

The manager smoothly offered folks free rounds, handed out cups of the artichoke cheese dip the place was famous for. May said something quick to Ced that made his face draw into the smallest frown. Todd had already gone outside with the other three cops. Contact was minimal. Berkeley dwellers, especially the white ones, didn't like being around medium or large groups of young blacks. But they had a wilting dislike of domineering police officers.

The extra-tall officer looked like he'd been around since the People's Park Wars. He made a right-this-way gesture with the last three fingers of his hand, then stood aside so Maynard and the boys could step by. Jess stood to follow Maynard.

The cop turned his palm to her, fingers toward the ceiling. 'Sit down, Jessica,' he said.

May stopped, turned around.

Jess said to the officer, 'Don't say my name.'

'Sweetheart, I seen your wedding picture up at your father's office.'

Jess didn't look shocked. She remained standing.

The cop said, 'Sit,' like Jess was his Doberman. Then moved his fingers at Oscar and Donnell and Cedric. Maynard gazed at the cop with even, old-fashioned restraint. Jess sat down. Ch'Rell, who'd said nothing almost all night, crossed her jiggly legs like there was a point to it.

Jess answered Ch'Rell's gesture with, 'I know. Fools speaking to me like they know me.'

When the boys and the cops had been out of the restaurant for about six seconds, Jess was immediately up, and us behind her. We got out there, stood about twenty feet from where the guys were.

Jessica walked closer. One of the black cops, with a crunchy shag haircut, told her, 'Move,' and he sounded like a foghorn. She took a baby step back. I never knew what kind of black girl from Oakland, even a dentist's daughter like Jess, blasted Carole King from the stereo of her fly-ass car. Paige and I would be humming the melody, but Jess sang the crying songs word for word, her hair permed all the way to pure white girl.

She always said there was more to life than being some UPS man's baby's mother. And that she didn't want to be an Oakland Xerox or Clorox or FedEx wife, didn't see herself working retail in the city during the holidays so she could buy gifts on her employee discount and be satisfied with a house on Upper High. She'd never graduate from USF, she said, or take the GMATs, go to biz school, go to networking mixers, or be a sharp cookie. Alamo, Jess said, was a pit stop. She wanted to stay Above Upper High forever. She wouldn't be seen at Red Lobster on Sundays, dipping crab legs in fake butter for a treat, getting hips like battleships.

'Fuck a Hyundai,' she said to Paige and I once, laying on her horn and passing a red one on the freeway. 'And anything that would be in one.'

The cops were going through Oscar's wallet paper by paper. All four of them—Oscar, Maynard, Donnell, and Cedric—were seated on a curb, which looked fucked up but was better than them being on their knees, in their good clothes, fingers laced at the base of their skulls. Every other second a whisper of water slipped up over the rocks and onto the walkway. Maynard stared ahead. Donnell looked at

Ch'Rell. Oscar stared ahead. Todd was in the backseat of a plain cop car.

Ced watched the cops, looked like he did when I used to catch him watching girls at parties. He loved to catch a female sticking two fingers down her cleavage and then putting them to her nose. It jarred him when a girl absently pinched at a spindle of tummy fat. He told me it was kind of sexual, yes, but it was more about seeing people messing with what makes them them.

In front of Carlos O'Rourke's, Ced sat on the curb, jolted but patient. He glanced at Paige, but she was looking at her husband. The cops were down to Donnell. Cedric was next for the pat-down, the wallet check, whatever else. The seat of his pants was soaked. Pacific water trickled down the back of his legs. Must've felt like cold piss.

THE next day, I went by the courthouse, where Paige sat on white steps waiting. She worked at a realty data company owned by Ham and Septima Wright. They bought properties in distress. It was a six-person office. Everyone from Texas, and related to the other, except Paige.

She clipped foreclosure notices from about eighteen papers. Called mortgage companies to see if it was the first or second or third loan that had been defaulted on. Called to see if there were tax or utilities liens. Sometimes she walked the two blocks to the courthouse, to look up the title. Paige said it was better than working at Diamond Pool.

I walked back toward the office with Paige, on lunch from Planned Parenthood. Sunshine yellow and strong as teeth.

'Why'd you even come to work today?' I ambled along like I was free. Paige looked pretty, and businesslike. Whenever I saw my sister in work mode, I was more objective about her. I could look at her like I didn't know her, see her round features and her own life. It shook me, and it loosed me some.

'What can I do at home? Oscar's dad is nosy.'

'Do you want to go down there?'

'To County?'

'To see what's up with your man, maybe.'

'Oscar doesn't want me down there,' Paige said, 'waiting on him like some—'

'Dope dealer's wife.'

'If I'd wanted to say that, I'd've said it.'

'I just don't understand why May's out. My friend at work told me she saw him over on Keller getting his car detailed.'

'May's out? Why didn't you say that, Pinch? When you know that's what you came down here to say.'

'I was about to say it.'

Back at Realty Data, the air-conditioning made me tense. Ham said hi to me, then asked Paige about the auction that was supposed to have happened on the steps. Paige told him it had been postponed, and he snapped his fingers like he was right about something. Ham and his wife, Sep, lived way Above Upper High, not too far from Jess's parents. I rolled a chair up to Paige's cluttered desk.

'What if they make him stay in jail?' She was whispering.

'They won't.'

'Do you think I'm stupid?' She didn't have a rhetorical tone.

'For what?'

'For everything,' she said. 'Marrying Oscar, not being in school, dealing with what he does.'

'Not stupid. More like . . . tired, maybe.'

'Tired.'

'Like you actually need a break.'

'From working thirty hours a week?'

'You'll go back to school. When you can, I guess. And Oscar, he'll go back, too.'

'So what he does is some kind of phase.'

'I'm not saying that, I'm saying—wait.' I pushed back

from the desk. 'Hold up. Are you mad at his morals?' I don't know why that would have offended me, but it would have. 'You and me, we're so above what he's doing?'

'He's above what he's doing.' She didn't look in my direction when she said, 'But then sometimes I don't want him to stop.'

'The money?'

She shrugged. 'If he stopped, and became . . . a regular person, a person with a good job, he'd probably want a regular girl to be with—'

'You're regular! You have a job.'

'No, you're right you're right.'

'I can't believe you're questioning your whole relationship at the first sign of trouble.'

'All of a sudden,' she said, 'you know about relationships.'

'I just mean that Oscar's good, is all. If you hate me, you know, if you don't like my comments, I could go live in Seattle.'

'Seattle? What are you talking about? That boy Evan? You still talk to him?'

'Sometimes. He lives right in Davis, goes to school there. He's *from* Seattle.'

'It doesn't seem like you'd go to Davis or Seattle by yourself.'

No, it doesn't.

Paige scooted up to her phone, beeped Jess, and put in her code. We watched the black thing like it was human and had a secret.

JESS called back.

Paige said, 'So May's out?'

Long pause.

Then, 'I guess I do need to go up there.' That was Paige's way of asking for a lift.

Pause.

My sister said, 'Yeah, she's here, but she has to stop back by her job for a minute.'

Longer pause.

'What'll you do with your free time if I learn to drive?'

Paige went to speak to Sep. I called Ch'Rell at her job. She was pissed and hissing.

'May's a punk,' she said.

'Don't talk about him like that.'

'Okay. Then I'll talk about his tragic mulatto wife.'

'Ch'Rell. Are you not mixed?' I had to laugh. Ham looked at me to get off the phone. I smiled. He left me alone.

'My daddy wasn't all . . . into being white. Bringing me up in white ways . . . all up on Upper High, passing along white shit to me, passing on that the-world-is-mine attitude. My dad came over to the dark side. He's crazy, and maybe that's why he came over. Or maybe coming over drove him crazy. But Jess's mama, she went the other way. And she got a silly daughter to show for it.'

'She's your sister-under-the-skin. You need to take her under your wing.' I laughed.

'Nothing's funny, Pinch. I need for Donnell's ass to get out. What if there's bail?'

I didn't know what to say to that. 'Want me to ask Jess to come get you? She's on her way to pick me and Paige up, run me up to Planned Parenthood so I can give them a dramatic emergency story. Then she's going to take us up to the jail.' I whispered *jail*.

'Jess called here a minute ago, supposedly all worried about Donnell. Whatever for that two-faced shit.'

'Why's it gotta be two-faced?'

'It just is. Where's Ree in all this?'

'She said she was dropping him by her mom's.'

'Must be nice.'

'You're just mad right now, because Donnell's—'

'Yeah. Because Donnell's still in there. Oscar's in there, and Paige needs to be mad, too. If Ced had the sense to have a girlfriend, *her* ass should be mad. May's out and about, though, isn't he? So no, I *don't* wanna go down to County. I can't leave work, and when I do leave I have to pick up Yan, and anyway, what am I going to do down there but act a fool with the damn guards . . . or with whoever. Donnell'll get out and he'll come home.'

'Rell still wanted Donnell to be Maynard as badly as Donnell wanted it himself. Jess and Paige always said that Donnell and Ch'Rell got along only because their names rhymed.

As I placed the receiver in its holder, Paige walked up with her purse on her shoulder. 'Sep said it was cool for me to leave. What did 'Rell say?'

'What you'd expect.'

'Tell her to stop complaining and lose that baby weight. Jess happens to understand the concept of exercise.'

'Ch'Rell's problem is more with May.'

Paige handed me my sweater. 'Soon as this jail thing passes, Ch'Rell will crawl right back up May's behind.'

IN THE waiting room at County, Jess, Paige, and I had to show ID and sign in, and then we sat by a window that didn't open. On a low table there were ancient copies of *Time* and *Jet*. Reagan getting shot and Bill Cosby.

There were fifteen kids there. Six adults. Two white women, one Mexican man. One white man. Two black women. All the children but one some shade of brown. Place smelled like armpits and Doritos, thin coffee and rash powder. Chewed-up drinking straws on the floor.

Jess said, 'My mom and I came here to get my dad out of jail once.'

'I can't imagine Dr. Roland getting arrested for anything,' Paige said. 'Except for maybe driving under the influence.'

'You know my dad doesn't drink that much.' Jessica gave her a look. 'Except for when I'm marrying May. Me and Mom came to get him out of here because he hit somebody who said something negative about Mom. Mr. To-the-Rescue,' Jess said. 'Always standing up for the black thing, always Mr. White Man Who Understands.'

Dr. Roland was half Italian, half Irish. Always wore his waved nougat hair combed back and smoothed down with what smelled like Vo5. He was from Oakland, had gone to Bishop O'Dowd High School, in Upper High. Our mom had graduated from Castlemont, down the hill from O'Dowd, and remembers how Roland would be at Castlemont after school in his Volkswagen with a black friend, one of the few blacks at O'Dowd at the time. Roland watched the kids from Castlemont until everyone had milled away except for a few girls sitting at the bus stops along MacArthur Boulevard. Then he'd pull up and offer rides. Played the charming chauffeur, my mother said, but always looked like he'd been let loose in a carnival, and like the tickets cost more than he had.

Gigi was at the bus stop when Sandra and two other girls accepted a ride from Roland. He'd leaned out his window and promised them 'a ride home even if you live in Hayward! Or Fremont!' My mom described Sandra as tall and black as black was gonna get. Apricot lips. Long, ashy fingers always wrapped around a cellophane bag of clay. Hair in a high frothy ponytail. Mom knew Oscar's father from back then, too. Or at least remembered him from parties and stuff, said he was always with his older brothers, and that he always had a lot of girlfriends. He joined the army because his brothers had. Mom said Oscar's dad's personality had been too subtle for Oakland, that he came home after his stint, fell into drinking and getting pregnant with Oscar's mom, ran back overseas somewhere for a couple of years, then came back, Mom said, sad about having been happy. Started doing every drug known.

Jess's parents met up again when Roland was at Cal and Sandra was at the College of Arts and Crafts. They were doing a voter registration drive or planning a fund-raiser or something real sixties, and they got married four months later, Jess already in Sandra's tummy. Paige had one of the squat, smooth bowls Sandra's known around the Bay Area for making. Jess gave it to her when Oscar and Paige got married. Paige put gardenias and warm water in it sometimes.

In the waiting room, Jess breathed in her surroundings. 'I've been having this idea that Mom is some kind of sucker,' she said. 'Like she got caught up in his need for some black and started being that for him.'

'And if she did?' Paige said. 'What if that was his need, and she liked satisfying it? What if she needed something from a white man that she didn't even know about until she got around one?'

'That's sick,' Jess said. 'Like what?'

'Like protection. Like love, I guess. Like feeling more than just normally special.'

If homeboy wasn't beating her ass, and was letting her mold pots from clay while he went and filled cavities, then that was reason enough to be with him. I listened.

'It's sick if it's true,' Jess said. 'My dad always says how it was Mom's skin, her *aura*, her scent, her cooking—'

'That's what a lot of men say,' Paige said. 'When they're in love with somebody.'

'Her black skin her bushy hair her foreign fragrance,' Jess said.

'But she *is* black,' I said, and they both looked surprised. 'So she wasn't going out of her way to be that for him. She's black for everyone. For herself, especially.' *Why am I talking?*

'And he can feel superior with a black wife.' Jess didn't

look at Paige or I. 'He can feel good for giving up his opportunity to be a normal white guy *and* have an extra measure of mystery and specialness—*because* of his ebony wife. He can be this guy who *must* believe in real true love or else why would he marry—'

'Would you have had him have sex with her until the excitement wore off? You wish they never met? That they fell in love and then said, No, but we can't marry because—'

'But the reasons they fell in love seem so—'

'Tainted? And Paige's reasons for getting with Oscar? Why didn't you pull yourself back from May because he—you know? That's not as bad as being white?' *Need to shut up, be quiet. All in everyone's business. I want to talk today. Quiet now. Quiet.*

'Part of it is a response to not being white.' Jess sipped her Crush through a straw. She had her mother's face and her father's skin. Roland and Sandra had lived in North Oakland when they were first married. Mom used to see them trudging down College Avenue, looking in store windows, dripping with ice cream and a pale kid. Mom said the couple looked worn down and had fingers tangled together.

Jess took her voice down to a murmur. 'That's what my dad said . . . about guys like . . . May . . . in general. May has this dream. He wants to be where his dealings with white people are from a position of power.' Then she shrugged her shoulders, spoke extra softly. 'I mean, if May can get money from the situation, why shouldn't he? Isn't it better to make money than to be smoked out?'

'There's space between selling and smoking,' Paige said. 'It's called a job.'

Jess said, 'Like your job?' Paige and I could barely hear her.

'What did you say?' One of Paige's eyes had gone into a squint. She'd heard. Paige found lemon hand cream in her purse, dotted some on the tops of her hands, massaged it until it disappeared.

'What was May going to do?' Jess said in a hurry. 'To get real money, I mean. To be stable, have power.'

The smell of Doritos had left the room. It was getting to be late afternoon, and sweaty Burger King aromas replaced it. I looked at the round clock on the wall. Paige sighed.

I said, 'So Maynard has power?'

'Power as in freedom to do what he wants, without white people checking him. Without anyone checking him.'

Paige said, 'Where are we right now?'

Jess put her shoulders up like, Huh? Her pink lipstick had a vague shimmer. Eyes lined against the upper lashes with dark blue kohl.

'We're in jail,' Paige said. 'Where brothers get checked. Maybe you're right, though, since May's out already. Maybe he's got some power.'

'Where is May, anyway?' I said. 'Do you ever know where he is?'

'Pinch, you have your nerve talking about anybody's situation. Last time you had a man was . . . never?'

Second time today. Okay. 'I don't need a boyfriend to know the boyfriend deal. You think I don't see? I watch.'

'No, Pinch. You cannot talk what you don't know.'

'Oh I know.' *How could I not know?*

'You've never even stepped in. What are you, twenty? Twenty-one? Have you had sex? I know you've had sex.'

Wow. All in my business now. I guess I'd gotten in hers. 'I've had sex.' *I had. Big deal.*

'So what then?'

'I haven't met a guy I want to be all into.'

'Have you had sex more than once with the same guy?'

Paige said, 'Jess, shut up.'

'Or have you had sex with a chick?'

'Jessica. You need to shut up. Shut. Up.'

'No Paige, it's cool,' I said. And right then, it was. 'If it's your business, Jess, I like boys. I wish I did like girls because then I'd be—'

'She'd be safe,' Paige said.

'Love is treacherous, regardless,' Jessica said. 'My dad always says, When two people love each other, there's no happy end to it.'

AFTER a trio of echoing clicks from the thick gray door, my brother-in-law walked out. He smelled like other people's alcoholic breath.

Oscar put his arms around Paige. 'I don't want to hug you,' he said. 'I'm filthy.' But he inhaled at her neck, clasped Paige hard. Then looked at Jess and me. 'I don't know why,' he said, 'you guys came down here.'

I was so happy to see Oscar. He had a genuine interest in my sister, and since I was my sister's, he had an interest in me. Maybe she wasn't scared of him. I wasn't anymore.

He gave me a soft pinch on my upper arm. How stupid am I that tears came to my eyes.

Donnell walked out, nodded, saw that Ch'Rell wasn't there, and then went directly to the pay phone. I went to hug him but ended up popping him lightly on the back of his neck while he was talking to his wife.

'We came down here to make sure you guys were all right,' Jess said. 'Where's Cedric?' She handed Oscar the soda she'd been sipping from.

Donnell walked up, slacks a mass of creases. 'Who's gonna give me a ride to my car?'

I said, 'Where is Cedric?'

Oscar said, 'Let's talk about it later.'

'He's not getting out?' Paige said it, pulling on Oscar's shirt.

'How long is it going to take him?' Jess said. 'We can wait, right?'

'Let's go,' Donnell said, and he had the nerve to sound irritated.

'Did you ask somebody?' Paige said. 'Did you see him back there?'

'It's not about asking so many questions,' Oscar said. 'Let's be out.'

In Jess's car, Oscar was at the wheel. Jess up front with him. Donnell, Paige, and I in the back. We darted between trucks on the Eastshore Freeway, the stretch set against the bay, and at late afternoon, a rusting sun. At the Berkeley Marina, Goosey's was closing but O'Rourke's lot was filling up with people looking for a happy hour. The boys had been so sharp the night before, pressed, manicured, and redolent with the rosemary–olive oil soap Paige, Jess, and Ch'Rell had started buying. Finally we all stood in front of Donnell's ruby 280ZX. Looking at each other. Way past Ivory and Zest, we were in a new circumstance.

'Todd,' Oscar said, 'was about to get out when we did.'

'Forget Todd's rambunctious ass,' Donnell said. He flicked a lighter off and on, like he was pleased to have it back.

'Todd was talking a lot about May,' Oscar said.

'Where is he, anyway?' Paige said. 'May.' She pulled her sweater around her, looked toward Oscar's car. Not at Jess.

Jess said, 'Home, I think. Why don't you guys page him. What all was Todd saying?'

'It wasn't just Todd,' Donnell said. 'Cops were saying it, too. That May's the smart one. And that Cedric wasn't going *any*where.'

Jess said, 'What kind of shit is that?'

Oscar looked at Jess and said, 'Fools just talking.'

'So Cedric's not getting out for a long time?' I said. *What's he doing in there? Is he scared?*

'He's in trouble?' Jess got paler. 'Like trouble for real?'

'Why?' Paige wanted to know.

Unlocking his car, Oscar said, 'It's just kinda fucked up right now.' He kissed Jess on the cheek, said, 'Go home.'

I kissed her, too. Her skin was cooler than the air.

Jess said, 'Pinch, I'm sorry.'

On the way home, Oscar said, 'Why's Jess apologizing to you?'

'She's always doing that,' Paige answered for me. 'In her undercover ways, to everybody.'

CHAPTER 10

Everybody but Jessica was at Oscar and Paige's.

This is how I live. What I do. Who I do it with.

Desperation is the raw material of drastic change. That's Evan's recent one.

With his garbanzo-bean head and Tic Tac teeth, Donnell was on the couch, drinking more than anyone should.

Maynard was in pleated ivory linen Bermuda shorts, and a pink-and-green short-sleeved plaid shirt buttoned to the neck. New K-Swiss, and short white socks fresh from the package. Nails manicured. Feet flat, knees splayed. Scarred arms buttery with baby oil.

Ch'Rell had new pointy black shoes and a fresh perm.

My sister was in the kitchen. Refrigerator door opened, *thwuck.* Closed, *thwuck. Cli-pat* went her sandaled feet. *Pa-click.*

Oscar read at a sports magazine.

Cedric was still in jail.

What I understood, from Oscar's backhanded comments, was that Cedric had traffic warrants, and he'd had weed under his car seat that night at Carlos O'Rourke's. Also he'd had sixteen thousand or four thousand or fifteen hundred in cash in his glove compartment. According to what I could decipher or overhear, there had also been 'other paraphernalia.' Cedric ended up pleading guilty, and his sentence was six months to a year. He was in Santa Rita Jail, about thirty miles outside Oakland. Out past Hayward, Santa Rita was a long dingy tract of bungalows surrounded by cyclone fence and barbed wire. Cedric had been gone for over three months. I hadn't visited him. None of us had. His name came up among the girls, and we talked about him wistfully, like he was doing a semester at sea.

It was my birthday, though, in Oakland. Rosewatery summer evening. Sky petal-pink, bruised blue. This get-together at Paige and Oscar's was supposedly in honor of me.

Mom had been by the Pseudo that morning, brought iced carrot cupcakes and birthday candles, and the best coffee from a place I liked called Peet's. She gave me a pair of silver earrings and a matching anklet. Plus bras and socks for both Paige and I.

In Paige and Oscar's living room, Ch'Rell spread spiced cheese on a cracker. Bit green grapes in half, ate them like that.

Oscar's dad was on the tiny balcony, where he had a bucket of tomatoes growing. He'd been beating rugs out there, and had begun polishing his and Oscar's shoes. Puffing on a cigarette.

I watched him. He'd found a rhythm.

Paige straightened my collar from behind. 'Stop being negative,' she said, over my head, to Maynard. 'They might let him out sooner. It's not like Ced's got a record.'

'He's gone,' May said, 'for a while.' *When had he started punching his words out like that? Spreading a napkin over his knee and being so prickly about his food?*

Paige poured May two inches of Grand Marnier. He'd brought the bottle to Paige and Oscar's months before. Nobody drank it but him, and occasionally Donnell. I didn't appreciate the way May sipped it and then pressed his lips together.

'Task Force,' May said, 'is serious right now.'

As if 'task force' and being 'gone' were so familiar to him. As if we were involved in an ancient story that was playing itself out and we had no choice but to go with it.

'Cops is tired of niggas getting over,' May said.

'Cops told you that?' I was tired of his hot-air finality. 'That there's a special new mood amongst them all?'

'The Climate. I know what I'm talking about.'

Paige stood in the archway of the kitchen.

'You're not old,' I said. 'You don't know anything more about anything going on than any of us do.'

'You're right, I know nothing.'

'Because you dress better than you used to? That makes you wise now?'

'I'm from the Acorns.' Like it was a degree.

'And? You been from the Acorns before all this shit happened—fools going to jail, getting shot and all. Why now does being from there mean something so deep? How can you just know stuff all of a sudden? You're just as tripped out as we are.'

'I'm not tripped out,' Ch'Rell said. I didn't look her way.

May rearranged himself. Sat up straight, like it was time to act properly. 'Let me shut up, then,' he said.

I hate when people disengage because they can't hang with the conversation. It's a Mom trick, a Gigi game. May always used to listen. Have encouraging things to say.

'It's your birthday,' May said. 'Pinch Talks Day. Go ahead—speak, sister, speak.'

Ch'Rell laughed a little. Sucked down more grapes.

'Nigga bring his own food,' Paige said, 'he wants to act like it's his house.'

May snorted.

Donnell kept at his glass.

Paige went back into the kitchen.

Oscar's father was still out there, shining.

Doorbell rang. Oscar pushed the intercom button, and Jess's voice pierced the room. 'Me and Ree,' she said.

May, still on the couch, took care to have no reaction.

His wife walked in, pale full lips set, son on her hip.

'What's the word?' she said, making eye contact with no one, like she cared not what the word was. Jess clearly didn't care what the weatherman said. No rain for days, and none forecast, but Ree had on a yellow rain hat, was carrying a bear wearing a red one.

Ch'Rell said, 'May's talking about Ced's in Santa Rita until.'

Jess looked at her husband. He'd turned his attention to his Styrofoam container of fried snapper. Mixed Tabasco into his tartar sauce with a French fry. Paige had baked chicken, made stuffing and spinach. We had the cupcakes. Salty odors floated to the living room each time the oven squeaked open. May'd wanted fish, though, so he brought it from Felix's Fish House. He had a bright gold ring on his left pinkie. Ch'Rell'd told me earlier that it was twenty-two karat.

'Until when?' Jess said to May like she was warning him about something.

'Until until,' he said into his container. 'Homeboy's locked up tight.' And popped another fry in his mouth.

'And you're not worried.' Jess put Ree in Ch'Rell's lap. Yannick, with his broad, eyebrowless face, was asleep on a blanket on the floor. 'Rell hugged beefy Ree like he was her own, then took off his slicker, checked the label inside his corduroy overalls, inspected the logo stamped in his metal buttons.

'Ced'll be all right.' He knew more than she did, May's mighty look said, so she should be still.

In the quiet I heard Oscar's father, *buff-buff, buff-buff*. His back was to us all, but the glass door was slightly open. I knew he could hear everything.

'I guess,' Jessica said, 'you're secure in the fact that Cedric won't mention your part in this.' She looked at Oscar, then at Donnell, said, 'Yours either.'

Just inside the kitchen, Paige was slicing sourdough. I saw her stop.

This is stupid. I mean, are we in a gang? Ced's in jail, but damn, it's not like anyone was caught moving kilos, running guns, murdering. May and Jessica acting like the guys are big dope dealers all of a sudden. With pacts signed in blood, Colombians on speed dial, renegade cops with personal vendettas out to get them. Task Force is serious right now. Negroes should be in class, in cleats, bringing home milk and eggs, slouching under backpacks. Like I can talk about what anyone needs to be doing. This Climate has everybody confused. Mom and Oscar's dad, their age group had their own Climate. The way Oakland was back then—hippies, Panthers, assassinations, no birth control, no legal abortions, marches on this place or that in protest of this or that. OPD and Berkeley PD way more flagrant than they are now. Yes, I guess they had their Climate. So we can't complain about ours. To them, anyway.

'He won't,' Maynard said. 'And if they arrested me, who'd take care of Ree?'

'What does that have to do with anything?' Oscar said it. He'd long since put down his magazine.

Donnell scooped up snacks, sipped his drink. Tilted his glass back, so the ice hit his teeth.

Ch'Rell bounced Ree on her lap.

Yannick sniffled in his sleep.

'Who'd take care of *you*?' May said to Jessica. He leaned forward, knees against the coffee table. 'Your father? I thought you wouldn't take anything else from him. I thought you said one black woman idolizing him and depending on him was enough.' May brushed his hands with his napkin, balled and tossed it to the low table. 'But go ahead,' he said. 'Run on home to Dr. Roland.'

Donnell took one of Oscar's father's cigarettes from an open box on the table. Didn't light it.

Oscar's father stopped buffing, looked in the glass door from outside.

Oscar said, 'You all need to take a deep breath.' He wasn't eating or drinking at all, and I was glad about the last part.

Jess took Ree from Ch'Rell, sat down on a wicker chair. 'May's mad,' she said, 'because I always got somewhere to go.'

'Go, then. Leave my son.'

Pa-click into the living room. Paige looked at Oscar with eyes wide and mouth shut. Oscar looked back at her with a shrug on his face.

Paige took the few steps to me, stood directly behind.

Jess said, 'I'll do what I want.'

May said, 'You're mistaken.'

'Cut it out,' Oscar said. 'This is supposed to be Pinch's birthday.' He picked up May's and Donnell's glasses by putting his fingers inside, took them into the kitchen. Oscar didn't see the hateful look May shot him. I heard trickling into the sink. Knew that syrupy sound. Liquor's thicker than water.

'What's wrong with you?' I said to May. 'How are you acting?'

'The way you'd want me to, considering.'

'Considering what?'

'Considering that people act the way they want, say whatever they want. Bullshit about who they are and why they stay. But when I say what *I* have to say, then I'm the motherfucker. But fools just *talk*.' He growled it. 'They say fucked-up shit about who I am and where I might be and what they think *I'm* doing. When I ignore them, I'm wrong, and I get screamed on. When I say what's real, though, and hit a nerve, then fools want to curse me out even more.' He didn't look at Jess when he spoke. Nor did he look at me.

'I'm not people, or fools,' Jess said.

'And,' Maynard said, 'I'm not talking to you.'

Babyish. Both of them.

Was glad Paige chose that moment to produce a gift wrapped in lavender paper and an artistic, pink bow. I recognized the wrapping. Knew when I saw the box that inside was this Aunt Jemima–like teapot I'd been wanting. The lid was painted to look like a red bandanna. I'd been with Paige and Jess in one of the nice shops along College Avenue, and I'd seen it. The ceramic pot wasn't a real antique, but it had been displayed in a glass cabinet, which the elegant older hippie clerk opened for us. Then she spread a blue felt cloth on the counter and set the pot on it. The clerk told us, while lifting the bandanna lid and then pointing out the detail in the apron's bow, that the pot was a limited edition, and only such-and-such a number of the teapots had been made. The teapot came complete, she said, with a certificate. Then she flipped it over to show us a number impressed in its base. I wanted it. I even wanted the blue felt cloth.

At my birthday gathering, I slid loose the bow, then tore at tape.

Jess smiled my way. Ree was in her lap, twisted on his side.

May was tired, or was trying to look it.

Ch'Rell crouched in toward me, curious. She'd reduced the heap of grapes. Flesh hung from each green-black stem.

Oscar was in the kitchen.

Oscar's dad stood in the doorway of the balcony.

Yannick slept away.

Paige had brushed her blush on in a subtle way. Black eyeliner drawn thick and dark on her lower lid, exactly like Jess's, exactly like mine, exactly like Ch'Rell's. My sister's shoulder-length hair was loosely bumped under, in a style we called a mushroom. Her brown eyes expectant and bright in the way they got when she served food, or came out of her bed-room lotioned, perfumed, and dressed up. It was a yellow yield light that warmed Paige when she thought she might be happy and confidently normal for a few hours. It shone through her skin, turned it almost amber when she believed she had a solid chance of pleasing.

My sister pushed the reddish front of her hair back as she watched me. I'd begun really looking at her. In such moments, I knew why guys liked her. For a chance at that light. To see it, to maybe inspire it, however occasionally it shimmered. Maybe because of just how occasionally it did.

I tossed away Styrofoam nuggets. Saw the certificate, all done in calligraphy.

'Daaaang,' I said, pulling the pot out carefully. It was an adult gift. A real collector's item, for my collection.

'You like? You like? It's from me and Oscar.'

'Yeah. I love it.' My voice was croaky. I did love it. But didn't know how to speak with effervescence. I gave my sister a swift hug. We bumped and poked each other as we straightened out.

I tried to gush. 'Thanks, Paige, thanks!' Then ran from the living room toward Oscar to say thank you to him.

But I stumbled over something. Tripped and fell to my knees and palms. The teapot dropped.

Paige was right there next to me, on her knees, face near mine. 'You all right?'

The teapot had cracked into five neat pieces.

Maybe my foot caught the strip of metal that separated the wood floor from the kitchen linoleum. Stunned. Water welled. Came up off my hands, stayed on my knees, butt on my heels. Looked at the pieces of teapot strewn around the floor. Wanted to fake a laugh, but the idea wouldn't move from my head to my eyes.

Paige shadowed me, getting to her feet as Oscar and his dad helped me up. Like they were helping her rise, too.

Oscar's father brushed my knees with his hand, said, 'Come on, Birthday Girl.' Then tears came down my face.

From just beyond the kitchen's archway, Ch'Rell crowed. She pointed at me, covered her mouth with a cupped hand. French-manicured talons almost touching her earlobe. *Yowl!*

Hoo-hoo! Her every brutish rock forward said, *That's life. That's what you get, so don't even try and be sad about it.* Twit-taunt. Ha-ha. But I wasn't Ch'Rell's only target. Only this day's. She mocked any attempt at actual hope, any stumble into misery or fear. Ch'Rell laughed your something into her nothing, laughed so her painted bottom lip left red smears above her chin.

Through watery eyes, Ch'Rell's nose seemed a beak. Her dimpled brown face all distorted with snorting. When people make themselves so easy to see, they want you to stare. To know who they are.

I stared so hard I got cold.

But it was Ch'Rell who froze over. All fowly and fruit-eating. Claws clutching the armrests of the chair. Homegirl iced-up in my head, just like that.

I brushed by Paige, into the living room. Stood dead center, Paige immediately beside me. I almost rushed Ch'Rell, hated her. But like I knew my own name, I knew I could afford to be gracious.

As if he'd heard my thoughts, Donnell frowned.

Maynard wasn't laughing, but his lips were in a loose purse. They didn't have to move for me to read, *If you were a bit more chill, you'd still have your little Aunt Jemima.* The soles of his shoes faced us, a clean insult. He'd crossed his feet on the coffee table.

'Don't worry about it,' Paige said, tugging me toward the bathroom. 'We can get another one. They had four at that store.' Then she whispered, 'Fuck Ch'Rell. Trifling heifer. Shit comes back around.' Paige said it the way we said it: *triflin' heffa.* Emphasis on the first syllables of each word.

Ch'Rell was still laughing.

Oscar placed the sharp Jemima pieces in the box like they were heirlooms. He said, 'Donnell, tell your girl, Keep it down.' Then he looked at May. 'Watch your feet, man.'

'What's that?' May kept his feet where they were.

'Get your shoes,' Oscar said, still holding the box, 'on the floor.'

May didn't move. They looked at each other.

Oscar kept looking while May slowly let his feet drop down, one deadweight after the other.

Oscar walked back in the kitchen.

Ch'Rell sputtered, and acted like she had to wipe tears from her eyes. Yan woke up with his father's frown.

As Ch'Rell reached for her son, I pressed my fingers in her upper arm, hard. 'Keep laughing,' I said with what I hoped was cold radiance. 'Keep laughing.'

Ch'Rell jerked her arm away.

Only person who didn't look shocked was Paige. And Oscar's father. I wiped my face with my arm, didn't need to go to the bathroom.

Ch'Rell checked Yan's diaper.

Jess slid Ree back in his coat.

May walked to put his snapper container in the kitchen trash.

Oscar fiddled in a kitchen drawer, asked his dad about Krazy Glue.

Oscar's father went back out on the balcony and inspected the shoes.

'You all right?' Paige said. *How many times has she asked me that in life?*

I turned, looked at Ch'Rell. 'You through now?'

'The shit was funny.'

'But you're through now.'

Donnell slid the unlit cigarette back in the box, said, 'We need to go have some real drinks.'

'Rell didn't say anything. Flapped slightly, bounced her shoulders, like she might do something. But she was just trying to get comfortable again.

WE DROVE for drinks, because that's what we did all the time.

Went to West Oakland in three cars, down to Mexicali Rose. Left Paige and Oscar's apartment together, out of herd instinct. We were to split a pitcher of margaritas.

When it arrived, with seven glasses rimmed in salt, Jess said to Maynard, 'You didn't even ask who wanted salt or who didn't.'

I knew Oscar didn't like salt with his margarita. Ch'Rell didn't either. Oscar finally said, 'I'm gonna ride out to Santa Rita tomorrow.'

'Nah,' May said. 'He don't want company. It's embarrassing to him. Don't go out there.' Like he was anybody's father but Ree's.

It was almost eight P.M. Mexicali Rose stayed open twenty-four hours. It was directly across the street from the county jail. Cops ate there, and opal-eyed UPS guys. Munchie-soft students at the worn elbows of bail bondsmen. Dope dealers. Burnt bus drivers and buffed longshoremen. Lawyers with dirty cuffs and dazzling links across from ancient couples sipping tequila. Ruddy new couples breathed beer onto wan chicks, cold brothers, and wise kids who sat in burgundy pleather booths awaiting a beep or an appointed hour, anxious about the release of the troublemaker rabble-rouser rest-stealer heartbreaker who was across the street in the building with the barred windows. People who'd forgotten to eat all day packed in the booths at Mexicali Rose, ordered oval combination plates so hot the whispery waitresses served them with thick cotton pads. *Muy caliente.* Careful. Torn breasts or cactus or tongue drooped from tortillas. Orange rice and pink beans. Raw onion gone vinegar-limp and rosy with beet juice. Paige and May and Oscar and the rest of us, we ordered none of it this time.

My heyday, as it was happening. *Feliz cumpleaños.*

Oscar rose from the booth. Said, matter-of-factly, 'Me and Paige are gonna head on out. We got food at home.' Oscar touched Paige on the top of her hand. She stepped from the booth. I scooted over, ready to exit.

'Paige,' Jess said, 'call me tomorrow?'

May didn't look at Jess, said, 'You have things to do tomorrow.'

Unbelievable. The way he talks to her.

Paige ignored him. 'I'll call you in the afternoon.'

'I'm not understanding,' May said to Oscar, 'why you're getting up.'

I couldn't believe it when Donnell cracked his mouth to say, 'We ain't in jail, Cedric is.'

I was up. Paige had slipped into her jacket. Between our shoes and the tiled floor, coarse salt was being ground fine.

Oscar reached for his light jacket. Paige jiggled her coat zipper. I touched her wrist, felt her heart beat at a normal pace.

Ch'Rell was a statue that fascinated her baby.

Donnell watched May and Oscar.

'There you go,' May said. 'Track star. On the run.'

He didn't run when you shot Todd and Bam was going to shoot you.

Paige stepped back a half a foot, like she felt Oscar needed space.

Oscar shrugged into the jacket. 'Do I seem,' he said in the same bland tone, 'like I'm running.'

If Ced had been at Mexicali Rose with his smart remarks and huge smiles and deciphering ways, he'd've snuffed this iffy moment out. He might even have made it cool between Ch'Rell and me.

'Oscar,' May said. 'I'm talking to you about something.'

'You're talking loud.'

May stood up quick. Cologne-filled air hit me, and then Oscar's and May's chests were six inches apart. Bartenders poured drinks in slow motion, pressed register buttons that rang like slot machines.

Maynard said, 'I told that fool. He don't listen. You know it. You know it out of everybody. Don't stand up here and make it about me.' Then he looked my way, said, 'Say something, Pinch. You watch everybody like a fly, always up in everybody's business. Say something now. You know me.'

They were fighting about something I didn't know about, wouldn't know about. I didn't know what kind of ground he and Oscar were standing on. So I said, 'Stop being evil. It's my birthday.'

Paige, Oscar, and I left May standing there. Walked down Seventh Avenue toward the car. There were people standing across the street in front of the jail. Paige and I took a walk down Seventh once with her twelfth-grade class. A hundred years ago, one of the big railroads had its terminus in West Oakland. Because of the factories and trains, people from all over the world had lived here. The International Brotherhood of Sleeping Car Porters was based there—it must have been such a big deal to belong to that, or have your man belong to that back then. On Seventh, in Nannah and Grandpa's day, there'd been Greek clubs and jazz clubs right next to each other. I thought it must have been nice, but then the docent said to Paige's twelfth-grade class that there'd been lynchings, and that not everybody got to be a redcap, and even if they did, life was pretty messed up.

Paige had said, 'If it hadn't been messed up, there wouldn't have been the brotherhood.' Paige had also said that at least the porters knew who to fight, what the fight was.

There at the car, Oscar said to both of us, like he owed us an explanation, 'I'm not fighting unless I'm ready to kill somebody, or somebody's about to kill me. Or mine. A person doesn't have to act mad every time he gets mad.'

Paige said, 'When did May get like that? He didn't used to be that way. How come you're not like that?'

That's the kind of uncomplicated person Paige can be. Real basic questions. Real basic reactions. Sometimes she's that way. The kind of person who dragged me from the apartment across from San Antonio the Thanksgiving she was fourteen. The Thanksgiving when we'd walked in on Mom saying to us, *Shhhh.*

Seth spread on the couch, facing the back of it, one arm and one leg dragging the floor. Manila folders and graph paper strewn around. Tequila in a squat glass, pale as pee. It scented his breath and ruled the room.

Mom knocked back a short glass of apple juice, checked her face in the hall mirror. Stretched her mouth, squeezed shut, then opened her eyes wide like she might snap back into a Gigi or a Gwen she recognized.

Seth shuddered in his sleep. Half-turned. Mom reacted too slowly for Paige.

My sister snatched me from the apartment, and we ran out into the street toward the park. I felt the wind from the AC Transit bus on the side of my face. Heard the brakes scream and try. Looked up at a driver staring at us with rage and relief. Two people ran off the front, to see if Paige and I were all right. Bus hissed scorched rubber breath. Grill hot, and four inches from my hip.

Mom ran out yelling, 'Oh my God, I'm sorry!' to the driver. The three of us climbed in her car without completely shutting the doors, and rolled from the driveway without power. Paige asking me, 'You all right?' I wasn't even scared. The bus wouldn't have hit me. Life had begun to seem a series of close calls, near-disasters. That the worst could actually happen—the sudden death of me or Paige or Mom—rarely entered my mind.

Mom drove us to a hotel restaurant, and we ordered the Thanksgiving special.

After dry turkey, the waiter brought us identical slices of carrot cake. Mom forked chunks into her mouth like she was meeting a quota.

'I have my permit, I'm gonna get a job,' Paige said. 'If it's about money, we don't have go to St. J's.' It was six months before Ninth Grade Court day.

Mom looked like she needed ten naps. She knew what Paige was getting at. 'You can get a job if you want, Paige. But we can't leave . . . right now. You don't leave someone at the first sign of trouble. That's just not what you do.'

Paige got a job that next month, at the covered swimming pool in Diamond Park. She wore a red swimsuit and baggy red shorts. Mom would go up to the pool and swim and swim, up and down a lane alone she held her breath until gills appeared behind her ears, until her eyes were magnified and blurry under thick, clear mucus, until her strokes were teak blades, until the slap of her feet on the pool's skin was lonesome applause, until chlorine washed over and through her, rinsing beyond purity. Mom would rise shivering, sheets of wetness falling, water dark on her lashes. She sliced through the blue green toward something Paige couldn't see. It made my sister so surly, Mom stopped coming to Diamond to swim at all.

When Paige remembers her fourteenth Thanksgiving, she asks, 'Was Christmas better?' in that earnest tone.

I tell her that it was definitely more cheerful than Thanksgiving. And that we'd been at Gram Liz's, in Los Angeles with no Seth. I'd tell Paige that she herself hadn't been so sullen, but that Mom, in a skirt and a shimmery blouse, and dispensing gifts with wide gestures, had seemed with friends and family to be among mere acquaintances. Mom watched television, she watched the clock. Mom suggested parlor games unfamiliar to everyone, accepted none of the twelve or fifteen long-distance phone calls Gram Liz announced loudly from the doorway of her spartan bedroom. As Mom folded whites into cream for eggnog and proposed to wash, to dry, to taxi folks, bathe babies, box food, find extension cords, to empty trash, I was thinking, *Do we leave at the second sign of trouble? The eightieth?*

IN THE street by Mexicali Rose, with Oscar and Paige, by where the Brotherhood got started.

Where people came from all over to thrive and fail in Oakland.

To see drizzly green San Francisco and the still-pristine bay.

To walk by Lake Merritt when it was still a big old marsh.

To build what they thought were new lives in what was 'out West' to them. New golden lives in what was becoming my smothery hug of a hometown.

People strained, in front of the jail, to read pamphlets in the canary-black light. Paced and talked fast about shades of innocence. I kicked at dry, cracked condoms, and flyers advertising necktied counselors-at-law. And Gram Liz and Seth were stifling my brain and Paige was working that stupid job at Diamond Pool and Mom was swimming and swimming and nothing's really bad and nothing's really good. And newness rarely comes. Waiting for it is like waiting on the AC Transit No. 40 at three in the morning. It's going to come, eventually, but it's going to seem like forever in the cold, bad night, between rides.

Paige, Oscar, and I got in the car, went to their place.

We weren't there ten minutes before Mom pulled up. She'd been in Oakland all day on errands, she said, but I figured she wondered what we were doing on my birthday. We all stayed up late, had the dinner Paige cooked, and the carrot cupcakes Mom made. Sang the birthday song and everything.

Oscar's father gave me an asymmetrical ceramic bud vase. It
was one of Jess's mom's. Then Oscar and his father glued my
Aunt Jemima back together. It looked almost perfect, and I
was happy.

The next day, Oscar got up early, said he was going to see
Cedric. He stayed gone almost all day. A week later, Paige told
me Oscar had got a new pager number, and hadn't seen May
or Donnell. Oscar told Paige and his father that he'd decided
to stop selling.

I believed Oscar. That he would at least try.

IN JULY, Oscar started selling televisions and VCRs and
cameras at Whole Earth Access in Berkeley. It was a big ware-
house store. One side was basically the women's side: blenders
and food processors, Earth shoes, soft shirts, frames, candles,
and pajamas. The other side, where Oscar worked, had
stereos, tents, and computers. Couples came in, separated, met
back at the cash registers. Oscar was on an hourly wage, plus
commission. He worked there full-time for about two months
and then went to part-time. He was doing okay, but other people had seniority, he said, and regular customers. He came by
Planned Parenthood to pick me up one day, to take me to their
place. Paige would be getting off work. She'd quit the realty
company and begun part-time at Joseph Magnin's, a department store in downtown Oakland that served mostly old, old
white ladies. Paige sold the ladies pure-nylon panty hose, the
kind with no spandex. They didn't hug your leg, and they ran
easily. But Paige said they were the sheerest, and they were
classy. She promised to get me some, on her discount.

The phone rang as I was getting some lemonade. Oscar
answered.

He tensed, then said, 'Them days is past.'

Pause.

'Because,' he said.

Pause.

'I can't help you.' Calm now.

Pause.

'Donnell is where Donnell is.'

He was frustrated by the time Paige walked in. Having a beer. Flipping through a sports supply catalog. I had my lemonade, and imaginary view of the lake. It had its view of me.

'Hey,' she said. 'What's your deal?' Paige could have been speaking to either of us, but Oscar answered.

'Fiends calling here asking.'

'Did you tell them?'

'What you think? Yeah, I told them.'

'Well then,' Paige said. 'Word'll get around. Just like it got around the other way.'

Within two weeks, Paige got ten more hours a week at Magnin's, and Oscar resigned from Whole Earth. He talked about paying off his emergency loans to Nebraska, so he could have access to his transcripts, and then maybe transfer them to San Francisco State.

If San Francisco State was a person, he'd be tired of us lying about him.

'What was your major, anyway?' I asked Oscar when the three of us had settled into watching movies on Paige and Oscar's new VCR.

'Sociology.'

'To do what with?'

'Don't know. Be a social worker, I guess. Parole officer, something.'

Paige looked surprised. She said, 'Would you like that?'

'I don't know. Probably.'

Within another two weeks, Oscar was back running with Maynard and Donnell all the time. He was doing what he'd been doing.

OSCAR'S dad was on the balcony watering his tomatoes. He had basil and curly parsley, too. Paige was talking to him.

The sun was August frank, and relentless. I sat on the edge of a planter, bending basil leaves in half and holding them to my nose. Warm as it was, Oscar's father had a steaming mug in his hand, cigarette smoke seeping through his teeth. His recovery was amazing to me.

On one day over a year before, Oscar's father had apologized to Oscar for everything he'd ever done to him. It took a whole day and into the night. Oscar hadn't believed his father, had challenged him for weeks about dozens of crimes against himself and his mother. Oscar said stuff like, *I know you don't even remember the time you made me sleep outside on the porch it was November I was nine I was crying I could hear Mom screaming at you like you were trying to murder her she was crying I was yelping like a little punk banging on the screen door. Mrs. Dennis from across the street came over tried to take me to her house she had on that same tired sweatsuit she always wore you told her to leave me the fuck alone told her if she called the police you'd burn down her yellow house with all her dead mother's things in it. You told her she'd be standing there, with a piece of your world, and hers would be in ashes around her ankles. You got in her face and told her you would do it and feel no pain. Do you remember that?*

Paige was there and so was I, and Oscar'd said—looking cold at his father, who sat there giving his son unfaltering eye contact right back—*That's what I'm talking about, Paige. That kind of shit. Paige!* he'd yelled, and finally looked at her, mouth dry and tight like sweetness had never existed for him, like for my brother-in-law there'd only been rind and wrapping paper. I was astounded. Paige and I watched them like they were a television program.

Oscar's father said, 'I remember that. I remember that. I'm sorry. You were a baby—'

Oscar said, 'I was not a baby.' He took a deep breath and said, 'I. Was. Nine. You—'

'I made you stay out there all night. I was high.'

'Did you watch me? Did you know I wasn't dead or snatched? It was fucking freezing, I was up under the doormat.'

'Your mother watched you. Your mother—'

'Have you apologized to her? Have you got right with her?'

'Not yet, Oscar, but I'm going to. You have—'

Oscar interrupted his father, and Oscar's father let him, and after weeks went by Oscar told Paige that his father needed to stay for a while, indefinitely.

He arrived at their apartment on a Sunday when Paige was washing towels and the kitchen rugs. Winston in his mouth, he took the dirty things from her, laundered them and all the sheets and blankets in the house with detergent, color-safe bleach, and fabric softener. Scrubbed the bathroom with Ajax and a brush. Mopped the kitchen with ammonia. Threw old food out of the refrigerator, wiped it down with Windex. Sprayed Easy-Off in the oven, burnt sandalwood incense in every room. Oscar's daddy's jeans were fifteen years old, too big, and cinched at the waist with a thin brown vinyl belt. His luggage was a glossy black eel-skin briefcase he'd owned since the bicentennial, and a matching rectangular pocketbook with a wrist strap. In the small bag were some matches, the address book, and an expired job ID. In the case was clean underwear, a toothbrush, Vitalis, a leather cap with a small brim, and embroidered slippers from a long-ago Moroccan journey.

On the balcony, against the warm tomatoes, Paige said, 'Oscar thinks he can boss me. I don't like it.'

It was one of the reasons Paige was thinking of quitting Magnin's. If Oscar dropped in while she was at lunch, he'd stand in Hosiery until she got back, and then walk Paige outside, his hand on her upper arm. Always asking Paige where she was and who she was with when if he leaned in a little closer he could smell the Taco Bell in her sigh.

He told Paige, 'Talk to Oscar.'

'I did.'

'Leave him, then.' Oscar's father sounded almost serious, but really it was just a challenge for her to think about herself.

She and I went inside. Oscar was playing solitaire. Beef was roasting, red cabbage and iceberg lettuce sliced in a bowl.

Oscar said, 'What's Dad talking about?'

'Same old. And he asked about Cedric.'

Oscar said, 'Did he.' Distracted.

Paige had told Oscar's dad that Cedric was fine. She hadn't mentioned that Ced would be out in a few weeks.

'And he said if you don't get it together and start treating me sweet, I should leave you.'

'I don't think he said that.' Oscar looked black around the eyes. Beat. He spoke flatly, with fatigue. Had been out until almost dawn the night before. Walked in like he was climbing, smelled like brandy and weed and Smorgasbord.

'I'll make you a smoothie,' Paige said. 'Or you going out?'

'Going out later. Probably.' Of course he'd go out, and stay out, and she'd have me to watch TV with, and so it could seem like she didn't care.

Oscar's dad walked in, opened the oven, poured water and red wine over beef. Door buzzer went off, Paige buzzed in whoever it was without question.

'You're trying to get on my nerves,' Oscar said. He tensed. From the other side of the door, Donnell said, 'It's me. And 'Rell.'

'Don't let the meat dry out,' Oscar's father said, and then went to his room. He'd no patience for Ch'Rell or Donnell since my birthday. Not that Oscar's dad said anything, but he excused himself when even the talk turned to them or Maynard. I didn't hang out with Ch'Rell so much anymore, but Oscar's dad's action made me feel I should be doing something more drastically different.

Oscar and Donnell went into the other bedroom. Ch'Rell said, 'We just came from looking at couches when what I want to be doing is looking for a house.'

Paige said, 'Did you find a couch?'

'Don't you want a house?' Ch'Rell glanced around—tiled kitchen counters with spicy teas and things on the shelves, twenty-foot living room, throw rugs. 'Not that this place isn't nice.'

'I guess. At some point.'

'Have you been to May and Jess's?'

'I haven't,' Paige said.

'Neither have I, but Donnell has. He tells me every detail. It's not that big, but it has three bedrooms, a kitchen that looks out onto this patio that runs along the outside of the living room with a hot tub. Wall-to-wall carpet in the bedrooms, parquet floors everyplace else.' Ch'Rell was standing, gestured around like a game show hostess. 'Leather couch, big-screen TVs in the den *and* the big bedroom. They don't have any pictures on the walls yet—'

'He does tell you the details,' I said. I hadn't been invited out to Alamo.

'I make him. I want a house so bad. We're saving but it's like inch by inch.' To Paige, she said, 'Are you and Oscar saving?'

Paige shook her head no. She tended to spend her money. Not like it was much, but Magnin's kept her in tea and flowers and nice shoes. Oscar took care of everything else. Didn't give Paige too much drama about it, either. Except when he was coming up to her job, being dramatic.

'I don't blame you,' Ch'Rell said. 'I want what I want. You know?' Raised her eyebrows high. 'Jess has what she wants,' Ch'Rell said. 'I have to admit I'm jealous.'

Well, hallelujah.

'She found May and whatever he had he just gave it to her.'

Paige said, 'You think that's how it went down?' Paige didn't have her earnest tone.

'I saw it go down. You did, too. May saw that flowing hair, saw Miss USF. She played like she was happy dating those white guys until May started taking her out to Napa for the weekend and stuff, taking her into Saks, over to Pacific Heights—'

'Not like,' I said, 'Jess wasn't used to Saks.'

Ch'Rell shot me a look. 'She wasn't used to going in there with a big good-looking black man who everyone glared at like he was a murderer until he started talking softly and peeling off hundreds. Jess never dated a brother until she got with May.'

'I've seen her with a lot of black guys,' I said. 'Even before I knew her. So have you.'

Ch'Rell shrugged.

Paige sipped the smoothie she'd made for Oscar.

'So you think,' Paige said, 'that Jess doesn't love May?'

'She might now. But she didn't at first.'

Paige said, 'No one loves anyone at first.'

'Maybe not, but I know I love Donnell more than she loves May.'

As if you're the measure.

'So you,' I said, 'deserve a house more than she does.'

Ch'Rell had the sense to at least pause. 'I might not say it to Jessica, but yes. I do. I love Donnell and he doesn't have one-twentieth of what May has. That's pure love. And I don't think May wants Don to have more.'

'What does Donnell want?' I said. 'To be where Ced is?'

Ch'Rell shrugged again. 'Donnell says Ced didn't have to do the things he'd been doing.'

I wanted Ch'Rell to shut up, leave. She was desperate and transparent.

But Paige said, 'What things?'

'Cedric told May about some deal, some guy with all this, you know, dope or whatever, and May was dealing with the guy on it and I think Ced was feeling like he should have been having more face time with the guy or something, and so Ced was supposed to meet the guy and then he went out there—all at night by himself over there in Emeryville, where all those dead companies are, where the buildings look new but are empty—and I'm not sure if the guy was there or not, but Task Force was and they saw him and I guess they just waited until that night at O'Rourke's to get him.'

Paige said, 'Whose convoluted story is that?'

'It's *the* story.'

'It's somebody's movie,' I said. 'And you're sitting up believing it. Repeating it.'

'You can believe all that about money in Ced's car if you want to,' Ch'Rell said. 'But the truth is, Cedric had been tripping for a while. Acting out.'

I said, 'And you're saying all this now because?'

'Because I feel like it,' Ch'Rell said, going into the kitchen. 'Tired of this whisper whisper stuff. If Donnell wants to be mad, he can get mad. But I don't think he will.' She poured herself some juice. Paige looked at me like, *I know she's not going in my refrigerator without asking.* We stifled giggles.

'And where was Donnell when all this with Cedric was going on?' Paige said. 'And Oscar?'

Oscar said Paige's name. I wondered how long he'd been standing nearby.

'I'm about to run out with Donnell for a quick second,' he

said. And was gone before Paige could get it together to ask him anything.

Donnell and Oscar left in the Mustang. Ch'Rell and Paige left in Donnell's car to go get Yannick from Ch'Rell's mom's. When they got back, Paige installed 'Rell and baby on the couch, and I leaned back in Oscar's pseudo-La-Z-Boy.

From his room, Oscar's daddy complained loudly that his beef was a little dry, but the wine sauce saved it. Then he hummed along with the Doobie Brothers for a long time. *What a fool believes / He sees / Is always better than nothing.*

In the dark apartment, Doobies in the background, Yannick fell into a phlegmy sleep. Paige flipped channels in her room. In the La-Z-Boy, I pushed the sheet down to my waist. Listened to Ch'Rell's Ethan Allen dreams until they melted into my own.

CHAPTER 11

That next morning I woke even before Oscar's father. Stood out on the balcony, looked at the park. Orange sun rays turned leaves, grass, and even the corner traffic light an olive shade. I washed up and put on some of Paige's clothes. Not my size.

Jess picked Paige and I up while Oscar was still asleep. Ch'Rell and Yannick had left with Donnell in the middle of the night. Oscar's dad drank coffee and smoked. Toast popped up over his talk-radio station as we walked out the door.

The three of us plus Ree rolled to San Francisco, then took the ferry, with the car, over to Sausalito for brunch and mango margaritas. We stood on deck in the usual cool brilliance and the misty breath of the bay. Once docked, we walked to the big restaurant, Jessica looking happier than she had when she picked us up. Ree was in his stroller, hands loosely curled, smiling with his tiny teeth, clapping just off the beat of a song from a nearby radio.

When the patio of the restaurant was almost deserted, Jess shouted, *Fuck shit fuck!* at the sun right in front of her child. We sat in fog. Jess breathed it in deeply, seemed disappointed as it began to warm and evaporate.

'The sun's mean to burn it away, isn't it, baby boy?' She sang to him, something about high hopes and a rubber-tree plant. Swung his arms, mirrored his seated, wobbly dance. A cold lick wrapped us again. Then the sun beat its way through once more.

'I want to know,' Jess said, looking at Paige, 'if you've heard something.'

'Heard what?'

'That May's fucking someone. A girl with glasses and a bob haircut. My dad saw a girl who looks like that driving May's car.'

Paige said, 'I haven't heard that,' though truly I'd been at the bar in the Claremont Hotel with Oscar and Paige when Maynard came in with a girl who had short hair and old-lady spectacles. He introduced her as Kimya, bought a round of drinks even though me, Oscar, and Paige had barely touched the ones we had.

I thought Miss Kimya seemed annoyed, and that Maynard talked in front of her like she knew a lot of his business. Paige and I went to the rest room. She checked her widow's peak for dandruff. We came back and Oscar said, 'May knew you were pissed.' May and Kimya's tumblers were empty and so were their chairs.

'And?' Paige said. 'You're not?'

'May's business,' Oscar said.

'He must not want it to stay that way.'

In Tiburon, Jess said, 'I can't trust my dad, though. He's always trying to find some way to make May seem bad, or like May's getting the best end of things.' She inhaled fog again. Waved through it, tried in vain to grab some. 'Maybe May is getting a good deal. Dad tries not to act like it, but I know he thinks that I'm somehow . . . better than May, as if there were such a thing. He can't see that May loves me—'

Paige said, 'And you love May.'

'Yeah. Like you love Oscar.'

'Yeah,' Paige said. A brown seal poked its head from the bay. Water beaded on its whiskers. Heard a loud wheeze coming from it. Paige looked at me and said, 'I don't know if sea lions wheeze, or if the thing is just tired.' She might not know about love, but leave it to my sister to know the difference between seals and sea lions. 'I just don't love all hard for a long time all at the same level. Love gets bigger and smaller,' Paige said. 'And hopefully bigger again.'

We were eating the last raw green onions and guacamole. Salsa and blue corn chips. 'Even hearing this bullshit from my dad . . . I love May all the time the same.'

'You must be tired, then,' Paige said.

'Sometimes, but May makes me happy.'

'How?' I said. Thinking of what stupid Ch'Rell had talked about. And of how, exactly, one makes another one happy.

'By him bringing out my true self.'

Paige said, 'How were you not your true self?'

'It wasn't me to be all sweet. Always trying to please. I got more comfortable with what I did and didn't want when I got with him. I didn't want to be at USF. Didn't want to be up under my mom and dad. I wanted . . . my own situation. I don't have to get to be thirty-five to have the time and money to get to know myself. I'm skipping the bullshit. I can be confident and independent now. I can live free and—'

'You can't skip stuff, Jess,' Paige said.

And how can you be independent and dependent on May at the same time?

'I have. And how do you know, anyway, Paige? I guess you know yourself so perfectly. All your beliefs labeled and filed.'

'I believe in tragedy mostly,' Paige said like she'd thought about it. 'It's the only constant.'

Oh so melodramatic.

Jess said, 'That's what you would think.'

'Irony,' Paige said, 'is second to tragedy. I guess they kind of go together. Good sets you up for bad. Great childhood equals fucked-up adult life. Fucked-up childhood means you get a fucked-up adult life except it surprises you because you thought fate would at least give you a decent adult life after a fucked-up childhood. Contentment—not paying attention, even for a second—means a serial rapist is wet-dreaming about you, means your boyfriend's going to beat you to death, means your car gets rammed by a semi, means your babies will come out retarded, means—'

'Jesus,' Jess said. 'If you could commit to life for five minutes, it would be different.'

'Than what?'

'Than this depressing shit. You waste so much time quote unquote paying attention,' Jess said, 'you don't even notice the . . . everyday good stuff. You talk about . . . big love small love . . . but I see how you keep Oscar at bay. Always presenting him with a meal instead of presenting him with you. You wonder why that negro comes up to your job acting a fool . . . and I'm not saying it's right, but it's because he doesn't know you, doesn't know if you love him, if you even really like him. And so he can't trust you across the goddamn street. But maybe I need to shut my mouth. My mom says some relationships are like that.'

I said, 'Like what?'

Paige was giving Jess a mind-reading stare. Could tell my sister was irked but curious. Didn't like what Jess was saying, but appreciated that Jessica, that someone, was analyzing her.

'I just think Paige hates to ask,' Jess said to me. 'And that's why her and Oscar get along—he hates to answer.'

Jess put a hat on Ree. He was asleep with a soggy chip in his hand.

Paige said, 'What if what your father says about May being with someone else is true?'

'I guess I'll cross that bridge when I come to it.' Jess let her ponytail out, then restlessly put it back in. 'If May wants out, he'll end up wishing I'd stayed sweet Jessica, Dr. Roland's lovely daughter. He'll wish I'd kept a hold of some of that nice.'

Paige sipped her drink.

'You better mark my words, Paige. Pinch, you hear me.'

Paige said, 'Do you know about this thing with Cedric? Like, why do you think May got out of County on the day the cops kept Cedric in for a year.'

'Why does it matter?' Jess leaned back in her chair. 'What's the mystery? Negroes break the law, then show out, then they go to jail.' She was suddenly as vaguely contemptuous as Maynard had become. 'Plus,' she said, 'I'm not in May's business like that.'

'Liar.' Paige said it with a smile.

'I'm a liar now. Okay. Let me be truthful, then.' Jess smiled back with just her teeth. 'I wouldn't be in May's business at all if I talked about it with everybody.'

Paige said, 'So I'm everybody now.'

'Everybody's everybody.' Jess said it looking at me, then at Paige, too. Jess got Ree together to go. We were quiet on the way home. Even Ree was asleep.

'There's no need,' Jess said when we were getting out of her car in front of Paige and Oscar's apartment, 'for us to start getting in these negroes' business at this late date, letting it affect us, and how we deal. And anyway, when May's fucking up with me . . . or with you guys, or with anybody, I set him straight. Watch.'

BACK in their apartment, Paige and Oscar said hi to each other, didn't eat or kiss or anything. I fixed myself a Monterey Jack sandwich.

Paige and I sat in the living room. Me on the lumpy fake La-Z-Boy, she on the couch with orange juice and Oreos. Oscar was in he and Paige's room. Oscar's dad in his, with the door closed.

I'd intended to go back over to the Pseudo, but all the way back from Sausalito, I'd wanted to ask Paige about Oscar. I didn't want them to break up. She'd need him if I got it together to leave Oakland.

'Paige. Today with Jess.'

'Right? I'd never ask whether or not Oscar was fucking around. Never let anyone know I was sweating it. Anyone but you, I mean.'

'Are you mad at Jess?'

'No,' she said in whine. 'I can't be mad at her.'

'Why are you mad at Oscar?'

'Does it seem like I am?'

'Not mad, but . . . let me put it this way. One time you said that you *would* love Oscar. Today you said you loved him but not all the time.'

'When'd I say that?'

'At the Pseudo you said that a million things about yourself and the world would have to change. For you to love him back. Did they?'

She wound her legs around a tasseled pillow from Pier 1. 'I guess they did. I think I decided to be totally into Oscar when he was flying to Oakland from Nebraska that time, like two months before we got married. I was sitting in that coffee place, Solid Grounds, in Berkeley. Thinking I'd left candles lit and that the Pseudo was in flames. Thinking that Oscar's plane crashed— maybe ice formed on the wings.' She pushed the cookies and juice in my direction. 'You know how I am,' she said. 'Sitting up there thinking, If I were a movie, we'd all be anticipating what my face would do when I got the message about the plane crashing to the ground over Idaho. Thinking, And even if the plane does land safely, I'm still stocky as a fireplug.'

'Why do you have to imagine stuff like that? And you're not that stocky.'

'I am. And I don't always imagine stuff like that. I used to do stuff, not be scared. Remember when I used to ride on the back of Lionel Johnson's motorcycle? Remember him? He and

I used to be rolling through Strawberry Canyon when it was like eighty-five degrees and there was almost no traffic. My hair whipping around my head, all in my mouth, in my eyes—like a whirling crown. Man! A sister had on black spandex shorts and a yellow basketball jersey with a blue No. 1 on the back.'

She laughed, and I did, too.

'I even fell asleep on the back of that bike once,' Paige said. 'On that curvy road home from Stinson Beach. It was cold and I was in leather gloves and one of Lionel's big leather jackets. Knit cap on inside the helmet. Fell right asleep. Lionel said I was like a sack of oranges. I still don't understand how I didn't fall off. Lionel said it was no big deal.'

'How could that not be a big deal?'

'Don't know. I woke up feeling like a miracle.'

For about three weeks, Lionel had been a security guard at Diamond Pool. Paige, for about five minutes, had been his girlfriend.

'He and I were both like, what? Eighteen?'

'You were younger,' I said. 'Way.'

'Lionel could kiss, though,' Paige said. 'Meaty lips, pillowy mouth. Homeboy was soft and fat, clean and quiet. A walrus without the fangs. Remember I went to . . . I think it was his uncle's wedding? Wore that mustard dress Mom gave me. It was on a white yacht, we cruised the bay for five hours . . . I couldn't believe I was under that glassy black sky. The moon looked like a giant aspirin and there were about twelve trillion stars. I can't remember what Lionel and I talked about. Not just on yacht night. But over the course of our whole relationship.'

'The whole relationship was like ten days.'

'And your longest relationship has been . . . a weekend?'

And if it was? 'Why'd you like Lionel in the first place?' I had my own theory.

'Because he liked me. Because he was weird. Lionel could draw, though. *That* was what we talked about. He had all kinds

of felt-tipped markers and colored chalks. Easels. Blazing
lamps. I sat on his narrow couch nude so he could draw me. I
wasn't all scary and covering my stomach. I had sex with him
maybe twice. There were issues with the condom . . . like it was
too small, and he did it to me from behind because he probably
would have smashed me. I wasn't attracted to his body when it
was naked. Clothed he was all cottony, a wall of comfort.'

'You hurt that boy's feelings,' I said. 'You made him fall in
love with you when you knew you didn't like him like that.'

'Pinch, if people could make people fall in love with
them, the world would be a boring place. No surprises.'

'You hate surprises. And you did make him. You . . .
charmed him, so you could be adored and have sex and not
worry about whether he'd hurt your feelings.'

'I charmed him.' I wasn't facing her, so didn't know
whether she was pissed or complimented.

So I went on. In an excited voice. 'You choose guys like
Lionel—who love you way more than you'll ever love them.
Even if they don't know it yet. You even choose guys who aren't
that cute.'

'I like a safe ride,' she said. 'And anyway, Oscar's cute.'

'Being on that bike wasn't safe. And Oscar's got your
number.'

'Numbers change,' she said. 'Sometimes I thought I was
riding on the back of that bike in next to nothing because I
had a death wish. I mean, I rode with Lionel all the way to
Sonoma County once. It was so hot I could see grapes turning
to raisins on the vine. A hundred miles an hour, we went. A
hundred fifteen. He *loved* me on the back of that bike. I have
never had so much joy. Overjoy.' She stopped for a second,
like maybe she was picturing it. 'All that speed and not a worry
in the world. I could cry thinking about going a hundred miles
an hour and holding on so loosely. When Lionel let me ride

without the helmet, the tears blew into my hair and into my ears. Dry almost before I felt them on my face.'

'You didn't have a death wish.' *More like a life wish.*

'Mom thought I did. One time, after riding all day with Lionel, after cruising that maze of turns up in the Montclair hills, I spoke to Mom about it. Told her on the phone all about my day. I didn't feel brave or like a daredevil. I just felt excited, free, like a magic hand had been keeping me from falling. I sat back in that motorcycle seat—relaxed, Pinch, *relaxed*—and inhaled those eucalyptus trees. I stared into the swells and the crevices of the hillsides, looked deep in the deep ravines. Just thrilled at life and not being sad and just being involved with the world and a boy. I was fearless. Pinch. Me. Leaning into the curves. I spoke to Mom—'

'Did you tell her how you felt? Or was the story like you were just hot-rodding?'

'I told her I'd had an adventure. On the motorcycle. Told her where I'd been and what I'd seen.'

'Did you tell her how you *felt*?'

Paige ignored me. 'Mom said, "You know, if a squirrel so much as crosses the road and that boy has to so much as swerve, you'll be dead. Or all your skin and flesh'll be torn from your bones. Or like Seth's friend Victor in a wheelchair for the rest of your life." '

'She brought up Victor?' Up in Sacramento, a tractor-trailer had kicked gravel in Victor's face when he was on the highway, on his bike, without a helmet. Even in goggles, he spun out of control. Not that I'd seen him since, but it took Mom to tell the story. Never mind talking about the gruesome stuff that had happened to her.

'Yep,' Paige said. 'And needless to say, I haven't been on the back of anyone's bike since. No bullshit. Not since that conversation.'

'And you hold that against Mom? She was worried. You'd expect that, right? You'd want that.'

She hammered her heel at the footrest of my chair, launched an attack on it, jerk wrench jerk. 'Why does she want to worry about squirrels crossing my road when I'm grown enough to be on the road on my own? When monsters were living in the house with us, where was the worry? Where could I run?' Since the chair had been forced back to upright, I was closer, and turned to face her. Paige took steady, shallow breaths. Her eyes stared right above mine. Hated that cold void look. Trying so hard for me to read her mind. I didn't have to read it. I'd been there for the engraving.

'I just remember,' Paige said, every syllable an ice cube, 'when Oscar got to Solid Grounds. He told me I looked pretty. And I decided to take it as a sign from the magic hand. You remember when we got married that morning by that young Asian judge. He took me and Oscar's hands in his—they were soft, that judge's hands, like a bar of soap—and he said, "Be scared. But know you can do this."'

The judge had said that, in just the humorless tones Paige was using to quote him.

'I held those silver flowers,' my sister said, 'and with Oscar as my man I believed there really were hours at a time that I didn't have to expect terror and death.'

'I'm going to get you some more juice.' I got up to pull a sheet from the linen closet. One for me and one for her. She'd stretched back like the couch was her spot for the night.

'Getting married was like being on that bike,' Paige said. 'Doing the scariest thing made me unafraid, for a little while, of everything else.'

A WEEK later Cedric got out of jail.

Maynard and Jess were the only ones not with us when we

got tipsy on Amaretto at the bar in the Lake Merritt Hotel and then walked down to the lake itself and pointed at its Necklace of Lights. I counted twenty-four lights strung between each showy pole. And it went around the entire lake. Every night at twilight, the bulbs were switched on. I knew from field trips that the Necklace had been up for many years before World War II. Then after Pearl Harbor, somebody thought that a Japanese bomber would see the bright circle from the air and figure it for a bull's-eye. So the Necklace was turned off, and even after the blackout years, Mom told me it was neglected. Bulbs broken and hanging.

When I was in high school, though, there was a jar on every store's counter: LIGHT UP THE LAKE. There was a billboard on Lakeshore Avenue in the shape of a lightbulb. As money was collected, the bulb was filled in with yellow paint. Seemed everyone took notice. Paid attention to the news when a company like Kaiser Permanente made a large contribution. In Oakland, for a lot of people, you didn't go 'to the doctor,' you went 'to Highland' or you went 'to Kaiser.' When Seth worked at Kaiser, it seemed like a prestigious thing.

Kaiser gave lots of money toward the Necklace, and I wondered, the night the flip was switched, and Lake Merritt was lit around bulb after brilliant bulb, if Seth had had anything to do with it, if he was on tiptoe, one of the cautiously expectant faces in the crowd. At one point, before he began to rot, Seth seemed to like his job, in the way that you can treasure consolation prizes.

In any case, the Necklace was a victory. People had really put in their quarters. I know I did. Even when Oakland got on your nerves, the lake at night could make you glad and proud of everyone. My roots were deep in a place where people pitched in toward even a hope of brilliance. I'd take that thought with me, if I ever left home.

Even in September, it's green as spring at the park around

the lake. Paige and I climbed the two-story Pinocchio and then slid down through the cylinders the huge boy has for legs. When Paige went off with Ced and Oscar and Donnell, Ch'Rell followed me over to the hollow cement whale, stood staring while I pretended I was Jonah and sat in it.

Then we all met up again on the damp grass and in our nice clothes pointed to tall buildings our parents used to work in. All of us thick, as Mom liked to say, as thieves. It was great to have Ced back, but May and Jess should have been there. Ced told us he'd spoken with May, and that he and Jess had a 'family obligation.'

We gazed at the aluminum face of the wide Kaiser corporate building, where sky and clouds were reflected during the day, like a mirror. I counted twenty-eight floors. We talked about Rhode's and Capwell's and Swan's, the big department stores now demolished or standing empty that we used to go to with our parents. Then Oscar and Donnell and Cedric walked down a skinny pier and sat. Paige, Ch'Rell, and I stayed on the lawn. Soon Cedric's chin was on his chest, shoulders curved and shaking. We all went to Merritt Bakery, after a while, for pancakes. The lake lights behind and above us, a better belt for Orion.

Cedric was bigger. We didn't ask him how it had been at Santa Rita. Ch'Rell talked about Yannick and her new sofa-loveseat combination. I talked about how Planned Parenthood was really Abortion Capital of the World. I was sick of the place.

'I'm glad for the abortions,' I said. 'Saves a lot of pain.' Thought about how some of the patients take the IVs and the jaded employee candor breezily in stride. About a girl dragging in for her fourth abortion. Heard a few audibly praying for miscarriages, seen them sick from trying to induce one with herbs or cleaning liquid or cough medicine or cooking oil. Some wept through the sonogram, then stiffened on the gurney like new corpses, expecting boyfriends who never showed. Girls slashed questionnaires with ballpoint signatures, cursed men who bounced in with bouquets. I'd wiped up after a chick whose eyes were dry and hard as peppercorns. She bled through three maxi-pads, through her panties and pants. Refused to believe she was miscarrying at all.

'You need,' Oscar said, 'a different job.'

'Have you ever had an abortion?' Ch'Rell asked me, suddenly hot.

Ced said, 'Hey, hey. This is how ya'll been acting in my absence? Pinch, you know you don't mean that shit. And Ch'Rell, let up.'

'No,' Ch'Rell said. 'Have you, Pinch?'

I said nothing. Felt blood making my earlobes hot. The answer was no, but I couldn't say it.

'Well,' she said, 'then don't talk.'

Donnell said, 'These two been at it for a while.'

'Ch'Rell, have you ever had an abortion?' Paige's voice was heavy and honed.

Ch'Rell didn't hesitate. 'I've had more than that.'

'Pinch can still have her opinion,' Paige told her. My sister seemed so satisfied with defending me. And I felt relieved. And lame.

'So,' Donnell said, 'can 'Rell.'

' 'Rell, get off Pinch. She's over there trying to make it nice for people. Right, Pinch? Donnell, pass the damn syrup. You guys are supposed to be welcoming a nigga home.'

Defending me. Tired of it, mad at it. No, I never had an abortion. No, I haven't had sex over three times with the same guy. No, I haven't had sex more than three times. And? And what?

Oscar talked about new wheels for his car and his time at Whole Earth. Ch'Rell warmed up again, and Ced laughed at everyone's stories like they were old jokes. I'd nothing to say. He had on brand-new clothes, a creamy leather jacket. Cedric's hair was not as golden. His smile was still too wide for whatever the occasion.

Month: June (1980)
Day: Hot Saturday, cool Satur-night
Attitude: Need a boyfriend

Today was uneventful. I got up and went to work at the pool. Had horrible nightmares last night. I dreamed (if I remember correctly) that I was raped in the swimming pool locker room. It was so vivid. Then I found out who the rapist was and it was a friend of this girl I know. So I went to see her, and in the dream she was staying, for some reason, at my great-grandmother's house. I was crying and swearing that I would kill her if I could only get my hands on a pistol. But she was saying, 'Paige, Paige, don't.' Then I found the guy who raped me, he was black with short hair and had brown eyes (but I don't recognize him from my real life). I was pointing a gun at him and screaming and crying. I can't remember if I shot him or not. Then all of a sudden I was in the swimming pool with a lot of the girls from school and they were trying to drown me. Anyway, enough about my dream. The pool was crowded today. And I love the people I work with. My boss Kirby is a freak, a flirt, a fool, but he knows it, so I still like him. This boy I like called tonight, but I wasn't home. From Upward Bound. He goes to a rowdy school, but we're both going to the eleventh grade. We've hung out a few times. He's nice, I think, and cute, but he probably 'wants to be friends.' Pinch took the message, anyway. At the risk of sounding very teenlike, will I ever, ever fall in love?

CHAPTER 12

THE FIRST time I saw Cedric after his big, emotional by-the-lake get-out-of-jail moment, he was driving a new Subaru Jeep. Red. The time I saw him after that, it was midday and he was coming from watching white girls practice lacrosse near Cal's Stern Hall, was free enough to give me a ride to the city.

Cedric and I took the long way—through Richmond, across the San Rafael Bridge into Marin County, past San Quentin. Stopped at the mall in Corte Madera, got frozen peach yogurt with fresh pineapple chunks. Looked in a place called Hold Everything and Cedric wanted to know what's the big deal about cedar hangers. Low mountains loomed to the right, and we agreed it was ridiculous that we hadn't been to Mt. Tamalpais since grade school. Reminisced about posing for photos surrounded by sword ferns. I asked him if he remembered searching boulders for emerald serpentine and laughing when the teacher said 'virgin' redwood. How we hoped to but never saw a gray fox or a bobcat or a mountain lion.

Through a short tunnel, and on the highway with the top off the Jeep, I waved at people on their ten-speeds. They were airborne almost, they looked like androids with their helmets on, legs lean and encased in tight kaleidoscopic shorts. The Presidio in the distance was like a tiny deserted kingdom, and if Cedric was white, his hair would be moving like crazy in the breeze. As it was, his short waves were gleaming. We stopped behind a parked yellow double-decker tourist-mobile. The bay before us cold sharky blue. I needed to get to Magnin's, but knew I wouldn't.

'It's just a little-ass bit of ocean,' Cedric said, looking out. The wind at Point Vista was damp and blowing rough. We wiped at the corners of our eyes. 'So how's you and Oscar?'

'We're getting along,' I said, 'keeping the place together. We're committed.'

Ced walked out by the edge of the ground, stepped over the chains that curved between the short poles. There was a steep incline, but he stood there like yards of level ground stretched before him. 'I'm recommitted,' he said, 'to making Cedric happen.'

'You haven't happened? In twenty-three years?'

'I'm committed—'

'To selling. You believe it's real, a job.'

'That's what I believe? Didn't know I rated so much consideration. What do you think it is?' He laughed hard. 'A hobby?'

'A phase. A spellbinding phase.'

'Now say what my daddy says. Say there's a tax on everything.'

'There is.'

'I paid mine. And you?'

'If there's a tax for me to pay—'

'And there is.'

'I paid mine early.'

My hand was sticky with pineapple juice. I reached to wipe it on Cedric's jacket, but he arced his body dangerously over the ledge to dodge me.

'Hey!' he said, then came back from the edge, stood in front of a telescope, put a quarter in, motioned for me to put my eye to the small piece of glass. I saw a speedboat flit across the bay. I wished I had some lotion.

He said, 'I swear to God I love Oscar.' Said, 'Oscar's my boy, he's like my brother,' and when he said it to me like this—

he'd said it like this three times to me over the years, all serious but dreamy—I knew he was about to tell me what mattered to him most, tell me his definition of self. So I already knew his definition by heart.

About how his mother, Irene, all wound up from lupus, had told Cedric a few days before she died that he needed to figure out what he wanted to be and then become it, told him to find a strong girl, a sweet, healthy girl with boobs and a brain, have babies and send them to good schools and 'give your father something happy to talk about at work.' When Irene said she knew her other sons' souls were living in Cedric, Cedric was crying and said, 'That's not what it is, Mom, I'm just me. Michael and Eric are somewhere, free.'

Irene and Darren had been married eighteen years, had buried two soft-skulled, squash-yellow infant sons, had walked every Sunday since forever over to the massive A.M.E. church on Seventy-third and East Fourteenth. They sat for service, dropped checks for five dollars in the plate, walked back to the yellow-brick cottage, rarely speaking of or to Cedric beyond school and money and upbringing, rarely speaking of the other boys at all. When Cedric spoke of his brothers, and he never did to his father, Irene was angry. When Cedric said *Michael* and *Eric* as he had in the hospital when she was at death's door, when he was trying to illustrate for his mother the idea that he, Cedric, had his own self to be, Irene said, 'Don't speak their names, Cedric. You know me and your daddy don't speak their names.' Cedric's tears came hotter and bigger for a long time until Irene told him, 'You're going to have to watch your father. Feed him. Don't run over him.'

Cedric had said, 'But Mom, I'm gonna run at Nebraska. Deal with the cold. Wreck fools at all meets, mess around and go to the Olympic Trials. Finally learn how to pace myself. Train hard.'

Before the disease got there with cracking skin and weak

breaths and Irene always tired, she would come home from work or the church or from over to her cousin's, clear the counter, and pack pork chops with apples and parsley while Cedric stood at the kitchen table chopping spinach, smashing garlic, and measuring out water for rice. Irene cooked what Darren liked, sat with him while he and Cedric ate it. She'd rinse the plates for the growling old washer, and as it ran, as Darren listened to the A's or the Raiders on the radio even though they were on TV, as Cedric watered the root vegetables and butter beans out back or talked on the phone or read his schoolbooks, Irene would unwrap and broil with butter and honey the biscuits from the morning, and drink white grape juice with seltzer. She called it her aperitif. When the people at Kaiser told her about the lupus, Darren went to the store at the corner and bought her the stuff for a real one.

Cedric said his mom had been the color of a peeled banana. Was stout, good-looking, and short with woolly hair pressed smooth and swingy. She gelled down the stressed hairs that fell at odd angles, then braided the heavy straightness into a dense rope, the end uneven and frayed. To Cedric, the brittle fan of hair escaping his mother's metal barrette was a fringe, an accent on a coverlet perfectly created for his mother's brief spine.

His parents used to sit on the couch and watch Jack Klugman as Quincy. Rock Hudson on *McMillan and Wife. The Night Stalker* and *McCloud.* His father would wind his mother's braid around his wrist and lightly pull until she looked at him to stop. Cedric's dad would stop, and then he'd start again, staring at the television the whole time. As far as I knew, Cedric had the cord of his mother's hair in a cookie tin. His father refused to touch even the door to the closet in which his son kept it.

Cedric's life, right down to the fact that his father is a bus driver, was just real old school, and normal. Almost mystical, with the Mom and Dad liking each other and staying together after the babies died of whatever they died of. Ced still being broken by his mom's death and his dad's sadness. It was like *Cooley High* or *Good Times*. There had to be tragedy, or else how could everybody arrive at a funeral already transformed by the lesson of death? The choir would sing, and the people who could sing well, but who'd been living sexy and wild, they'd be there all puddle-eyed, bodies demurely cloaked behind stiff, pleated robes. Some female would fall out at the coffin, writhing in misery. Maybe that's what Irene had done at her boys' funeral. That's the only thing missing from Ced's definition—a choir stomp-sliding to the notion of being able to lay down a sword and shield, down by the riverside.

Of course, I know Ced's definition by heart. Down to the last detail. After one time, a person could recall the broad strokes of his story easily. After three or four times, all the details would be crisp and simple to recount. And if this is what you always see, in photos, paintings, movies, in your psychic memory of all things Oakland-black and distressing, you can fill in your own details. A muted color here. An extra baby there. Specific kinds of foods. Or an emotional detail—like a husband's attachment to his wife's hair. People will believe you. Because they know the definition ahead of time. They've explained it danced it drawn it watched it breathed it changed it drowned in it as many times as you.

YOU could stand under Cedric's eyelashes for shade. His eyes were hazel cracked with dark yellow and clear and shimmering brown, and for once he wasn't using them to distract, was looking hard at me like he did only when Oscar wasn't nearby.

Cedric said, 'If we were in Mexico—Ixtapa, *man*!' Said, 'I know you'd tan up some pretty red, or like cinnamon.'

Then he said, 'You're happy, aren't you? I can tell you're happy right now,' and I said, 'I'm happy to be by the bridge, but I know if I stand in this air too long with the fog rolling in'—and it was falling over the green hills heavy—'my eardrums are going to start hurting.'

Cedric cupped both his hands over both my ears and he smelled like Grey Flannel or Polo or something soapy-grassy and he said, 'Can you hear me,' and of course I could, but I shook my head no, and he said, 'You can't hear me?' and I shook, and he said, 'Yes you can,' and I said nothing, and he said, 'Stupid, but I used to think you'd end up with me.' I looked up at him like I'd heard nothing, and he said, 'You heard me.'

The smell of him was making me ill, though, and I knew why. The smell of almost anything was making me queasy.

'You're truly pretty,' he said. 'Such a girl.' Put his hands on my shoulders, the weight of them made my stomach tight with small happinesses, with guilt, with nausea. 'You make me happy just looking at you.'

Cedric moved his fingertips in my hair on my scalp behind my ears. I could hear it in my head, a comforting static. I closed my eyes to try to see me how he did. Lips and big breasts and legs, which I knew how to accentuate. Plump waist and my nails needed a fill. Decent brown skin, loose, long hair. Nervous Nellie, Chatty Cathy. Unbeliever. Hopeless, stupid, sad, and crying. Always falling in with a negro who says, *Hey, I love you. I kind of know you don't love me but you will, you will.* Even I know that much about me. In the black backs of my eyelids I tried to see more.

My nose and mouth were against Cedric's sweatshirt and then I turned my face toward the water and could see Alcatraz.

And Treasure Island. Oakland, big as day. The side of my face was on his chest, his arms around me. Mine at my sides limp. I leaned into Cedric's squeeze, held my breath against the cologne. He was sweet and beautiful. And kind of simple, I thought, for making up a story around me that could give him a thrill.

Cedric said, 'I'm going to feed you, let's get out of this cold.' Said, 'You want what? Clams? Fish 'n' chips? Rum and Coke? Tapioca?'

The thought of my favorites made me queasier. But I started laughing, and we were back in the car, then at Horizons restaurant on the harbor sitting over crab Louies.

'I want to know how it was for you in Santa Rita.'

'It's not like being in state prison. I mean, I don't think it is. Fools acted up. I guess I had to act up sometimes. Everybody in there knows they're not in there for that long, so me and the few people I chilled with, we just got done what we had to get done.'

'How vague is that?'

'What do you want me to say? Time passed slowly? It did. I wished I was somewhere else? Of course. I was scared and couldn't act like it? Yeah. But isn't that life?' He put his fork down.

'Then why are you back sell—'

'Paige. I haven't seen you in forever.'

'Okay, but . . .' Pushed my crabby-smelling crab away. 'What would you be doing if you weren't doing what you do?'

'Driving a bus?' He brushed bread crumbs from the table with the pinkie side of his hand.

'If you'd graduated from Nebraska.'

'Track coach, teacher or something.'

'You can't still do that?'

He took a gulp of his lemon Coke. Pressed his lips

together like he was drinking alcohol. I hated that gesture. 'What would *you* be doing if you weren't doing what you do? If you'd graduated from Cal.'

Hadn't thought about that in a long time. Never thought about it hard. 'It wasn't for me to graduate. I didn't even know what college was—'

'Didn't ask you all that.'

'I wish I had the science head to major in marine biology, but I took that one organic chem class. Dropped it.'

Ced looked at me with impatience.

'I guess I'd want to work, at a library, or a museum,' I said. 'Or maybe be a teacher, I don't know.' I could work at a library, learn the Dewey decimal system. Or work in one of those offices at a museum where they decide what artifacts are going to be displayed. A natural history museum. Could be responsible for all the tour guides. Make sure they were enthusiastic. I'd seen people with jobs like that.

'You can't still do it?' Ced raised his fork and began eating again.

'It's hard to think about focusing on school, just with everything that goes on, you know, with everybody.' Even to myself, I sounded retarded.

'You're bringing me news?'

'What if,' I said, 'you didn't know May or Oscar or Donnell? Or any of us?'

'I don't think about it like that. I mean, can you sit up here and say how your life would be if you hadn't met Oscar? And what if there was no Pinch?'

'If I didn't have Oscar, I'd be sad, but I'd have to deal. Without Pinch, that's not a thought.'

It was, though, because Pinch had this thing in her head about going to Seattle, but really it was about going anywhere. I could see on her face she was sick of our friends. Was probably sick of me. Wanted to be her own girl. Not mine, not Jess's or

Ch'Rell's. My sister had started looking at me sometimes like she wanted to commit me to Highland Psychiatric. Looked out the window of the No. 40 like all of Oakland was Fairyland, and as cool as it was, the shit just didn't thrill her anymore.

On the bus just recently, going from the Pseudo out to Berkeley for pizza, Pinch and I were on Foothill, and we passed Casper's Hot Dogs, where Mom went for lunch when she was in high school, and then by Diamond Park, where I used to work, and where Pinch and I went to day camp when we were real young. We learned how to fry doughnuts, and swim in the deep end. Pinch said, 'Let's go up to Diamond Pool.' She was watching me like I might leap at her.

We got off on MacArthur and Fruitvale, and before we could even get to the park where the pool was, Pinch said, 'Forget it.'

'I thought you wanted to go.'

'Nah. I'm being stupid.'

The park was halfway up a hill, anyway. We were standing right in front of Diamond Bowl.

'Hot dogs,' I said, 'are good in here.'

At the door of the bowling alley, Pinch said, 'I know you think about Diamond Park and the pool sometimes.'

I shrugged. I had good times there, bad ones. 'I did used to work there.'

She looked at me like I look at Mom sometimes.

WE ROLLED over the Golden Gate Bridge, past the Presidio and into San Francisco, and Cedric's eyes began to corrode over. I was swimming in my own fluids. Everything in me sloshing, blood rushing, bladder full, mouth full, stomach acids splashing up to my throat. Forced myself to sit as still as I could in his Jeep. Bring all waters to a stop.

'Life is cool now,' he said in a quick swipe. 'I'm happy to

see you. You need to fix me up with somebody. Somebody to help me get right. Get the few things I need to get done, done. One of Pinch's friends, maybe.'

'You know Pinch's friends. You are Pinch's friends.'

Cedric dropped me at the Embarcadero Center, in front of the Hyatt Regency, where I remembered Gram Liz staying with her friend, Melbourne, when I was little. It was new then, and cost sixty-five dollars a night for a double. Gram had said, That's high living, yes it is, but that's my Mel.

I offered gas money to Cedric, who had his own money to burn. He kissed me, said, 'Say hi to Oscar.'

I kept looking at him.

Cedric said, 'I'm fine.' He kissed my cheek again, shaking his head at my dollar bills.

'Cedric. So I should . . . still trust May.'

'He ain't changed. Maybe you've changed. May is nobody's leader. I don't know when you all put him up there like that. Must be some shit that's gone down while I was away. And anyway, you don't trust anybody, so the fact that you don't trust May doesn't really mean much. If I was him and I knew you didn't trust me, I wouldn't even be offended. I'd feel included.'

'Yeah yeah.' *I trust Pinch,* is what I wanted to say.

'With my situation it's not all about trust in a particular person, it's about looking out for myself and having some kind of faith that I'm going to be all right.'

'For some reason I trust you.'

'Yeah yeah.' He said the two words fast, like I had. 'My man O got the love. I got the trust. And that's the deal with you, right? Outside of your sister, you don't love who you trust, or trust who you love—that would be putting your eggs in one basket, right? I'm just figuring this out right now.'

'You need to be figuring your own self out.'

'I had seven months. I did. And I know what I have to do

now. Make some money. Get my daddy right. Then get to Mexico for a few days, or Hawaii. Yeah. Maui.'

His gold bracelet was shining and thick next to the steering wheel. The sun was saying bye-bye bye-bye, all fiery peach and ferocious. Then he was lost in the purple black.

CHAPTER 13

Paige and I sat on a green bench in the Piedmont Rose Garden. Ch'Rell was supposed to pick us up near there a little later, take Paige to Magnin's, and me home. I wanted to meet at the garden because I felt like I needed to see the places I liked before I could even think about going to Los Angeles, or anywhere away from Oakland. Even just to a different state of mind.

The night before, rain had fallen hard until dawn. Loud drops. Irregular rhythms. *Plat-pli-platting* in the dark green dimness of Funktown before sunlight. Evan was in my ear as drops hit Pseudo windows.

'You don't even remember,' Evan said, 'what I look like.'

'I remember.' Heart stretched open.

'Maybe you do, because you're never trying to see me.'

'I want to see you.' We'd been on the phone for five hours. I'd fallen asleep and woken up on the phone once already.

'Why don't you come up here to Davis, then? I ask you that every time I get you on the phone. I have about four cents in my bank account, but if you get up here, I'll get you back.'

I need to get a bank account. 'Maybe,' I said, 'if I come to Davis, I won't want to come back.'

'So you say. Where's your sister?'

'About her business. With her man.'

'Where's your friends? Jessica? Ch'Rell? Why're you home?' So much sun in his voice. He was pleased with himself for knowing their names.

'I've been spending time by myself more lately.' *Such a complete lie.* 'Plus my friends have been . . . going through their own things.'

'People starting to prioritize themselves over the group.' That's how he talked.

'There's no group. I mean, there is, but . . . people have kids now, and Ced's back and different a little. And Jess and May are having their problems.'

'And what about you?'

'You've asked me that thirty times in thirty different ways. I'm the same.'

'Life is difficult.' He said it like anyone else would say Life is good. 'It's another quote,' he said.

'Like "Home sweet home." '

WE HAD cool coffee in white card cups. Paige said she was pregnant. I repeated the word *pregnant* without adding a question mark, but she said, 'Yeah,' like I had.

Paige sipped. 'I told him and he said, "What are you going to do?" Then he said that we'd figure it out.'

'You heard him say "we"?'

'Yeah.' But I knew that by the time he'd said *we,* Paige would have been the way she was in the rose garden now— dead about the eyes and deaf to everything.

'When'd you find out?' I wanted to know. 'When'd you tell him?'

'A week and a half ago.'

'When's the last time you all spoke about it?'

'When I told him.'

We sat there in the garden, where a wedding erupts every summer weekend. Where perfume sways like heat, light keels through trees and splatters finally on brides' crepe de chine. Standing near where buds tied with wire and ribbon are held waist-high with relief or smugness or dread and sometimes love. I was thinking, How insane are those two to be in that apartment together, married, not talking about a baby living right inside Paige. Felt air pushing in on me from all sides. But it was like the air was in tight balloons, so I felt no breeze. The skin on Paige's face was usually almond, with dark yellow slightly showing through the brown, but at the rose garden she was dead brown old brown the brown that's left after all the brightness and beta carotene, all the good's been stripped and put to use elsewhere.

'How do you feel?' I said. 'Are you sick?'

'It's not gonna work out.'

'What's not? The relationship?' I walked a few steps, and faced her. It was chilly. We both had on coats zipped to the neck. 'The baby?'

'I can't picture it. Either one. Can't see it in my mind. What's Oscar going to say or do, anyway? He's not pregnant.'

'He's the daddy.' Even as I said it, I didn't know what I meant. But I had an idea, so I said, 'Maybe Oscar will say that he loves you and maybe he'll have ideas for names. Maybe he'll act right.'

'Maybe he'll say, "Paige, you should get an abortion because we're not ready to have a kid. And because you're psycho."'

'That's what you want to do?'

'I can go to Abortion Capital of the World. On your discount.'

'Don't say that like that.'

'You say it all the time. Not everyone needs to have kids.'

'Some people *aren't* ready. Some girls don't know how to make kids . . . grow up right. They weren't taught how. Maybe their mothers weren't taught how.' *Some girls.* Air pillows pushed in on me. I wanted to block them out with my elbows.

'You're fidgety,' Paige said.

She got up from the bench, and we walked from the rose garden down Lakeshore Avenue, looked in the sewing-machine repair shop like we had a reason in the world. We walked and talked like Paige wasn't pregnant, and then she said, 'Everything's gonna be fine,' like I was the one who'd made the announcement.

I pulled her into my usual check-cashing center. It was in a mini-mini-mall with a Laundromat and a closet of a dough-nut shop that also sold every kind of candy and every flavor slushy. I had a check for fifty dollars from Gram Liz. *Toward rent,* it said on the memo line. The check cashers worked be-hind Plexiglas. Once you got your photo taken and received a membership card, of course you could cash your check there—every tenth one for free. You could pick up food stamps, deal with Western Union, buy stamps, pay the phone bill, every-thing really, except have an account. Next to a bulletin board with enlarged versions of bad checks and handwritten updates regarding the perpetrators, there were smiling Polaroids on the wall of everyone who'd won Quick Cash at the check-cash-ing center from the state lottery.

In line with me, Paige said, 'Can you picture me a mom?'

'Like whose?'

'Just a regular one. Like Jess.'

Yes and no. Yes but no. I hope so. I said, 'Yeah,' but had hes-itated and she noticed. *Not yet. I'm sorry. Not yet.* 'After you have the baby, or decided what else you're gonna do, then after all that, when things are calmer, maybe I'll go away for a while.' My voice sounded foreign as I said it. But then it was like I'd gone to another country and was surprised at my own fluency. One person ahead of me in line. I changed my mind. I'd go to Wells Fargo. Mom had been telling me since the dawn of time I could open a savings account for fifty dollars. Then when I had a hundred, I could open a checking. Got out of line, began walking out of the center.

Paige just followed me, no question.

'What do you mean, "away"? Oh. Evan.' She said it that knowing way May used sometimes. Like she knew the deal already, had been knowing it. Knew how things were, how they would go down. Is it an Oakland thing? To act like you know? To—in some private, mental, graduation-like moment—accept that all you've seen is all there is of any worth that there could be? And what you assume from your East Oakland, West Oakland, North Oakland, Berkeley, San Leandro experience, what you assume from your life as a kid, is enough on which to base life decisions and lifetime attitudes? *Cops is tired of niggas getting over. Task Force is serious right now. That shit was funny. Not everyone needs to have kids. No. No. No. Spanish girls and bullfights. Knowing what the fight is. You don't have to act mad every time you get mad. Life is difficult. Be happy now, you'll see.*

'You don't even know anybody in Seattle except for homeboy.'

'I've told you and told you. He doesn't live there. He's from there. He's just told me about it. I'm glad to know about a different place.' I was going to have a bank card. That I could use at the outdoor computer tellers.

We ended up in front of the Grand Lake Theater. It's where Ch'Rell was supposed to pick us up. I looked up and down the street for her. No 'Rell, and Paige was going to be late. Stood behind the bus bench. I was looking at my nails when Major pulled up. I was surprised but not shocked. At some point, in Oakland, you end up seeing everyone.

Major didn't look our way as he came to a stop, the nose of his mother's car pointed just to the right of us. He got out, locked his car door with his key. Then it was, 'Oh, shit,' and he loped over, pulled Paige into an embrace. He had shoulder-length dreadlocks.

Paige said much later that he'd felt like a warm dream.

Major kissed her on the cheek when she was in the hug. He grabbed me up, too. His body was softer, more forgiving. I could smell the musk oil that the Muslims sell at flea markets in Berkeley. And there was cocoa butter in the breeze his body movements created.

'Dang! Right? How've you been?' *Always amazes me, a comeback.*

Paige looked frightened, like he might hit her.

'I'm fine,' Major said, with a big boom in his voice. 'Wow. How about you two?'

I said, 'We're good. You know. Paige is married and everything.'

'Yeah! I heard that! Congratulations! Wow, *such* a big move. So, like, about having *faith* and believing in somebody. *Wow.*'

'Just trying to do my thing,' Paige said.

'My*self*, I been clean for eight months. *Just* over that.'

'For real. Man,' I said. He was adding to my no-more-check-cashing-center gladness. 'So excellent.'

Major pulled one of Paige's hands into both his huge ones and said, 'How are *you*, though, Paige? *You* was my *girl*.' He shook his head without letting go of her hand, amazed and thankful. Emphasized words, almost sang certain ones. 'This is incredible. You *look great*. You, too, Pinch. It's a *trip* seeing you all. Just on my way to the *bank*, and *damn*!' Major was shining down on Paige, and I swear she took a half step back into the shade of the building. '*This* one?' he said to me, bragging. 'She was with me through some *bad* times. But you know, Pinch. You *know*. I remember some times—boy! Paige was my *rock*. She had to be tough, too—you know how she is, Pinch—she had to let a brother find his own way.' Then Major held each of her hands in each of his, swung them. Looked at her. His big smile was a beacon for me right then.

'I'm at this professional agricultural kind of school, down

near Barstow, it's great, it's different. It's what I'm doing right now. A decision I've made.'

'That is so good,' Paige said through her teeth.

'I been through it, no doubt. But you helped me so much, that's why God put me here today, to see you—and you, Pinch—and to tell you thanks.' He shook his head, still with the rock-steady grin. 'It's just great seeing both of you,' Major said, and I could tell he wasn't just saying it because it was the thing to say. Hugged me with his eyes closed. 'Always the quiet one,' he said.

And then kissed Paige again.

Paige and I sat back down at the bus stop. She slouched, feet way out in front of her. 'I wanted to mess up Major's little flow so bad just now. He doesn't even know.'

Had her hands burrowed in her pockets. Face open and accepting the sticky cold.

'I wanted to tell him right then that I watched a roach crawl right across his forehead once at the Pseudo, the very first time he came over.'

'What?' Tight emphasis on my *t*. She didn't hear me. Sat up straight, brought her hands from her pockets, grabbed the tops of her knees.

'Watched that roach like a movie. Helped him so much! I woke up and saw it come up from the back of his head and make its way down by his ear, and then up and across his forehead. I should have told him! Right now. I should have told him. *His girl?* If I was, I would have yelped and hit it, got it off him. But I let that roach walk on Major like that fool was trash or old grease.'

I could only look at the crowded triangle of sweat beads between her brows. With the back of her hand, she wiped the spit from her lips. Shoved her hands back in her pockets like she was punching somebody.

'Some of his friends had told me he was living in L.A.,'

she said, rocking back and forth. 'After that time I heard he was cracked out in San Francisco, sleeping at a church, trying to be a cook at a shelter. Then I heard he was working on an orchard out near Coalinga, picking strawberries and lettuce.'

I'd no idea she kept up with Major, thought about him. I would have thought Teddy. Paige licked her lips. Wiped at them again.

'"All he knew was football," Major's friend told me one time. "It's the only thing anybody ever wanted to deal with that nigga on." I thought of Major like that all the time, getting black in the sun, living a migrant's life, purifying his soul, finding meaning in simple things.'

A tiny victorious jump from my sister. She pulled a tube of lotion from her pocket. Flipped up the cap, squeezed out pale yellowness. Then the tube burped out clear oil. She fiercely rubbed it in. Tangled and untangled her fingers, massaged each thumb into a palm. Wrapped each thumb in a fist. Thrust both hands, with the tube, back in her pockets again. Looked ahead into the street, not at Major's car, nor at me.

'And now,' she said, rocking again, 'with those snaky-ass dreads, and that massive smile. He looks like a big, stupid chocolate sun. I hope I looked normal, but I was all sweaty, saliva was coming up from under my tongue. Like I was hanging out the window of the Pseudo, blouse filthy, mouth slimy, hair wild, hands ashy, and here comes Major—hot, tainted, safe, and saved. He's the fucking crack boy. Major should be melting himself. He ought to be running in milky rivers at my feet.'

Ch'Rell rolled up in her new Prelude. She was more than proud. Ch'Rell looked at her pager, said it was Donnell and that we had to find a phone. I hopped in the backseat.

'We saw Major,' Paige said, in her regular voice. She slid into the front. 'He looked fine.' Her eyes were still on a voyage elsewhere.

'It must've been a trip to see him, huh, Paige? Surprise, surprise.' Ch'Rell giggled. Her pager went off again. She looked at it like, *All right already.* 'Major was your big love thing.'

'He wasn't,' I said absently, not knowing if I was lying. Just wanted Major not to have been, so that Paige's words would mean less.

'Pinch, please,' Ch'Rell said. Her pager was blowing up. Desperate little bird. 'Back then? Major? Yes, he was. That was your sister's man.'

'He was not,' Paige said, looking for a radio station and then trying to check her lipstick in the mirror. 'He was not.'

WE STOPPED at a phone booth right before we got to the bridge. Ch'Rell jumped back in the car. In a hurry, she reported that Donnell had said Jessica was in the hospital. A private place called Providence. We turned around, rolled there directly.

I asked Ch'Rell, 'What *exactly* did Donnell say?'

'He said, Come on.'

Yannick was asleep in his car seat. Paige rubbed lotion— pink, from another tube—into her hands, said, 'It can't be that she's sick, so it must be that she's hurt.'

I wanted to say, *Stop! with the lotions!* But I said, 'Paige, shut up! Shut up!' at the same time Ch'Rell screamed, 'Be quiet!'

'You don't know.' I leaned forward between the seats and growled at my sister's defeated face. 'There is *no way*, Paige, that you can have any idea what's happened.'

CHAPTER 14

In the elastic hours before Jessica died, I crept from floor to floor. Jess needed more things in her room. To make it pleasing. My clothes were binding, so I stripped down to my stretch pants and sleeveless undershirt, stepped outside, for real air, and autumn winds showed up. My arms folded loosely around myself. Was just for show. I felt no cold.

May was out there while Jessica was in surgery, folded low in his Benz with a small brown bottle of liqueur. Lite jazz leaked from a thin opening at the top of his window. Ced sat out there, too, on a stone chair, except when he was going to the pay phone, answering pages. Oscar's dad leaned against a gray brick wall with his Winstons.

Padded over to the plush green lawn in Providence's parking lot. Sat down and felt chill wetness go directly through my pants to my skin. Who was I to complain of mud streaks, or cold. I was Pinch, but Jessica was dying. On long strides I was back in the waiting hall.

Maynard ran into the hospital behind me, panting and moist at the armpits. Like he'd had a vision. Or like he thought we might keep something from him.

He looked at everyone. No one looked at him.

Dr. Roland had already clenched Maynard's shoulder. 'Are you gonna tell them what happened?' I swear his teeth were chattering. Eyes charged. 'Tell them the truth. Tell them right now.'

May snatched his shoulder away. 'Or you will?'

In the hallway, when Paige, Ch'Rell, and I first got to Providence, Jessica's mother glanced at Maynard and the rest of us like we were due some pity, but that she wouldn't dredge it up. Sandra had on jeans with ankle zippers and a plain T-shirt. She had all Jessica's gold chains on her own wrist. When the doctors were with Jessica, her mom sat back to the wall, the crown of her head touching a cork bulletin board, chin tilted toward long rows of humming light. Then she'd lower her face, watch her husband watch himself shiver. She looked at jogging doctors as if they carried tools of slate and bone.

When he was able to rise from his chair, Dr. Roland went to the cafeteria and got heavy blueberry muffins, and tea and boxes of orange juice for his wife. She took none of it. He went outside to speak to Maynard, who pressed the button that wound up his window. Then Dr. Roland would stand just inside the door of Jessica's room, glance back at his wife. She'd say something like *They're helping her We need to stay out Let her concentrate on getting through the day.* Sandra would come in Jess's room by herself most of the time, and Paige and I would leave the bedside without having to be asked. One time we bumped into Maynard as he walked in Jess's room. We were on our way out, and away from him.

Jessica'd been shot. In she and May's rented house in Alamo. May was there, had gone with her to the hospital in Alamo, in an ambulance. But then Dr. Roland wanted her in Oakland. And he was with Jess and May when they got to Providence. This is what I'd gotten from Donnell.

May's head was turned from us. He was saying to Jess's father, 'I hear you. Don't say that to me again.' Maynard walked dead into me, and Paige seethed. 'Why are you talking to Dr. Roland like that?'

'Why,' he said, 'are you talking to me like you're talking to me?'

Square-faced nuns moved around in suede hippie sandals, wooden crucifixes over their bellies. White and placid as
pearl, the sisters seemed, in a way that was infuriating, to
already know the background and outcome of our story.
Ch'Rell, Donnell, and Yannick were dolls on a shelf. I trailed
Cedric as he paced the immaculate halls. He touched picture
frames and interrogated nurses about weekend drives to Napa
Valley and the moral mechanics of keeping wicked people
alive. Then I slipped into Jessica's room with cafeteria lemon
wedges for the water pitcher at the foot of her bed. Jess slept
and woke up. It was a tan, calm room except for the chirping
equipment, barred bed, and sour-cherry odors of free blood.

'Familiarity breeds contempt,' Paige said. She flicked a
remote at the suspended television Jessica'd never watched.

'Seth used to say that.' *It's a quote.*

'It's true.'

'Why are you thinking of that right now?'

'You heard the police are asking May about if he did it
or not?'

'I don't feel like he did it. Something like this.'

'He shot Todd.'

'Shut up saying that right now.' Brought my voice down to
a whisper. 'That was in the foot.'

'He could've taken a step up to bigger things.'

'May's not like that.' I wasn't as sure as I was trying to
sound.

'All of us should see less of each other while this is going
on. It's like we're stranded at sea with the drinking water dwin-
dling. Somebody'll be the devil. Somebody will be God.
Somebody'll be sacrificed for the survival of the rest.'

I tried not to think of that movie where the plane crashed
and the people ate the ones who died.

Oakland police were in the hallway talking to May. These
were different cops than I was used to seeing. No uniforms.

One white, one Chinese. They were less bossy-acting than the few officers I'd ever had contact with. Sounded like it was taking every effort just for May to put sentences together.

In her room, Jess's face creaked open. Her breath gurgled. 'Is Ree gonna be fine?' She lifted her head like it was two-ton.

Paige said, 'Yeah, Jess, yeah,' and Jess put her head down and was quiet again and still breathing. A braid wet as eels lay on her collarbone. Sandra had done it. Who knew how long we'd been there. Inside the hospital was an eternal predawn. I was sleepy and trying to remember what noons had looked like.

'May had been trying to get me to go,' Jess said. 'To leave Ree.'

'Jess,' Paige said, 'don't talk about it.'

'Where's my mom?'

I stood up and turned to get Sandra. I thought she must be with Ree.

'No, don't get her,' Jess said, suddenly not gurgly or any more tired than if it were any early morning. 'But she's all right?'

'Of course she is,' Paige said. 'Pinch, go get her.'

I stood in the doorway.

'No,' Jess said. Her arms lay at her sides, palms facing her thighs. An arm pale enough that you could see veins, the big one, especially, that the sac was feeding. 'Talking about we'd gotten married too fast. Saying he'd give me money so I wouldn't have to go back Above Upper High. I'd been screaming about that Kimya.'

Paige said, 'Don't talk, Jess. Get rest.'

My sister didn't want to hear the story. I felt guilty for wanting Jess to go on.

'Said I could see Ree when I wanted to. Like May's the only one who counts. I told him he could see Ree wherever I was going to be.'

I put some of the lemon-water near her. She didn't look at it.

'Told me I needed to start fresh. "You don't need to go into something new with a baby you had by the kinda nigga you had it by." That's what he said.'

I said, 'Did he sound serious, like he was in his right mind?'

'He sounded . . . practical. But still scary. Mostly because that gun was on the dining-room table in front of him.'

'What gun?' I said. 'The one he—'

'Pinch, shut *up* about that,' Paige said.

Oh now the Todd thing is off-limits.

'He'd already made a show of taking it from the hardware drawer and slamming it down,' Jess said. 'It was kind of like a souvenir-thing, that gun, and as far as I knew, there were no bullets in it. You know I wouldn't have a loaded gun in the house with Ree. May had agreed with that.'

'Jess,' Paige said, 'stop talking.'

'I will. But don't you guys leave.'

We sat. Seemed like she might have fallen back to sleep.

'May told me I had to go,' Jessica opened her eyes and said. 'Like he hated me.' Her voice had come back brittle. 'Went to pick Ree up from his playpen, and I said, "Don't fuck with me, May." He said, "Leave what's mine here. And keep your mouth shut about my business when you're in the streets." Like I'd say anything.'

'Jess,' I said, 'you should calm down.' Not like she was excited. But she seemed exhausted.

'But I did say, "What are *you* gonna do? Shoot me in my foot?"'

It sounded so stupid when she said it. Such a pitiful turning point.

'The thing is, there's this cord that's too short for the distance between the outlet and the table with my big lamp.'

She's delirious.

'And May came at me, pissed, so like he wanted to kill me he was almost roaring. He stepped down on that cord, or tripped over it, and the big gray light my mom gave us tipped to the floor like *boom*, like a bomb. Bulb glass and clay flew out everywhere. *Boom*.'

I'd seen that lamp on the gift table at Jess and May's wedding reception. That heavy lamp, with the mirrors pressed into it, and the shade with all the pretty slits. It had been waiting to fall since the day it was given.

'Shard from the lamp sliced Ree's leg open to the bone. He didn't even scream loud, and his leg, his little knockwurst leg, it was just split. Cut so clean it took a few seconds to bleed. Do you know how I was trying not to panic? I saw all these dots and dashes of blood all over Ree like some kind of pox. May ran from the room, I thought he must be getting help from one of the people on the block and I thought why would he when we'd never even said hello to any of them. I thought I heard chairs being moved in the kitchen, my metal kitchen table being rushed across the floor. I heard all these fast words, not even words I could make out, but expressions, they sounded mean and all this was happening fast, and I heard May yelling something and I wondered what he could be doing when Ree was starting to really bleed, and then I heard another voice, it was muffled and weak and trying to compete with May, and then Ree started to yell, and I'd already reached in the pen, thought I'd press the afghan against that biggest cut.' She paused. *'Then he moaned like a grown man.'*

Tears rolled down Jess's temples. Neither Paige nor I said anything.

'I heard a snap like wood popping in a fireplace and at the same moment I got shoved over the low plastic rail and into the playpen.'

'I don't understand,' Paige said.

Jess was lost. High, or in pain, or numb. 'Ree was surprised into serenity,' she said. 'By the noise, I guess, and . . . the pain.' She touched at her thighs through the blanket, as if to make sure she could still move, or feel. Maybe to make sure she was still there. 'Felt like someone had dripped boiling oil in my stomach,' she said, 'my breath lurched up wet in my throat. Then the pain started pulsing from a single place beneath my breast.' She tried to move one hand toward her belly, but weak as she was, and attached as her arm was to tubes, Jess just lifted it a bit from the blanket. 'I figured, with the noise, that I'd been shot. I grabbed Ree by his good leg, but I couldn't pull him to me.' Tears fell down the same tracks. 'I could only inhale a little at a time. Not breathing equals dying. *So this is dying. If I can't pull him to me, I'm at least going to look at him.* That's what I was thinking when I was laying there, but my eyes must have been closed.' In the hospital room, they were open and red under the bottom lids. Jess began speaking much faster.

'Then May was pulling me from the playpen and putting me on the floor and the afghan was under my head. He was on the phone saying, "My wife has been shot," and saying, "Jess, breathe, relax, breathe," like he had when Ree was being born. Then I woke up here. On these papery sheets.' Struggled to give a little laugh. Brought pain to her splotched, pasty face.

Paige said, 'You didn't see who did it?'

'No. But it wasn't May.' Jess got a smile to her face. 'See what happens, though? I just might live, but this has happened to me. I guess you're right, too, Paige, about tragedy being the only constant. I should have been on the lookout for all this, right? That would have stopped it.'

Jess tried to roll her eyes at Paige. I felt they might stay toward the back of her head. Sandra walked in, so Paige and I walked into an adjoining room to see Ree, who'd been set up in there. Sandra didn't even look at us.

When the doctor stitched up Ree in four places, we'd heard him crossly tell Jessica's parents that tiny pieces of glass would push themselves out of Ree's skin over the months and years to come. The doctor'd said, 'He'll get a pimple, and inside will be a fragment of glass or clay so small you'll barely be able to see it. Like this,' he said, rubbing his thumb and index finger together. 'You'll be able to feel it between them.'

Oscar's dad came over, gave Paige and I each a paper cone filled with water. Cedric and Oscar hung in the doorway. We had to speak softly. Ree was asleep. Thick white pad and gauze around one thigh.

'Is there some way we're supposed to be acting?' Paige said. 'Something we should be saying, something regular people would do?'

Cedric said, 'We're acting right. You see Ree is fine. Jess is gonna be fine.'

Oscar said, 'She better be fine. OPD's—'

'It was an accident,' Cedric said.

Paige snapped, 'You know that?'

'You know something else?'

'Where is he right now?' Paige said. 'May.'

'Out front,' Oscar answered. Cedric nodded.

Paige said, 'Guilty.'

My sister got up and went to the doorway of Jess's room. I followed, and Sandra waved us in. Her face held no more disdain. Her eyes were as adrift as her daughter's.

Paige had torn off her loose acrylic nails, so her hands were gross, randomly declawed. Her clothes were wrinkled and damp in places. We stood stiffly. Not entering. Dr. Roland was in shock, or what shock looked like to me. Zombie.

Then I heard our mom's voice, in the hallway. She was there, talking to Oscar's father about Where's my girls. Mom

walked over, said, 'What's up, Miss? Are you hangin' in there?'
Her voice was perkier than was warranted, but I was glad to
see her.

'Mom, how did you know?'

'Your sister called me,' she said, looking over at Paige.
'Upset.' Paige gave her a dry look that said, Don't brag. 'Plus
it's Sandra's daughter in trouble. Your friend.'

Mom was there. *Jesus.* Made me feel like Paige and I
weren't just out here, hanging. What did Paige expect Mom to
say? *Hi, my daughters! Are you all right? Is there anything I can
do for you? Come here, put your head on my lap, let me stroke
your hair. Kiss kiss hug hug. I love you both dearly and I am so
proud of you both for forging ahead through times of craziness.
Hug hug. I know you have a few problems right now, but
I am here to help in every way I can. With my heart, with my
mind, with my checkbook. Here are some ideas I have about getting you two back on track! Let's go see the counselors at Cal
and at Laney and do whatever we have to do to get you reen-
rolled. And I want you both to graduate and become profession-
als and be successful in life. I want you all to travel and see the
world. Be adventurous and studious and, please, come to me for
motivation and encouragement.* I don't know whose mom Paige
thought she had. I mean, Mom could be helpful. Sometimes.
She was just very sink or swim.

But Paige had called her.

Mom had keys in her hand. She had on white tennis shoes
and loose pants, bright smocklike shirt and hoop earrings. She
had postwork tiredness in her gestures, though, so I figured it
must be about six P.M. Mom went and talked to Sandra, they
seemed to remember each other. Sandra began to tremble, her
feet softly stomped the ground. Mom put a hand on her shoulder. Dr. Roland said, 'Gigi, you're lucky. Your girls, they've
been . . . wonderful. So present.'

It's not that we're wonderful. It's that we're not dying. Anything's better than that.

The temperature of the hospital in that last hour was so perfectly tepid I couldn't figure out where my skin ended and the air began. By the time Jess started talking about big abstract things and addressing comments to the wrong people, Dr. Roland was suddenly nowhere around.

Ch'Rell and Donnell had taken Yannick home. Mom was in the hall, I hoped with Paige. Oscar's father was standing by the bed where Sandra was seated. She leaned on him some. Wide tears ran down her cheeks and along her jawbone. Oscar's father tried to hand Sandra a handkerchief, but she didn't seem to see it. She'd been offended by us when we first got to Providence, but she didn't have space for it anymore. Maynard wasn't leaning on anyone or anything. He seemed rooted in an active fault, though, was biting down on his tongue with his side teeth.

Jessica's words were swirly and full of air. 'I try to be about other people,' she said, 'but I don't even know if I'm really like that with anyone, even Ree. Is love humbling yourself to the other person's ways? Giving the man what he needs you to be, even though you know it's not you, it's what you seem to be? Or wish you were? I thought me and May were doing that, but . . . I love you, May. I love how you made up this whole big persona for me and for everybody. I'm tired of not letting people know me, but maybe I did. I'm sleepy . . . worried . . . I'm like my baby, Paige, I don't know the difference between being nice and being weak . . . between being in love and allowing someone to pull me, biting and scratching, from a cave.' She was silent for a second. Then she said, 'What was I supposed to do. I didn't know.'

Oscar's father said, 'You had love, sweetheart, you have love. You have everything. You can have the things you want from life, do the things you want to do. Do anything in the world.' And I let myself believe he was talking to me, willed myself to believe that what he said was true for me, and that's when I really started wailing, but only for a second, or at least it seemed like a second or a minute. I stopped because it seemed pathetic to go on. I never really heard that kind of stuff to even know what it sounded like, to know what I was missing if in fact I was missing anything. Jess had probably heard it a million times, and look where she was.

Oscar was looking at his dad with suspicion. Like, *All of a sudden, you're Mr. Comfort-Giver, Emotion-Haver.* Oscar turned and left, maybe to find Paige. I couldn't blame Oscar for that fast, mad look because I was feeling torn-up myself. But like dramatics were unnecessary because I had life, I wasn't paralyzed or without my hands and feet. I wasn't shot. My baby wasn't sliced and stitched up and in pain. I wasn't sexually molested, nor did I have rickets from being kept in a basement for months at a time. My own mom knew, had always known, that I'd pull it together, handle it. She knew that about me and my sister. *That's not a bad thing. That's not a bad thing.* I started crying again. I was unbelievable to myself. But Jess was really going to die. It was clear to everyone. A nun-nurse paused in the doorway. She knew exactly what in Jess's body had been savaged. Maybe even knew who'd failed her.

I hated that. Wanted to tell that nun to share the information, or keep moving. Or she could tell me if Jess had failed herself.

I've never heard anyone's last words, but the last words Jess said in front of me were, 'Stop looking at me like that. I know I'm hurt. Go on . . . come back in a little while when I can sit up.' I don't think Jess died right then, but she was still. Sandra shook and shook. Dr. Roland was still missing. Maynard was frozen. I wanted to go to him. Jess was his wife. But I didn't know anymore what he would or wouldn't do. What he had or hadn't done.

I went in the waiting room, where Paige was sitting near Mom and Oscar, folded myself down on an ottoman. Paige came over, eyes pink. 'When I die,' my sister said to me closely, 'don't sit up and think about what I could have been and get all sad. Don't try to live your life better just because you see how quick it can end. Don't make me some moment of realization.'

I was going to implode. Everybody was accepting everything. Maybe Sandra acted sad, but no one was upset *enough*. *We can react to life. We don't have to be jaded, or even so mature that we take all that happens as just life. This is not life. This is not even difficult life. This is death. It trumps everything, right? This is fucked up and I do not have to put on a smiling face for anyone.* And if Jess had been in her right mind, if she'd been kicked back with a margarita and with Ree on her lap, she would have flipped her hair over her shoulders and cursed Paige for saying something like that to me. *I believe in tragedy.* That's what Paige says. *Shut up!* Jess called Paige on her cynical shit all the time. I mean, Jess was Paige's friend, but I used to hang around them and I remembered the hair dark on Jess's forearms, her short rounded nails when she let them go back to natural after Ree was born. The way she kissed her son with her whole face. The way she looked everyone in the eye at her clumsy wedding reception, the beautifully conceited way she looked when brothers checked her out on the street, in her clean-ass car.

She sat up and got snooty. Smiled to herself, and for them. Jess might've checked her lip gloss, maybe she changed her music from K-ROQ to K-JAMS. She'd raise her eyebrows, or poke out her chest. It was fun to her. It was living. You always love people more who don't love that many people. And she loved us. And she was gone. I heard the beep, saw blue scrubs hurry to the room. Sandra didn't scream, *No!*

I barely heard her, but Sandra said, 'Yes, Jessica. Yes, yes, yes indeed.'

s k y sprayed drizzle into scolding cold air.

The death markers, decked with links to the living, seemed to chug toward me on the thump of underlying heartbeats.

At Jess's burial, I was hazy.

This was it for me: the funeral, and then Good-bye. I would go to L.A., stay with Gram Liz until I got a job and could get a place on my own. I wanted out.

From a plain car, OPD surveyed the proceedings. Not with telephoto lenses or anything, but there were lots of dope dealers at the burial. Plus no one had been arrested for Jess's death. Mom said it was going to be ruled accidental. May wasn't saying anything to anyone about anything.

Cedric, lightning-eyed and silent, stood near Maynard and Oscar and Donnell. Mom was at the cemetery, sitting with us. Oscar's father, crisp under a brim and in his son's navy blue, sat on the aisle. Sandra was up front in sunglasses, looking like she'd tip over from the slightest breeze. At the church she'd bumped into a pew, run her stockings at the knee. Forehead on the back of the first pew, she'd quietly cursed and cried.

Wide-eyed and rashy, spine curved, and fingers raw, Dr. Roland looked to be on some drug I didn't know about. Because the doctor was useless, at one point Oscar's father said he was going to move up closer, to see if Sandra was all right. Mom told him he might want to stay put. Why he listened to her, I don't know.

I had the feeling chips of glass were in my eyes, so I closed them. Paige let me lean. It's why I was able to rest my eyes in the first place. Mom looked serene and in control, not like when I was nine and Mom was feverish, falling shoulder and breast from her orange cotton robe, forcing ten dollars on Paige while Seth tugged on her arm. At the funeral, this is where my mind went.

Mom was weak, had some kind of infection, so she was stumbling and Seth was calling Paige and me and Mom names like naive and moron and self-centered witch. Paige had already been shoved so hard in the chest and arms and neck with his spike fingers, she was sucking in air. Then he came at me saying, *What the fuck are you looking at.* Paige picked up a foot-tall wooden pepper mill and hurled it toward Seth's head. The mill missed him and shattered the vinegar and vegetable oil and steak sauce bottles that crowded the Lazy Susan, and the kitchen smelled like dinnertime. Seth told Paige, *You're not fucking leaving this house,* and he said that Paige didn't deserve to go to the sixth-grade picnic, where they had bowling and horseback riding and an ice rink. Told Paige that she wasn't shit, that she was a punk, and that her friends weren't shit either because if they were they wouldn't have invited her to anything.

At the funeral I was leaning and limp. People probably thought it was over Jess, and it was, it was about my friends, about Paige's friends.

How could Paige leave her mother at home sick, Seth wanted to know. *Look at your mother.* He had Mom by one arm and shook her into display. *She's a mess.* Mom was sweaty, her hair was damp around her ears. She threw Paige the lunch money and said, *Paige, just go, I'm fine, just go. Take Pinch. Get out.* Paige ran out the door alone. I thought she was running to school, but she got in Mom's car, it was parked halfway down the block. I ran out, and Mom came lurching behind me. Paige hadn't quite shut the door, sat in the passenger seat, her forehead on the dash. Tears and snot fell over the top of her mouth. Paige's eyes went scarlet, yellow-white mucus came to their corners and stretched between lashes. Her body boiled up a soft sweat. She shook me off and then shook Mom off. Paige said, *I don't even want to go now, I just don't want to live in this crazy house. I hope everybody dies.* I was scared and she finally said, *Not you, Pinch, not you.* I ran back, ahead of Mom, who was walking back to the house in bare feet, looking like she was about to faint. I grabbed Paige's bookbag and ten dollars. By the time I got back, she was standing by the car like it was a whale she'd beached. My sister smoothed her hair back into her ponytail, wiped her face of everything but heat. I was in the fourth grade and I went to the sixth-grade extravaganza. The bowling alley was a million of us and echoing pins and the high rapid ping of pinball scores. Fluted tin ashtrays and black wax pencils. We touched the fuzzed warm sponge of mare noses, ate corndogs with stripes of mustard, had money left for cola and ice cream cones.

In wobbly line on the rink with Paige's friends, we fell in a pile and rolled on smooth ice, electrified.

Was still on ice. Still running from home.

With Paige's friends, burnt to a crisp in the cold.

MY SISTER nudged me to sit up. When I opened my eyes, Evan was there.

It's not like homeboy was my man or anything, but he had to get on a bus from Davis to come there, and I'd only spoken to him once since Jess was shot. That was for a split second, and I hadn't told him what was going on.

Evan was taller than I remembered. It was the first time I'd seen him in daylight, only the second time I'd seen him ever. He looked pure and durable, as if born a windy yesterday.

'You want to go for a ride?' he asked me.

I looked at Paige, and then at Mom, and they both said, 'Go.'

Evan held my hand. I stumbled over a little dip in the gravel.

He helped me up, dusted off my dark green skirt, held my hand more tightly.

'How you managing?'

'I'm good.'

'I had to come down, see what I could do. Even up in Davis folks are talking about it. As soon as they said her name, and May's, I knew those were your people.'

'Talk about something different,' I said. 'Talk about Davis. Tell me a quote.'

He was still holding my hand. So tight it hurt but hurt good.

Evan told me that his new classes were fun and that he was learning about Caesar. Evan couldn't remember if Marcus Aurelius had been a good guy or a traitor to Caesar, and I wondered why it would matter today, at Jess's funeral, but Aurelius had said, at some point, something like the art of life is more like wrestling than dancing, and that the key is to always stand firm, and be braced for attack.

Evan stopped and waited until I was in a relaxed stance, feet set apart, and comfortable on asphalt.

'Life is more like wrestling,' he said, 'than dancing.'

It was the lift in his voice that made it sound like he said, Life is a struggle, so we struggle, and then we dance.

I'd danced with Evan. And I'd wrestled. Both were hard to do. Hard to brace. Hard to let go.

'You can get through this,' he said. 'You're braced. And you're better than all this, better than any girl in Oakland, in Davis, Seattle, better than any girl I ever met.'

'You don't even know me,' I told him, but even at Jess's funeral, Evan'd made me think about myself. And this time it made me happy.

'I almost know you. And I have this idea that you can handle anything.'

'Tell me another quote,' I said.

'"Humor is the last vestige of the nonconformist mind."'

That made me laugh, the way he said it, so proud he had another to tell me.

'I'm dazed right now by the funeral, by you being here, by me just wanting to go away from where me and my sister's friend is dead.' *From where even in this cold, I feel Oakland's July hand over my mouth and nose.*

Evan said, 'Hey girl, look.'

In what looked like his high-school graduation suit and brogans, with his duffel bag in the backseat of a borrowed car, Evan pointed to the sun. Too yellow to look at, it brought fever to my face, and sand went liquid in my hips and knees and eyes. Fuzz in my ears dried to fine powder. I shook it out, squinted my eyes, stretched my body.

Didn't turn back toward the funeral or Paige or Mom or anybody. I wanted to kiss Evan but didn't.

Looked up instead. Directly into the sun this time so I saw nothing but fireball and halo. It made me dizzy, had to shut my eyes. But I didn't fall.

From continents away, I thought I heard Evan say my given name. Jesus, it rang! Sounded so new it gleamed, made me want to look.

So I opened my eyes, and everyone, everything else was lost in a radiance of black light. There was just me, the hot kernel of me inside, and my name. Above me the sun hung ringed and radical as Ezekiel's wheel, way in the middle of the air.

Month: Same as it was yesterday, still 1982
Day: Fuck the day
Attitude: Can you not tell by now???

Am I supposed to just be the absolute worst
person in the world? Am I supposed to listen to the
stories Mom tells and just accept them? Am I the kind of
person who just takes shit and takes shit and then ends
up killing herself, supposedly on accident? Mom doesn't
say NOT ONE SINGLE WORD about Seth. DOES SHE HAVE
AMNESIA? I wish I did. I hate St. J's I hate Diamond
Pool I hate everyone but Pinch. Pinch brought me
almond lotion today.

CHAPTER 15

OSCAR AND I got up early the Saturday after Jess's funeral. He drove south, passed Monterey before ten o'clock. I curled next to craggy stones, lay on the beach hidden by sand grass. Highway 1 was curve twist slow turn curve, and over the side sometimes a thousand feet down was water like weak ink, so I dove in, got bluer. Made myself a crown of kelp, dove with otters for abalone. Underground mountains stuck their heads up offshore, and I was atop one, shivering and searching above for upper and high. Came back on land among the red rock red dirt and redwood trees. Then I stretched flat and spread out like a veil over everything.

'See the water?' I said.

Oscar was moving at forty miles an hour. Speed limit was twenty-five. He glanced out my side window, said, 'Yeah, that is pretty.' But mostly he kept his eyes on the road.

I looked at the speedometer. 'It's not like,' I said, 'we're even going anyplace.'

'We'll be fine. We're not going to crash over the side.'

'Why would you even say that out loud.'

After a while, an RV in front of us kept Oscar at the limit. Forearm muscles tense and fingers clamped on the steering wheel like he wanted to mow it down.

The hills were draped in clouds and smoke from a fire somebody was talking about on the radio. Feeble flowers, a few hungry bees. Fog on the horizon, where the ocean softened to milky sky. I didn't know enough about geology to know why land stopped where it stopped in the way it stopped, random jutting broken grandeur. To make a coastline. A boundary, an end.

Endangered brown pelicans bobbed on swells. 'Where're we going?'

Oscar said, 'We'll get there.'

At a house in San Luis Obispo with olive trees in the front yard there was a moving sale. Oscar picked up an old milk bottle and I got happy. He picked up a pair of shiny, Asian-looking hair combs, and then candlesticks that looked like men with sombreros. The house with its porch and no other house for a while. Daffodils and a clothesline. I didn't know why the family would ever move or throw any of their things away.

Oscar bought his picks for six dollars, said, 'Let's go,' like a kid and grabbed my hand.

I started getting sad like a cornball and Oscar held on to me.

'That's why we came out here,' he said, 'to get away from all that. Think about what we're going to do about us, and the way we're living.'

We checked into an inn, drank iced tea with mint leaves and slices of tangerine. The room was small, with green apples and red pears in a wooden bowl. The bed was the same color as the apples and the coverlet was the plumpest and laciest I'd ever seen. Oscar stripped me down, stripped himself down, unhooked my bra, held my breasts up with his hands. It was a joy to not feel the weight of them, like two five-pound bags of C&H sugar, hanging from my chest. We stood there for two or three minutes, until he carefully let them go. Then Oscar lay on his belly, his chin on the pillow.

'It's not fair,' I said, 'that May has Ree now.'

'Let it go. Even if it's just for today.'

'No. I don't care what anyone says, May killed Jessica and we're all acting like he didn't.'

'We don't know. May says he didn't do it.'

'That's all he says.'

'Come lay by me.'

'I hope somebody shoots him in his heart. I hope he dies over and over again in a painful way every time.'

'May's your family. You've known him as long as me.'

I slipped back in my top, sat on a huge chair in that and panties. 'I kept it together, right? At the funeral. I didn't accuse May. I saw his fake sadness, I saw him look at Dr. Roland and Jess's mom, they were just in a daze, like an inch away from coma. They didn't even have the wherewithal yet to try and stab him in the face with a fucking rake.'

'Paige. With the melodrama. Please come lay down by me.'

'What is it with the "Come lay by me"? What will that do?'

He sat up, hung his legs over the sides of the bed. It was so tall, his feet grazed the braided rug. 'I'm not going to talk if you yell.'

'Can I be upset? How can you not be upset?'

'I am upset. I can't believe I know someone who's suspected of killing someone else I know. Right now I can't believe I sell crack, my friends sell crack, Jessica is dead, and all I can do is run down the highway with you like that's gonna fix something.' Flopped back on the bed, face to the ceiling. 'I want to move.'

'Like you moved from Nebraska.'

'I moved from Nebraska because I wanted to be with you.'

'We got married fast. Almost like—'

'Like I was looking for a reason to get away from Nebraska? I know I know we've had this argument ten thousand times.'

'So it's just fuck something up—then run. Then fuck something else up and then run some more.'

He got up off the bed. Took a few steps over to the bureau, turned apples over in the bowl. He pulled his gray jersey back over his head. I tossed him his underwear.

'My friends—'

'Aren't your friends. Aren't my friends.'

'I was gonna say my—our—friends are changing. We used to have . . . other plans. Get in, get out. Get through school. Find some shit we liked to do.'

'Why'd you start selling.'

'I don't *know*.'

'Who said it? Who said, "You know what we should do? We should sell dope"?'

'It wasn't like that.' Oscar sat back down on the bed. 'Donnell—'

'Donnell?'

'Donnell was always trying to impress May. And after May had shot Todd, we were just high on life. I was bugging. On some level I was amazed that we'd done something so . . . concrete. It was a reaction what we did, but it was still an action. We—or I should say, I—didn't feel like a kid after that. Didn't feel like some run-fast nigga who lucked out with the scholarship. I was supposed to be so grateful. Always, always, it's been for me to feel grateful. For the free tutoring at the boys' club. For the fact that my mother was what they called functioning instead of a nonfunctioning . . . drunk. For the fact that I got what they tell me was top-notch therapy because of this program where psychologists donated their time to kids of addicts. Here was me—always saying thank you so fucking much. People had the nerve to say to me, Oscar, you're so lucky. I wanted to say if I was lucky, my dad wouldn't be off fiending, my mom wouldn't be living for Cutty Sark. But say all that and a nigga's feeling sorry for himself, so shut up, shut the fuck up and be happy, count your blessings, go off to Nebraska. Right? Right. But after May shot Todd, I didn't have to feel lucky. Fools were scared of us. And just because of that feeling . . . of being, I guess, feared, I felt grown enough to be married and take care of a wife. But I had no way to do it.

Being there when May shot Todd, and not being able to give you what you wanted—those two things didn't go together.'

'What did I want.'

'No worries,' Oscar said. 'A life.'

We sat there.

'Don't give me that fucked-up look,' he said. 'That dead look.'

'What about Donnell?'

Oscar sighed a short strong sigh. 'Don had actually been making a few . . . runs for this nigga from his neighborhood. You know I was making mine, too, from when I got back from Nebraska. And then at some point, Don said something like, *Fuck Todd.* Maybe it was that day, after you, me, and Pinch went to the aquarium. We—I—started saying, "How's Todd paid and we're not." Things escalated. May started saying he was tired of school and not having any money and Donnell was tired of school and I guess so was I. Supposed to be the cool-ass athlete, but it seemed like the coach couldn't stand me after he'd been so backslappy when he was recruiting. And there were guys on the team who were like . . . I don't know, they just seemed way faster and more committed. Cedric and I, we had each other, so we didn't fall in with the other guys and there were all these white girls trying to get with us and it's not like I wasn't fucking them, I was fucking them all the time. Was I playing myself? Yes I was playing myself. The white girls that liked me truly for my . . . self, or seemed to, I didn't really like and was laying up with them, anyway. And the ones who I could tell liked me because I was black or fast or different or exciting, those were the ones I found myself liking more. To be held out like that as special . . . you know this, why am I telling you this again.'

'Just tell me.' I'd heard it before, some parts of it. But I'd listened in bed, when we'd first met, when everything about him sounded foreign and dramatic. I needed to hear everything again, outside the glitz of lovey-doviness.

'I was starting to smoke all the time—weed, not crack, you know I wasn't smoking crack—but I wasn't going to class. I didn't understand what they were talking about in there, I didn't understand how all the other kids seemed to just read the books and take the tests and go to practice—the white ones and the black ones. I wasn't getting it and Cedric was no help. Pretty soon the coach sent me to some counselor for the athletes. And she didn't know, she *couldn't* know shit about my life, at school or at anywhere. And May was calling all the time from home, talking about Hayward and just seeing everybody we know all the time. I was running up phone bills calling folks here. It's stupid but I guess I was homesick. Felt like I was disappointing everyone, was about to disappoint everyone, and at the same time it was like who gives a shit if I make it through Nebraska? Nobody would really give a shit if I completely fucked it up. And I was mad at myself for thinking that it was anybody's job in the first place.'

'Why'd you start selling dope.'

'You want to know what you want to know.'

'I want to know you better.'

'The reason I sell isn't the road to that.'

'It figures in.'

'The road to knowing me better is listening to me.'

'Then tell me the rest.'

'I started because it was easy. I could, I can do it in my sleep. I do it when normal people are sleeping, anyway. You buy it from some fool who's more evil and fearless than you and you sell it to fools who think you're more evil and fearless than them. It's not scientific. You buy it you cook it up you bag it you sell it. You make a lot of money, you try not to get caught. You have to trust your friends.'

'You don't trust me.'

'You don't need to know the bullshit that goes on. You

need to listen to me. You used to talk. About you, about me. Back when I was visiting you from Nebraska—'

'That's why May shot Jess. She knew the bullshit that was going on.'

'Say that as many times as you want when we're down here, Paige. When we get back to Oakland, you can't be saying that. You're not listening to anything I say.'

'I thought we were moving.'

'Don't say that to anyone, either. Will you just come over here by me?'

I went over, sat on the bed near him. Looked in my purse for cucumber lotion with lanolin and rose hips. Worked it into my toes and heels. You have to work it in, really let it absorb.

'There you go,' Oscar said, 'rubbing stuff into yourself.'

'Is that what I do?'

'Like it'll make you better. You're supposed to let your man rub you, hold you. That's how you feel better.'

I kept massaging it in. 'It makes me soft.'

'On the outside.'

'So I'm hard on the inside?' I wondered what he knew about my insides, aside from him, inside me, making a baby. I stopped rubbing. 'What about you?' Pressed out more lotion for my hands.

Oscar took the bottle. He looked at the label, then placed the container back on the fringed stand exactly, and began turning it, like he could screw it in. The lace doily began winding. Oscar stopped, like the screw had hit steel. 'You're questioning me,' he said, 'about why I do what I do and how I deal with *our* friends and I guess you're asking me about my conscience or my morals or maybe you're wondering exactly how I was raised. Maybe you think I'm a coward, a follower, or I'm too trusting of unworthy people. Maybe you think I'm on some all-the-white-man-has-left-for-me-is-selling-crack type shit. Maybe you think

I'm stupid because I couldn't hang with school, maybe you feel sorry for me because my father was a smoker and my mother drinks. Maybe you think I'm smart and I have so much potential—if only I'd get a real job or go back to school. Maybe you think I'm one of these people who's in it for the thrill. Maybe I'm all those things. You fell in love with those things. Be in the bed with those things. And you look disgusted with me right now.'

He was still on the bed, deep in thick poufs. Kept talking. Every word round and complete.

'You, though,' he said, 'you're above it all. Paige prances around like she knows who killed who. Raises her eyebrows and makes like she'd never sell dope. You have a look on your face like you know who the fools are and who they aren't. Paige. So what about you? How'd you come to find yourself married to a dope dealer? Why are you crying at the funeral of a girl you think was murdered by a friend of yours? Why do you still live in tired-ass Oakland why haven't you graduated why are all your ex-boyfriends crackheads buck-toothed bull-shitters fat boys, jokes? Why do you look over your shoulder like a monster is chasing you? Putting yourself around people you feel better than. You kill me, wife. You wouldn't know yourself in the mirror. You think you know everything. Who killed Jessica. How Cedric got put in jail. You think you know everything. You don't know a goddamn thing.'

He inhaled, then blew air out like there was a balloon at his lips.

'I was going to say that I hope you die, too,' I told him. 'But no. I don't. I'm tired. I can't talk anymore.'

Oscar fell, arms out, back across the swells. I wished I could hate him.

I picked up the lotion, kneaded it into my cuticles, said, 'You still want to leave?'

He said nothing. I was sitting up. He was laid out, his expression in the small of my back.

I said, 'You still want to sell?' Because nothing he'd said changed the facts of anything.

'I don't know what I want to do.' I believed him.

We slept awhile, and then from the edges of the bloated bed, Oscar and I inched toward the kind of clear, sticky sex we hadn't had in a while. Smelled like mint in middaylight, like moist minerals in clean, wet dirt. Oscar said, 'Say you don't want me to die,' and I said I didn't and I meant it.

In the morning, Oscar took a shower and then called May. As soon as their conversation began, I went to the bathroom. Came out wrapped in a towel appliquéd with blue and green fish. Wanted to steal it.

'May says shit is crazy.' He was dressed already.

'I bet it is.' I'd oiled myself in the bathroom, away from his sight. Began getting into my clothes.

'Him and Ced have some things they need me to take care of. We need to get on back up to the bay.'

In my pants and top, I stretched out across the ridiculous bed. The sky outside was hard and lined with tan and gray, like real turquoise.

'You don't want to go.'

'It's what you want to do.'

'It's not.'

Oscar and I hopped in the car, and I felt huge relief when he continued south, away from Oakland. It wasn't until Pismo Beach that we started seeing palm trees. We stopped there, sat in the car, watched waves whip and darken and dissolve. A group of students listened to a red-bearded tour guide say that 'pismo' is from the Chumash *pismu*, which means tar, for the natural oil seepage near the shoreline. Someone asked, so the guide said also that a marsh is where salt water meets fresh. In green rubber boots and shin-deep in water, the man tugged at tall stalks, and spoke in the paced tone of someone sharing a worthy if narrow expertise. Marsh plants such as salt grass can live in salty soil, he said. The roots take salt in, and the blades sweat out crystals for the rain to wash away.

Oscar took the car out of park, said, 'I never knew that. That makes sense to me.'

WE DROVE the coast. We could get gas and end up in Baja.

The junction for Los Angeles, 6 MILES. That's what the green-and-white sign announced.

'You want to go meet my grandmother?'

Oscar was surprised but said, 'Why not.'

I knew the way there, and figured Gram Liz would have just got off work. Sure enough, when we pulled up, her face was in the trunk of her Oldsmobile. She saw us, and said in her scratchy voice, 'To what do I owe the pleasure?'

I kissed her quickly on her lightly rouged cheek, and she shook Oscar's hand.

'So you're the one who stole my grandbaby away.'

'I guess so.'

'Come on inside,' she said.

I hadn't been there in a while, since high school. Gram looked good, asked about Mom, about Pinch. She didn't say, *What are you doing here all of a sudden?* Her house was immaculate, as it had always been.

I didn't have that much to say. Didn't know why I'd wanted to come. Oscar picked up the slack.

'We might be going away for a while,' he said. 'Moving.'

'Moving, huh?' Gram Liz said. 'Where?'

'We're thinking New York City.'

She didn't blink. 'That's a big move. When's all this happening?' She looked over at me. 'You taking your sister?'

She said it like I'd never leave Pinch. If Oscar and I left for New York, for San Diego, or for anywhere today, I could leave Pinch. She'd be okay, maybe even better.

Or maybe she'd come with us. If I asked her, maybe she would.

So I rolled with Oscar's flow. Didn't know if he was telling the truth or making up stuff.

'Pinch,' I said to my grandmother, 'is into the idea of me and Oscar getting away.' We were in her spotless living room. On new chairs as plump as the inn's.

'So we're leaving,' Oscar said, 'probably in the next few days.'

Then I was shocked. Gram saw it.

'So what's your plan?' she said to Oscar. 'Do you have money?'

'We have some,' Oscar said. 'Yeah.'

'A place to stay?'

'We will.'

Gram Liz looked at me. 'And what's your mother say? She's worried, I bet.'

'About what?'

'About you going off to the other side of the country. In the next few days, no less.'

'She'll be all right.' If a squirrel jumped in the road this time, it was my skin and flesh to lose.

'I like your husband, Paige.'

Oscar produced a smile.

'I just hope you're not running from your mother.'

'There's a lot of stuff going on that you have no idea of, Gram, and Oscar and I, we need—'

'Okay, okay. I know you feel like no one else has lived but you. No one else has got married young or dropped out of school or had to help with their sister or had to work penny-ante jobs they didn't like. No one else has ever had a lot of stuff going on. Have you ever thought somebody might be able to help, if you asked?'

'When did we become the helpful family.'

'Sometimes we don't get what we want, Paige, we get what we need.'

'Thanks, Gram, for that wisdom.'

Oscar said my name.

'You are so . . . pissed,' Gram said. She waved her hand. It was dismissive and empathetic at the same time. 'I guess you can be what you want to be. But the fact is, you needed to be out of that house with Seth, and you even needed to be away from your mother.'

'Is that a fact.'

'It is. And you sure didn't need to be with me. Evil as I am, and as much a mess I made of Gigi. Don't be mad at yourself, though, for being strong enough to deal.'

'Don't,' I said, 'be happy with yourself for having had Pinch and me deal with shit that you all should have handled.'

Oscar slowly stood. 'We probably better go.'

Gram stood up, too. I didn't hate her. I just didn't know her. Didn't know what I'd hoped for by coming to her house.

'Are you all really going to New York?'

Oscar said, 'Yes.'

I said, 'Sorry for cursing.'

'You been cursing me,' Gram Liz said, 'since you were twelve.'

And then Gram got on the phone with a travel agent. It was decided Oscar and I would leave the car at her place, take the one-hour flight to Oakland to get some clothes, and so Oscar could get his money, and then we'd fly from San Francisco to New York. The next morning. Tomorrow. Six hours in the air. I didn't know whether to be happy Gram Liz was taking so much interest, or sad that she was pushing me off again.

At the Los Angeles airport, after we picked up our tickets, Gram said a warm good-bye to Oscar and then said, 'Walk me to my car, Paige.'

Once there, she gave me twenty dollars. 'I know Oscar has

money,' she said. 'And I think I know why. He seems like a nice boy, but let me tell you something. You get to New York. You get a job. Get your own money. It'll be good to get away from your sister for a minute, away from that responsibility.'

'Pinch lives on her own, Gram. It's not like Pinch is my . . . exact responsibility anymore.'

'You think that, but you listen to me.'

'No, Gram, Pinch isn't a drain. She never has been.'

'You love her, she loves you. That's forever, and you're lucky. But you get out to wherever you're going and you think about you. Marriage is fine, but marriages come and go. You think about you. Let Oscar think about Oscar, let Pinch deal with Pinch. She probably needs to see who she is without you, anyway. And if that boy gives you the least trouble, you call me, and between me and your mother, we'll get you back to California so quick—' She stopped, like she was catching herself. 'I know you're not one to ask for help, Paige, and like you said, this isn't the most helpful family. But being lost around the corner is one thing. And bad enough. Being lost out on the other side of the country is something else.'

'Oscar's not going to give me trouble, Gram.'

She got into her car. 'Don't be getting pregnant all fast, either,' she said as her window whined down. 'You have plenty of time for all that.'

WHEN WE got on the plane to New York, the first thing I did was imagine the crash, of course—got that out of the way. Then I read the safety instruction booklet. The beverage cart inched toward us.

'You know,' Oscar said, turning to me, 'we need to talk about the baby.'

I pulled out my crossword puzzle magazine. Held my pen in my hand, got all accustomed to the *grrrrrr* of the engines, and I started figuring out six down and eleven across and then looked out the window. Disturbed by the rumbling stillness. I was glad for Oscar's presence but scared enough to be relieved when I looked down and saw lights organized enough to belong to a familiar civilization. Sipped my Lipton with the red plastic stick in it, relieved, too, that I must be still alive and of the earth if not on it, and hopefully not dead a second ago and experiencing the last moment of perception allowed by God and the devil. How could I know that a second ago the plane's engines hadn't exploded? I've known since I saw that snake in the road in Sacramento that horrifying death would happen in a moment when I was comfortable with the sound and speed of living.

24 Across. Searched my brain for a seven-letter word in which the second letter was *t* and the fifth letter was *i* and the last letter was *n*, but what showed up in my head was Seth pointing to the night saying *What's that* and I'd say Sky and he'd say *After that* and I'd say Stars and he'd say *After that* and I'd say Planets and he'd say *After that, stupid* and I'd say God and then Air and Atmosphere and he'd say *After that* and I'd say I don't know and he'd say *That's the kind of shit you need to be thinking about instead of sitting up in here with that bullshit Nancy Drew.*

Coast of agony. That was the crossword clue.

I'd already imagined, on purpose, that Oscar and I would have the baby. It'd be a girl, she'd be cute, and Oscar and I would find a two-bedroom apartment and he could find another Whole Earth Access, appliance-selling-type place to work and we'd just be a family. Oscar didn't have enough money to last forever, but I bet he had at least forty-five or fifty thousand dollars. After the baby, I'd get a job, too, and the girl's hair would curl and gleam and escape from green barrettes. Her face would have cheeks so swollen they sagged, and her eyes would be gray like Pinch's, bright as stainless steel. She'd gnaw on plain crackers like Ree and I'd come home from my job—at a big natural history museum or zoo or a library—and bathe her in the kitchen sink. Sipping my tea, I thought about all this.

Oscar said, 'You won't even discuss it? Time's passing.'

I nodded slowly, like, I know time's passing. I got the clock in my belly.

When we got in the cab in New York, I wanted ginger ale. Oscar got some for me at a deli near the hotel, sat by me in the room while I sipped it. It was one of those hotel rooms with a mini-kitchen. Embassy Suites. 'So we're going to have the baby,' he said.

'What would it be like?'

'Like Jess and May used to be when they first had Ree. Cool.'

I pulled out my crossword again. 'And if we didn't have it? We're about to the point where we have to,' I said. 'But if we weren't.'

'If we went to a clinic? It'd be all right.' He seemed to have no agenda. Wanted just to settle on one way or the other.

'It wouldn't be kinda sick? Wouldn't we be dancing to the music and not paying the piper?'

Oscar said, 'The piper isn't as mean as you're thinking.'

In the puzzle, I penned in *Stygian*.

'We'll get settled,' Oscar said. 'Get our heads together, and then we'll . . . decide.'

'Do you *want* to have it?' I finally asked him.

'It's not a hundred percent up to me. But yes, I want the baby. Hell yeah. I want you to be . . . happy about it, though, and if you're not, then, well, we can make that other kind of decision.' He was tiptoeing. Oscar looked at me and pictured me a crazy mom. I knew he did.

Stygian shores. That's what Seth used to say lay beyond the beyond. *You have to think about stuff like that. All this . . . shit you do means nothing.*

Nodding heavily with each slow stinky breath.
Head back with the inhale.
Head down with the exhale.
Life is jam-packed hell. Beyond life is empty hell.
And what, I wondered, was after that.

PINCH had that patient kind of breathing going when I told her it was probably for the best that I was in New York because I hated everyone now—Ch'Rell and Donnell for acting like May was normal. May for being a murderer. Jess was dead. Cedric was selling dope like the world was on his string. Mom was chilling in Walnut Creek. I was pregnant and hadn't been to the doctor yet and was losing weight from not really eating because even the smell of food was making me nauseous. If the baby got here, what would I do, how would I raise it?

I asked Pinch this, on the phone. She said, 'Come home, we'll figure it out.'

'I'm not worried about the money,' I said, 'or Oscar. It's more *how*, in what *manner*, will I make the baby a regular person?'

What would I say to it? What if it did something wrong, how would I tell it?

What if it did something right?

And the really sick part was, what if Oscar liked the baby better than me? What if I hated seeing Oscar being nice to it? I finally knew a man who was somewhat regular and then I'd have to see him being nice to the baby and I know I'd be jealous, I know I would be, I'd be mad looking at the baby with a dad that liked it.

That's the kind of sick shit I was feeling, so I was embarrassed to be in Oakland, really, where people knew me and would be able to see through my bullshit. Or I should say, I'd be ashamed in front of my sister.

'Have you seen Ch'Rell and them?' I asked Pinch. 'May?'

'May came by the Pseudo. He said he doesn't know why you and Oscar had to run off.' She was remote. 'Why do you care, though? Don't you have your own issues? Like with Oscar, for example. And with being gone all the way across the country?' There was something I'd never heard from her, directed at me. It was envy, when she mentioned me being across the country.

'You're mad I didn't call before I left?'

'You could have. I could have gone with you. You were in Oakland for a night.'

'I don't remember you inviting me to Seattle.'

'I didn't go! Didn't go to Seattle, didn't run off to Davis.'

'So you think we ran off, too? How about we just left? And if we did run, so what? Running is all right. You run when something you can't control is coming for you. You run when getting away is the only way. I know about staying and fighting. But wives are supposed to run if a husband beats them. People run from a shooting gun. Why does running have such a bad name?'

'You're running up your bill.'

'Huh. Me and Oscar are about to take a walk.'

'Why'd you take so long to call?'

'We've been here a day and a half. And anyway, you know what Seth used to say. If the plane had crashed, it would've been on the news.'

I was like my Gram Liz. I hadn't meant to sound so insensitive. At the same time, I knew it was a mean thing when I said it.

OUR hotel was near Times Square, so we walked around. I hated it. Oscar and I went into a theater, saw a movie about a white girl who wasn't supposed to be dating the boy she was.

The wrong boy was frail, dressed in odd clothes, and liked to read. His rival was also white, had muscles and a convertible and rich parents, and at the end the girl defies her own parents and rides off to California on a raggedy motorcycle with the wispy one. I was happy after the movie. Read each job title in the credits and imagined the different professions people could have.

Afterward, Oscar and I held hands, gazed at billboards that puffed smoke and shifted images. In the Formica and polyester hotel room, we kissed until we were perspiring. Oscar started peeling back underpants, and I felt queasy. We went to sleep.

Woke up holding my abdomen. Lay on my back for maybe a half hour, thumbs and index fingers framing my navel. Ironed sheets covered our legs. I had on a pink cotton nightgown. Oscar slept without a shirt, his body curved around a white pillow. The skin on his face was dry from the heater. His bristly chin was almost touching my elbow.

I moved to get some Tylenol from my purse and by accident shook Oscar.

'What's wrong?' he said.

'Nothing.'

'You all right?'

'Yeah.'

Waking Oscar was a clear sign that I wasn't to take the painkiller. If it had all gone smoothly, it would have been meant to be. Oscar curled closer to me, stretched an arm across my ribs. His sighs moistened the border of my breast. When Oscar nestled an inch closer, I cringed. He opened his eyes, frowned, and then turned away from me with his pillow. No part of him was touching me. The ceiling was a perfect rectangle of cream.

I lay there.

Felt like I was starting my period. Things were turning

over. Dislodging. Except for occasionally grabbing at my belly flesh with my fingers, I refused to squirm or moan.

Seemed like ten moons shone through the window, each pulling my fluids in a different direction. Everything waist to knee was humid with blood or perspiration or both, and right when it got so I could feel an oily pool building between my skin and the stretched sheet covering the mattress, I wanted to push, and leapt from the bed. Oscar said my name but I was already in the bathroom, door locked. Calm as hell.

'Paige! What are you doing, what's going on?' He was at the door but not banging.

'I'm fine.' Hair fell to my face, tickled my nose. Chest on my thighs. Was on the toilet doubled over. 'I'm okay, okay? Just a little sick. Girl stuff.' The hairs on my arms were on guard. Vomit wanted to come up, didn't.

'There's blood in the bed.'

It must have hit him as he said it.

Thirteen weeks slid from me like a tiny pliant bowling pin. I closed my thighs. What if it was living? A smooth little sea lion is all I could picture. Inquisitive and needy. Whiskers. No natural fear of humans. Gazing up from the water. What if it looked at me.

I sat there. Warm blood fell. I could hear it. Fast, fluid rhythm.

I sat. Hunched over. The flesh around my toenails was pale. Dimes of blood on the tan tiles. Drying kisses and licks of it on my inner calves.

'Paige let me in.'

No. I wasn't crying. There was no more pain. I straightened up, reached behind me, pressed the flusher. Heard it suck and whirl. Wrapped toilet paper into an oblong wad, pressed it between my legs. Took tight steps to the door, opened it. Oscar looked at me. What could he have seen? He ran to the phone.

They took me down in a freight elevator. Canvas attached haphazardly to the metal walls. Visible cables looped and unlooped. I was standing on my own feet, but the security guard with his severe haircut and burgundy blazer and walkie-talkie, he had his hand on my arm like I was under arrest. I bled on the floor in the elevator. I bled on the seat in the taxi. At the hospital, a man who looked like a doctor attached me to an IV. He made Oscar leave the room. I knew the blood they were giving me must be infected, but I didn't say anything.

A blonder man in white came over, said he was the doctor. He said, 'Tell me exactly what happened.' I told him. He asked what I had seen in the toilet. Asked if I had brought it with me.

'We could have examined it here,' the doctor said, 'and seen if it was everything.'

I had the feeling I was about to go to jail. Then my mind ran to the time I'd been on a drive with Mom and Pinch to Palm Springs. 'Let's go just for the drive,' Mom had said. *To be somewhere else.* Crooked stitches of copper and lemon cracked the early dark. That trip was the first time I'd seen lightning with no rain. Quick light that sucked air and scented the sand. Was the place to be, somewhere else.

'People do that? Bring it in?'

He placed my bare feet in stirrups, looked inside me with a flashlight, said he was going to have to go in, make sure all that was supposed to be gone was gone. There were no more cramps, but I said, 'Okay.'

The first, fake doctor gave me another IV. When I opened my eyes, Oscar was there. He unclenched his face, said, 'Don't worry. You're fine.'

I told him I'd done it on purpose.

He said there was no way I could have done it.

I told him I hadn't even tried to help it.

'Sleep,' he said. 'You've been through a lot tonight.'

I told him I'd done the whole thing on purpose.

Paige . . . Paige . . . Oscar made a tune of it. Over and over he said my name, his mouth right at my ear. He stretched the word like it was a dainty piece of elastic, made it long and taut, then limp again. He made it warm and steamy, cupped it around my ear like a muff. He made me want to cry because all I could think was that he needed to be a better judge of character.

I had to spend the night and most of the next day at the hospital. I kept thinking they were giving me dirty water, spoiled food, drugs to which I would turn out to be allergic or addicted. Every time I told Oscar that I'd killed it, he told me that I couldn't have. He was getting tired of it, I could tell. If he would have just said he believed me, then I would have stopped telling him and we could have moved on.

After Oscar and I spent ten days in another hotel, he found a small place for the both of us that I wouldn't move into. One of the security guards at the hotel had told him about it. I never even saw the place.

So he found me an apartment on the Lower East Side. A cupboard of a studio on the top floor of a small four-story building. You could see the East River, the super said. We didn't have people called 'supers' in Oakland. Oscar stayed with me some nights at first, but then I got a job at a huge bookstore near Union Square, ringing up books and putting books away. Oscar'd paid three months of my rent, so I was fine. But I volunteered for extra hours anyway.

One day I worked from open to close, ten in the morning until ten at night. For at least seven of those hours, I read. Finished half of a biography of Lou Gehrig. Six chapters of an illustrated book about the 'Indians' who lived in California before California had a name. Went to African-American Studies, thought about Pinch, who would have changed the little sign to read AFRICAN AMERICANA. Picked up and read

about the day-to-day life of female slaves in Mississippi. Right
before closing I read a coffee-table book, with etchings and
photographs, about men who'd gone to work in the morning
to build a bridge, fell in the water, and were never seen again.
Oscar came by the bookstore that night, found me in Children's, reading *Bread and Jam for Frances*. It was about a
badger family. They were so proper, and smart. And ate together all the time.

'You're the only one who can be going through it because
the baby died?'

'Why are you saying that so loud?'

'That's what you're worried about? You haven't seen me
for a week, you don't know how I'm living in this city where I
don't know nobody but you, and you want me to lower my
voice?' He hadn't been talking that loud to begin with.

I was sitting on a toddler chair. 'I don't know what to say.
Not just to you, but to anybody. Just for right now.' It was true.
I hadn't been answering my phone. Hadn't returned any of
Mom's calls. Gram Liz had phoned twice. I couldn't even
speak to my sister. I knew her calls. Heard her voice in the
rings. She was mad at me. Because I was in New York. Because I was in New York without her. Because she was in Oakland. She wasn't upset because she was without me. She was
upset at not being in Seattle or wherever it was she wanted to
go, alone. *Ring-ring-ring.*

'You didn't want to speak before this happened. You don't
want to speak now. Tell me why we got married.'

I got married because he liked me. He said he loved me.
And I knew if I hadn't married him, he would have stopped.

Oscar waited on an answer. I played Pinch, said nothing.
He looked at me for a while. Then from the top shelf, he
picked up a book with cardboard pages. Knocked over all the
books up there. Not violently. Oscar tipped one over, watched

them fall against each other like dominos. Watched them fall to the floor.

It was closing. I wished the shroud around me wasn't so fastened to my body with gum. Figured I should go down, cash out my register. Act like I worked there. Oscar walked to the down escalator. Paused. Let his fingers dust the revolving belt. Then he stepped on.

Oscar had started to believe that I'd done it on purpose. Or he believed that I believed it.

I had done it.

One of the main things I believed was that anything I believed in wouldn't come true. I knew God wouldn't let me see into the future—that's why I constantly imagined bad things, so they wouldn't happen. I'd imagined the baby for weeks. The cuteness. The niceness. On purpose.

And so I lost it.

I didn't imagine, for example, that Pinch would come visit me in New York City. And then there she was.

I wasn't acting perfect when she got there. And she looked exhilarated, like she'd done something incredible. Nails perfect, as usual. Tight pants, new bulky sweater. Eyes bright and oblivious to the cold. And she didn't wander into my apartment, she about danced. She hadn't asked me if I needed her to come. She was just there.

'Negress,' she said with a vibrant smile, 'you cannot hide from your sister.' All Oakland hip-shake, and this-is-a-money-day Oakland attitude. When you're in Oakland, Oakland ways are everywhere, so they aren't special. In New York her strut and shrugs stood out in sharp relief. I realized in that moment that I had a hometown, and that the reason people claimed their stomping grounds was because if they didn't, everyplace else was as pretend as Fairyland.

All I could say was, 'How'd you get here?'

'I took the No. 40!'

We dragged her stuff in and we laughed and for a little while I was Pinch's big sister, so I quizzed her about her flight and her cab ride and about Mom.

'Mom gave me some money,' Pinch said. 'She said you needed rescuing and that you wouldn't have anyone rescue you but me.'

'Gotta give Mom credit,' I said, 'for that.'

Then Pinch gave me quiet for a minute. And it was enough just to be seen, and not have to give details. Because even though Pinch hadn't been there for the baby, she was my witness. In her company, no one could deny the facts of my life, or hers. I had one to protect and to protect me. Even if I killed somebody. And I had.

'So you gonna show me around,' she said, 'or what? Can we climb the Statue of Liberty see the Apollo go eat some real Italian food?'

I had every intention of taking her out, maybe even going to see Oscar, so I called in sick to the bookstore, and tried to wash clothes, so we could do all that. But I ended up between sheets gritty with graham-cracker crumbs, reading recipes for bouillabaisse and duck with prunes.

Pinch stayed in with me, though. Even though I wouldn't go with her to the Empire State Building. With my dirty clothes mounded on the studio floor, and wrinkled yellow M&M bags on the counter. Gray light dusted the olive bean-bag she sat on. It alternately blurred and brightened her. Pinch washed my plastic dishes, talked about her coral nails, read at paperbacks I had about the wills of the rich and famous and about Josephine Baker. She let me hold the remote. Holed up and vaguely hungry, we didn't have pepper-oni pizza or see Central Park. I didn't take her on the Staten Island ferry, which I often rode back and forth to be someplace where Oscar couldn't call, so it wouldn't matter that he didn't. I hadn't unrolled the poster Pinch brought me from home. I tried to explain to my sister that my depth perception was off, that I hadn't known, ever since the baby, the difference between what was close and what was far away.

I looked at Pinch, tried to see her as a stranger might. Blue stretch pants and yellow silky blouse. Yellow tennis shoes. Like Jess used to wear. But even looking away, my sister was watchful. Her eyes past tired. The light she had when I'd opened the door was sucked by my gasping need for a lifeguard. Sitting in that apartment getting full off sharp photos of sugar tarts, and tearing up over the kids on *Sesame Street*, who must be grown now and normal adults, I thought for the second time in my life that I was holding Pinch down, and not just holding on.

Sunday morning, before she left, I got it together to shower and dress. I did have to go to work. Was supposed to be there by noon, and was running late. I was going to call one of the car services, but Pinch wasn't having it.

'I got from JFK airport in a yellow cab,' she said, 'and I can get back.'

'You have enough money?'

'I think so, yeah.'

I wanted to cry. I wanted her to stay.

'You know you can come home, right?'

'Not yet,' I said. 'I need a minute.'

'I know what you mean.'

A cab rolled up.

'I'll be fine,' Pinch said. 'I'll have a glass of wine and be asleep the whole way.'

I didn't know what to say except, 'You don't need to be drinking on the plane. You should have your wits about you when you fly.'

CHAPTER 16

Late morning in Oakland. The sky went on white-gray, gray-white, heavy and lowering. Water fell steadily, straight down, no angle. I'd been back from visiting Paige in New York for almost four weeks. Jess had been dead about seven months. Didn't think things would brighten at all.

I'd just hung up the phone with Ch'Rell. Had barely seen she or May or Cedric at all since Jess's funeral. Oscar's father had stopped by the Pseudo a few times, brought me some meat-loaf once, a two-liter bottle of 7-Up another time. I'd been working like a maniac at Planned Parenthood, got myself another little promotion, was paying my whole rent. I had plans, big plans to go to Los Angeles, go to the city college down there. Get into psychology and figure out a way for girls not to end up at Planned Parenthood in the first place.

Mom came by way more than she had before Paige and Oscar left, brought me ice cream and of course bras and socks and panties. I talked to Evan about every other day. He called from one of the buildings on his campus, where he worked as night security. He was a Campus Cadet or something. Was thinking about going into law enforcement, he said.

I hated to, but I dialed my sister's 212 number.

It was time for her to come home.

Since I'd been back from New York, I called her about twice a week, and she told me about the bookstore, and about how Oscar had taken her to lunch or dinner and how they argued. That wasn't going to be today's conversation.

Connection. I could just see Paige in that tired apartment, deciphering coded rings, noting the level of each party's frustration. She'd got to where she hated voices—Mom's, our friends', mine—hated for us to say anything that proved we knew her. The rings she detested most were from people who rarely called—Oscar's father, or Cedric. They'd no code but determination.

'Hello?' Paige had probably said the word loudly six times before she picked up the phone. But I could still hear the crust on her voice.

I said, 'What're you doing?'

'What are you doing?'

'I think Cedric is dead.'

Felt her tiny hope. 'You think he is?'

'This is what I hear. On the TV.' I was normal. Paige, too. I said I hadn't seen or spoken with Maynard.

Paige said, 'Call Oscar on the three-way.'

Oscar picked up his phone laughing. We heard chuckles in his apartment. She said, 'Oscar it's Paige,' he said, 'Hey.'

My sister's voice broke and it could have been because of Cedric or it could have been the way Oscar laughed before he said *Hey*. His world seemed okay without her and here she was about to rock it. Paige said, 'Have you talked to anyone from home?'

The laugh evaporated. 'My dad. Why?'

'Pinch just called and said she thinks Cedric's dead. She's on the phone.'

'Who told her that?' he said. 'Pinch, who told you that?'

Paige answered. 'She said it was on the news.'

There was a click on his line and he had us both on hold. Paige and I said nothing to each other. I pictured her looking at the black-and-white poster of Lake Merritt I'd taken to New York. I was still eight blocks from the real thing. There was a rumor that the Oakland Police fished a severed hand out of the lake. The story'd been circulating since we were kids and probably before.

Oscar came back on the line with 'Yeah.' Then he said, 'It's true.' His voice was slow enough that I knew his mind was already ahead of it. 'What exactly did they say about Cedric on the news?'

'Convicted drug dealer, execution-style slaying—like that,' I said.

Paige said, 'Are people saying May did it?'

Jesus. 'I spoke to Ch'Rell. According to her, May was in Tahoe. Supposedly someone told him right when he got back. He was getting his hair cut over on Shattuck Avenue and he ran out of there with his head half-cut.'

Paige said, 'Supposedly?'

I wondered whose hand was in the lake, if the cops had really found one, if it was salt-whitened bones when they got it, or still fleshy and full of story.

Oscar said, 'Paige what are you going to do? Tell me now, because I won't be calling you back—'

I should have got off the line, but stayed on. No one said, *Pinch hang up, we're about to get personal.*

'—because I know your ass hates to pick up the phone in a crisis,' Oscar said. 'You'd rather make stuff up that's worse than the truth.'

Paige said, 'I prepare myself for the worst.'

'Are you prepared for Cedric being dead?'

'Aren't you?'

Isn't that why you guys left Oakland in the first place? is what I wanted to say. *To dodge calamity? To pretend you could outrun it?*

'There's such a thing as dealing with life,' Oscar said.

'And death. But that's a whole different set of encyclopedias for you.'

'I have that set.'

'Read them, then.'

'Did. And don't believe any of it.'

'You're not going to Oakland, then,' Oscar said.

'There's nothing for me out there. But Pinch, I mean. Pinch?'

Oscar had practically hung up in her face. Mine, too, technically.

I could see if she was really experiencing New York, making friends, and figuring out her life. But she wasn't doing shit out there but complaining about how ugly and dirty it was. Going to and from that bookstore and trying to act like she wasn't missing Oscar.

'You know what I should have done, I should have married Obe from Bret Harte.' Paige and I were still connected. 'He deals in tropical fish now. I could have lived with him in Fiji for two years, where he learned how to catch cichlids without killing them, learned a way to pack and ship them so they could breathe. I could have married him when I was twenty or so. Then when Cedric ends up killed and Oscar goes to Oakland for the funeral, I wouldn't have known any of them. I would have been just back from Fiji, living in Monterey, helping my junior-high-school man clean our fifty-gallon tank. I would have been happy, looking out the window at the kelp beds, hoping to see an otter. Cedric, Donnell, Ch'Rell and May and Oscar would be somebody else's life. I would never have met Jessica.' Her voice was starting to break again. 'That would have been fucked up, but seeing how things are, maybe it would've been better.'

I hate when Paige talks about some other way things could have happened when they've already happened. I don't indulge in that kind of stuff. Paige called me the next day, though. Said her phone had rung seventeen times and then she picked it up. Said nothing.

'So he starts shouting my name, telling me he was sick of my paranoid shit. He said he got me a ticket, and I was going to Oakland, and to the funeral.'

'What did you say?' *You know you're glad.*

'I told him I didn't think so.'

'And he said?'

'He said, "Oh no, you're going. Get your stuff together."'

So she and Oscar would be coming home—as a duo. There was another funeral to be gone to, after all. Fools to be faced.

I hung up the phone. Sitting there in the Pseudo. On the big flowered chair. Television on mute. Saw his name and mug shot again. Rainy as it was, I walked over to the lake. The skin of it was like faintly rippled steel.

Silvery ashen sand and lawn, the sky was smoked white wax. Even from three thousand miles away, I knew Paige could see it. The Necklace of Lights was slack and dripping. The clear bulbs were dim, of course. It was late afternoon. At least I thought it was.

'All things going as they should,' Paige had told me, 'we'll pick you up on the way from the airport.' First Jess, then Paige's baby, now Ced. My Los Angeles plans were trivial.

Yes it'll be fine I'll come by all the time bring you what you need you all are smart and responsible then when you're eighteen you know what my girl says God bless the child that's got his own work it out I'm so proud of how this place looks you all are sisters for real everybody always talks about how close you are and wants to know the secret wants to know why you two are always together never fight or talk bad about the other that's how you were raised is what I say love your sister no matter what someday she may be all you have . . .

Let's just go to the Pseudo! You all got it made. Your own spot and everything! Tired of these damn Acorns, let's go to the Burrito Shoppe, get extra everything, watch Miami Vice . . .

You don't want to come work at Realty Data with your sister? Come on up to the house, see what you can get when you're smart, save your money, stay up on the foreclosure market. You know the No. 40 doesn't come up Above Upper High, now . . .

Your sister wants you to come stay with us. She loves me but she needs you. I knew you two were down like peanut butter and jelly from the word go . . .

Of course you can go with your sister, Pinch. I'll speak to her teacher. Mrs. Loftus will want you to see the aquarium with her. She knows you're a quiet one. I'm sure you'll interact more if you go on the field trip with her . . .

Pinch, just come up to the pool with me. What are you going to do at the Pseudo by yourself? Plus I miss you when I'm up at Diamond. You can watch me work. I'll show you how to swim.

Oakland is home. And unless the world tilted off its axis, neither me or Paige was going anywhere.

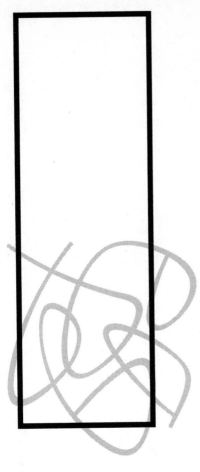

PART II
THE NOW

CHAPTER 17

Supposedly May wasn't going to show up at Cedric's funeral, because the police were questioning him, in jail. I heard this two days before Paige and Oscar arrived in California.

According to another dirt-disher, May was hiding out in Alamo, worried that whoever shot Ced would, at the cemetery, shoot him.

Heard also that May was definitely going to show up at the graveyard—to shoot the person who'd killed Cedric. May and Donnell supposedly knew exactly who the murderer was.

Another line of gossip maintained that May had shot Cedric over money, and that Ced's father knew it. Ced's father supposedly forbid May, Oscar, and Donnell from the funeral.

All this, even with Jessica's story still wet on the mural.

Oh, there'd be a Jess mural. Right next to the OAKLAND IS PROUD mural on Foothill. And across from the La Raza mural on the underpass at Grand Avenue. There's always a mural.

REMEMBER ME WHEN I'M GONE AWAY, FAR AWAY INTO THE SILENT LAND. That's the kind of stuff they paint. Rest in peace.

I was about to step on the No. 40. Go to M-B Mall. Buy a dress and shoes for Cedric's funeral.

PAIGE said that she and Oscar hadn't sat next to each other on the plane.

When they landed, he rented a glowing black Mustang convertible. Paige liked the wind parting her hair in different places. Oscar liked being surrounded by something low to the ground but slightly grand. They scooped me up, and we cruised west through the Flatlands. On our way to the cemetery. We weren't going to make it to the funeral.

'You gonna come back here?' Oscar wanted to know.

Paige said, 'Are you?'

I'd run a warm comb through my hair that morning, so the air was making it fan out, too, like Paige's. It was a typical, late-spring East Bay day—not cold enough for a sweater, not warm enough to go without one. The sun was high, though, and I had the whole backseat. My black-and-blue dress was a little tight for a funeral, but it was cute. Had royal pumps with a pointy toe and small, classy heel that made up for the clinginess of my outfit. Had to carry my bigger purse, though. I'd gone through my closet at the Pseudo inch by inch and gathered the papers I needed for either Mom or Paige. I wasn't sure which one.

I was glad Paige was home. Checked out her tapered slate skirt and blue satin blouse. She'd stopped with the acrylic nails, so her hands looked natural, soft and strong. Her pumps were very Perry Ellis, her hair recently clipped to the shoulders, and flipped up. She looked like she was going to work at Magnin's, had on the super-sheer hose they sell there. I coveted them as we passed three separate Church of God in Christ storefronts with hand-lettered praises.

'Tell me one more time,' Paige said to Oscar, 'why I had to come to the funeral.'

'What were you gonna do? Stay locked up in that apartment?'

Paige seemed to check herself in his rearview mirror. Her eyes were unfocused, though. Then she faced the windshield again.

There were men in front of the Foothill Narcotics Anony-
mous chapter, where Oscar's father still sometimes went to
meetings, so Oscar beeped at them. The place had blacked-
out windows. Had been a Hells Angels club room, and a sandwich shop before that. As usual, Impalas and Caprice Classics
were parked on oily wooden blocks in the side lot. With the
same haircuts they'd had since Vietnam or Panther meetings
or their last everyday job, the men puffed on cigarettes and
squinted until they recognized Oscar in the rented Mustang.
Then they walked to the curb, slacks soft from wear and washing, and gave swaggering salutes. Oscar did a double-toot, and
we pressed on along the boulevard where girls with permed
locks pushed strollers with French-fry-fat babies and white
bags full and filmy as clouds.

I put my silver cat-eye shades on so I could gaze without
being screamed on, and once they were on my face, I felt like I
was profiling a little too cool—with Cedric being dead. Told
myself he'd want me to be that way. Want me to roll up to his
funeral cute and cool, like he'd show up to mine.

Oscar said, 'Paige. You know you miss Oakland.'

Still looking straight through the front window, my sister
said, 'Yeah I do.'

Oscar could have jumped on the Nimitz freeway and
we'd have been in Berkeley way sooner. But he was taking the
long way.

Paige said, 'May's not sad.'

At a red light, I spied a girl with a paper-wrapped burrito in
her hand. Standing, she scanned the bus-stop bench. Didn't
want to sit on gum. Paige and I used to forget to do that, and end
up on the bus embarrassed. This was before we started rolling
with guys with cars. Before Oscar and Cedric and Maynard and
Donnell. Before Ch'Rell and Jess. The Burrito Girl sat down on
the bench, was overly aware of ordinary hand gestures because
her nails were three inches long, curved, rounded at the tips, air-

brushed mocha. I wondered where she got them done. Homegirl picked at her coat zipper and then at bits of her burrito like
a finicky goddess, skin nutmeg and gleaming from long rub-
bings of petroleum jelly. I thought I knew the girl from somewhere. She didn't watch for the bus. The No. 40 ran on Foothill.
It would be by like clockwork. I looked at her harder. Had never
seen her before. She was overflowing her clingy blouse, and sad
but satisfied with her big food, impotent hands, and trip on the
bus. The No. 40 was only going to the end of Foothill, though,
and then right back down it, the other way. Mustang surged. It
aggravated me that I knew exactly how the 40 ran.

I faced forward. Wind filled my face. *It's the wind, got to be
the wind, snatching my breath away.*

'Paige you don't know what May is.'

'Truth's 'bout to come out,' Paige said. 'About everything.'

'What truth? Why don't you tell me your truth, Paige, now
that Cedric is dead. Why are you about to cry?'

'He's dead. Can I cry over that?'

'That ain't why you're crying. You're just mad. You stay
mad. At me, usually. And now it's May.'

Another red. I looked over the door of the car. Four girls at
this bus stop, each different from the other as possible except for
the flawless nails and the eyes feigning indifference and the
jeans tight as possible and the brows plucked skinny. They
didn't look at me, didn't want to seem like they were jocking the
car. It's how I would act. The girls were dazzling and yearning
hard as Oscar and Paige and me used to for a brand-new Jetta
with fog lights from Pep Boys Auto Supply. Not that we were
near it, but bus 40 stopped right in front of the Smorgasbord.

I had a craving for the place, hadn't been there since
Oscar and Paige had split. Missed the high chairs at every
table and all-you-can-eat chicken wings aged in Lawry's sea-
soning salt. Mashed potatoes from the box with floury gravy,
frozen yogurt in a chubby swirl. Kids wild and wild and wild.

Didn't know how it would be in there without the cushion of crew. Me, Ch'Rell, Paige, Jess, flashing our nails for Ced, May, Oscar, and Donnell.

Oscar got over to MacArthur Boulevard, pulled into a Giant Burger parking lot. Paige hopped out, went next door, paid for some flowers, and came back. People sat in their cars slashing at apple pie, sucking back berry shakes. Oscar ordered us all jumbo dogs split down the middle, grilled to puffy and black around the edges. There were emerald pickles, and diamonds of white onion. We ate standing at a scratched counter inside. Oscar'd let his hair grow in. His arms had softened some. I watched his brows bend as a boxy sedan passed on MacArthur. Could about hear him saying *Task Force* in his head.

Before we stepped back in the Mustang, Oscar nodded at a chick he looked like he almost remembered. Her moon face lit up like it was night.

'I like that car,' she said. 'But then you was *al*ways rollin'.' She paused. 'Where you at if a sister needs—'

'I don't live out here anymore.' Like he was waking up to the fact.

We pulled from the lot with Oscar saying, 'Paige, wipe your face. You've got lint from the tissue all on your eyelashes.'

'How are you so composed?' Paige spoke sharply, leaned over to peep in the mirror again, touched the pulse in her neck, pulled down the skin beneath one eye with an index finger. 'You're not sad at all.'

Into the gusts, Oscar said, 'I've been sad since before we moved.'

'You were gone.' Paige's shirt billowed like a parachute— cobalt silkiness fluttering like it could let us down easy. 'You know how to let everything go so everybody else is supposed to.' At the red light it lay quiet against her curves again.

'If I was gone,' Oscar said, 'you chained the door.'

We got onto Telegraph Avenue. Oscar had the signals on his side, and our stomping grounds were flying by. Paige's shirt was rippling again. I inhaled fresh mud plus roses blackening. Saw shiny limousines.

Paige said, 'Do we have to go to the cemetery? Do we have to talk to people when we get there?'

'Yes, Paige.'

'Will you stay by me?'

'Yes, Paige. We're almost there.'

'Do you still think I liked Cedric?'

Yes, Paige.

'I never thought that,' Oscar said. 'What I knew was that you liked him liking you. You like anybody liking you. Proves to you you're here.'

She looked in her pocketbook. Found vanilla hand cream, rubbed the backs of her hands, dug some more out of the small tub, got at her elbows. Pink tulips lay on her lap, sweating in crisp cellophane.

He turned up a low hill toward a band of tombstones. Same cemetery as Jessica's burial. The three of us got out and walked. Paige and I on tiptoe over the squishy lawn.

Oscar looked toward the gathering.

Cedric's new cradle a split in green velveteen.

We lingered far from the huddle. Paige held the tulips. Cars tootled along the borders of death. Cemetery bled right up to a public sidewalk and slow street. People shouted directions or about their cousin who said hi. Folks went on, testy and proud, Baton Rouge and the knobby hot places of East Texas pulling at their celery-salted syllables like three generations hadn't already been young and old in California, like there wasn't a crowd of the ever-silent on our side of the leaning cyclone fence. Like Cedric was dozing and wouldn't mind being shook.

The noise was disrespectful. It seemed to itch Oscar, too.

'I told you what he said, didn't I?' Oscar stopped gazing at the casket. Looked at me and my sister. Paige had already told me that Cedric's dad hadn't asked Oscar, Donnell, or Maynard to be pallbearers.

My brother-in-law looked at me. 'That day when you called New York, Pinch, and you two got me on the three-way.' He was agitated. Eyes stony, hands messing with his belt.

'He didn't mean it when he said it,' Paige said. 'Ced's father was upset.'

'He meant that shit. Ced's dad said, "You're calling now for what?" That's the first thing he said to me. Then he said, "You're not calling to know if it's true Cedric's dead, because you know it is." I called him 'cause I *know* him,' Oscar said. 'Long as I been friends with Ced, his daddy says to me, "Read the paper, find out about the service." He said, "Come bow your head if you got the sense your mother gave you, but don't bother me. Tell your partners the same thing." That's how he was talking to me. He could have asked me how I was doing.'

'He knows how you are,' Paige said, 'with your friend dead. Just like you know how he's doing, with his son gone.' She touched his arm, but awkwardly, because she had to lean to reach him. She, Oscar, and I stuck in grassy mud.

Ch'Rell and Donnell were both there in big sunglasses and patent-leather shoes. Donnell was fatter, the pleats in his pants weren't hanging right. Ch'Rell's hair was in a natural, tapered afro. Walnut-sized plastic pearls in her ears and around her neck. Lips lined, eyebrows arched. I could tell they saw us by the way Ch'Rell and Donnell didn't move their heads at all.

That girl Kimya was there, and didn't glance our way, either. She hung back from the cluster of people around the grave, as we did, but set herself up far from us. May's sister Teeara was there, with the dark, dark shades that she was rarely without. Todd loped around heavy and limping, shaking hands with and embracing people, trying his best to look sad.

He kept his distance from Teeara and May. Nodded toward me, I gave him a nod back. Todd had on leather pants and a leather coat. Thick oval links hung around his neck, and a palm-sized *Africa* silhouette carefully cut from leather dangled at his sternum.

'Oscar where's your father?' I wanted to know.

'He'll be around. Tomorrow, maybe. He wasn't down for all this again.'

The grass held shivery water gems. Dandelions dipped heavy heads. I thought Paige had welled up as much as she was going to, over her hot dog at the Giant Burger, but here Oscar was, passing her balled-up tissue, and squinting himself. Then he bent to remove his shoe. I thought he was going to shake some of the mud off. To balance himself, he put one hand on Paige's shoulder.

Hundred-dollar bills had been cushioning his right heel. He handed them to her, folded, damp, and curved. 'In case we get separated,' he said. 'Or something happens. It's seventeen hundred.'

Something like what?

'You kept a good amount for you?'

Oscar stuffed the money way down in her purse. 'Let me worry about me.' Gingerly slipped his foot back in the muddy shoe. It was one of the brown kid loafers he'd worn when they were married.

Walked nearer the grave site. Closed umbrellas and *He restoreth my soul* and a disk of carnation heads resting on a tripod. Cedric's father seated with a handkerchief across one knee, like he was waiting on lunch to be served.

Paige had the four pink tulips in her hand. She'd taken them from their wrap, as if to walk up and lay them on the casket. But then it was *Surely goodness and mercy shall follow me all the days of my life,* and the casket was sunk into the ground.

Cedric's father allowed people to pat him. He folded his hand-kerchief until it was small, then put it in his fist.

Maynard walked over to us. His eyeballs looked in need of an injection. In need of fluid or air or whatever's supposed to fill them and make them round. I saw Paige and myself in his eyes, cartoony and caught behind a dusty piece of sepia glass.

'Missed y'all,' May said toward Paige. 'At the church.'

Paige bored through Maynard's cheekbones then his fore-head then his chin and his nose with her own eyes. Stared at whatever was on the other side of his face. Paige said, 'Re-member how you used to treat us all to captain's platters?'

He kind of laughed. Said, 'Huh?'

Paige told me later that she'd wanted to ask Maynard if he remembered sitting at the big polished table in Spenger's Seafood—him loud, shirt draped open to his belly—telling us about calamari like we'd never had it. But then she felt the tulip stems darken and collapse in her hand.

What Paige said at the cemetery was Maynard's first and last name, and he looked at her with his eyebrows raised.

'They found Cedric on a road facedown,' Paige said, 'with the back of his head shot off, right?'

Ch'Rell and Donnell kept their distance. Kimya hovered. She wore a hat with a gray angora stripe—like somebody's mother would wear. Wore a look of calm that had to be false.

'Neck all but gone. Right, May?'

Oscar said, 'Paige, come on now.' People craned their necks toward us as they walked back to their cars. Some stopped altogether but didn't come over. Cedric's father was gone. Maynard kept his gaze on Paige. His hands settled loosely in his pants pockets.

'You think he was on his knees when he died?' Paige said. 'Or was he on his belly, face all dented in by gravel, peeing on his self?'

I grabbed her right wrist but knew she'd yank it away. 'I'm not talking about the pain,' Paige said, 'I'm talking about the *end*. About not knowing what that even is. Talking about not seeing anyone ever and not even knowing you're not seeing them. But there's not enough time to flesh it all out, is there? If you're about to die. Just tears and too much spit in your mouth. And why this why now why me.'

Paige did jerk away from me. Then inched nearer Maynard. Oscar stood next to her. He looked at me, then quickly took in the whole graveyard, like a Secret Service agent would do in the movies.

The top of Paige's body was pushed forward. 'Can you reason with your teeth in the dirt, May?' Her lips were dry from all the movement. Tulip petals faced the ground like doll skirts.

'Girl,' I said. 'Paige.' If she heard me, she didn't turn my way. I could have stopped her. But I was tired. Couldn't lay in the mud, couldn't run through it.

'Was Cedric hoping the killer would see past what he did? Did Ced hope he'd end up back at his own place? All, Christ, what a fucking scare! Right? Him all thinking, I thought I was dead for sure, but damn, here I am with cable and a Corona. Was that his desperate little last dream? What do you think, May? Did the killer beat him, did he taunt him? Was the killer scared himself of killing Ced? Maynard! This is your homegirl from the old world. You can look me in my face.'

'I am looking you in your face,' May finally said, and he was. 'So you need to calm down.'

'You calm the fuck down,' she said, like he was ranting. 'You're not looking at me. You're doing what you always do. Looking through somebody at what you'd rather be seeing. Being someone you'd rather be being. All's here is graveyard, Maynard. And Cedric's right here dead.' Oscar put his hand around Paige's left bicep, but he didn't pull. He and I both repeated her name in different tones, hoping she'd respond to one. Paige inched even closer to Maynard, who stood there, in his charcoal suit, rooted.

'Did he know about dying, May, or was he just gone?' She wasn't crying, but she was crumbling. I wanted her to give me the tulips at least. Paige's mouth closed. She ran her tongue over her top and bottom front teeth. She licked her bottom lip and then pressed bottom and top together. She still hadn't looked at Oscar or I. Kimya came to stand behind and slightly beside Maynard. Donnell was beside Kimya. He looked at me first like I could be of assistance, then with a loose loathing I'd only seen him direct at Ch'Rell when she told him that if he didn't stand up for his, he'd be next-to-nothing forever.

'You know you know!' Paige slowed down. 'I know you know. Ced. Dead. Jess. Dead. Your people. You changed shit. You changed everything.'

Oscar snatched Paige from where she stood. Maynard had raised his hand like he would have hit her with the back of it. I didn't think he'd do it, but I wasn't sure.

Paige whipped herself toward Maynard again. She said, evenly, 'You're gonna hit me?' She was burning from the inside out. Hot hate. It was only worse when she directed it to a mirror.

'Maynard, first of all, you won't be slapping anybody.' It was me talking, saying the things I thought would come from Oscar's mouth. I pulled Paige from Oscar's grip, from Maynard's range. I hated to have spoken at all.

'We need to leave,' Kimya said. She was pissed in her grown-up hat.

Bolstered, May gave a smile, put his hands back in his pockets, said, 'Bye-bye, Paige,' like he was happily watching her get hauled off in a straitjacket.

Paige stared hard at Maynard. He said, 'Find somewhere else to look. Get her comfy, Oscar, she needs to relax.' He was still with the rancid grin. I looked at him for some trace of the boy I stood next to, panning for gold. I saw him in there. Half-gifted, half-starved, at risk, upward bound.

Oscar was supposed to be a man and tell Maynard, *Fuck you, apologize to her*, or Oscar should hit Maynard. It was a cemetery though, and maybe Oscar was trying to be serene. It was a punk move from him, regardless. Paige was behind Oscar, looking at his back like she was trying to remember where she knew him from. I was thinking of Vacation Bible Camp, and the story of Job, when God was sending him all this bad luck, torturing him really. At some point either God or Job said, *My face is foul with weeping, and on my eyelids is the shadow of death.* It's funny what comes to mind after a long time. And what sticks and sticks forever.

Oscar faced May, looked like he was trying to figure out what to do. Maynard reached toward Oscar, to put a hand on his shoulder. Maybe to say, *Sorry*.

May faced Paige directly, Oscar between them. With a frown, May said, 'What's up, Paige, you all right?'

Oscar turned to Paige from Maynard, who'd caught him-self, and gone back to looking amused.

In a hurry Oscar pulled tissue from his pocket and wiped at my sister's bottom lip and chin. Paige shivered. Oscar put both his hands on her shoulders. A glycerin drop of saliva had stretched from her mouth down to her blue blouse, she must not have felt it at all. She stared through Maynard as Oscar steadied her. The wet on the satin was dark and spreading. Tulips, fuchsia and darkly creased in queer places, fell to the drenched green ground.

Oscar said, 'Paige, come on, let's go.'

Maynard beamed, his teeth iridescent. 'Why you looking at me like that, girl?' he said. He was facetious, cooing. Like an evil father. The tip of Maynard's tongue was on his own top lip. Oscar wrapped Paige in his arms, put his mouth to her ear.

'Swallow,' Oscar said. 'Paige. Baby. Swallow.'

CHAPTER 18

Cedric's death was ours. I didn't want it added to anyone's chart or graph or argument proving that crack cocaine killed either by ruining families or by violence or through addiction. Hated that when history was written, Cedric's murder scene could easily be in a picture in *Life*—an illustration of an era, a single death proving a broader point. Jess could be in there, too, above a different caption. All of us in an old magazine. I didn't want that. Some grainy candid shot of us at a club with blank eyes and drinks held high, in clothing of the period. Looking pitiful to scholarly types who'd been discovering Chutes & Ladders when we thought we were ruling things.

THE funeral was over. Paige, Oscar, and I were eating at the Smorgasbord.

At normal post-funeral gatherings, like my nannah's, and then my grandpa's, you can count on confrontations, macaroni, and pans of clovey sustenance. Reliable as sex, the mix got everyone sleepy, silly, or sadder, led to folks arriving home satisfied they'd met tribal responsibilities, if not quite paid respect. Cedric's father hated us, though, so the Smorgasbord was the closest we were going to come to all that.

Oscar brought Paige chicken-fried steak with gravy. Got himself the same. I'd filled a bowl with applesauce. Too sweet, put the spoon down. I'd have to find an apple tree, then pick, peel, chop, and simmer. Even then it wouldn't taste exactly like Nannah's. *It would be mine, though.*

'Eat,' Oscar said, setting down ginger ales. He knew Paige and I figured ginger ale to be a restorative. And for a funeral day, it was less casual than Pepsi or grape Crush.

'So you were gonna let May slap me?'

'I thought you might slap him,' Oscar said. 'He wasn't going to hit you unless he's really lost his mind. And then I'd've had some decisions to make.'

'You'd've had half a second.'

'And it would have been enough, Pinch.' He sliced meat with the side of his fork. 'I see you,' he said to Paige, 'looking at me like you're changing your mind.'

'I been changed my mind. About you. I didn't expect help. I've been on my own. Was on my own when I was with you.'

Peeved as I was at Oscar, I wanted to say to her, *In what way? You sound just like Jess did, talking about her independent self when she was dependent on Maynard, clear as day. You depend on Oscar for money and for a ride and for his affection, but then you want to act like you're so on your own. Just because we weren't dependent on Mom for the normal things, or on Gram, that doesn't mean we have to fight it all the time. Oscar's been helping you, helping us both. But* I guess being dependent on people is bad. Even though you and I lean on each other still.

On accident, I'd said the last two sentences aloud.

'It's not dependency with us. It's more like we had to . . . rise to the occasion. It's how we were raised.'

'I'm more than an occasion, and I'm more than how I was raised.' *And so are you.* But if I said one nice thing, I wouldn't say anything else about how I felt. 'We could've lived separately. I could have stayed with Mom.'

'But you didn't.'

'No, because I was scared of Seth, and because—' I stopped.

'Because what?' She was cocky. With that wet spot still dark on her shirt.

'Because I was scared of what you might do. How you'd end up.'

'Scared of how *I'd* end up? You came with me because if you hadn't, you'd have been by yourself.' She was still in that graveyard mud. 'I could have been by myself.'

Oscar said, 'You think?'

'I know.'

'Then why didn't you just keep going?' I asked her. 'When you were on your way? That day after the Ninth Grade Court. Why didn't you just get on something other than the 40, and really just go?'

Oscar said, 'Ninth grade? Keep going where?'

Paige looked at me like *Game over.*

'Hey.' Oscar softly pushed my sister's shoulder. 'Keep going where?'

She didn't take her gaze off me.

'*You* feel guilty about Ced. That's why you've got May on death row. You think it was *your* job to have told Seth to calm the fuck down.'

'Shut up.'

'Many a day I've had to keep you on this planet. Today's another one.'

'Are we counting days? Fuck all the days I had to tell you what to do and how to act. When I was getting you money when Mom wouldn't give it or didn't have it.'

'Like Mom didn't give you money. Like Oscar didn't just give some to you. I benefited. But you worked, I worked. We had to raise each other.'

'Like that,' Paige said, 'makes us special.'

I was about to say something else, but Maynard walked in. Didn't hesitate to come over. 'How long y'all in town, any-way?' He wasn't warm, wasn't cold. He was with Kimya and

Ch'Rell and Donnell. They all nodded some vague salutation. Ch'Rell did at least kiss my cheek.

'Not long,' Oscar said.

'Not sure,' Paige said. 'I have to make sure I get by to see Jessica.' Then, in a chirpy voice, she asked Maynard about his son.

Ch'Rell said, 'He's big,' like she was Ree's mother. 'You're not going to ask me about Yannick? Paige? He's a real little man.'

'You go see Jessica,' Maynard said. 'Give her my love.' Then Maynard said to Oscar, 'So you two are back together?' Like them being back together was the stupidest thing he'd ever heard.

Oscar pulled cash from his pocket, put it under the napkin container. 'Any other day,' he said, 'we could go right on outside. If that's where you felt you needed to take it.' Oscar patted pockets for his keys. 'Not today, though. It's a funeral day.'

Paige had my purse and hers. She let Oscar hear his keys clink together in her hand. I yanked my bag from her. Didn't want her holding my stuff anymore. Plus I had papers in it she didn't need to see. Oscar looked at me like I was crazy. Paige looked at me like she'd looked at May at Ced's grave.

I saw May see me. Arranged my purse on my shoulder.

May had never seen Paige and I fight. And honestly, outside of bullshit over borrowed clothes or the telephone, she and I never argued. I may have told her about herself in specific moments. But I'd never stepped to her about how she was as a person. And she'd never stepped to me.

Held my bulky purse like it was precious. Maynard's slick face had fallen. I hadn't seen him look so disappointed since Teeara got her glass eye.

May took the tiniest step aside as we walked out of the Smorgasbord.

Donnell and Ch'Rell took the secondary position to Kimya. Just like they used to take with Paige.

PAIGE, Oscar, and I drove across the Bay Bridge with the car's top still down, through the center of Yerba Buena Island, which, in order to hold up the bridge's middle, had been tunneled through in some way I couldn't imagine. Once in San Francisco, we took the spiral road up Telegraph Hill to Coit Tower. Oscar parked, and we stepped onto the bedrock of the monument, and no one had spoken a word since I'd snatched my purse from Paige. I stood among other deep breathers with hands on hips and looked out at the bay. Another funeral day. Not that I'd seen Cedric in the weeks before he died. If what happened to Jessica hadn't happened, I guess I would've been more in shock about Cedric. Maybe I was devastated and didn't know it.

We rode down through North Beach and then onto Geary Boulevard, almost to Fisherman's Wharf, where Joe DiMaggio's father and brother used to bring in nets full of snapper. We would have walked along the waterfront, maybe through a funhouse called Ripley's Believe It or Not, which I loved and Paige thought was too much like a haunted house. If we'd gone down by Pier 39, there would have been crab cocktails with sharp ketchup from a cart. Velvet-covered card tables with silver bangles on sale from Deadheads come home. Bumper cars. Sea lions barking from below the piers for fish, for scraps of anything.

But instead Oscar made a left before the piers and zoomed over the short curved highway that led to the Golden Gate.

We pulled onto a narrow sightseeing area, just past where the bridge ends on the Marin County side. Of course, there were the same old heart-shaped steel telescopes along the ledge that you could put quarters in to see the bay all choppy and dotted with sailboats. People traveled from all over the world to see this. The Golden Gate. The Bay Area. It stood up to any postcard. Took myself out of being Pinch for a moment, tried to look at it like I hailed from elsewhere. Was difficult. From the dusky moon to the darkest part of the bay, there were at least forty shades of blue. But I'd counted those blues before.

Oscar got out, stood before an ancient brown iron chain curved in a smile between waist-high cement poles. Was there to keep folks from falling into the beauty.

Paige turned the radio up loud.

Some of the other viewers, in windbreakers, and with the lock-kneed, glassy-eyed stance of the awed, got shook by the noise and drifted away. Paige began to transform another tissue puff to a sodden wad. Moisture in various states of drying mottled my sister's blouse. The stains a map to how we got here.

Oscar walked over, clicked Paige from her seat belt, led her to where he'd been standing. It was getting chilly, but he stood with his face to the wind, then stepped over the chain and onto the hard dirt just before the precipice. There was a way to get down toward the ocean if it was daylight and you had a guide. If you had gloves, rope, proper hiking boots, and had made peace with yourself and your enemies and so had no fear of dying.

Paige stepped over to join him and they both took three more small steps toward the edge. I couldn't tell if they were about to fall or if they were going to walk out onto the air and leave me among the living. Paige took one more step outward, and I watched Oscar watch her. Paige hugged herself against the cold, brushed longish bangs from her face. Then she stretched her arms above her head.

Oscar went behind her, put his arms around her middle.

His chin was on top of her head. It looked like he was holding her back, and then like he was just holding her. They stood there awhile, Oscar's mouth by her ear, then Paige squirmed, tried to escape the wrap. Oscar locked his arms tighter, and I wondered if it was inches or a foot they were away from the end. I finally turned the music down and heard Oscar widen the word *What?* twice, like Paige's answer would be so deep as to solve everything.

Back in the car, Paige put her hand on Oscar's thigh for a moment, and then she dug her nails in. He brushed it away, put the car in reverse. Neither of them had on their thin wedding bands.

The convertible top came up with a push of a button and the snap of two levers, and we took the long way through Corte Madera, then past San Quentin's brick and barbed wire, then over the scrawny San Rafael Bridge and past the C&H refinery by which we inhaled air whipped through with confection. *C&H / Pure Cane Sugar / From Hawaii / Growing in the sun / I see sugar / Growing pure, fresh, and sweet / C&H / Pure Cane Sugar / It's the one.* Knew it like I knew the birthday song. In New York I'd seen 'Domino' sugar, no California & Hawaii brand, anywhere.

We were nearing Mom's house, plowing through the one-story pitch-flatness that was Walnut Creek at midnight. Oscar floored it, and Paige was tense but said nothing.

God help us if Paige yanked up the emergency brake while he was going full speed. In her mood, she might've. It would be worse than a gory pile-up if she turned to him after a spinning stop and deadened his *What?* with a *Why?*

CHAPTER 19

It was late, but Mom was up.

Paige and I were speaking, somewhat.

Mom let the couch out in the third bedroom for Oscar, had already made up the second one for Paige and I. In the morning we'd sit out on the deck. If it was coffee, we'd drink it pale with milk. Tea would be hot, milky sugar water with a quick dip of Earl Grey.

Out the wide-open window, a crescent moon clung to sky. In four hours the universe would turn hot blue, unblemished by cloud or visible impurity. It was always warmer or colder in Walnut Creek. Only ten miles over the hills of north Oakland, the bedroom town—in the summer especially—could feel like a whole different kingdom.

Paige liked to point out that until the 1900s, not that many people even lived out in WC. The Berkeley–Oakland Hills were daunting back then. 'There was no Caldecott Tunnel burrowed through,' she'd say. 'People needed stagecoaches or ox-drawn wagons to deal with Summit Road.' It had become so you just needed a car or BART, and a desire not to be loud with the sweaty scent of Oakland.

She flipped through her raggedy hardbound copy of *Bread and Jam for Frances.* Mom had it out, along with my Easy-Bake oven. Scrubbed and taped, they were as much artifacts as my Aunt Jemima teapot. Paige's book was about a badger who refused to eat anything but bread and jam. When Frances's mother started serving bread and jam to her three times a day, Frances got sick of it and started eating meat and fruit and whatever else well-drawn badger moms prepared. It's *propaganda,* is what Seth used to say. *Frances* was all about white people telling black people, *Look, eat what we give you, or we'll stuff you with your own shit until you come begging back.*

While I soaked in the tub, Paige flossed her teeth until they bled, then gargled with salt water.

'You left stuff at the Pseudo.'

'Junk,' she said.

'Real stuff.'

'Can't be that real, or I wouldn't have left it.'

'You should have it. Was in the closet.'

'Then it's not even taking up room. Why you telling me now? You about to set it on the porch?'

Back in the bedroom, I popped chunks of green gum into my mouth, watched a movie on cable in which people were naked in conditions that called for clothes. Heard Oscar snoring. Mom opened and closed drawers, putting away laundry, or maybe sifting through the cast-off costumes of her veiled youth. I switched to *The Best Years of Our Lives.* That's what Paige liked. Gray people with no forearms. High-waisted pants, women in gloves on their way to volunteer at the Red Cross. Dad comes home from war, drinks too much, is saved by Mom and Daughter. Betrayal and suffering stomped out by integrity, long love, triumph of spirit. Neither Paige nor I slept. Dawn crept around, anyway.

I was the first one down to the wood deck, then Mom in her yellow terry robe.

'Sleep good?'

'Not really,' I said. 'What about you?'

'I slept fine.'

'You always do.'

'How would you,' Mom said, smiling, 'know what I always do?'

'I know.'

The small wooden deck was overrun with lanterns, fig-urines, and hoses unattached and poised to bite. Paige came down in lavender pajamas. I had on the same ones as Paige, but in silver. Mom had given them to us, in piped green department-store wrapping, the previous Christmas.

'Aren't you two a picture,' Mom said. She went in the kitchen and I heard the *click click click* of a gas burner lighting. She returned to the deck carrying trim, carefully arranged albums of real pictures from me and Paige's infancy and early grade school. Placed them within reach, along with a few loose school photos from our early and late adolescence. In the best ones, we looked stunned, in the worst, unfriendly. She went in the house again, came back with round teabags, hot water, sugar, and milk on a tray.

Paige fixed and finished hers quickly. 'I want to call the police,' she said. She didn't look at the photographs. 'The whole thing is unfair. The way May's getting over. I hate it.' Paige spoke fast because she was seething and because Oscar would soon walk out on the deck, and then she'd have to slow down.

My elbows were on the wooden table. Mom set out sliced pineapple. I wished for the pastels of half a cantaloupe filled at the center with bland applesauce.

'Aren't the police,' Mom said, 'doing what they're sup-posed to do? I don't understand why you can't leave it alone.'

Photos of my sister and I in bloomers. Eyes of oolong and of chamomile. We were simple, impish, sun-squinting. Stood under dangling trout and leaning rods. Or beside Easter bas-kets. Born-yesterday tender. Sweet as if molded from different batches of caramel. I couldn't look too long.

Paige said to Mom, 'I'm not gonna talk to you about this anymore.'

'Because you know you're overreacting. Taking all this on. Unless there's a way you're at fault that you haven't said.'

'You tell me, Mom.'

'Tell what?'

'Say whose fault this whole situation is.'

Here we go.

'You know better than I do.'

'No,' Paige said. 'I don't. I'm talking about the *whole* situation.'

'I'm going inside,' Mom said. Shook her head but didn't move.

Paige was seated. Had the top segment of her thumb sideways on her front teeth. She moved it to that space between the bottom of her nose and her upper lip. Kind of bounced the side of her thumb there. Paige looked straight past Mom.

'Paige,' I said, 'don't start.'

Then my sister sat on her palms, leaned forward. Spoke quickly. 'I appreciate you, Mom, for thinking I'm so able to withstand anything. I guess that's a big compliment to me. But I'm not like you.'

Mom made the smallest move—took her hand from her teacup—and Paige took it as a contradiction.

'No. I'm not strong. I'm weak. Sorry but I am. It's a sign of weakness that I reel from shit, right? Not like you, who can just wash shit off. I want to know where is that motherfucker now, anyway.'

'Stop cursing,' Mom said. 'And if you're talking about your friend, I don't know where he is. If you're talking about family business, there's a better time.'

'When? Is he dead? Just because you don't need a person to recognize your life . . . maybe that fool said something to you that made it all—"

'He didn't apologize to me,' Mom said, like she was sick of saying it. But she'd never said it to us. 'He's alive. He's still drinking.'

'I don't even want to hear his drunk ass say sorry to me. I'm wrong for cursing, Mom, but fuck it. I don't want to mess up your life the way you've made it normal. I want Yes I saw it yes it was bad yes it happened yes you happened.'

You're not saying it right, Paige.

'Okay,' Mom said, looking through the screen door to the kitchen, 'but right now I see your husband's up. You might want to ask him if he wants some breakfast.'

I shook my head.

Oscar walked onto the deck, said, 'Good morning,' to everyone like he knew we hadn't said it to each other.

'You hungry?' Mom was making me mad.

Paige put her hands on top of her thighs, said, 'This is why I'm going back to New York. Not because of Jessica, not because of Ced. This is why I'm on a plane tonight.' She was talking about Mom but wouldn't look at her.

Oscar fell still with so much grace, he seemed carved from wood. Hands lightly on his hips like he was ready to defend a righteous person. I didn't know who among us qualified.

Paige fiddled around under the table with her feet, looking for her slippers. There were sequins on them, in a rainbow pattern. Her teeth were deep in her bottom lip, her breath short, in and out fast through her nose.

Mom suddenly with hot, horrible red eye sockets. I knew the look I knew the look. Stiff but slightly trembling under scrutiny, afraid she wasn't living up to whatever the rules were for being right, being smart, being the mom of those two well-mannered girls Paige and Pinch. *Hell yeah, we were well-mannered, we were on guard.* And Mom next to us at any given function anxious herself, hoping for the best, saying, 'Part of being an adult is putting on a happy face when you're not

happy on the inside,' and she knew we were big girls and we
could do it just for a little while.

*Jesus. This is how my head works. This. Is the only place
my brain goes. I think of me, think of Paige, and what follows
is this same set of scenes, same scratched record of conversation
scraps. This can't be all there is to me.*

I put down the stack of high-school photos I'd been bending in my palm. Paige was as motionless as Oscar, eyes
focused on some piece of air in front of her.

*But I'm like Paige, don't need an apology. I forgive every-
body for everything. I forgive even me for whatever my part was
in anything bad that's ever happened to me or Paige or Mom or
Jess or Ced or anyone.*

*But even that proclamation is bullshit. If all one had to do
was think forgiveness, all in every person's life would be forgiven,
and this would have been some other world all along.*

'Pinch you don't have anything to say?' Paige turned her
eyes to me, but she squinted, like I was hard to make out.

*Fuck what Paige said right before Jess died. I am trans-
formed by Jess's death. By Cedric's. By my own. I came close to
dying when I was twelve. Am close now to coming back to life.*

'I was doing,' Mom said, 'the best I could.' She'd stopped
trembling.

'The best you could? We had food and clothes and school
and some fun. We just had the shit kicked out of us, and humiliation after fucking humiliation.'

*Mom could have helped more. Should we have hoped for
that? Were we supposed to take for granted that Mom was getting her ass beat, too, that she was too wrecked to make a move?
This was my weakness, my death. These questions.*

'If you'd let me speak.'

'Speak about what, Mom? What're you going to say? Get
it out, Mom. Say you're sorry. Make yourself feel better. Sorry
I can't curse Seth out, but you're the only one here. Ask us what

kind of perfection we expected so we can feel grateful for the good stuff we did have. Go ahead. Say how much worse kids have it in Ethiopia. In Lebanon. In the Acorns. Say how some people's kids end up dead or see their mothers killed . . .'

I never heard Mom say anything like that.

'. . . Say how much more fucked up shit could have been so we can all feel good about how tolerably bad we had it. That's what I tell myself already, Mom. It could have been worse. But you tell me, so it sounds true.'

Mom was stone. Sun on her face, and she wasn't blinking. Oscar relaxed his stance, went over to my sister, stood behind her. Mom blinked. Her posture relaxed, and became stronger.

'I was stupid,' Mom said. 'I used to tell you that all the time. I was doing the best I could.' The raw way Mom spoke, I knew she believed it. Paige had stripped her, but not naked.

Mom knew what her life had been before Seth during him after him. It was only a mystery to us her reasons her rationalizations her responsibilities to different kinds of love. Obviously Mom had been through more shit than we'd seen. Or why else? I had to believe there'd been things neither Gwendolyn nor Gigi nor Mom could win against. There had to be.

And when she said to Paige in a tight sad self-conscious voice, 'There's no reason for you to go anywhere right now,' I knew she was telling the truth. She included Oscar and I in her gaze. 'You all can stay here with me for a while.'

But why didn't she say that at the motel that time, the day after the Ninth Grade Court? Why didn't she say it at Diamond Pool? It was too late by the time Paige graduated high school, and for me, it was too late now. To stay.

I'd found a way to draw on my will. Mom was doing the best she could. I kept that fact high in my mind, spelled out in tall yellow light. In the back of my mind I burned the following: Mom's ashamed because we've seen her failings. Paige and I saw her weak and degraded and incapable.

Mom knew we knew. It was penalty enough. I didn't know if any of it was forgiveness, if it was better than forgiveness, or if forgiveness was even something we were supposed to go for. I didn't know how much was family shit people are supposed to just get through. But I was doing the best I could.

'Stay with you? For what? You don't say *anything*,' my sister said to my mother. 'Why don't you say something real?'

'Paige,' I said, 'leave Mom alone.'

O S C A R retied the drawstring of his sweatpants, said, 'You all are having quite a morning.' He could be real Jethro sometimes.

My sister brushed past him on her way into the kitchen. Pans came screeching from a cabinet. Heard her whipping raw eggs in a bowl. Caught the hiccup from a vacuum-packed biscuit canister as Paige pressed a spoon, for maybe the five hundredth time in her life, against the cardboard seam.

Mom pulled her face together, asked Oscar about his father, about what he was doing in New York. Oscar was working for a liquor company, rode around in a company car and checked on the liquor stores in some towns in New Jersey. He delivered posters of girls in red bathing suits sitting atop huge bottles of beer, checked refrigerated cases to make sure the real bottles were in straight lines at the front of the shelves.

When Oscar said he wished he could go back to school, finish up, Mom said, 'That sounds good, keep it all in perspective.'

'Here,' Paige said, and set out plates and a skillet of eggs with cheese. She went back and forth to the kitchen three more times, crowded the table with the rolls, margarine, grape jam, grits, and a jug of ketchup. Oscar waited for Mom to get hers and then started spooning up. It made me think he was lucky, the way the food lit him from within.

Paige said, 'I'm still going to the police station.'

I said, 'For what?'

She spoke directly to Oscar. 'To tell them May either killed Cedric or had Cedric killed. Gonna talk to them about Jess, too. How she died.'

I ate. Oscar forked food with precision. The surface of Paige's grits gelled to skin. Mom padded to the doorway. Slid the screen door shut behind her.

'You have everything decided,' Oscar said. 'So you must've figured out what you're gonna tell the police about me.'

Paige pushed up the broad sleeves of her pajamas. They slid back down. 'That you have a real job now,' she said.

'One,' Oscar said, 'I don't have a real job. I have a job. Two, you're not going to talk to any police because who you gonna tell on? Everybody? You gonna tell on your mom, too?'

'You do need to think about what you're doing,' I said.

'You tell me to leave Mom alone, but what you want is for me to shut up in general. *Shut up, Paige. Whatever's bothering you, put a happy face on top of it.*'

'That's not what she's saying.'

'Don't tell me what my sister said.'

'I was just saying that maybe you need to relax a little, think about the consequences of what you do.'

'Why is it my job to think about consequences? When I was scared, when *we both* were, who was thinking about consequences? Who was even thinking about the *moment* fucked-up shit was going down? Does May think about consequences? But I've got to think about the costs of my actions. That's my job.'

'Only,' I said, 'if you want it to be.'

'That's cool. No one's on my side. Weren't you going to Seattle, Pinch, to be with your non-boyfriend? He's probably got a happy face. Why don't you go up there.'

I WALKED the short path out to the beige-green meadow just beyond Mom's yard, before the thin creek. Oscar followed me. Paige stayed at the breakfast table. We sat out there, backs against a bench, two fools together.

'Before this place was named Walnut Creek—for the nut trees and all the creeks—when it was basically where a road from Martinez met up with a route to San Francisco, this area was called the Crossroads,' Oscar said. 'No houses out here at all.'

'So you listen when Paige talks.'

'Ha. Yeah. There was a post office out this way. So you could send something, or wait on a word. For a long time, people didn't live at the Crossroads. They picked a direction and kept on stepping.'

'You trying to tell me something?'

'Or tell myself.'

Mom leaned out, now sporty in vivid workout gear. 'Sandra's on the phone for Paige.'

She hopped up from the table without a glance at Oscar or I, ran into the house barefoot, slippery rainbows in hand.

We started walking back toward the house.

'Jessica's mom wants us to come visit her,' Paige yelled through the screen. 'This afternoon.'

Oscar picked up dishes to bring them into the kitchen. I followed, began rinsing and placing them in the dishwasher.

He didn't offer, so Paige said, 'Oscar, will you take me out there?'

'Yeah. If that's where you want to go.'

'Are you coming, Pinch?' Slyly, like she was triumphant in some way.

'Yep I am.'

Within an hour we were going through the Caldecott Tunnel, top down, directly toward Upper High. Above Upper High.

Traffic was flowing. Paige, hunched down in her seat, found a tube of lip balm and applied it twice. Oscar drove beyond the speed limit, even through the tunnel. Fumy air grazed my face. Paige still had no idea how to drive. I'd no license and no car. Whenever Paige or I wanted to go somewhere, it was at the courtesy of someone else. Oscar was lucky, in some ways. He had the nerve and the inclination to get places on his own.

RIGHT before we left Mom's, I went up to her room. Folded clothes were everywhere. More than laundry. Seemed like every stitch she owned. Paige was in the shower.

'What are you doing?'

'Rearranging my closet.'

'Why?'

She paused. 'I never ask myself that.'

'I have to ask you something.'

She stopped folding. Found a clear space, among slips and pullovers and sweatpants, to sit on her bed.

'Do you want this?' I handed her two manila envelopes from my purse.

'This is what? Your will?' Her laugh came out like a cough. 'A letter to me?'

'It's Paige's.'

'Paige's what?'

'I'm trying to . . . help, Mom. This stuff isn't even for me to give.'

'And what if I don't act exactly how you want me to after I look at it?'

'I don't know. But maybe you need to . . . just know some things. The way I need to know some things, straight out.'

'And what do you need to know?'

Everything. About you, about me and Paige's real father,

about Seth. Why. I need to know why everything. 'Basic stuff, Mom. Like how many happy times is a person supposed to have? Did Paige and me miss a lot, or did we miss just a little? Are people supposed to count happy times from birth on, or do you start counting when you're old enough to create happy times for yourself?'

'I missed a lot. Of you and your sister.'

'And what do you do about it?'

'It's late now, Pinch. So I count every happy time I can remember.'

CHAPTER 20

Lamb roasting and chopped mint on a wooden block. Marble countertops. Sandy sponge-painted walls and a thick round table looked like from Mexico. We sat around it, with heavy empty chairs between us. Everywhere Sandra's own blunt, glazed pottery. We were in her breakfast nook. Paige and I had barely spoken to each other since we left Mom's.

'Teeara brings Zachary by to see me all the time,' Sandra said. 'To see us all the time.'

Kitchen had a new toaster made to look old-fashioned, and a real terra cotta–tiled floor. Bushy braided throw rugs and the faucet with just the one arched handle that goes left for hot and right for cool. We had Cokes. Sandra'd offered goblets, but the small icy bottles fascinated me.

'Zachary always has on the nicest clothes,' she said, 'and he speaks much more clearly than other children his age.' Sandra had no clay under her nails. She wore screeching pink lipstick and no other makeup.

'So Ree's good, then,' Paige said.

'Yes he's good. His little teeth, and his hair's always trimmed and shiny. And that scar on his leg has softened to the thinnest . . . almost saffron line.' Oscar pushed a goblet toward her. I sipped my Coke, wanted to keep the bottle.

'You talked to May much?' Paige asked.

'I speak to him frequently. We speak to him frequently. Of

course we do.' She sat with her hand around her drink. 'We appreciate him a great deal.'

'That's different,' Paige said.

'I invited you up here because you were Jessica's friends. And because Maynard will never tell anything. Through all these investigations, I see him. Cool as he can be.' Sandra looked around like she'd just noticed the clanky jazz falling through her house. 'I'm going to tell you something,' she said. 'But ahead of time you should know that as far as any police, or the courts, I've never said anything.'

What? I couldn't believe Paige was right. My sister looked shaken. Oscar sat back in his chair.

'The day of the shooting,' Sandra said, 'Roland went over to Jessica and May's. To take Jessica a gun.' She looked at each of us.

'A gun for what?' Oscar said when her glance fell on him.

'Roland felt Jess needed one. As he put it, she was "out there in Siberia." Roland also felt like Jessica was mad at Maynard, afraid of him.'

I said, 'Afraid of him why?'

Sandra lifted her shoulders slowly. 'This is what my husband felt. Because Jessica told him that Maynard never talked to her about his feelings. Or about his . . . job. Maynard wanted Jessica to spend only his money. Jessica told her father that Maynard could be unpredictable.'

'What's that mean?' Paige again.

'Kicking over furniture. Threatening to take Zachary someplace far. Maynard ruined some clothes in her closet when he found out Jess was using the AmEx Roland had told her to keep for emergencies.'

'Ruined clothes?' Paige could believe May had something to do with killing Ced and Jess, but not that he ruined Jess's clothes.

'I'm not trying to prove to you what anyone did or didn't do. I'm telling you the information people were working from.'

'What people?'

'Paige,' Oscar said. 'Let her talk.'

'Jessica complained to me, too,' Sandra said, 'that Maynard drank. Too much. In the day. She didn't like that. Jessica felt she couldn't do anything to make Maynard happy, and, I know now, Maynard felt nothing he did was good enough for her.'

I didn't like Sandra's expression. Nostrils flared, glowy chin, lips lopsided.

'Jessica was sure Maynard had a girlfriend.' She paused, looked at us. We looked at her to continue.

'She wouldn't leave May, though,' Sandra said. 'Roland and I suggested, then we asked, and then we pressed Jessica to come back here with the baby. At least for a while. My problem was more with Maynard's lifestyle than anything my daughter was complaining about. His dope-selling. Your dope-selling.' She kept her gaze broadly fixed. Sandra's cheeks were chafed, her hair was back in a fiery bandanna. 'The numbness the boys all have to manufacture in order to be out there doing it. The way it's rubbed off on you girls. But who am I to judge. I never asked Roland not to take Jessica the gun.'

What are we talking about?

Oscar said, 'Where is Dr. Roland?'

'Roland's here,' Sandra said, 'and he's not.'

I looked out at two dangling birdhouses and a kiln like a red igloo. The birdbath was dry and spotted with muck. Beyond all that was a slope of iceplant and then a sheer drop and then the General Douglas MacArthur Freeway moved four lanes east toward Hayward and another four west to the Bay Bridge, and nowhere out there was Jessica. Ree could squat on Sandra's red-orange floor with pots and a wooden spoon from now until, but we'd all seen Jessica's coffin

wheeled from the hearse, seen the purple-eyed Dr. Roland
damn near feverish with hives at the grave site, watching his
daughter lowered. The house's sick melody seemed louder
than before. A brush smoothed over a snare so repeatedly,
with so exactly the same *whisk whisk* each time, it burned like
an iron on my ear. A trumpet and a saxophone howled. There
was a giant bass being plucked, too. The song was garish, but
Sandra stood up from her chair as if framed by Mohave quiet.
Walked to open her oven door, inhaled the hot meatiness like
it was the best thing she'd ever breathed.

'I know you loved Jessica,' Sandra said, looking at Paige.
'And Maynard. That's why I called you.' She straightened up,
tugged down her tan blouse, and daintily adjusted her pants.

Paige walked to the window nearest Oscar, looked toward
the lap pool. It was clean, beyond clear. I wished Sandra
would say what she had to say so we could leave.

'Jess,' Paige said, 'told us it wasn't May.'

'You don't believe that,' Sandra said. 'I see it on your face.
And I saw the way you dealt with Maynard at the hospital. I
heard about Maynard's friend Cedric. People think May was
involved in that, too. I'm sure he wasn't.'

Oscar stood to put his bottle on the counter.

Paige started to speak.

Sandra put her hand up. 'Maynard allows people to think
he had more to do with Jessica . . . not being here. He allows
people to think he had a hand in Cedric's death. That's how he
is, is what I'm trying to say. He needs that. I know him better
now.'

We were all suddenly motionless, like there'd been a
blurred noise. Looked instantly at each other. A clay tureen in
a dish on the floor made rough clanking noises. Dishes clat-
tered, glasses shuddered and clinked in a credenza. Outdoors,
birdhouses swayed slightly. Spinning music skipped into
silence. One of Oscar's knees bent, and Paige's teeth were in

her tongue. A mile-long rolling pin revolved beneath our soles. Stressed plates under us shifted. The fault wheezed. No time passed. Years went by. Then the rumbling came, for a moment, to an end.

'A tremor,' Paige said. She'd swayed with the small quake like an accomplice.

Sandra took a few steps in each direction, glanced around for damage. 'Do you want to call your mother?'

She must have caught our blank expressions.

'To see if she's all right? To let her know you're all right?'

Paige nodded, but neither of us moved.

'Mom knows we're fine,' I said.

'She's in Walnut Creek now, right?' Sandra walked out of the kitchen, and we followed her. She was looking at her shelves, righting things that had fallen over, noting the glasses that had broken into pieces. I picked up some books from the floor, and she looked at me sharply. 'I'll get that,' she said.

'Mom's been out there awhile now,' Paige said. Oscar sat on a painted wood bench in the foyer.

'I miss your mother sometimes,' Sandra said, suddenly jovial. 'Not that we were real good girlfriends, but we'd hang out after Glee, or Art Club, wait on the bus. Does she still paint?'

Paige and I both shook our heads. Oscar belted out a huge laugh. The conversation, the visit, was bizarre. And then it began to rain.

'Not even sometimes? I'm surprised,' Sandra said. 'It wasn't her life, but she enjoyed it. Your mother was with me the day I met Roland.'

We said nothing. We knew nothing about Mom painting, or her glee.

'You knew that. And Gigi wouldn't get in the car with us, because she was going with your father.'

I couldn't look at Sandra, turned my attention to the falling water.

'Where's my purse?' Paige asked Oscar.

'In the car.'

'Get it for me?'

'No.'

'I need my lotion right quick. And my lips are chapped.'

'Live through it. Sandra, Paige and Pinch never did meet their father.'

'Hmm.' She was about her business. Almost humming. Checking the fireplace, looking at the walls for cracks. The quake wasn't even big enough for all that. 'Maybe I have too many secrets to spill today.' She picked up broken glass with her bare hands. Held shards in one palm.

'You aren't talking,' I turned to her and said, 'about Seth, then.'

'No. Seth, I guess he was a doctor? No. I'm talking about your father.'

'Was he nice?' I didn't know what else to ask.

'I didn't know him except to see he was sad. Gigi liked boys who didn't have lots of friends. Then she could be their whole world.'

How is she just bouncing through my life?

'You don't know Mom like that,' Paige said.

'I told you earlier. I'm not trying to prove anything to you. I'm just saying I used to see your mother all the time. Probably right up until she got with Seth. We'd run into you all at Fairyland. I'd have Jess, and you all would play for a minute in the sandbox.'

'No way,' I said.

'Yes,' Sandra said. The memory seemed to make her genuinely happy. She held her hand out, like the glass was a gift, but she must have squeezed it, because a thread of blood was about to drip to the floor. 'You two with your long braids and Gigi pleased as punch. She looked tired, no doubt about that. But everyone always told her what gorgeous little girls she had, and she always had you all dressed so perfectly, and she was always petting you and always made you two introduce each other: This is my *big sister*. This is my *little sister*.'

Of course she did. How else would we introduce each other?

Heard brakes whining to a stop. Car door opened, then slammed. Car door opened and slammed again.

In a rush Sandra said, 'Roland is responsible. For the accidental death of our daughter. Roland went over there, he stupidly went over there with the gun. He heard a noise. He says there was crashing and confusion and he thought May was hurting her. He says he shot into their living room. That's what he says. That May came into the kitchen and Roland was going to shoot May and May pushed a chair or something into his knees. And he did shoot at May and the shot did go into the living room and hit . . . my . . . daughter.'

Paige said, 'That doesn't even sound right. Nothing you're saying sounds right.'

'No,' Sandra said. 'It doesn't. But I'm not trying to convince you. I'm telling you what I choose to believe.'

I also choose to believe.

Dr. Roland walked through the door with his grandson on his hip. Ree's lips were orange. There was a silver cloud on his forehead. His cheeks were painted with blue lightning bolts.

'Do you think it's what I would choose?' Sandra's pink-slashed mouth stretched wide, like she was screaming. Her voice was a squeak. 'Over the other possibilities? Unless it were true?'

Dr. Roland took us all in, was about to hand Ree to Sandra when he saw the blood.

'Sandra, what the hell.' He handed Ree to me and opened a closet near the stairs, pulled out some towels. Gently he turned her hand over into one, so the glass fell in, along with a spoonful of blood. He loosely wrapped the hand with another towel. 'What are you doing?'

'Did you feel the earthquake?' Sandra held her hurt hand in the other. Spoke giddily.

'It was a tremor,' Dr. Roland said. 'We were on the freeway, didn't feel a thing. Heard about it on the radio.'

'How was the carnival?'

'Booths and a merry-go-round and people on stilts.' He looked around the house, and at us. 'How's it here?'

Oscar extended his hand, which Dr. Roland shook. 'We were at Cedric's funeral yesterday.'

'I heard about that.' His hair was pushed back from his forehead. It was thin enough that I could see where his fingers had run through. His collar wasn't pressed. The cuffs of his white shirt were streaked sticky with candy, and sand bound to that.

I said, 'I thought we might go by and see Jessica.' Ree was heavy and grimy and quiet.

'Zach and I were by there this morning,' Dr. Roland said. 'Between us and Maynard, she's rarely by herself.'

'Maynard's been good,' Sandra said. 'I spoke with Bill—'

Oscar said, 'You talked to my dad?'

Oh now it's not funny.

'He's who felt I should ask you all by.' She glanced at her husband, then looked back at us. 'You all are funny. Think Oakland is brand new. I've known Bill for years, since high school. For longer than I've known Roland.' She took a breath. Her cut hand looked bulky in the other. 'But you all knew my daughter, in a way I didn't. Now I want—we want—to know you.'

'But,' Dr. Roland said, 'I won't hear anything negative said about my grandson's father.'

Ree wanted to get down. I held him tighter.

'If I'd reached out to him before, if I'd ever tried to know him, a lot of this'—he motioned roughly toward his wife, and then myself and Ree, and then in the direction of Oscar and Paige —'might have been avoided. Maynard is a decent person.'

Paige said, 'All of a sudden.'

I said, like a tattletale, 'May has done some crazy things.'

'I know about Todd,' Sandra said, like by her knowing it, it had less meaning. Then she said, 'You think Teeara didn't tell me how she lost that eye?'

It was raining in bursts. Thin streams of water entered the lawn like glass. Wondered if the ground would become over-saturated. An inch of rain on damp ground can cause a short wall of water to rise in minutes. Can move smothering mud down a hill in a second. You drain and you mop. Rays warm your back. As you forget, clouds like dead mice on their gray backs float together. The wind whips or it doesn't. You stack your sandbags, you pray it be quick. Fingers in mud, you think lovingly of dust and then of the flames fathered in drought. Sandra was living it. We all were. And this happens all the time in California.

Sandra was trying to be everybody's friend, make every-body her family. And she was exasperated by us. She came over and took her grandson from me, handed him to Dr. Roland.

All in my face she said, 'You believe May would kill some-body?'

Dr. Roland walked from the room with Ree.

'You all were May's friends,' she said. 'Weren't you?'

CHAPTER 21

The day after the tremor was another day of visits.

Bright day, big day. Pyrotechnic pinwheels and primary signs. Dead people wandering. Living people happily half-blinded by the long hook of life.

Me, Mom, Oscar, and Paige all went to see Jessica. Then Mom was going to walk over to her father's grave. I'd paged Todd the night before. He hadn't felt the earthquake but was surprised to hear from me. Todd and I had plans to meet for food.

Mom brought daffodils, and Paige had a thick softbound book about California with color photos, pullout maps, and histories of interesting points. She had cheese sandwiches, and plans to sit with Jess awhile.

'We saw Ree,' I said in the direction of Jessica's tomb. 'Looked like he'd been having fun.' I put some of the yellow flowers on Jess's marker.

'You got Cedric, now, on your side.' Paige spread her sweater on the grave and settled down right on top. She cheeped along like Jess would answer back. 'You two are probably having a good time over there.'

Oscar stood next to Mom. Restless, and with faces pushed in, they looked as I felt. Embarrassed and experimental, talking to the dead.

'She might just be able to hear,' Oscar said.

'What do you think, Mom?' Paige looked over at her. Testing. 'Can Jess understand?'

'It's fifty-fifty,' Mom said. 'So why not talk to her. Just in case.'

But since I didn't know whether Jess would be happy or sad to hear me say that Oakland was just the goddamn same, I said no more.

'Jess,' Oscar yelled, 'give a sign!'

We waited. It was early. So just the same slow symphony of traffic beyond the fence. Mom had called in sick to work, but wore the same kind of ironed, beige, low-heeled outfit she'd sport were she going.

There was no one but us breathing in the cemetery. As far as I could see.

After a few minutes, Mom re-hoisted her tote to her shoulder. 'Where I'm going,' she said, 'is all the way on the other side.'

I said, 'You want me to walk with you?'

'Go on ahead with Oscar, see your friend.' Then she looked at her son-in-law. 'I'll expect you in what, an hour or two?'

'Y'all are gonna stay in the cemetery for two hours?' He shook his head.

'What are you going to say to your dad, Mom?' Paige asked. 'When you can barely remember him?'

'Don't know. Maybe I'll wait on a sign.' She started walking away. 'Paige,' she called over her shoulder. 'Sit tight.'

My sister with hair pulled from her forehead with tin combs from Chinatown. Eyes heated and hard. Mom didn't wait on Paige to answer. Disappeared into a dip.

'You're gonna be all right up here?' Oscar asked. 'We'll be gone awhile.'

Paige nodded.

I was glad to see a middle-aged man setting seashells on a

greenish tombstone. We weren't the only ones in Oakland trying to communicate with folks no longer here.

'You won't get spooked?' I said.

'It's a cemetery in the *day*time,' Paige said, looking past
me. 'Plus, all the bad's been done to get here.'

We left Paige on a puddle of gold sweater, shoulder to
Jess's stone.

L A D Y Esther's Southern Cuisine is a shack bound to a store-
front where you could buy life insurance from a man who
looked old and sour enough to have been denied work on any
one of the bay's bridges. Dogged enough to have finally gotten
on at the Standard Oil yards during the forties before his second wife left him for a Virginian who bought fur-collared coats
and beat the wife broken. Cold enough to have left the Virginian bleeding to death on Negro Night at a dance hall called
Melody Lane. This was the tale that always got told.

Oscar dropped me. 'Beep me when you're ready,' he said
before burning off in a U-turn. 'Or when Todd acts a fool.'

The insurance man gazed at me, eyes gray on yellow, as I
walked into the restaurant. Then he looked back at his papers.
He'd been behind that spotless window since Paige and I were
tiny, used to speak to my great-grandfather. The insurance
man didn't believe in guns for any reason. He'd cut you if you
looked at him wrong or asked him about himself beyond How
are you. My great-grandfather told me this last part, so I figured it to be exact.

At the restaurant Todd ordered us a mound of chicken
with a bowl of gravy. Grits on the side. Lemonade. His sideburns and hair were trimmed so precisely it all looked painted
on. Todd's shirt was of a turquoise fabric I thought would be
cuter as a dress for me.

Todd had been running thick with Bam all along, and

now Bam was doing twenty-five to life for a murder of some-one I didn't know. Not that I knew Bam.

'Homeboy might never get out,' Todd said. 'Was a close call, too, for me.' He stuck the last part out like meat on a stick. Stuck it out blandly, knowing it would still tantalize.

'You were with him?'

'Don't ask me ridiculous stuff,' he said, snatching back.

Did you kill somebody? Did you almost kill somebody? Did you dime on your so-called friend? Cough it up, spit it out. I'd wanted to ask Todd if he knew what really happened to Ced. Wanted to see if Todd had been changed by his shuffle, by time, by people we both knew dying.

'So the fireworks started after I left the funeral,' he said. Dipped a piece of thigh meat in gravy. 'Oscar and May getting into it at the graveyard!'

'More like Paige and May.'

'Sounds right. I'd heard that, too. Eat,' he said, waving at the food.

Put a wing on my plate. 'I know you heard something about Ced.'

'I heard what everybody's saying, but everybody's saying something different.'

'What'd you hear from people who'd know?'

'That's why you called me?' He sat back, faked mortifica-tion. 'To quiz me?'

'I need to know what happened.'

'And you knew I'd know.' Todd was glad about having that value. Wiped his fingers on the napkin in his lap. 'I heard shit.'

Jesus, stop relishing. 'I want to know.'

'Whoever killed Ced made him eat mud. Literally. They took his bracelets. I heard they asked him something, I don't know what it was, but then Cedric spit on the ground. They told him to find it. Get down there and find it.'

What kind of sick shit? He's making this up? 'You know all this because?'

'Don't ask me shit like that. I'll tell you about your other friends. Know you ain't been rolling with them. Donnell got picked up over in north Oakland, thought he was going to be gone for a while, but he ended up with work furlough. Ch'Rell works at a bank in San Francisco during the day and does something for a construction company at night.'

I know all that. Any chick at the nail shop knew that.

'May and Paige ain't cool no more?' Todd said, motioning to the waitress for hot sauce. 'I always thought them niggas shoulda fucked and got it over with. It's what everybody thought. Or that they did it a long time ago.'

'You're asking me? Ask my sister. Ask Maynard.' *Something about my sister I actually do not know.*

'May got him a new one now, anyway. Kimya.'

'That's his girl.' Waitress brought lemonade. Crowded with lemon quarters wrung to the rind, in my first sip, granulated C&H crunched between my teeth, melted on my tongue.

'His girl like Paige was his girl. Kimya's older than him, she watches his back, he watches hers. Or seems to. You know the drill. May keep one for making babies, one to be his mama.'

'Paige isn't older than May. And she wasn't his mom.'

'What was she, then? What was she to you?'

Fuck you. 'Me and Paige are sisters.'

'I guess. All y'all up under each other like puppies in a litter. No tit to fight for, though. So then you all bust out like raw dogs.' He laughed at his little distillation.

'Anyway,' I said carefully, 'Paige is mad at May like maybe May hurt Cedric.'

'May didn't do anything to Ced.'

'Who did?'

'Does it matter?'

Yes. 'Was it you?'

'Was it *you*? Shit. Ced got caught out there. You thought niggas who run like we run gonna come out safe, on top? That's not what you thought. I know that's not what you thought.' Waitress slid a check under Todd's plate. 'You know the truth,' he said over crisp heart and gizzard. 'That's why your ass be on the sidelines. When you run the streets, though, when you be out there with fools creating they own hell, or fools allowing mufuckers to put hell on them, you know for sure there's a real hell waiting for all us that contributed to this Climate. All us that accepted it, used it, danced in it.' Todd looked at me steady. 'Need to shut my mouth, anyway,' he said. 'To you. You half-up outta this shit, I can tell. Looking good, looking grown. Laying low, changing friends.'

'I haven't changed my friends.' I didn't eat, or drink any more lemonade.

"Who you talking to?' He snorted. "Cause I don't be around you, I don't be around?'

'Stop being stupid.'

'I want to stop. But you know what I want more than that?'

To walk like you used to?

'To get back with Teeara,' he said. With a serious face. 'I'd take care of her. I've told her I was sorry a million times. I bought her and the kids all kinda shit. She keeps it, too. I mean, she should. I shouldn't have brought that jack inside the apartment that day. I was mad. New to things.'

It was like he was explaining why he was late for class. Like he'd a real reason for being late, but like he wasn't one to take the bell seriously, and he'd never ask what lesson he'd missed. Todd must have seen my mind wandering because he said my name.

I hunted inside my head.

Pinch.

There's Nannah. Put Gram Liz out when she was seventeen. There's Gram Liz. Put Mom out when she had two babies, no man, and a new job. There's Mom. Let Paige and I go when we were still kids.

Pinch.

Sink or swim. Moms are required to create individuals who can survive. As fast as they can, they make sure we know how to survive, then force us to go for it. Mothers aren't required to create perfect individuals. They're required to feed, clothe, and teach. That's love. Jessica had the add-ons. She was petted. Taught to thrive. To drive. And where was she except in heaven. I'll take Gigi, Liz, and Nannah over Sandra. I don't need a bright lamp if it's only going to come crashing down in the end.

Hunted my head for another way to look at things.

Nothing.

Except *Pinch.*

I'd pressed and pressed and made it like *me too I can take it like Paige and Mom I feel the pain. Because you didn't put it on me doesn't mean it isn't there.* The third grade. That's when I began to pinch blue posies in my thighs. By fourth grade they bloomed on the baby-skinned pudge of my arm.

Ah yes.
Press.
Sigh soft.

No burn, no sting.
The buds welted, rose up sometime.
At me, if I did it right.
Pressed for a long time.
Or sucked until ducts broke burgundy under my cream-of-wheat skin.

Wispy-looking. Breathe on her too hard and she'll break. In elementary school, that's what people said. What Seth said.

But outside Paige's JC Penney fitting-room door, Gram Liz said, *Paige is stocky, built to last.*

Paige says I was silent back then. I guess I was, from like ten to twelve. In therapy I played with wooden toys, fantasized through a dollhouse with a coaxing blond lady. A teacher at my school had told Mom I was 'withdrawn,' so Mom called out to Cal, and Paige took me to a counselor-in-training there, once a week, after school. Didn't know what a sliding scale was back then, but that's what I was on. That lady was nice to me, had me drawing with colored pencils. I told her about Paige, and how I wished Paige could come. But because my teacher had spoken to Mom, I was considered a part of some program. That lady told me to tell Paige to draw or write about her feelings, and that's what Paige did.

I didn't tell the therapist I grew the posies myself, but maybe she knew. I got to go to stupid counseling because I wouldn't talk and because of the bruises. My sister talked all the time. Paige's grades were good, so of course Mom thought she was fine. Paige's teachers thought she was a prize. Paige talked to everyone about otters and old goldmines, Cannery Row and the Golden Gate Bridge. So clever. No one saw her dark bouquet but me.

I T W A S Paige who started calling me Pinch, and I liked the name because no one ever got it.

Paige'd be all, Pinch this, Pinch that. We had an inside joke.

Pinch this, Pinch that.

It caught on.

The last time Paige called me by my real name. I don't know.

'PINCH,' Todd said. 'Do you think Teeara'll take me back?'

'If she's lost her mind.' He saw I meant it.

He put money on the table. I put down ten dollars of my own.

I got up from the table, went to the pay phone out front, put my code in Oscar's pager. Todd limped out after me. He and I stood in front of the insurance guy's window. NOTARY PUBLIC—LIFE INSURANCE was painted in neat letters on the glass. I watched the street for my brother-in-law.

'Tee'll be back,' Todd said. 'She hates me right now, but pretty soon she'll need to be with the brother who made her like she is. No one else can tell her sorry enough times. Tell her every day. She'll get her pride back, take off them glasses, when me and her get back together.'

I loved Oscar for pulling up right then in the Mustang. Leaned back in his seat, light canvas jacket half-zipped up. Oscar said, 'You ready?' He didn't lift his shades, but said, 'What's up,' to Todd.

'You, man, obviously,' Todd said, limping over a little closer, and smiling at Oscar like he could spit on him. 'New York nigga back in town in a big way. Talking shit, making waves.'

I got in the car, buckled up.

'Pinch,' Todd said, 'what we were discussing about Ced. Regardless of what you think about me and what I say—I handled that, for real. That's why I know what I know.'

Oscar turned down the volume on the radio. 'If you really had,' he said, still not looking at Todd, 'you wouldn't be saying shit about it around me. If you'd done anything to Cedric, you'd be shitting on yourself right now because you'd know I was about to run your ass over and not give a fuck because the car isn't mine, anyway.'

Todd put his good foot behind him. The bad one flopped so it lay across a crack in the sidewalk, pointing in. 'You act like you shot me,' Todd said with a short crow. 'Let me hip you to something—May did it. While your ass stood by like a boy. So your show right now is weak. You *still* behind May. Behind Paige, too. Got your wife cursing niggas out. I'mma tell you right now—May didn't do shit to Cedric. He ain't hardcore like that. I'm telling you because I know.'

Oscar shook his head. Spoke absently, as if to himself, but loud enough so Todd could hear. 'Hobbling on the corner in front of Lady Esther's. Gimpy, punk motherfucker. Mufucker who put his son's mother's eye out gonna try and talk to me about my wife.'

I liked how Oscar referred to Paige as his wife. But I said, 'Come on, let's go.'

'That's why your ass'll be back in New York,' Todd yelled. 'Or wherever the fuck you ran to. You can't live this Oakland shit.'

The insurance man walked out of his building. I hadn't noticed him come from behind his desk. He stepped directly to Todd and said, in a weirdly youthful voice, 'What happened to your leg?'

Todd was caught off guard, but this was his favorite subject. 'It's my foot,' he said. 'Something that happened a—'

'Is that why you and this other one are hollering in front of my store?'

Todd started in with 'We was—' and the guy kicked Todd's healthy foot out from underneath him. Todd fell on his ass and the heel of his palm. He didn't shout. His face caved in like another obscene thing he'd suspected about life had been confirmed.

Oscar got out of the car. He put his hand out to Todd, who got to his feet with the help. The insurance man's skin was like a paper bag wrinkled and mottled with grease. The wiry white hairs in his eyebrows stood out from the black ones. His slate eyes were keen, his lips soft like he was nineteen. 'I'm so tired,' the old man said, 'of all you fuck-ups.'

Todd dusted at his pants.

Oscar walked back toward the driver's side of the car. The man opened the door to his insurance office and then stopped when Oscar spoke. 'Where's the love, Mr. Black Business Owner? Sir Stab-a-Motherfucker. Ain't you supposed to be passing down some wisdom? Each one teach one?'

The insurance man turned, said, 'I got your wisdom.' He pointed an index finger toward his temple, jerked down his thumb.

OSCAR and I. We sat in front of a bakery where the coffee of the day was hazelnut. Next door was a place to buy Rollerblades, then a store in which the mannequins posed in gauzy dresses and the kind of wide-brimmed straw hats I never saw anyone wear. Oscar and I waited for his father to come out of the big Episcopalian church in the Rockridge area of Oakland. I always thought of Rockridge as one of the nice areas. Was near where Paige had got my Aunt Jemima.

'What're you gonna do?'

'Can't stay here,' I said. 'I love . . . Oakland. But I need to be somewhere else.'

'You'll be all right without your sister?'

'I'll find out.'

'You will. I've been other places, though. And nothing's wrong with Oakland that can't be dealt with, one way or another. Ain't nothing wrong with coming home.'

'You're coming home. I've been here all along.'

'Think your sister wants to be away from Oakland, all this shit that's gone down?'

'Make her talk to you. After twenty twists and turns, she'll finally say what she wants.'

'You're tired of talking to her.'

'I'm tired of her being the only person I can talk to.'

People from Oscar's father's meeting trickled out, holding wilted paper cups of coffee.

'How was it?' Oscar said to his dad.

'Same. Fine.' He got in the backseat, put his flat eel-skin bag on the seat next to him. Pushed my head a little, said, 'What's wrong with you?'

'Just tired.' Decided to tell the truth. 'Pissed off, really. And just want to be gone.'

Oscar said, 'She fell out with Todd.'

'Maybe I'll go back to New York,' I said. 'At least I've been there.'

'You could, but if you're running from Oakland, believe me, you take it with you.' Oscar maneuvered out of the parking space and eased into the traffic on College Avenue.

'If you're gonna go,' Oscar's father said, 'then really *go* someplace.'

I said, 'I could, huh, Bill?' *I can.*

From the backseat, Oscar's father tugged twice at my ponytail. It didn't hurt at all. Tears came to my eyes.

We were going to get Paige and Mom from the cemetery. Paused at the signal near MacArthur–Broadway Mall. My nail spot was inside. My café au lait panty hose on rack in the Woolworth's. Thought I saw myself, in a cute outfit from the Ten Dollar Store, getting on the No. 40. I had an Icee. Was going to see my friends. Would lay up on somebody's couch. Talk about what we were going to do that night. How we were going to do it. Probably not do it at all. Put my fare in the box. Barely kept my balance as the bus pulled off heavily, wheezing exhaust and leaning hard on the driver's side.

The No. 40 pulled on down Foothill Boulevard. Groaning. But I wasn't on it. *I'm going in another direction.*

Looked up at the light. Red flashed off. In the instant before it changed, I wanted to yell out 'Green!' like Paige and I used to for my nearly blind grandpa.

Oscar's father passed me his frayed address book.

His son burned rubber into the empty intersection.

I wanted to stand up and scream it.

Green green green.

Month: April. Feels like January.
Day: Weird Friday, diary in the morning, for a
change
Attitude: See below

This dream was about a school bus shaped like
a key. Pinch and I were standing at a bus stop that
didn't look like any stop we've ever been at, and we
were with some kids I've never seen. The bus was
shaped not like a key really, but more like the space
through an old-fashioned keyhole. Bulb-like on top,
rectangle on the bottom. And so it was me and Pinch's
turn to get on the bus—the line had been moving slowly.
The bus driver didn't have a face that I can remember.
When Pinch and I were on the bus steps, I heard kids in
front of us whimpering and I started getting scared.
When we got up by the driver, at the place where you
would put in your fare, the driver handed us keys,
regular metal door keys, and we were supposed to
swallow them. Pinch looked at me and I didn't know
what to do except put the key in my mouth and try to
swallow it, and there was no chewing it, so I tried to
swallow it whole. Of course it was hurting me and tears
were coming to my eyes and I was trying to use the
muscles in my throat and it seemed like the key was
cutting me but I kept trying and trying and when Pinch
was about to try and swallow hers I woke up. What is
that about? Who has this kind of a dream?

CHAPTER 22

IF I FELL asleep in the graveyard, the guy on the giant lawn mower might just fold me into a hole. I stretched out, though. The grass smelled like raw spinach. Jessica was beneath me in a cold nap.

'I knew you'd be here,' May said. He stood above me. Sneakers brand new. His voice relaxed and familiar, like he was running into me in front of the Rusty Scupper.

I wished I'd been leaning against Jess's tombstone, staring into the distance pensively, tendrils of hair gently blowing across my face. I wished he'd caught me arranging Pinch's flowers, eyes wet with remembrance. Instead I was splayed out like a psycho with old books and crumpled wax paper. 'Yep,' I said. 'Here I am.'

'You think I'm not supposed to be here.'

'She was your wife.'

'And I shot her, right?'

'That's for you to answer.'

'Why should I when everyone answers it for me?'

'You got Sandra and Dr. Roland on your side. She's telling the truth?'

'That's a way of putting it.' He had sad daisies. And some bubble gum. Sat them on the smooth top of Jess's stone. JESSICA MARY, it said. LOVING DAUGHTER, WIFE, MOTHER. REMEMBER ME FOR THY GOODNESS' SAKE. May's skin was like he'd been living in a basement. 'You want to go over to where Ced is?' he said.

I looked around, didn't see Mom trudging back. 'Yeah.'

'Pinch up here? I know you're not still fighting with Pinch.'

'Pinch is about her business.' Put my stuff in my pack. He leaned to help me gather things, but I looked at him and he stopped. He put his hand out to help me stand and I took it. May's cuticles were pink and frayed. I hadn't seen him in need of a haircut in at least five years, but he needed one now. The gray patch was a tiny bit longer than the rest of his hair. He had on glasses, too, thick. We walked down a wide gravelly road. Tombs went on for a mile in every direction. But May knew where to go.

'Oscar wasn't going to let anybody hit you. He's still your husband.'

'But you were going to hit me.'

'No. I mean, it was a reflex. A new one. You were trying to make me say stuff—'

'That you didn't want to say.'

'That wasn't true.'

'And that's a reason to slap somebody? When did you get like that? When did you get that way about me?'

'When did you get the way you are about me? Believing I'd kill somebody?'

'You shot Todd.'

'Did I kill him? And I never touched Jessica. Never hit her, never . . . shot her. Our relationship was me looking at her, and her looking at me, both of us trying to figure out how we got what we got.'

'You were drinking. Slinging. It changed you.'

'Did it? Maybe I'd changed, and that's why I started.'

Cedric's stone wasn't up yet. The mound of dirt had almost flattened, but some of it crept into my sandals. May crouched, patted the soil. I stood above him for a while, then kneeled on the grass, feet under my butt.

'What'll it mean,' May said, 'if I confess?'

'I'll feel better.'

'Than what? Jess's death was officially "accidental." And if you'd been here the last few months, you'd know Todd's the one going around saying he . . . shot Ced, or knows who did. But I don't know who put Cedric here. I wish I did know.'

'So you could feel better?' Heard the mower, off in the distance. Wondered for a second how I'd find Mom.

'So I could let fools know they don't fuck with my friends.' He stood, pulled a small, opened bag of popcorn from his pocket. It was the kind dipped in sugar syrup and studded with almonds. 'At least I know what I want to know, and why. You just want to know so you can accept someone's apology. That's what makes you feel "better." You wanna forgive somebody? Feel righteous? Forgive Todd. Forgive me. Oscar? Who else? You sound like you're mad at Pinch, which is beyond me. Forgive her, too.'

I hated that he knew even one thing about my sister or me. 'Shut up.'

'I guess I better. Don't want you going off on me again.' He pulled clusters of popcorn from the bag, popped them in his mouth. Made noise chewing.

'There was no real reason,' I said, standing, 'for all of us to ever be friends.'

'You're right. Except for you and me. You knew who I was when you saw me at Upward Bound, before I ever said anything to you. I saw you looking at me.'

'Maybe I liked you.'

'You know that's not it. You hoped I wouldn't say anything to you at all. You didn't want me to ask you about that man who slapped you, at Bret Harte, by the Ninth Grade Court. I saw it in your face when I spoke to you and Pinch at the bus stop that Tuesday. It was a Tuesday. This whole time I've known you, I've never brought it up, right? That's what I could do, to keep proving I was your friend.'

'Why are you bringing it up now.'

'I want my transfer back.' He smiled to himself. 'I gave you a transfer that day on the playground.'

'I remember. I used it.'

'I hated that man. Whoever he was. I felt like a punk that day. He made me feel young and weak. After that I needed to get strong so I could . . .'

'So you could what?'

'So I could get between that kind of shit, if I saw it again. And when I saw you again, you and your sister, I wanted to stick around. Watch out for y'all.'

'You were just happy to hang out at the Pseudo.'

'That, too.' He shook his snack around, looked in the bag for a prize.

'They're not Cracker Jacks,' I said. He picked out another glossy piece. 'So you're innocent.'

'Of murder,' he said, 'yeah.'

The lawn mower man had shut down.

'You had your person on the side. From Jess.'

'I never did. Kimya's my . . . partner, kinda. That was in Jess's head about Kimya and me. She's got a man, and a kid. I need somebody like her to watch things. I let Jess believe her own noise after a while. To make her mad.'

'While you had the benefit of knowing you were loyal,' I said. 'You like taking credit for being evil.'

'Somebody's got to. Oscar wanted only the least amount to do. Just to pass bags, get money, and get home. And Donnell, I love him, but the nigga's shortsighted. All he wants to be is me. Kimya watches, counts, works. I trust her. Ced always wanted to hang out later, start shit with niggas from other areas. I used to make him mad when he'd call me from jail . . .

I'd say, "Cedric, you wanted to go to jail. You where you want to be."'

May balled up the bag of popcorn. Held his shoulders like a rod ran through them.

'Pinch said you and Donnell aren't that cool anymore.'

His turn to shrug. 'Donnell's back in school. Ch'Rell'll leave him when he stays broke too long. Or she won't. I don't know.' He crouched down again, forced his fingers into the mud of Cedric's bed. Curled them around what he could, held it in his fist. May straightened up, nodded his head away from Cedric's tomb. We walked toward the main gate.

'So what are you about to do?' he said.

'I'm trying to figure that out. I need to go back to school, someplace in New York. I want to be a person with a job, or classes.' The entrance to the cemetery was deserted. Grass grew through chipped curbs. There was a big black arch with the name of the place, and a booth at which someone might collect tolls.

'I meant,' he said, 'what are you going to do as in, How are you about to get where you need to go right now. Because I got a run to make. Toward San Jose. If you're going that way—'

'I don't need a ride,' I told him.

'You need a ride. You and your sister always been scared to twist the wheel.'

He glanced at his pager. His Benz gleamed like a grand prize. May reached in his car and pulled out an open bottle of water, set it on the roof of his ride. He unballed the popcorn bag, pulled at the bottom seam, looked in, then poured in his mouth whatever was left. May coughed like he inhaled crumbs. Reached for the water bottle, knocked it over. Water ran across the roof, dripped into his open side window. Things slowed, went crooked. Seemed like the world was tilting.

May hacked. I picked up the bottle from the ground, felt

the damp dirt from May's hand, from Cedric's grave, fall in my hair. Saw it drop to the asphalt and break into black powder. May choked and I stood there with his little bit of water. One of his hands was on the side of his car, and the other was stretched taut, at a low angle. His mouth a protruding O. May's upper body kept lurching forward. I glanced around and saw no one. He couldn't verbalize anything.

He choked harder. Huffed in little bits of air. When I could tell he was trying to speak, I leaned in. All I could make out, though, was him trying to say, Help. Give.

I am poured out like water, and all my bones are out of joint, my heart is like wax, it is melted in the midst of my bowels. I saw those words in my head, printed on a blackboard. What could that Bible-school lesson have been about? What was I supposed to have learned from that?

The earth quivered beneath me. Trees fell over with snaps and rustling crashes, the cemetery arch collapsed. I spread my feet to get balance as the ground opened. Graves lay exposed and filthy, there were creaks and moans and tremor after tiny tremor. I got behind May and pressed in on his belly with my arms, but that didn't feel right to either of us. After the exertion of trying to shove me off, his arms dropped to his sides, limp. It seemed like May's cough had been going on for a long time. It was weaker but wasn't stopping. I expected to see blood come out of his mouth.

I'd been through earthquakes. Felt that fantastic roll and shake. Scary as it is, in the right stance, you can ride it. Because before you can formulate a panicky thought, the ground goes quiet again. From the corner of my vision I saw someone running toward us.

At the same time I said, 'Be still,' I heaved May against his car. Then put the bottle of water to his lips and poured. It ran down his chin and wet his shirt. He took a deeper breath, spit up some water, and the coughs tapered. I was relieved. Even free.

The someone was Mom, a beige blur. Her tote bounced on her hip as she ran.

May leaned forward with his butt against his car, his hands right above both knees. Slid into a sitting position with his legs bent. Took breaths.

Mom stood there, panting. 'What happened?'

'May was choking.'

'I saw you helping him.'

I patted May between his shoulder blades.

'Took her long enough,' he said, looking at me. 'Was that supposed to be the Heimlich?' He hacked out a few more coughs, rubbed his chest with one hand.

'It's not like you were going to die,' I said. 'But I was scared.'

Mom said, 'I would've been.'

May stood up. 'I need to go.' I could tell from the way he hesitated that he didn't know how to not offer us a lift.

'You go on ahead, Maynard. Oscar's coming back by to get us. Paige and I are going to take a walk, anyway.'

I said, 'Through the graveyard?' When what I thought was, We're going to take a *walk*?

Mom had started down the street, though.

Beneath the arch, I hugged May. His arms came stiff as pincers around me.

'You're not my friend anymore,' I said.

'Nah. But I will be. Call me when you believe me.'

'I'm starting to.'

'Call me when you really do. One day you will. When we're old. Then everything that's gone down will look small, and not as pitiful as it does now. You, me, Pinch, Oscar, everybody. We'll have to hang out then—way in the future. No one else'll understand.'

What bothers me are aftershocks. They tilt you lopsided and keep you respectful of the Big Ones. The shudders come to

increase the earthquake damage, to cause fires, floods, and keep
you in a horrid state of expectation. Aftershocks come sure as
lies after deeds. Sure as disbelief at being returned to life.

It's the earthquakes that surprise you.

I caught up with my mother.

Month: May(day)
Day: See above
Attitude: See above and below

. . . *I decided on the Berkeley Marina, but then got off near Cal, where Pinch goes to counseling for not speaking enough in class. I always take her to counseling, know my way around Cal because I mill around when Pinch is in session, and when it's really hot I get in the fountain on Sproul Plaza. The college kids get in with me sometimes, and Pinch'll run out, roll up her pant legs, and get in, too. Pinch doesn't have braces or retainers or rubber bands on her teeth, but 'orthodontist' is code in our house for 'counseling.' Mom doesn't want Seth to know Pinch is going. He's being played for a big fool. Doesn't he ever think, Where are the braces?*

I know my way around the area of shops and dorms and lots that surround the campus. I know that the libraries and restaurants stay open late, and that the students walk around at all hours. I went into a department store to pee, and when I came out, a lady employee who had blisters like razor bumps on her chin and neck was staring at me, so I looked in a mirror and saw that my eye was puffed out like somebody had socked me, and I almost started crying when I realized somebody had. And that I wasn't home.

But I wasn't about to start crying in front of that lady, so when she walked toward me, all concerned and erupting, I ran back to the rest room and put my clarinet case in a low cabinet behind some paper towels. Waited in there by the sink, breathing through my mouth. She didn't come in after me.

Crossed the street and sat on the steps of Sproul
Hall until the admissions employees filed out, chatty and
sighing. It was almost dark, but not, and I went two
blocks over, where mimes performed and kids danced for
money. Sat there until this longhaired, sleepy-eyed
Chinese boy who didn't seem much older than me asked
if I was all right. You know I didn't answer. I went to
the next block, where there was an open-air market.
People sold terrariums and batik skirts and leather cords
with brass lockets. I wound them around my fingers
until a vendor thought I was going to steal one. He had
on a shirt that said BUILD SCHOOLS NOT BOMBS. I wondered if the Chinese boy was Theo, and that made me
cry. I tried to stop, tried to go back where the boy had
been sitting, but couldn't.

But then I watched a puppet show near the market.
Watched it until the air was clingy, until the moon had
swelled to twice its size. A man came out from behind
his cardboard puppet stage. His skin was soy sauce. His
wide-brimmed hat made me think he had adventures.
His belt was like what a construction worker would wear,
except where there would be hammers and wrenches
there were bottles of rouge and mucilage, yarn balls and
toothpicks bundled by rubber bands. There were puppets hanging there, too, like charms on a huge bracelet.
One looked like a dolphin, and there was a dog with
macaroni teeth. There was a lion, too, but without his
shoestring tail, he could easily have been a sun.

The man asked if I liked his show, which I'd thought
was silly. The puppets were half-stuffed, decorated socks,
but they had good jokes, so I said I'd liked it. In a quiet
way, the man seemed glad that I'd stuck around until
the end.

You've been sitting here awhile, he said, sifting with

pocked hands through the coins and rare dollars in the basket he'd set out for tips. Then in a syrupy voice he said hello through a puppet who announced herself as Bernadette. He'd pulled her from his pocket, and she looked relieved to be free. Bernadette made a show of shaking her head, to clear the lint.

Why are you here by yourself this late? she wanted to know.

I told Bernadette I was a student at U.C. Berkeley and could be out as late as I pleased.

Bernadette shook her head and curled her mouth. Where's your momma?

I looked at the puppeteer but he looked toward Bernadette as if to say, She's talking to you.

Bernadette had been flitting behind that stage all night, spinning riddles and having the last word on everything. She wore a swingy plum skirt—her waistline being halfway between his wrist and his elbow. A necklace of paper clips and speckled beads dangled almost to the ground.

Home, I said. My mom's right at home.

She's not looking for you? Bernadette's sequined eye was bent and brilliant.

I told her I doubted it.

And your daddy?

He lives in Oregon, I said from my seat on the ground. He left Berkeley in the 1960s because they wouldn't let him walk the street with his eagle on his shoulder.

I lay down on my side. Head burning. With my index finger I pressed in on my cheek. Didn't know what I was touching. Hot, smooth, and puffy, then at the temple torn skin dried upright from gummy flesh. I'd been hit before. I'd been hit in front of my friends. I'd never had this kind of wet, visible mark. I kept grazing the stiff skin with my fingerprint. The ground under my head was like a pillow.

I told Bernadette that on his days off, my dad had walked around the Berkeley campus in cutoff trousers and a tie-dyed shirt—with his eagle, no matter what the police said. They took it away from him after a while, on account of the fact that it is the bird that represents the country, and so my father moved to Oregon. My mother had left him long before that, when she was six months pregnant with Pinch. At least that's what she says. Bernadette was listening like she was interested and sympathetic. I hate for people to feel sorry for me, but right then I took pity no problem.

Looked up at the puppeteer. I didn't tell Bernadette that I always pictured my father as a milk-chocolate man with a big afro and a mustache, a man who needed more freedom than even wild Berkeley would allow. I pictured him up there in an endless emerald Northwest, minding a chicken coop and purple onions and crooked rows of corn. Out there working one day, he'd find himself a still-wet baby eagle, shrieking from a halo of broken shell.

Bernadette was bald gray where she should have been fuzzy pink. She cocked her head and asked me again about my daddy.

He's up in Oregon, I said.

She opened her mouth up wide. She didn't scream, just opened her mouth and looked indignant.

I said, My fake father's at home. Talking crazy to my sister, who's not listening to him or saying anything in return. He's waiting until my mother gets home from work so he can lie to her about where I am.

And where are you?

I looked at the puppeteer again and he was looking

*at me like he had the same question. I said that I was
running away. That I was tired of Seth. I wanted him to
be in a hell where the drinks didn't work, where liquor
was like Kool-Aid and he didn't understand why.*

*You better go on home, Bernadette told me, and I
said, No, I hate it there. I can't stand my mother for
keeping us there. Seth loves hurting me. I don't know
him like my mother does. I don't have any money either,
I told Bernadette, and I can't walk from here.*

*She put her mouth in the basket and picked up a
dollar, then dropped it back in. Bernadette said, Sit up.
Get up. See what happens if you ask. She nodded
toward a chubby white girl coming down the block
with a book bag.*

*Hi, I said to the girl, who looked only a little bit
older than I did. I stood up and felt dizzy. Felt stupid.
But I said, I ran away from home and I don't have
any money to get back. The girl focused in on my face,
handed me a dollar like it was a leaf I should press
between pages. I said, Thanks, and she walked on.*

*Bernadette was gleeful. She danced. She smiled. Her
neon eyebrows, painted on like two sideways parenthe-
ses, were lifted in approval. The puppeteer was doing a
happy dance himself. You'll give that back, Bernadette
said about the dollar in my hand. Don't feel bad about
asking.*

Why am I going home? I asked her.

*Where else you going? It's late, Bernadette said, her
head turned inside out as it came off the puppeteer's
hand. I could hear her from inside his pocket, Where
else is there?*

CHAPTER 23

SEEMED TO ME Mom was trying to get away from that graveyard as fast as she could.

'Can you wait up? Where're we going? Oscar and Pinch are coming back.' She paused at a corner, and I finally stood next to her.

'I'm not worried about that.'

We crossed the street. Walked for two blocks without saying anything.

'Why are we walking?'

'When we find somewhere to sit,' Mom said, 'we will.'

We walked for more blocks, had to be a mile. Finally got onto Shattuck Avenue, which runs through downtown Berkeley. Campus loomed just east of downtown, green and old, a preserve.

'Your stomping grounds,' Mom said. 'So where should we go sit for a minute?' She tried to sound bouncy.

'Let's go on campus, then.'

Walked in through the west entrance, which was all shrubbery and trees. Followed the creek, heard squirrels. She followed me without a question. Got to the Campanile. Tall, Washington Monument–like structure with a clock on top. We sat on a bench nearby.

'You know you can go inside the Campanile.'

'Looks closed,' Mom said.

'They had to put bars up there, because students have committed suicide. Jumped.'

'That's why you brought me here?'

'You said you wanted to sit.'

She reached in her tote bag. Handed me two familiar envelopes.

'Say you didn't read this stuff.'

'I can't say that.'

'Where'd you get it? Pinch.'

'I think she found it in your room. At the Pseudo.'

'So you and Pinch are in cahoots now. That's funny.'

'Your sister was trying, as she said, to help.'

Shook my head. 'So then Pinch read this, too.'

'When's the last time you read it.'

'I don't have to read it. I wrote it.'

Pulled some of the pages out. Loose-leaf, ruled paper from my high-school three-ring binder. Handwriting big and neat. A few smaller spiral notepads. I had a system. Always noted the month, not the date, because to me, the days were all the same. Always wrote down the weather, because that was the only thing that separated the days. Felt I was demonstrating discipline by making myself define my attitude in one sentence. It was also so that when I went back over the diaries, I could pick and choose whether I wanted to read about a good time or a bad time or a weird time. It was an index.

'High-school bullshit,' I said. Flipped through some pages. I'd written down quotes I liked, song lyrics, test scores. I rated boys. Used my diary mostly to record the dreams I had at night. Gaudy, three-dimensional, tiring dreams.

'It goes into college, too,' Mom said.

'Oh, so you weren't just skimming.' I was kind of glad. It enraged me. But I was glad. Now Mom knew where I'd gone on Ninth Grade Court day.

'Pinch gave it to me the other day. I been at it since then.'

'Fun for you?'

'Those are yours. Neither Pinch or I should have touched them.'

'Give me your private papers, and then maybe we can have a conversation.' I tried to keep my voice tight and angry. I would not break down. Get emotional. That was for her to do.

'I don't have private papers.'

'Give me something, Mom.'

'You've seen too much of me, as it is. In the worst situations.'

'So you're embarrassed? No, Mom. Too late for that. Who are you? That's what I want to know. I need the background.'

'I'm not going to talk about your father.'

'Talk about him, Mom. Or at least talk about Seth. Talk about why you put him before us.'

'I didn't do that. I can't explain to you because *I don't know.* Can it be that I was just stupid? That's what you want me to say? Again? That I was weak and maybe too . . . prideful to ask anybody anything. I have to sit here and tell you that when you've seen it for yourself. I look at you right now and you look at me the same way you did when you were two, when you were five, when you were ten, fifteen. Mad and frowning.'

'That's why you can't look at me.'

She looked me in my eye. 'I can look at you.'

'Why didn't you run?'

'I didn't know how.'

'That's weak, Mom.'

'It is.'

'Why can't you talk about Pinch's and my real father?'

'That same weakness.'

'I'm supposed to feel sorry for you now? Feel bad for

whatever you've gone through. I'm supposed to let go of how I feel. How Pinch and I . . . were just . . . out here . . . like we were grown when we were kids dealing with all that shit that at the time I thought we were handling just fine, but now, the way things are, I don't think it was all right anymore. Somebody's wrong.'

'I'm wrong.'

'Don't say it like that, Mom, like I have to feel bad for you.'

'Don't feel bad for me. Feel bad that you're going to let the way your life has been affect the rest of it. Feel bad that you're going to let your anger mess up the best thing in your life, which is your relationship with your sister. Whatever the circumstances of how you all ended up as close as you have— what*ever* the circumstances, you have Pinch, and she has you.'

'Don't flip it.'

'I'm flipping it. Feel bad that because you are so pissed off at me and at Seth, you'll leave Oscar, who seems like he has the patience to deal with you.'

'And I him.' I wouldn't look at her.

'I see that. And it makes me proud that you aren't in a relationship where the man wants to hack away at your happiness.'

'I don't have a lot of happiness for him to hack away at.'

'You will.'

'How do you know, Mom?' I hated that I had to ask her anything. That she could know.

'Maybe I don't know it. Maybe I believe it. And it makes me sad, because sometimes, when I've seen you happy, up at high school, or just you and Pinch chitchatting away, I know I haven't had too much to do with how you and your sister turned out.' This was a little bit. I'd always been cool with a little bit.

'It's not like Pinch and I are perfect, Mom. You and I are sitting up here at Cal, and it's not like I'm alumna. Been running around with dope dealers, going to funerals, basically floating along and fucking up.' I didn't go into dating crackheads, losing babies, and waiting for Oscar in the jail waiting room.

'Like that's new.' Mom looked at me funny. Couldn't place the expression.

'What's new.'

'You are young. Thinking that because you're doing something, that's the first time it's ever been done.' She was looking at me like I was a child. Like I was blameless, and needed guidance. She'd been looking at me like a grown person for as long as I could remember.

Before we got up and started walking again, I looked through more of my papers while Mom watched me for my expressions. I didn't say a word. It was too much for me, really, feeling even cautious gladness about Mom.

I came across a quote, neatly printed on the inside back cover of a notepad decorated with stickers of rainbows and Hello Kittys.

> What are the wild waves saying,
> Sister, the whole day long,
> That ever amid our playing
> I hear but their low, lone song?

THE night I went west, after that day on the Ninth Grade Court, I was out by Cal, wandering like an idiot. This is what I told Oscar, when I finally decided to tell him everything.

I was sitting there watching a puppet show pack up when Pinch found me. I knew she would.

She sat down. 'Where we going?'

'I don't know. I have a transfer, though.'

'Doesn't matter. I brought your bus pass.'

'Gonna use this transfer.'

I told Oscar that the bus we got on had been damn near empty.

Driver said it was twenty-two minutes after one in the morning! like he was excited about it. We rode up front near him, a brown man about fifty with a shiny process and a gold stud in his ear. He loved it when there was no one at the stops. He'd just barely pat the brake to see if there was no one disguised by night, and then press back on the gas, like the No. 40 route was a game, and he was winning.

Pinch and I were on that bus a long time, passed the stop by San Antonio again and again.

'You wanna go to Diamond?'

'Dark at the park,' Pinch said.

'I have keys to the office.'

'Gotta walk through the park to get to the office.'

'We're going to Diamond.'

'But you look . . . you don't look right. You look tired, like you need to lay down or go to the hospital or something.'

'You wanna go home? 'Cause if you go home, you're going by yourself.'

'You both need to be home,' the bus driver said.

I told him, 'We live over by Diamond.'

I told Oscar how we got off the bus, waited for the bus driver to pull off.

It was dark, but I could see. Knew exactly where I was going.

'Wait up,' Pinch said.

'Come on.'

Oscar wanted to know if I was scared.

No. I walked. Over grass in some places, sand in some places, and long stretches of dirt. Finally got to the door of the pool. Pinch and I walked through it. I put the latch on.

'I want to swim.'

'Now.'

'Yeah.'

I went to my locker, got my suit. It was sour. Slipped out of my clothes, put it on. Out of shoes and into flip-flops. Pinch watched me.

'I don't have a suit,' she said.

'I know.'

'What about . . . your face. It could get infected.'

'Chlorine's probably good for it.'

I'd always told people that I'd been a junior lifeguard at Diamond Pool. Used to tell them long stories about how I'd walked around in a swimsuit with a bullhorn hollering, *Hey, no running!* When Oscar and I were first getting together, I told him that I'd made people take freestyle tests so they could swim legally in the deep end. I told Maynard the same, and Jess and Ch'Rell and Donnell, too. Truth was, I was a locker-room attendant, and gave out orange locker keys for people to pin to their swimsuits. In stiff blue plastic gloves, I scrubbed toilets and showers with concentrated chlorine. I never told Oscar, or anyone, that I saved a life, though. That would have been going too far.

At the pool, we called the patrons 'fish.' And sometimes, before opening or right after closing, when there were no fish in the water, a pool staff member who hadn't done so was goaded into climbing up on the roof. There was a leaf of thick fiberglass over the pool that slid open for ventilation and sunshine. We'd all cheer for the person to plunge through. I used to tell people that I'd dove in like an Olympian.

Told Oscar that I cranked open the fiberglass cover.

The lever was behind the counter. Took both hands. Heard the fiberglass sheaf above us screech into its cement port. I started up the rusted ladder that stretched up the wall to the ceiling. There was a hatch for me to go through, and then I'd be on the cement part of the roof. Looked back. 'No, Pinch,' I said.

'I'm gonna watch you.' She had a foot on the bottom rung.

'Go out on the deck. Watch from there.'

'I wanna come up. I don't want to be by myself.'

'Be by yourself for five minutes.'

'You don't look right. You look . . . funny. What if something happens.'

'If I look funny, that's how I feel. Get your foot off the fucking ladder. I don't want you to come with me.'

'Just wait.' She looked scared. Face still, eyes steady and full of water. What did she have to be scared of?

'Pinch, go!'

'Paige, uh-uh. Can't you think about it for a second.'

'Think about what.'

I lost my flip-flops climbing the ladder. As I walked across the cement roof, twigs attached to my feet.

I told Oscar it was nice up there, and the air felt good on my face.

And through my hair. I was dirty, had been too much on the ground. Breeze cleared my head. I brushed myself off. Paced along the ledge. Could see the Mormon Temple's five towers, lit up so grand. Looked in the direction of Lake Merritt but couldn't see it from where I stood, so hurried to the other side of the roof. Walked the perimeter, all along the edge.

Then I heard someone yell, 'Don't walk on the fiberglass part! Stay on the cement!' as I stood above what seemed a giant's bowl of honeydew liqueur. Beneath me, the water went down about eight feet, which I knew wasn't deep enough to jump into. I'd seen others go in through the roof, and I knew you had to propel yourself forward, to where the pool dipped to fifteen feet. I spotted a drain shimmering at the base of the deepest part. It could have been a silver saucer I was trying to save.

I told Oscar how people were down there, urging me on. Even Kirby was there. Kirby who played Big Kahuna to our *Gidget and Friends,* a guy at least thirty-five who should have gone to a managerial job at Parks and Recreation years ago, but stayed around Diamond Pool because he liked the freedom, he said, of ruling the cement pond, as well as watching, we said, girls' breasts fall free of their tops. I heard Kirby's booming voice, he was encouraging me, 'Come down, Paige, come down.'

Told Oscar that I knew everyone had made the drain the mark.

So I made it mine. And as I backed up a few feet to get a running start, someone yelled up to me not to run because I'd hit my head on the other side of the opening and knock myself out.

I still couldn't see the lake. Touched my face. Walked to the very edge of the roof again. Saw leaves in the gutter. Long oak leaves with rounded lobes.

Overhead lights flashed on. Noticed a revolving red light, too. The kind a police car would have. People below me screamed, 'Take your time up there.' They screamed loud, but I was focused, didn't need coaching. Was ready to dive in and

swim up and down those lanes. Back and forth in the chlori-
nated clear water until I was disinfected, healed, and so
exhausted I remembered nothing.

With their palms visors against the light, it seemed they
were saluting me. There had to be a way to do it. I knew because I'd seen three people jump in the bluest part of the
green pool, curled up tight, cannonball style, like that would
save their legs or spine from shattering if they hit the bottom
of the eight- or nine-feet. They'd all come up, though, ecstatic
and relieved, everyone else cheering, Kirby tapping the alarm
button so it sounded like a big goose was hooraying us, instead of like *Lungs filled with water, pull 'em out, here comes the
ambulance,* which is what the button meant, really. A deafen-
ing siren was loosed when it was pressed in. Fish did drown
sometimes.

Then Pinch was next to me. What did she need?

I inched closer to the hole in the roof.

'If you go in,' Pinch said, 'I'm going in, too.'

'Everybody that works here has done it.'

'And if you do it, I'm going to.'

Now people were yelling Pinch's name. I hated the way it
sounded. It wasn't her name. Why was she making it like this?

Inched closer.

'Mom's down there,' Pinch said. 'I called her.'

'She shouldn't come up.'

'That's why I came.'

'Don't follow me.'

'But I always follow you.'

Told Oscar I stepped over the lip, into the air.

It was miles until my shins slapped water. So softly my
knees hit the very bottom of the pool. Everything cold. Eyes
closed. I liked the cold, the bubbles, no breathing. Why did

Mom swim, I wondered, when she could have just stayed under.

Then a surge of fizz near me. Mute wet explosion. Knew it was Pinch and she put her scrawny arms under mine and tried to lift. Pinch tried to pull me up. She was disturbing me. Opened my eyes and pushed at her. Cheeks bulging, her eyes barely open against the water. I got her around her waist. Held her. She squirmed. She was easy to hold. It was harder to keep myself down. The water lifted me up closer and closer to the top.

More fizzing. Grabbing, yelling. Kirby's voice, bossy and panicked. Pinch and I both above water. I wouldn't let go of her. He pried. Pinch's eyes were closed. She was limp. They couldn't pry her from me.

Felt Mom's thin fingers pulling at mine. Bending them back. Pulling at my wrists. Heard Mom's voice, so shrill, and actually scared. Yelling my name in desperation and shame.

Told Oscar I knew that tone.

It had always moved me. I let Pinch go.

EPILOGUE

The only part that's new, really, are the cigarettes.

I've always made boys I like drive me along California's snaky coast. It's a kind of test. I have to see how they respond to what I see and what I love and what I hate.

I don't take them through the callused-over patches—the industrial knuckletowns of Lawndale, Richmond, Hawthorne, Simi Valley, Artesia. I go on the big roads—Highway 5 is a spine going up the middle of the state. The California Aqueduct crisscrosses Highway 5, a visible topless pipeline that feeds Hetch Hetchy Reservoir and Lake Shasta water to thirsty cropland all along the way. Cotton almonds oranges tomatoes. Buttonwillow, Coalinga, all those truckstop wannabe towns up through the San Joaquin Valley. Greyhound buses and Foster Freezes. Rank beef plantations. Power phone towers wreak static through all the Christian or classic rock or Today's Talk radio stations. Slim Jims poly seeds and Snapple from the gas station. Crop dusters and you can get to the bay from L.A. in four hours if you have a radar detector. Highway 5's a flat and boring ride, some of the boys have said, not even relishing the geometric beauty of the straightaway. I crossed them out real quick.

Two boys have passed my little test, though. Major, who took me to see the otters in Monterey, and living shrimp—who ever sees swimming shrimp? Oscar took me to Carmel and Calistoga and San Luis Obispo. At the rainbow bridge over

Bixby Canyon right as you come out of Big Sur, I stood with
both of them, the Pacific eating at the rocks hundreds of feet
below. The sea the clean wind the steep red wall of dirt and
stone, the arrogance of the long-dead men who tied two protruding pieces of the state together—it all seemed to symbolize
an evolving permanence. More like a forever solid sweet as
Tijuana flan.

The best way to Mexico, or to Oregon, or to anywhere, is
U.S. Highway 1, the Pacific Coast Highway. It's easy to love
because when you roll along it, you own the shore. You see it
like California does the blue sky reflected in the water and
maybe you wonder, Is that ocean her eyes? But I've seen Lake
Tahoe—an immaculate mass fringed with eyelashy firs and
pines and in the morning of winter with the snowy crust of
sleep. And even though almost half of Tahoe is in Nevada, that
shimmering puddle is California's eye if she needs one. And if
it cries, it's because Cali still feels the pain of Highway 1. You
can hear her screams from the days when workers red brown
and white tore at her sandy flesh, at the softest, most delicate
part between the quiet waves and the baby mountains, where
she was sliced and dug at and then tar was poured like salt in a
gash. You can picture the forty-niners, the real ones, riding out
to the coast on their exhausted donkeys and yelping with joy at
what they saw. At what the Franciscans and the Chumash
before them claimed in the names of various gods. California
laughed back then. Roared and rolled like she was touching
herself. She never imagined pain. Her oily blood had not yet
been tapped. Her dry and dusty parts were not yet packed with
masses of people places and things.

OSCAR and I sit out on Stinson Beach before we get on the
road for real. We eat sandwiches. He eats Skittles from my
navel. Then we get on a freeway that will take us to a freeway

they used to call El Camino Real—the Kings Road—before it was paved. PCH. I've got my Winstons my bare feet on the dashboard we're zooming. Oscar's got a 9mm holstered in the glove box. He never had a gun when he was dealing. It's like he has to have something so as not to be totally normal and law-abiding. Plus, he refuses to be helpless. We fight over him having the gun. But then we fight about a lot of stuff. Couple stuff.

Like bees Oscar and I buzz along. And don't think he isn't pushing ninety. A guy and a girl in a black Beemer pull up behind us real close like an inch away from our car's rear bumper. Then it zooms around us, humming. Oscar's pressing on the gas eyes darting from the rearview mirror between us to the mirrors attached to the doors then back to straight ahead at the Beemer it's fat fast moving—like one of those beetles with wings it's dusting us and suddenly we're square behind an eighteen-wheeler full of frozen Burger King we almost hit it but Oscar swerves we're going from lane to lane and crossing back. I'm screaming but it's a roller-coaster scream Oscar's mind is on the road he's sitting up now we're at 110 about three car lengths behind the Beemer and I wonder if the other drivers are in awe because we must be making quite a movie and Oscar is right behind the guy who switches lanes really fast but so does Oscar and the Beemer goes to the next lane again and so does Oscar and I mean to say we're on this guy's ass like close like his shadow like he cannot escape and the guy is smug and his car is super smooth and his girl looks bored like not even doing 110 on a fairly busy highway could rouse her and the Beemer steps on it and so does Oscar and while the Beemer is in the next lane with no cars in front of it for like a quarter of a mile we're trying to get over there and we come to within one foot of this mammoth open bed truck carrying three-foot-tall pieces of pink slate for some big building's lobby I guess and I see this blond chick's face in a green Chevy next to me and I know she's writing me off as dead for sure I see her eyes already full of the story she's gonna tell when she gets to where she's going 'cause I mean we were about to hit that slate truck but unbelievably I trust I'm going to be okay and if I'm not, *well then fuck it God take me right now please right here five miles from the water where I'll forever see hillsides thick with poppies and paddle cacti where the sun works tirelessly and without vengeance just steady and warm.* Oscar steps on the brake a little bit and we swerve a little bit and almost hit the chick in the green Chevy but we get in the lane behind the Beemer chase him yeah we were at like 120 when the guy puts two fingers up near his rearview mirror, like Peace. Oscar slows down I think I hear him say *motherfucker* under his breath, he says out loud *Can't mess with the Ponycar,* laughing. I put his hand on the inside of my thigh we slow to seventy. Finally we're on Highway 1. 'A farm,' I say when we pass one, like in my life I haven't seen a million. Oscar says, 'Too big, though,' and I realize he's actually been listening to my sandy little dreams.

Where Oscar and I spend the night, there's a cricket living under the bureau. Oscar lets it be. Stars come out on the ceiling. He and I talk about how our life can be, together. Mom says we can stay with her for a while in Walnut Creek, and maybe we will. Oscar's dad likes our old apartment, he has a job now, and we want to start someplace new.

Oscar and I are almost back to Los Angeles. Going to get our car from Gram Liz's. In Oxnard, we are near the coast. Top's still down floor's sandy sky's purple velvet with an orange slip moon's a pearl brooch California's ready for evening. Oscar still in his sunglasses. I'm telling him about the kind of madness that goes on in my head when I sleep. Even as I speak I'm forgetting half.

It was the end of the world in my dream. The earth and the sun revolved extremely close to each other and at a

faster rate every hour. I was with some people I didn't recognize, but in the dream they were my friends. We could feel
the earth spinning beneath our feet and had to walk carefully. Sometimes we were at a sort of clubhouse, or a decent,
spread-out hotel. We were nervous but not scared of the
world ending, or of dying. We partied, tried to relax, took
walks outside, and giggled at each other as we tried to balance.
Day and night changed every few minutes. We scrambled up
humps of rock until we squeezed onto a tight plateau and
reached, fingers spread, for the fast, giant sun. On the television they announced with calmness that the huge day was
coming soon, and we were happy that the hot star bulged
because night came less frequently. We reveled in the odd
heat. It got brighter, but never blinding. Warmer and warmer
but never hot.

We did begin to feel small, though, so devised ways to
climb higher even as it became more difficult to walk. The
ground was speeding up always, getting from place to place
was like marching on a merry-go-round. We moved upward
anyway, holding tight to natural turrets and orange cliffs, urging each other on. To bring the collision on even faster, that
was my dream within my dream. Plus the rays had begun to
look solid and I wanted to touch one.

Higher we climbed as the world spun faster. The rays
were solid. We began to have to duck them, felt the soft winds
they generated as they came for us, giant blunt swords revolving in the newly touchable sky. We got happier—it seemed
we'd helped along the convergence by climbing, by not just sitting still and waiting for the end of everything. I reached out
my hand finally and touched a ray, it was warm, smooth as a
mirror, soft as wax firming to candle the closer they came. The
sun started to spin more slowly, stopped and started again as it
sheared tops from mountains and then like a horned wheel
impaled the fields around us, speared the ocean beds, then

swept the earth up and out of its orbit. The sun spun away with us and we didn't die, at least not then, we held on to a slippery massive ray thrilled and staring out into a horizonless universe. There was no night coming. We held on and saw everything. Though we were spinning slowly, the ground seemed still and I woke up.

And so maybe I'll love Oscar all the time. Maybe he'll love me. I don't know a lot, but I do know Oscar knows how to make crack and sell crack and then stop. I know he knows how to get a job. He knows regret and discretion and real fear and some of the other things that equal up to the better part of valor. I mean, the free counselor at the church is cool, but she's extra. I have to talk to me. Maybe to Mom. Pinch. And to Oscar, even more than I have. I know he could graduate if he wanted to, that he's built for speed, and but for grace and God, would have been dead or shut down a long time ago. Have you seen this man drive? Has he held your hand bought you tacos sang a song with your name in it? I *do* love him, for what I know about it. I see, in his brown eyes, a bona fide gleam of *moving the fuck on*. He pulls me in with that. Pulls me out. Please, please let it be that I do that for him.

Oscar and I are going to get it together, rent a place in Oakland. Not by the lake this time. Maybe in Rockridge or out near Alameda. And when I'm not in school or at work or trying to Rollerblade or some shit that gets you to like yourself and make new friends, I'm going to swim at Stinson Beach no matter the cold. I'll sit on the mossy floor of Muir. One thrilling dawn—beyond the pumpkin fields and Christmas tree farms—I'm going to leave my footprints in the pebbly sand at Half Moon Bay. If it's true that the longing for paradise is paradise, as the fear of hell is hell, if I've got to believe—which must mean, at the root, Be Alive—where else would I go but here? Where but home?

Oscar says, 'Yeah, yeah, as far as the dream. *You* are a ray of sunshine. I don't think it's true. I don't dream it's true. It is true.'

He pulls over at a rest stop so we can look out, so he can pee against a tree, so he can take my photo while wind blows hair from my face, and the smoke from over my head.

I ask him if I look romantic.

He says, 'What does that mean.'

I ask him if I look like a real girl, like a regular girl that he would want to be with if he didn't know me already.

He shakes his head with a little laugh and says, 'Here's what you really want to know about.' Holds out his hand.

I take the keys from his palm and he says, 'So are you rolling by yourself, or am I getting in with you.'

'You have to get in with me.'

'I'm going to stand right here and watch you.'

'And I'm just going to drive.' I say it like I know it's impossible and like the concept is funny. And like because it's ridiculous, it has to be easy. I light another cigarette.

Oscar says, 'You gonna get in the car or what.'

'I've got to stop smoking.'

'You will,' he says. 'When you get tired of it.'

I know how to put the key in the ignition. I know which is the gas and which is the brake. We're in a parking lot off a short, bristly stretch of beach. There is an old van, and a Datsun with a bike rack. I have room to make mistakes.

Pinch would scream if she saw me. She would laugh and scream and be excited and maybe cry. I wish she were around.

Out goes the cigarette. Start moving slowly. Forward about twenty yards. Make a wide turn toward the exit.

Oscar waves wildly, yells, 'Where you going? Where you going?'

I turn the car back toward him and I'm laughing. I stop

because I'm laughing so hard. He jogs over to me, seems proud and nervous. He's in a T-shirt and gray V-neck pullover, jeans and loafers. He has his wedding band on a thin gold chain around his neck. Oscar says, 'You were driving. I can't believe it. You can go wherever you want. You could leave me right here and ride off for good.'

'I'm a long way,' I tell him, 'from the highway.'

We learned state songs when I was at Bella Vista Elementary. Texas's wide, high prairie sky. Wind sweeping down the plains of Oklahoma. There being nothing halfway about the Iowa way of thinking. Then *Each morning, at dawning, birdies sing and everything is sun-kissed.*

Oscar says, 'Why are you humming that?' He smiles a smile from a long time ago, a smile for a long time from now. He says, 'Who *are* you? That you hum corny songs like that.'

I pop out of the car with the motor running. *Right back where I started from.* We search the backseat for fruit juice not yet fermented by the sun. A breeze comes up, kicks papers and empty plastic bags from the floor of the car. We chase down a few dollar bills, but the rest we leave caught in the wind. In New York City, the berries tasted like fuzzy mistakes. The ones I'm eating now, we bought at a stand, and they taste about as good as the ones that used to grow in back of the clothesline at Nannah and Grandpa's. Of course the sea is before us. Of course I am wishing an otter will walk right up onto the sand and want to be my pet. Oscar's fingers rest in my hair and I have on clothes that I think make me pretty.

And can you believe I called Obe? He's the same tropical fish–loving Obe he always was. Talking to him is like being on the Ninth Grade Court, having a normal time, all over again. As a grown man, he still goes on about the cichlids as usual, about how they lay eggs in a hollow in the sand and then either the husband or the wife cichlid carries the eggs in their mouth until they're hatched. It's extraordinary, Obe says. The care they take.

Pinch, who's on her way to a big international life now, says it happened, all of it. Diamond Pool. The puppeteer. She says I talked to her about him for months and months afterward, and that the story was long and in depth and there's no way I could have made it up. Pinch says she dreamt of that man with the paint and the paste all the time after I told her about him. Says she entertained people's babies at Planned Parenthood with a sock on her hand.

And Pinch says—see how much she talks now?—that I should let it all go, she's trying to. Says I should pick up the clarinet again. She talks about the night we jumped in through that roof at Diamond Pool. She'd called the police when I went on the roof, and then Mom was there with them, screaming for me to come down. The police had called Kirby and he came roaring up, wondering loudly how I'd opened the roof when usually it takes a grown man, and how the hell I'd climbed up top, since they'd been trying to make me do it for months and I'd been too scared to even climb up, let alone jump through.

Pinch says I had my arms out like I was on a tightrope, that I was staring at the water like it was the only place I could be and be all right. Pinch says all she could think about was how we used to walk sometimes from Nannah and Grandpa's up to Mills College. For like fifty cents we played in the shallow end of shimmering turquoise, looked up at the mile-high eucalyptus trees, inhaled chlorine. Two brown girls each with two dark brown braids in the clear, clean water with a troop of longhaired nosy funny white girls. I think I was nine and Pinch was almost seven when we used to walk home from Mills down MacArthur Boulevard, bath towels rolled like tiny sleeping bags under one arm.

Pinch says no, she didn't almost drown, she passed out, and then so did I and we both had to go to Highland and Mom wasn't hysterical but worried and cursing out doctors and then Gram Liz showed up and got everything as right as they could make it. Pinch says I wouldn't quit that job because I never wanted to ask anyone for anything extra. Pinch also says I wasn't trying to let May choke to death at the cemetery. Says I probably moved much faster than I think I did. Hope so.

I say to Oscar, when we're on the road, 'Can I believe Pinch, though? I mean, really.' He and I both fell out laughing when I reminded him that Pinch didn't talk for two whole years to almost anyone but me.

I know Pinch is scared but glad about leaving California. She'll come home to Oakland, though, if only to see me and Oscar and Mom and Bill and have presents and laugh tears and eat Dungeness from gumbo and cruise Foothill and breathe home until she's silly and then ready enough to leave again.

The night before Pinch left, Mom made tacos and French fries. Bill was there, with his Winstons. Pinch's friend Evan was just off the bus. He told Pinch when she was wavering, not to be scared, to just go. I'm glad he said it because I wouldn't have known how. Mom was kind of brisk, and sad, but she played music and served ice cream, told Pinch it's a big world over there, and Pinch said that's why she was going.

We were the loudest things in Walnut Creek that night, which wasn't hard. Toasted Jess, told stories about Cedric. It's what things came down to—tall tales of adventure in the streets of Oakland, some true romance, brand-new legends that proved, or at least illustrated, what friends we'd been.

It was almost midnight when Pinch held out her wine, said, 'Here's to my sister.' I put my own glass up. Oscar was across the living room with his father. Mom was near them, her face as partly cloudy and awkwardly pretty as Oakland.

Pinch looked separate from me. Pale brown skin and hair in that tired half-wet ponytail. Thin, pretty face, a rare smile. A nervous, big one. I was happy. Didn't want her to go. How could she be leaving when I felt for one small moment like there was no other, better way we could have turned out to be.

My sister waited on me to speak, then she started being silly. 'I *said*,' and she gave the two words four syllables, 'here's to my sister.' I wanted to tell her that I loved her and that I'd miss her. That I'd braid her hair in the morning before she left. If she had time, if it's what she wanted. I was shivering because I swim with Pinch every day of my life. Always have, always will. Been through whatever will go through whatever. Icy turbulent warm brutal lulling—the well's never empty. And if we can't feel the bottom, big fucking deal. I'm in it with Pinch. We get through what has to be got through.

I love you, baby sister. You're a superstar. My best friend till the bright shining end. Don't go.

My glass was up. I said, 'And here's to mine.'

Because Pinch and I don't talk about that kind of stuff. We know how we feel.

WE GET back in the car, Oscar at the wheel. I twist in my chair to sift through stuff in the backseat, to pull out what we need. A new junction is coming up, and until I get my license, I'm still copilot, and the best one.

Oscar has his eyes on the road, says, 'Where we going? What the deal?'

Out the back window are rumbling trucks with yellow eyes, and behind them the mountainside is transformed by darkness into monsters that would lumber after us.

I can't find the map in the back, and really, I think I know the way. One third of the moon has swum to the corner of the windshield. A blue, pearly light is on Oscar's face. I resist the impulse to look in the mirror behind the visor. I know I am in the car, navigating. In the lovely dim, I am, for the moment, clear.

Oscar says, 'This doesn't feel like running.'

'It isn't running.' I say to him. 'This isn't running at all.'

Paige,

Thanks for the seventeen hundred dollars. It's pinned in my bra. I only have but so much money after the ticket (even though Oscar did give me some more, ha! And so did Mom) and I will *not* be getting it snatched. And tell Oscar thank you for taking me around to get my passport and all. I still can't believe I have one. There's another letter in here for Bill, please give it to him when you see him. At the airport, it looked like you and Oscar were you and Oscar again.

When the plane stopped in New York, three black girls got on. They look like they're in college and making a trip together that they'll remember forever. I know I'm about their same age, but I feel older. Or maybe it's younger. No matter, I'm going to go talk to them when I finish this letter. Maybe in Milan I can hang out with them. For a little while, anyway. I have to get a bus from there to Lake Como, where Bill's friend lives. She seemed nice over the phone, and since she said I could stay with her until whenever, who knows when I'll come back to Oakland. Homegirl doesn't know what she's getting herself into (smile). Lake Como. I wonder if it's like Lake Merritt. If they have a Necklace of Lights. If it's the kind of town where the people would put money in a basket toward one. I guess I'll see.

Right now, below me there are all these little islands and channels or skinny rivers. I guess they're really huge rivers. I don't see bridges. I need bridges. Looks just like all the maps I've ever seen. Except colder. I don't understand a landscape like this. It looks mean and uneven and ragged, like no one could ever walk on it or live on it or build on it or even breathe on it.

Okay. It's ten minutes later. Out over the blue now.

Love always,
Your sister,
Pam

ACKNOWLEDGMENTS

The thanks go back way further than this book. And for my mom, back to May 1945.

I live in gratitude to the following people, and to many others, for their support, patience, and encouragement:

Janelle and Reginald Jones.

Raquel, Parker, and Marco Williams.

Lottie Charbonnet Fields. Victoria Jones and Brandon Wells Jones. Robert and Cherrie Carter. Nicole Janée Jones and Keith Reginald Jones. Khalief Brooms and Maiya Askew. Amorette Brooms. Pedro, Shanette, Jahmad, and Kaya Balugo. Theodore and Louise Balugo. Betty Reid-Soskin. My aunts, uncles, and cousins on the Jones side, the Balugo side, and on the Allen and Charbonnet sides.

Gail Clifton. Robert Soller. Mary Fletcher and her family. Romaine Clifton.

April Jones and Karen Lewis.

Wendy Washington and Dayna Clark.

Carl Lamont Posey and his family. Karen Renée Good. Candi Castleberry-Singleton and Alex Singleton.

J. H. 'Tommy' Tompkins. Lee Hildebrand. Quincy Jones. Ann Powers. Alan Light. Norman Pearlstine. Jackson Taylor. Linda Walsh. Bobby Pope. Rose Larson. Roberta Blatt. Phyllis Theroux. Raymond O'Neal Jr. Cory Halaby. Charles Muscatine. David S. Mills. Earle Barrington Sr. The staff of *Vibe*—editorial, art, and publishing—1997–1999. The National Arts Journalism Program.

My agents, Paula Balzer and Sarah Lazin, for believing from the ragged start.

Mrs. P. J. (Dorothy) Balugo, Eugene Leocaddio Balugo, Jaime Juanillo Balugo Sr., Lottie and Dorson Charbonnet, Thurman Dorson Brooms, Louise Latimore, Mitchell Dickerson, and Lesley Pitts, for living in my memory.

Libros son grandes, pero la vida es más grande—para mi amor, Jerry Rodriguez, las gracias son solo el comienzo.

Finally, I thank my relentlessly enthusiastic editor, Chris Jackson. He continues to provide guidance, to see what I can't. And what can be.

MORE LIKE WRESTLING
Reading Group Guide

Pinch and Paige are sisters, growing up on their own in the crumbling poverty and breathtaking beauty of Oakland, trying to build their lives on the fault line of a violent childhood. Betrayed by their mother, who is unwilling to leave an abusive relationship that is killing them all, the girls become everything to each other—so closely entwined they don't know where one begins and the other ends—and begin to assemble a makeshift family from other down-and-out young people in their neighborhood. But gradually, the sisters find themselves entangled in the fast-money world of drugs, and as marriages, arrests, pregnancies, and murders shift the landscape of their group forever, Pinch and Paige must struggle to make sense of their past and chart a route that will carry them forward. Told from the alternating points of view of each sister, *More Like Wrestling* is a novel about loyalty as well as the dangers of apathy and the ultimate necessity for forgiveness.

    Raising each other in the bungalow they call the Pseudo, by the ages of fourteen and sixteen Pinch and Paige know that there's no going home again. Their mother checks on them once a day like a camp counselor, but they're on their own to find a path, any path, that will lead them out of the despair and monotony that hover over Oakland. Paige is the dreamer, the wordsmith, the sister whose anger is so deep and wide that it threatens to drag her under completely. Pinch is the pragmatist, the follower, the silent one, who knows clearly that she needs to leave her hometown but cannot bring herself to make an escape without her sister. Between trying to unravel the pain and mystery of their childhood, and trying to keep their volatile group of friends from becoming unhinged, the sisters have no energy left for planning a future. And as tragedies begin to multiply, fueled by the crack epidemic wracking Oakland, Pinch and Paige are dragged apart and forced to see themselves as individuals with free will and the choice to move on or give up. Their haunting first-person narratives, interspersed with excerpts from Paige's childhood diary, tell an unforgettable story about love, with all its potential for salvation and all its limitations.

Questions for Discussion

1. The Oakland we see in the novel is a muddle of contradictions: poverty, devastation, cynicism, and a gory drug epidemic, mingled with deep blue lakes, gentle mountains, gorgeous skies, and the lights of San Francisco and Marin twinkling in the distance like a promise. Smith treats this landscape almost as a third central character in the story. What relationship does each sister have with this "character"? Does it change? How does it affect their decisions?

2. The two sisters have very different requirements for inner peace. Paige is invested in the idea of justice, and often demands a clear delineation between good and bad. She is able to commit facts to memory "as long as they come in the form of a story in which the right people halfway triumph." Pinch, on the other hand, is more interested in letting go and smoothing over. She says, "Not looking back—that's still my definition of joy." How do these differences affect each girl's relationship with their mother?

How do they affect each girl's role in the gang of friends? Does one attitude seem preferable over the other? Why?

3. Nannah, Gram Liz, Mom, and Pinch and Paige are four generations of women who have experienced abuse, adopting evasion as a survival skill. Each mother has kicked her own daughter out at a tender age to fend for herself. By the end of the novel, Pinch has convinced herself that this behavior is preferable to the nurturing and petting that Jessica was given by her mother. "Sink or swim. . . . As fast as they can, they make sure we know how to survive, then force us to go for it. . . . That's love." Do you think Pinch really believes this? Do you think Nannah, Gram Liz, or Mom regrets her actions?

4. When Major melts down, Paige is forced to confront the fact that he has a crack addiction and that she has no interest in helping him find his way out of it. This is when Paige has her first experience of not being able to see herself in the mirror. What do you think this episode is about? Why doesn't Paige share this frightening experience with Pinch?

5. "If you're a dope dealer, you sell for the freedom of the money, the standing, and for what you believe is the standing up," Pinch says. "I wasn't going to look down on our crew if they did start moving crack." As the women in the group realize that more and more money is appearing almost magically among the men, they are paralyzed. While they don't approve of the dealing, they also recognize "the warped, strengthening sense of purpose" it gives these men who have never had anything to be proud of. What do you think women in this situation should do? At what point does turning a blind eye become what Pinch calls "secondhand selling"?

6. An ongoing question throughout the novel is: When is it time to leave—a person, a place, a situation, a decision?

Her mother's injunction not to leave "at the first sign of trouble" rings in Pinch's mind, but she asks herself, "Do we leave at the second sign of trouble? The eightieth?" Is the question ever answered? Is the answer different for different characters?

7. Why does May allow people to think he had a hand in Jessica's death? Is it an attempt to bolster a dangerous reputation, or is he trying to protect Jessica's parents?

8. Why does Smith wait until the very end of the novel to explain the origin of Pinch's name, and to reveal that Pinch's childhood trips to the "orthodontist" were actually visits to a counselor? Has Pinch's self-mutilating impulse subsided by the time we meet her?

9. What is the significance of Paige's last diary entry, in which she talks to a puppet about running away from home? What lesson was the puppeteer trying to teach Paige by encouraging her to ask a stranger for money? And why do you suppose Pinch felt it important to show Paige's writing to their mother? What effect does it have on her?

10. It can be argued that Oscar's love is the only constant in the girls' lives, outside of their relationship with each other. Where do you see examples of his devotion? Do you think he and Paige will make it as a couple at the end? Has Oscar taught Pinch anything that she will use on her solo adventure?

11. Has Pinch forgiven Paige for nearly drowning her at Diamond Pool? In what ways do they replay the dynamics of that night over and over in their adult lives?